Dream
Matthew A

Copyright © 2022 by Free Minds Publications, LLC
All rights reserved. No part of this book may be reproduced or used in any manner without written permission of the copyright owner except for the use of quotations in a book review.
For more information, address: freemindspublications@gmail.com
FIRST EDITION
www.freemindspublications.com

Chapter 1

EBJAN ORBIT

    Daleth attempted to distract himself from his unrequited longing. His entire life he could never figure out what the longing wanted, only what it didn't want. He lay on his back in the dim light that crept through the tattered makeshift curtains. He stared at the scar on the back of his hand, one of the many scars he carried on his body. He pressed his trikilldo against the scar, the point not piercing the skin but making a barely visible indentation. A faint tingle was all that he was able to register from the long-ago severed nerves that failed to fully come back to life. The sensation faded quickly. The trikilldo had a sharp needle-like point with razor-sharp curved blades on either side. It was these curved appendages that allowed the trikilldo to inflict the worst pain. Daleth pressed one of the crescent-shaped sides of his weapon against the scar, peeling away a thin slice of skin ever so slightly. Nothing.

    He was about to dig deeper when Lorelei jumped onto him and straddled his flexed abdomen. He felt her vulva underneath her satiny lingerie. As it pressed against his skin, it radiated warmth which contrasted the drafty air in the room. Her long brown hair cascaded down in front of her shoulders as she looked down at Daleth. The minimal street light which remained this late in the cycle illuminated Lorelei's delicate features and created a foil to the deep shadows Daleth's angular face cast.

    "I'm worried about you. You're too isolated. You need to start dreaming." Daleth's brow folded heavily at Lorelei's words. "I don't mean with me."

    Daleth relaxed his face or at least as relaxed as it ever got. "Good. Cause I don't dream anymore and even if I did I don't consider you that kind of relation."

Lorelei pulled a slip of paper out from between her thong and her pale smooth thigh. She held it in her outstretched hand. "Here. This Upright would be good for you to dream with."

Daleth snatched the piece of paper. "You must be joking with me." He looked at the scrap which had the word 'Armonia' written on it along with sector coordinates he recognized as belonging to one of Ebjan's moons. "You know ones such as us are just the tattered waste products of the system, left to slink in and out of dark crevices to feed off the shadows."

"You're especially bitter this cycle. At least think about it, and please put that thing away. It doesn't sit right with me when I see it."

Daleth stuffed the piece of paper into the sheath for the trikilldo and jammed the weapon in behind it. Lorelei rolled her eyes as she unclasped her brazier and tossed it casually on the floor. She clumsily climbed off Daleth and with a huff laid down next to him.

Daleth placed his sheathed weapon on top of the empty crate by his side of the mattress. He ran a hand over the boney crests that protruded through his coarse hair braids and sighed. He looked at Lorelei who was already unconscious and wondered how one such as them could settle into rest so quickly. He closed his eyes and shifted his body on the lumpy bedding as he tried to find his rest.

⟪ ⟫

OROGUNU ORBIT

Micah stepped off the hovercraft. It was, fortunately, a short ride from the Prep Center to the cooperative he was assigned to. The fresh air which hit his nostrils carried the savory aroma of the cove berries and ocun blossoms. The fields just outside the small town, where the inhabitants worked, stretched as far as the eye could see. Greens, reds, browns, and whites filled the landscape against the yellow sky. Micah couldn't imagine living in a better Orbit in the system. Orogunu was the biggest food producer, so it had many open areas where crops were grown and one could take in the splendor of the natural world. The other Orbits which encircled Iris were either much more densely populated or much harsher.

DREAMING

Micah had, like all Uprights, been born in a genetic lab called a hatchery. No natural birth had taken place since The Spark appeared in the system to show everyone how to live in peace and find immortality utilizing The Way of The Light. The hatcheries genetically designed Uprights, like Micah, and placed them in Prep Centers on the Orbit that they would be best suited for. After leaving a Prep Center an individual was free to migrate to another Orbit if they felt so inclined but the hatcheries chose right in his case, for sure.

Micah knew this from an early age. In the Prep Center, along with other young developing Uprights, he was instructed on how to function within the system. Besides lessons in farming, since it was a Prep Center on Orogunu, they were taught arithmetic, language, technology, the culture of the different Orbits, and most importantly how The Spark gifted the system with Light to find their way out of the darkness.

Before The Spark, millions upon millions died in the conflict between the empires of Gremoilio, Fimeger, and Ebjan. If one didn't die in the battles that raged around the bright ball of light known as Iris, then one was likely to die from the countless plagues that besieged the populace. The Spark appeared in the system from Iris itself to cure the maladies and make the peace between the warring empires. The Uprights of each Orbit were given their own domain to govern how they saw fit. Now everything was wonderful in the system and Micah looked forward to starting a new life on Orogunu.

A crowd was forming at one of the market stands inside the quaint town which served the local cooperative. The Uprights there were shouting and jostling each other, some held up signs which had slogans scrawled on them such as, 'Feed Ourselves First' and 'More Food Means More Farms'. As Micah passed the unruly mob it brought to mind an instructor who toward the end of his time at the Prep Center had talked about how there was some issue with too many Uprights within the system. Something about the formulas used by the companies which ran the hatcheries, and the Prep Centers too, being slightly off for some reason.

The formulas were used to determine the optimum quantity of Uprights in an Orbit to maintain and manage the resources. The Orbits, of course, traded with one another and there was travel between them but the formulas ensured even distribution so that all got a chance to find immortality by following The Way of The Light. The Way of The Light was a methodical process of self-realization and one needed to live life to fulfill that process and fully realize it. Once their Light was unencumbered they could become an immortal Twin Flame. This had been in place since The Spark's arrival and had always worked beautifully. Micah was led to believe in the Prep Center that the issues with the populations throughout the system were minor and simply just needed some tweaking to set things right once more.

The faces of the Uprights in this crowd seemed quite upset. As Micah observed them the distinct impression formed that this was a drastic dilemma, not a mere bump in the road. What seemed like an abrupt metamorphosis turned an agitated group of Uprights into a melee of violence. The cacophony of bones cracking and produce being squished echoed in the air. The red mist of blood erupted like mini geysers within the throng of Uprights. The storm of swirling limbs engulfed Micah without warning. All he could think to do was squat down and curl into a ball. He was taught in the Prep Center that everything was peaceful and happy, but this was not remotely of the sort.

He couldn't tell how long it took for the guardians to show up and stop the fighting. "You alright?" one of them asked. He was so frazzled that the only response which could be mustered was a weak nod.

⟨ ⟩

IRIS ORBIT

From all over the system ships streamed toward the cluster of artificial structures that revolved around the shining orb of light called Iris. Surely Grevolios played a part in the uptick in activity. The inhabitants of the system were busy preparing for the great celebration which not only marked the start of a new gremrev, the time the planet Gremoilio took to make a full trip around Iris, but it also was the anniversary of the appearance of The Spark to bestow upon them The Way of The Light. Uprights often made a holy pilgrimage to the sacred seat of The Spark during this jubilee.

But there was another reason Iris had such an influx of activity, a far more somber one. The population of the system had grown to a point that it had begun to put a serious strain on its resources. In each Orbit, things had slowly but surely gotten more difficult for all. Now delegates poured in from all ten Orbits to hold a special summit conference with The Spark so the situation could be addressed.

High Councilor Zean arrived with the other High Councilors from Ebjan selected for this most important meeting. Almost immediately after disembarking from her inter-Orbit craft, she stopped at a Grevolios mirror to check her attire. Her hands swiftly swiped along the fabric of her finest suit to smooth out any creases that had formed. She picked a few fibrous strands off herself which must have clung from the seat cushion of her craft. She disdainfully let them drop before continuing.

She walked past the tables with trays of delicacies that crowded the usual spacious halls of Iris. Her stomach had no room for food so she made her way to the Room of Enlightenment where they would all gather to confer with The Spark. She wondered if it would not have been better for her people to send the Panel of Judgement instead of the High Councilors but she knew that the Panel of Judgement must pertain to matters of the Orbit of Ebjan. They could not be spared for what would surely be a lengthy and heated discussion.

Zean made sure the coil of silver hair atop her head was neat and in place before she reached the doors to the Room of Enlightenment. She took a deep breath and straightened her broad shoulders. She opened the doors to the monumental space. Zean gazed at the immaculate high-backed golden chair in the center of the room where The Spark would soon be seated. Several circles of gilded stools surrounded the throne and Zean guessed this was where Twin Flames, who wished to take an audience, would sit.

Around the perimeter of the room were several benches, which seemed almost never-ending. These circular benches had a wall in front of them about half the size of Zean herself and there was a ledge jutting out from the wall. Zean surmised that the ledge was designed to allow those who sat to take notes or perhaps layout materials. Zean squinted and noted the bright lights that seemed embedded in the high domed ceiling and wondered if the brightness came from Iris itself rather than artificial lighting. Silk banners hung high on the walls around the room and alternated in color between a deep red and vibrant yellow. They swayed ever so slightly from the air that was constantly circulated through this artificial structure that housed the moral guideposts of the system. A tangy aroma in Zean's nostrils became apparent and it made her contemplate if that was always the case on Iris or if it was done specially for this occasion to soothe the tension of the gathered delegates.

Many of her fellow High Councilors had lagged back to mingle with the delegates from the other Orbits or sightsee but Zean was focused on the task at hand. This was not a time to talk about trade matters or brag about progress in The Way of The Light.

The long circular benches were cordoned off in various sections for each Orbit. Zean took a seat on one of the benches in the Ebjan section. She straightened her spine as more and more delegates filled the circular space. She noticed a robed Upright making his way toward her. She did not recognize him but from his green garments, she could tell he was from the School of Prosperity, one of the three schools that oversaw the watery Orbit of Baabcrest.

"Hello, neighbor," the Upright greeted her warmly.

"Do I know you?" She smoothed her form-fitting suit.

He smiled, and the small whiskers around his mouth became sharply angular. "I suppose not. Your reputation precedes you. I am Magistrate of Prosperity Molomew. With our Orbits being adjacent I have heard of the up-and-coming career of High Councilor Zean."

Zean's thin lips couldn't help but curve at the ends. "You are a part of the School of Prosperity so I would imagine you would be keeping close tabs on the movers and shakers of the other Orbits."

"I would be a poor Magistrate of Prosperity otherwise."

"So what do you make of how this will all play out?"

"I fear this will be a true test of how we walk the path of Light." Molomew brought his hand to his chin in contemplation. "I suspect there will be much blame passed around. The outer Orbits will accuse the inner Orbits of leading a too-backward life and not graduating enough to Twin Flame status. The inner Orbits will accuse the outer ones of too much excess."

"Circapto will of course shoulder a great deal of blame too," Zean added coldly.

Molomew nodded in agreement. "But we must get past the blame."

"Indeed. It will not help us muster up the courage for the solution we all know is necessary. To close the hatcheries and grant temporary Orbital control over to the Twin Flames and The Spark."

"I feel that would prove to be quite difficult for many."

"We must have faith in The Way of The Light," Zean said with purposeful emphasis.

Molomew gave pause and seemed to weigh his words. Tensions even among like-minded individuals could be dangerous. "I have my faith and you have yours but I don't believe all the others have the same faith you and I share."

Zean saw the choice of words being used. Even those who shared similar aims saw different trajectories to get there. She agreed with Molomew that now was not the time to debate faith. That would come soon enough. "I hope you are wrong, no offense."

Molomew chuckled to alleviate the tension. "I hope I am wrong too. I should get back to my section. I believe we will start soon."

Zean gave a slight nod of approval as Molomew made his way back to the others from Baabcrest. The room had become a symphony of banging and footsteps as the final delegates made their way to their respective sections. Zean focused inward to shut it out so she could prepare herself.

As the last delegates took their seats other Uprights began to file into the room from a door that opened up in the floor. Zean could tell these were Twin Flames from the customary shiny white robes they wore and the tiny flame tattoo under each eye. This was only a small grouping of the many throughout the system but it was important they bore witness to what was about to transpire as an example of what one could become with The Way of The Light. They stood along the rows of stools until the last one was in place. In unison, they gave the familiar greeting of the Twin Flame, "Look deeper." Zean's palms were sweaty with anticipation. A bright light sculpted in the form of an Upright ascended from the staircase below the floor. The room became heavy with stillness as all held their breath at the luminous sight of The Spark. The Spark walked to the golden chair at the center and stood there. The Twin Flames began the recitation of the creed of The Way of The Light. Every delegate in the room joined in.

"The Light watches over this system. It saw our suffering and sent a piece of itself to show us The Way of The Light. This Spark guides us toward immortality and peace. The Spark will always be a beacon and all we need do is turn toward it to know the Way before us."

With the creed finished The Spark sat and spoke, "Let us shine Light." With that, the meeting commenced.

⟨ ⟩

GREMOILIO ORBIT

Grevolios was in full swing on Gremoilio and had been for several cycles already. The inhabitants weren't going to let the overpopulation issue ruin their party. Mirrors were hung on every door. Huge spotlights swayed back and forth when Iris was not visible. Parades with people wearing iridescent costumes and carrying torches were a regular occurrence.

Daleth sat in a tavern on one of Gremoilio's moons. Although the small space was brightly lit for Grevolios, the stale scent which hung in the air and dark stains on the wood of the bar Daleth hunched over betrayed the usual decor of the establishment. Many of the tiles were chipped and the walls were a faded brown. This was how Daleth preferred it, a quiet hole in the wall to hide within. At the present moment though, his eyes felt tight and his head throbbed from all the lights reflected every which way. He had forgotten Gremoilio started Grevolios so early. The view screens which hung on the walls flitted between Grevolios events and coverage of the deliberations on Iris. He was about to leave to head back to his ship when he heard the door behind him open and a voice bellow, "You're Daleth last of the Followers of Vuhox. Aren't you?"

Daleth straightened his posture but didn't turn around to look at the source of the voice. There wasn't a need. A large statured Upright with thick muscles stood tense with a snarled face aimed at Daleth's back. Daleth fed off the fear of the crowd which began to gather behind him. The barkeep's words couldn't even distract Daleth from the feast he was secretly savoring.

"Are you really the infamous Daleth, last of The Followers of Vuhox?"

"Yes. I was their greatest disciple."

"Hey! We're not afraid of thugs like you here on Gremoilio," came the voice again still saturated with hatred. A thick group of people now blocked the exit to the tavern as all those gathered were focused on the confrontation at hand. Despite the hostility in the room, Daleth remained almost motionless. He steadied his breath and utilized his training to feed off the fear that the group was so desperately trying to hide. It was a basic tenant of The Followers of Vuhox to gain power from the energy of others' pain and fear. The air was electric with it and he drank it to his full advantage.

The patrons chanted, "loodeev," a bastardized version of the familiar Twin Flame greeting used by commoners to encourage confidence. "We're going to send you to join the rest of your plague of a cult."

Daleth with a steady hand discreetly reached into the pouch at his waist. The five crystals he held would end this scene at any time he wished but he wanted to prolong the meal for as long as he could. He softly closed his eyes. The more hateful the insults hurled at him only meant an increase in their fear. Daleth squeezed the crystals in a clenched fist to feel their weight and steady himself from all the energy that flowed into his being.

Once more the barkeep excited in anticipation of a brawl interrupted Daleth's trance. "If you were their best why did I hear you killed them all?"

Daleth opened his eyelids. The look in his eyes was so icy it made the barkeep shift away from him. "Because I was their greatest disciple."

The shuffle of feet next met the ears of Daleth, in response he opened his hand. By his command, one of the crystals shot out toward the leader of the rowdy bunch who now advanced on him. It then returned just as quickly to join the rest of the crystals. The crowd was hushed in silence. The hulking figure who had started the commotion stood starkly still. Everyone saw something whiz through the air but it moved at such a speed that none could determine what it was or the path it traveled. The Upright who started everything suddenly became aware of a stinging sensation on his neck and put his hand to it. It felt sticky and wet. He noticed others in the tavern now staring with open mouths at him. He looked at his hand and saw smears of blood. He shifted focus to the floor below where a lock of his once white shoulder-length hair now lay. His eyes darted up to Daleth who still sat stiff and motionless. A lump formed in the usually confident Upright's throat and he sprinted toward the door, the rest of the patrons quickly followed his lead.

Daleth sighed and slipped the crystals back into their pouch. The banquet was over for him. He gulped down the remainder of his drink and tossed a few halos onto the counter in front of the barkeep who now tried to hide his tremors.

Daleth walked outside into the steamy air. The faint scent of tar and burning wood became apparent now that he was in the unfiltered open air. Gremoilio was always humid and quite warm despite being the second farthest Orbit from Iris. This was due to all the thermal vents and volcanoes which allowed heat from the active molten core to escape into the air above the surface. Much of it then was held in by the gas cloud which not only encircled the main Orbit of Gremoilio but engulfed the moons as well. Thus a warm blanket for the entire Orbit and its inhabitants was always present. Daleth patted the moisture already on his face with his cloak as he strolled the streets which looked almost like Iris shone even though it was the dark period of the cycle. This was thanks to the myriad of Grevolios decorations.

A shrouded figure stood in an alleyway and called out to Daleth. "I saw what you did back there. You handled it with deftness."

Daleth made his way over to the Upright and noticed that they wore a tunic much like himself which covered the majority of the body. This was a rarity in the system since almost everybody but Twin Flames showed off and enhanced their physical appearance to attract a partner to reflect with in accord with the doctrines of The Way of The Light. Still even with everything covered he took note of practiced muscle control. There was also a stifling of not only fear but all emotions. He wondered if he was interacting with a member of the heretical Order of Consciousness.

Daleth narrowed his eyes and delivered a measured response to this stranger. "Situations like the one you witnessed are fairly common."

The unknown Upright shifted her body away from Daleth's intense gaze. "Irrational minds are far too prolific in this system."

Daleth's muscles contracted as his suspicions increased about this stranger's allegiance to the subversive group. "Everyone judges, I only asked to be judged fairly." Although the Order of Consciousness claimed to be free of emotions, including hate, Daleth knew well that they saw him as a dangerous wild card and resented his infamy. It was well known the Followers of Vuhox originally sprung out of the Order's ranks. The shrouded individual lifted their head slightly to acknowledge Daleth's proclamation and to encourage him to continue. Daleth decided to continue to play this game out of curiosity. "Is there more you require from me or was your aim only to pay me a compliment?"

"I require your services."

"And who is requesting them?"

"Such information is not necessary at this time but I can tell you the payment will be well worth your trouble."

"Need someone killed or something stolen?"

"Someone found."

Daleth let out a grunt. "I don't do search and rescue. Call a guardian."

"This matter is better left to one who comprehends the value of discretion."

"I usually do jobs with a little more action." Daleth made sure to punch the last word.

"You live on the fringes of this system and get by on the darkness others wish to hide. Can you afford to be choosy?"

The contemptuous tone made Daleth's skin flush. "I am no lost and found." He was done and turned with dismissal.

"I already informed you the completion of this task would substantiate you generously. Haven't you always longed to hide away from the system?"

The truth in the last remark made Daleth turn his attention cautiously back to the stranger who now held out a miniature computer. The small screen was thrust in his face. On the display was an account with twenty million halos, enough to support him for nearly an entire gremrev.

"I don't use accounts", Daleth coldly stated.

"Take it however you want, that is your business."

Daleth chewed slowly on his tongue for a moment. The dull pain helped him think. He inventoried the figure before him who stood steadfast. The balmy air was on fire with the tension between the two. "Anything I need to know about this Upright I am supposed to find?"

"All I can tell you is that she will most likely appear feral and will be trying to keep below the scanners."

"Well, under the scanners is where I like to be but you got to give me more to go on."

"I am sorry to say there's no more information I can give you. Hopefully, this will be of some help though." Daleth was handed a cylinder about the size of his forearm. It looked simple enough, a smooth black casing adorned with a crimson bulb at one end that flashed now and again. "The light will pulsate quicker as it grows nearer to her genetic signature. It will be lit without interruption when you are upon her. Between the device and your unique talents you should be able to locate her eventually."

Daleth knew if this cagey Upright had the genetic signature of the Upright he was supposed to find then there was much he was not being told. Likewise, Daleth knew that his would-be benefactor would have to know this fact and was simply counting on Daleth being discreet out of habit. He did not appreciate being manipulated this way. His lips parted to refuse the assignment but before he could his enhanced intuitive abilities told him to speak other words. "When I find her what do I do?"

"Bring her to the southernmost pole of the moon of Baabcrest which houses the School of Knowledge." Now Daleth was sure he was speaking to a member of the Order of Consciousness. It was well known the secret sect had infiltrated the School of Knowledge significantly and used it as a clandestine base for their seditious operations. Still, Daleth sensed no trap and detected the desperation that the Order member was trying to conceal. If his target caused desperation amongst the Order perhaps he could use that as leverage for his own ends and this would be the last foolish errand he would be obligated to endure. If he was somehow misled by his training and this was indeed a trap he doubted it would successfully ensnare him. The Order was crafty but they were not warriors.

"I'll find you. Don't find me."

As Daleth turned to leave the Order member added, "Make sure she is brought there alive and unharmed. Otherwise, our arrangement is null and void." Daleth raised his hand in a gesture of dismissal and headed toward his ship.

《 》

IRIS ORBIT

High Councilor Zean sat with a stiff poise watching the deliberations go around in senseless circles. Her thin lips pursed as she evaluated the undercurrents which steered the proceedings. Circapto, Fimeger, and Gremoilio had formed a curious and unexpected trifecta against the suspension of the hatcheries. It was not a surprise that Circapto fought to keep them open. After all, the company which ran them was based on Circapto. The Orbit attracted the best and brightest of pioneering innovators. Those who worked at the hatcheries prided themselves on the varied creations which populated the system. They surely wouldn't want to see their masterpieces cease.

The more peculiar development was Fimeger and Gremoilio joining forces together since there remained bitter resentment between the two. Zean surmised that the trio had formed an uneasy alliance out of convenience. Although Circapto was the second largest Orbit and the economic and scientific center of the system, it still needed the two other heavyweight Orbits to avoid accusations of only materialistic interests. Empress Rushi, as well as the royal couple from Fimeger, most likely feared that the current situation will inevitably lead to them turning over their power to the Twin Flames. Surely the rulers were scheming behind the scenes to accelerate the process of The Way of The Light so they can quickly achieve Twin Flame status themselves. As soon as one ruler did they would shift the Orbit's stance and leave their rival in the lurch with Circapto. Such was politics.

Zean's jaw clenched at the mockery they were making of the sacred Way of the Light. To hear these discussions showed all too clearly how much work those who oversaw the Orbits still needed to do to rid themselves of all darkness.

Empress Rushi of Gremoilio now had the floor. "We cannot snuff out entire mechanisms because of a strain on them. The people will find a way to adjust."

One of the tribal leaders from Dooga responded. "We on Dooga pay attention to the systems of the natural world to ensure the safety of our clans. When a means becomes strained it eventually breaks and such a thing is far worse than the removal of a process no longer thriving."

King Hyron now stood with the regal air so famous on Fimeger. "What my equal from Gremoilio meant," he could barely hide his bitterness calling a Gremoilion ruler an equal, "was The Way of The Light will guide us as it always has since The Spark arrived."

These certainly are unique times to trigger such a farce, Zean thought, staring with scorn.

Hyron went on to address The Spark directly. "Doesn't your Light still shine on us? Didn't you reveal to us a way to prosper without war or plague?"

Zean leaned forward and craned her neck as The Spark replied, "I gave you the Way. There are still many shadows cast in this society by those that get distracted. Until all find their way to the Light there will be complications."

A representative from Washa now spoke, "We have sterilized our populations as The Spark instructed. But there still needed to be life so we entrusted measured control of it to the geneticists of Circapto. They are who failed us with their greed."

Zean couldn't help but smirk. *Leave it to a Washan to state things so simply.*

Murmurs echoed and bounced off the high ceiling. Queen Zayn with her nose held high in the air came to the defense of her ally. "They regulated based on the need of all the societies moving through The Way of The Light. Not based on Uprights living like superstitious ancients as some Orbits still do." The dig at the end further scoured the line between the inner and outer Orbits.

It was now Orogunu's turn. "We on Orogunu can see the pressure on our crops from the populace. The ships go out fuller and fuller but come back quicker and quicker. It is good for our people in the short but not in the long. The soil will eventually tire. For all our sakes the hatcheries must be brought to a halt."

"We should not act rash and simply prune ourselves till nothing will remain but twigs", replied Queen Zayn.

Zean could hold her tongue no longer. "The Way of The Light is a duty we all have. We were given it so we could achieve immortality. If we fail to look within ourselves we doom our society to darkness and death. The Way of The Light was never meant to be easy but it is far better than the alternative. If we turn away from it now by ignoring the wisdom of The Spark and instead heed only our egos, we will fall into the chaos of our ancestors and leave nothing but empty orbs around Iris."

The hall was still as Zean slowly sat back. She had cut through the differences between the Orbits to speak directly to what binds them, The Way of The Light. Not an Upright in the room wanted to go back to the ancient ways so they knew she was inevitably correct. Zean believed she had finally brought the endless roundabout to a close. She couldn't help but beam at her apparent achievement.

It faded quickly when a Circapto representative sprung to his feet. "I breathe today so today is a good day." Zean rolled her eyes at the old maxim of Washa being used in the manner it was. The representative continued, "Fear must not dictate for us. How about we make shorter life spans to encourage those to move quicker toward The Way of The Light." The room erupted into murmurs and shouts as the occupants argued amongst themselves once more about the new ludicrous proposal.

⟪ ⟫

BAABCREST ORBIT

Daleth stood on the shore of the western side of the Great Band of Baabcrest. The bright light of Iris being reflected off the water caused his skin to come alive with tingly heat. The humidity hung so heavy in the air that Daleth felt he was in the water rather than on the narrow land mass that ran north to south without breach on Baabcrest. It was the only significant landmass on the main Orbit. Although the three moons had few bodies of water, Baabcrest itself was almost entirely ocean. Aside from the Great Band, there were only small island chains scattered around the sphere.

Daleth dug his feet into the sandy coast, weighed down by the oppressive heat and thick air. A dense menagerie of saltwater plants created a mosaic of green, purple and pink behind him as towering walls of water curled and crashed to the ground in front of him. His glazed eyes watched as natives of Baabcrest rode the currents of the sea up to the top of the crest of waves and then down the backside of them before they stumbled onto land. Those placed on Baabcrest by the hatcheries were specifically designed to be hydrodynamic. The shape of their bodies along with the fins helped them glide through the primal forces that ruled the waters with ease. Daleth felt a knot form in his stomach. The inhabitants of Baabcrest were perfectly designed and suited for their environment. They knew where they belonged.

Suddenly Daleth became aware of a more intense burning on the top of his hand separate from Iris' light. He glanced down and saw the sting was the result of a baabcrest sucker which had decided to make a meal of him. He stared at the winged parasite for a moment and then with a quick jolt he pinched the skin around the proboscis so that the tiny fella could no longer retract but had to keep feeding. Daleth glared as the baabcrest sucker became engorged with his blood. It grew in size till it burst, leaving a dark red drop of liquid on the backside of Daleth's hand. He uncermoniously wiped it off on his tunic as he turned his attention back to the frolicking dwellers of Baabcrest. They still carried on seemingly without a care.

Daleth was fairly certain his employer was a member of the Order of Consciousness. With so many of their rank being embedded into the School of Knowledge they would be able to sift through vast catalogs of the system with ease. For them to need to reach out to the likes of him meant the target had gone underground. He had deduced that if someone needed to lay low and hide out the two easiest places in the system to do such a thing were Baabcrest and Circapto. Washa and Comqwo were also good places to lose oneself but the deserts of Washa and the tundra of Comqwo proved too much of a significant survival challenge for most. Due to this Daleth disregarded those two Orbits. He hoped his target would be on Baabcrest but he had flown his ship all over the ball of water with the tracking device his employer gave him making no sign of confirmation.

Daleth now had to muster up the will to go to one of the Orbits he despised the most. Circapto grated at his very core with all its noise and clutter. It attracted innovators but also derelicts who fed off those innovations. The only worth of the Orbit, in his mind at least, was the inhabitants were easily provoked into fear and suffering. The dwellers of Circapto feed off the excess of the Orbit and when Daleth was forced to visit there he in turn fed off of them. Still, he now tasted bile at the idea of traipsing around the suffocating gas ball. The only Orbit that would be worse for him to visit would be Fimeger.

He took the beacon he was given in his hand and raised his arm poised to throw it into the great waves. Carefree laughter wafted into his ears and almost against his will, his body turned toward it. It was a group of natives that splashed around in the breakers careening into the coast. His eyes burned at the ease they moved with. He stuffed the beacon into his belt and made his way back to the ship.

Chapter 2

IRIS ORBIT

High Councilor Zean rubbed her temples in a corner as her fellow councilors talked to the media about the results of the conference. The halls were so abuzz that Zean was surprised she heard her name called out. Magistrate of Prosperity Molomew made his way toward the High Councilor. "I wanted to compliment you on an impressive speech." The reserve in his voice from before the conference had left.

Zean balked. "It did no good."

Molomew blinked his eyes. "My impression was it put matters into perspective for the assembly."

"They just kept arguing the same points over and over. It was a mockery."

"Eventually it was resolved."

"It's only a partial measure to close the hatcheries. Resources will continue to be exhausted and we will be back here in less than point one gremrev. We needed to give things over to the Twin Flames so they can get us back on course."

Molomew sighed. "It certainly is a possibility that we will have to take more drastic action. The source of the problem has at least been addressed. Now it is up to us to steer the ship to the proper course."

Zean noted that Molomew's tone seemed more agreeable to Twin Flame control. *Does he see how utterly futile the leaders of the system were in the face of crisis? Or is this simply political feint?* she wondered. "I don't know why The Spark didn't just order us to do what needed to be done. It would have saved us all this trouble."

"You know that is not The Spark's way. The Spark came to show us the Way and guide us on it but it is still up to us to decide whether to walk it. I have faith we will live up to the task."

Zean could agree that a great deal of faith needed to be mustered for all. "Circapto will continue to recruit allies and push for the hatcheries to reopen."

Molomew shrugged. "They will need to reopen eventually."

So political feint it is. "Not if we all become Twin Flames, which was originally the idea if I understood correctly."

"The Twin Flames were meant to aid the rest of us but a society is needed to ask for aid."

Zean narrowed her eyes. "Uprights got greedy and desired too much. Perhaps we all should take a lesson from the simplicity of Washa."

"It would seem you and I disagree on the value of society. It is what makes achieving Twin Flame status worth anything. For without it there would be nothing to overcome. We need society so we can see the contrast between it and the Light. All that is required now is for us to temper it, just as Twin Flames have promised to only sparingly use the precious resources of food and water."

"Because they know the meaning of sacrifice."

Molomew jutted out his lower lip and clasped his hands behind his back. "True. But this goes back to my overall point. The Twin Flames are not as bothered by suffering for they have transcended the trappings of the world. We aren't as fortunate yet. Nonetheless, we all will get there."

Zean puffed out her chest. "I know I will. My reflection and I are in the final stages of preparation to join together."

Indeed it made Zean feel as though she was walking on air to just think of pouring her life essence into a special physical vessel to complete her journey on The Way of The Light. The end goal of all those who walked The Way of The Light was to gain immortality through the Twin Flame process. It was a right of passage for the true and faithful. You found somebody who could reflect your Light onto the darkness you still carried. You did the same for them. The two of you by reflecting Light onto each other's dark spots helped expel all darkness. Once you were fully beings of Light without any darkness whatsoever you were ready to merge your brightness and become a Twin Flame.

Jamila, Zean's reflection for a little more than a quarter of a gremrev, was equally excited to merge with her. The special bodies of the Twin Flames were designed by The Spark and were sealed with the special Light of The Spark at the end of the fusion process. The vessel began as any infantile Upright but it would not be prepared and cared for in a Prep Center. The responsibility would fall instead to Zean and Jamila. It would behave with a will of its own but still of Jamila and Zean. Over time as it matured more and more of its Light would flow into it. Finally, after it had been brought up to be a fully functioning member of the system, never straying from The Way of The Light, then the process would be complete. Zean and Jamila would be no more, their empty husks discarded. In their places instead would be them in one body and mind, forever a Twin Flame, the product of the intensity of both of their Lights.

The process was a daunting one and is only undertaken under the strictest supervision of a Twin Flame guide specialized in overseeing such an endeavor. Countless discussion sessions with Twin Flames as well as carefully monitored dreamings and other Light Ceremonies needed to take place before one is ready. Zean and Jamila weren't intimidated though. Their bond was strong. They had already seen that through the dreaming they had done together. They truly loved one another and were fully devoted to The Way of The Light. It would prove natural and easy to safeguard and support this extension of themselves with a mind of their own and also not of their own.

Molomew's voice called Zean back from her wandering joyous thoughts. "I shine Light on you for your good fortune. I too have been working with a reflection but she and I are not that far along yet."

"Stay true and shine Light everywhere within. You will get there."

"Well, I suppose we will just have to see on all counts. May you have a bright Grevolios."

Zean's mouth formed a tight-lipped smile. "You as well."

She watched Molomew disappear into the crowds and then turned to her associates. They were still preoccupied with the media and hadn't budged. Zean made an exaggerated roll of her eyes. They were intent on political wrangling and basking in the historic moment. Indeed the entire system had trained its ears and eyes on all who had gathered here but Zean wanted no part of the showmanship. She did her duty and that was all she was interested in.

She decided to head back to the ship to see if she could reach Jamila via the inter-Orbit communication transmitter. She hoped to catch her in-between guardian shifts. Zean was anxious to discuss the conference with her for she knew she would understand the frustration of it. The others would come to the ship when they were done soaking up the attention.

⟨ ⟩

CIRCAPTO ORBIT

Daleth weaved his ship around the other crafts and structures along the flight paths in Circapto's gaseous atmosphere. Circapto was the second largest planet in the system and had an extremely thick gas cloud around it which engulfed the majority of its sixty-seven moons. Circapto seemed nearly uninhabitable at first glance but thanks to it being the most technologically advanced of the Orbits it was also the most populated. An electromagnetic dome kept the volatile gas cloud dozens of kilometers above the main orb of the Orbit. This allowed those who dwelled on the surface to move about freely. They lived and worked in tall structures that nearly reach the top of the artificially created bio-dome.

You could not see Iris through the thick red atmosphere but it didn't matter. The entire planet was a giant city that never slept. Whatever you wanted, whenever you wanted it, Circapto could provide it. It was no surprise that it was the economic powerhouse of the entire system. A continuous stream of ships came and went loading and unloading cargo. Artificial satellites were strewn above the field that protected the populace as well as placed on the various moons. They hung in the vapors monitoring and stabilizing the mix of unpredictable elements so ships could safely navigate the Orbit. Most pilots had to move through this maze slowly to avoid the moons and other structures. Daleth's enhanced senses from his time with the Followers of Vuhox allowed him to reflexively navigate with ease.

Skirting the border of the electromagnetic field he kept a close eye on the tracker. As he passed over the equator the device began to extend its light. Daleth let out a groan.

As his ship circled he ruminated over his life. His shoulders and neck tightened when he remembered his time with Followers of Vuhox. He had entered that cult in the hopes it would offer him a way to take control of his life. *What a joke!* Now possibly a new avenue for him to assert some direction may have presented itself. He had heard the news of the decision made on Iris. If his employer was a member of the Order of Consciousness they would be all the more desperate since their sworn enemy will most likely eventually assert total dominion over the system. With the unprecedented move of closing the hatcheries, it seemed inevitable that the Orbits would eventually be forced to give over power. Daleth was approximately 1.33 gremrev's old, his life nearly half over. *How likely is it for me to find another opportunity like this? Even if one did come again, how long would I have to wait?* He gritted his teeth. *I will see this through come what may.*

Daleth passed over the same spot he had previously and sure enough, the tracker behaved the same. His target was down there all right. Unless this was all a ploy to bring him to Circapto. But if that was the case he still reasoned he had little to lose and much to potentially gain. He decided it was in his best interest to dock his ship nearby and continue his search on foot.

Daleth walked the crowded streets. Above him, the elongated yellow crafts with bulbous points went every which way buzzing to and fro in seeming chaos. They carried Uprights who had a destination beyond walking distance. Other Uprights jostled and rubbed up against him making the hairs on his neck bristle. Many of them, fortunately, took no notice of him, too engrossed in view screens or some other distraction. Indeed, Circapto was a hub of activity. You couldn't possibly take in all of your surroundings if you stood in one spot for an entire cycle.

Daleth tried to cut through an alley to get away from the crowd. His tracker flashed rapidly, almost solidly lit. He was close to his prey. As he made his way along the artificial canyon the pungent aroma that hung in the air made his nose curl. He stopped suddenly as a group of Uprights sprang from the shadows. This Orbit was rampant with ambitious Uprights fresh out of Prep Centers who tried to have some fun and make a name for themselves before they embarked on the more stringent life The Way of The Light deemed.

One of them spoke with arrogance. "Another who wants to use this shortcut but forgot to pay the fee."

"Get lost", Daleth sneered.

"Wait. I think this guy is that last remaining Follower of Vuhox you always hear whispers about. Damon or Queaf?"

"The name you're looking for is Daleth and if you've heard of me then you know you should let me be on my way."

The group snickered amongst themselves. "You don't scare us."

"I know I don't. I taste no fear from you."

"You won't intimidate us with your nonsense. You're the past. We're the future." The gang brandished sophisticated laser guns and electroshock gloves. It was quite the display of technological fortitude but it meant nothing to Daleth and the gang of youths in front of him did not pick up on that most crucial fact. "The charge to cross is fifty halos. Pay up or find out what we're made of here on Circapto."

The gang of six stood confident across the narrow alleyway. Daleth glanced at the tracker on his belt. It had not changed which meant his true goal was stationary for the time being. He decided he could spare some time for a quick meal before he continued the hunt. Daleth steadied his breath and drew up the energy he had stored from the base of his abdomen. He used it to first shield his body. Their guns may be top of the line but he had much in reserves. The energy he used would provide enough protection so their blasts only did superficial damage, at best.

"We need an answer, dimwad." As if in reply Daleth reached into his pouch for his crystals. "Burn him up! Loodeev!" They opened fire with their laser guns but the blasts of energy didn't even register. Pain meant nothing to Daleth anymore.

The crystals flew out of his hand and with the most natural of efforts zipped through the air. They deflected laser blasts, cut flesh, and disabled the energy packs. While they did their thing Daleth unsheathed his trikilldo and joined the fray himself.

One of the gang members tried to use her magnetic palm plates. She called a piece of rusted metal toward her hands and electrified it. She swung the weapon at the swift crystals but they easily avoided her swipes. Daleth kicked the piece of pipe out of her hands. He sliced at the plates she wore with his weapon. The curved blade of the trikilldo in combination with Daleth's ferocious strength quickly destroyed her toys. She let out a cry as they shorted and scorched her hands. She threw them off. Daleth grabbed a strip of leather which hung out of a nearby trashcan with his free hand. He whipped it toward her so it wrapped around her throat. Her hands instantly shot up to try and untangle it but Daleth yanked so hard that she slammed into the wall. Daleth could tell from the sound that echoed in the concrete and steel canyon that her shoulder had dislocated.

Another Upright with a round face approached him. Arcs of electricity ran across his gloved fingers. Daleth couldn't help but be amused that this Upright thought electrified hands posed a threat to one such as him after what he just did to this young Upright's companion. The Upright lunged but Daleth moved with a quickness that startled the youth. Daleth tripped the Upright and drove the hilt of the trikilldo into the back of his spine. He heard him cry out in pain and fright. Daleth drank it in. He didn't paralyze him for he didn't want to risk any annoying investigations by guardians. That being said he ensured his back would be sore for several cycles.

All this time the crystals were cutting up the other four. None of the injuries would be permanent but it was enough. Daleth's reserves had been greatly enhanced from the fear and pain of the group which now scurried away. He drank it in and savored it. If they ever encountered Daleth again they would be afraid, they would know to keep on moving.

The one Daleth assumed was their leader was all who remained. He was nervous now and Daleth savored it. The crystals swirled around him like insects drawn to a rotting carcass. The laser gun he held had been severed from its power source by Daleth's crystals. He chucked it. The leader held out his hands and tiny darts shot out of gauntlets around his wrists. The crystals deflected all of them before they reached their intended target. Daleth grabbed the leader's throat and dug his pointed fingernails in so blood trickled on his hand. A tight beard outlined an elongated face, all underneath a neat crop of dull orange hair. Daleth violently thrust his captive up against the wall and brought his face in close. Daleth could see the young thug's blue eyes growing more black as his pupils dilated. Daleth could smell the punk's hot rancid breath. "Is this the best Circapto has to offer?"

"Alright, I give up you can go through," stammered the leader.

"I know you're afraid. Maybe you missed that part of prep class but we Followers of Vuhox feed off fear. Pain too. It's like special food to us. It energizes us. We can use that energy to shield ourselves, enhance our senses, and wield the crystals." Daleth brought the trikilldo up to the leader's cheek while he held him fast to the wall. The shadows covered most of their faces. The little bit of light that trickled in from the streets glinted off the weapon.

"What's your problem?" The quiver in the voice was unmistakable.

"Since your technology failed you why don't you call on the Light? Light casts out darkness, right? Look into my eyes. Do you see anything but darkness?"

The gang leader shook his head slowly. "I'll follow The Way of The Light. I promise."

"I couldn't care less." Daleth shoved the point of the trikilldo into the leader's shoulder as he covered his mouth with his other hand. The gang leader screamed bloody murder and Daleth pulled out the blade and wiped the blood on the leader's clothing. "Too bad you didn't get to see what this thing can really do."

Daleth released him and the gang leader sprinted out of the alley. Daleth summoned the crystals that floated in the air back to his hand and placed them into his pouch. He sheathed the trikilldo. The detour had provided a satisfying energy boost but he needed to return to the matter at hand. He pulled out the tracker and continued down the alleyway.

A whimpering sound mingled with the thud of his heavy boots on the pavement. He strained his sight within the shadows and saw a trembling mass huddled amongst broken crates and smashed-up boxes. He was about to continue on his way when he glanced down at the tracker which was now solidly lit. He walked over to the sobbing mass huddled in the dark and said, "You're coming with me." The lump of flesh sprung up quickly. Daleth stumbled back. He was not used to the experience of being taken by surprise. Before him, was an Upright with fiery wild hair and eyes to match. Small needle-like teeth protruded out of her thin mouth. Her fingers had claws but Daleth noticed they were filed and not natural like his. She wore a black leotard and a mottled leather jacket. Her black boots seemed a size too big for her. She made an odd specimen.

"Who are you?" she stuttered. Daleth felt no fear from her which he thought peculiar. He noticed the remnants of tears across her sunken cheeks.

"It is not important who I am."

The stranger began to weep. "I wish I knew who I am. All I know is the hurt."

"That is not my concern." Daleth stepped forward to grab her. Before he could, she clutched her head and let out a blood-curdling scream that ripped through Daleth's skull. Daleth pressed his palms against his elongated ears. He was fortunate that Circapto was so noisy and callous. Another Orbit and that scream would have caused dozens to come running.

He watched with wide eyes as the odd Upright tossed herself against the wall. Daleth couldn't recall ever interacting with someone quite this peculiar. Several moments passed until she stopped and leaned still against the concrete. Just as Daleth once more tried to advance she began to jerk violently. She turned to Daleth, her eyes saucers. She began to bounce back and forth on the walls of the alley. "I have to get out of here. I have to find the way out. Just don't stand there like a stone. Help find a way out will ya!"

"I have a ship. Just come with me and I will take you away from here."

"Shut up! A ship won't help me!" Those crazed eyes spied the hilt of the trikilldo and lunged for it with such a quickness that Daleth had to wrest it from her. So jarring were the actions of this stranger that out of the sheath came the piece of paper Lorelei had given Daleth. She bent down and looked at it. "Armonia? I like the sound of that word. I think I will call myself that."

"Whatever you call yourself is space dust to me. Never go after my trikilldo again or I'll give you more of it than you ever want."

Armonia still gave up no fear toward Daleth but instead began to jerk violently once more. She stopped and glared at Daleth. "I'll decide for myself what I want," she said in a velvety voice.

"What is your problem?"

"Life. I want ya to use that weapon to end mine."

"As much as it would please me I can't. My employer gave explicit instructions that you be delivered unharmed."

"Then you're a coward!" snapped Armonia. She lunged for the trikilldo once more and Daleth pushed her away. Armonia licked her lips as she stared at Daleth. She then squeezed her eyes closed and screamed once more. She blinked her eyes open and pointed at Daleth. "Don't you understand how doomed we all are? Especially me! Even if I somehow get out of this dungeon of a realm what life is there for me?"

Daleth shoved his trikilldo back in its sheath. "Get out of this realm? What are you going on about?"

Armonia began to speak quickly in a language Daleth had never heard before. She paced back and forth moving her arms erratically through the air. Daleth stroked his chin trying to figure this strange creature out. Armonia jolted to a stop and began to shake violently. She stopped and stood motionless for a moment and then put her face in her hands and began to weep again.

Daleth stood there transfixed. "Leave me alone. Please just leave me alone", Armonia murmured.

"I thought you wanted me to kill you?"

Armonia turned to Daleth. "Yes, please kill me. Get it over with already!"

"I already explained to you I can't harm you, although you are sorely tempting me."

Armonia stomped her feet. "Then what good are ya?"

"I am very equipped and could end you ten times over before you took a second breath."

Armonia jerked violently once more. She walked toward Daleth and ran her nails over his arm. "Show me."

Daleth snatched her wrist. The tiny hairs on the back of Armonia's neck sprung up at his touch. He meanwhile eyed Armonia to discern what to make of her. He still sensed no fear. She suffered for sure but had no true fear. He for some reason couldn't feed off her pain try as he did. "You're not afraid", he whispered.

Armonia smiled slyly. "Maybe the others, they're weak. I'm the strong one, the one who won't let myself be hurt anymore. But you can still try and make me afraid."

"If you won't let yourself be hurt then why do you want me to kill you?"

"So the pain will end, silly."

Armonia pounded her forehead with the flat of her free hand and wrenched her other hand from Daleth's grip. She grunted and whimpered and threw herself against the wall repeatedly.

"Stop that this instant!" Daleth yelled. "I told you I will get nothing if you are harmed even by your own inept self." Before Daleth could reach her Armonia launched herself against the wall and hit her head. She fell back unconscious into Daleth's arms. Daleth checked her vital signs. She lived and seemed to have no visible injuries.

Daleth looked around the alley. He took off his cloak and wrapped her in it. He then picked up a hat that one of the gang members had dropped in the alley when they fled. He pulled it down as far as it would go to obstruct his face. He slung the cocooned Armonia over his shoulders and made his way back onto the streets hoping no one would recognize him and just assume he was transporting a piece of furniture or something.

〈 〉

ONCE MORE ON THE SHIP, Daleth gripped his crystals in a clenched fist as he waited in line to approach the checkpoint for Circapto's Orbit. Most Orbits allowed ships to come and go at will. Since Circapto was the biggest importer and exporter they employed more stringent methods to monitor the comings and goings. Daleth had stowed Armonia who was still, thankfully, unconscious in a secret hollowed-out compartment underneath the floor of the bridge. He wished to pass through the checkpoint with minimal trouble. He was certainly no stranger to death but killing a Circapto trade official was bad for business. In his line of work as a mercenary, his victims were always the dregs of society or involved heavily in the darkness trade. The various governments and even The Way of The Light tended to look the other way.

Daleth slowed his ship and entered the station he was directed toward. The stations were giant scanners that orbited Circapto just below the protective bubble that surrounded the world. The airlocks sealed as soon as his ship entered the station to prevent him from making a hasty escape. The air pumps were then turned on. Daleth used his skills to keep focused on the present moment. He would have to be ready to think fast if they detected his prisoner. The sonic scanners Circapto used began their scan, and sound frequencies beyond the hearing scale of Uprights bombarded the ship. They provided an echo image of the layout, as well as all its contents. The compartment Armonia had been placed in was made of special soundproof material you could only get in the darkness trade. It was an old smuggler's trick to have a tiny compartment or two made from such material onboard your ship, often called a snuffer. Daleth didn't do much smuggling but he still found it useful to have on board from time to time. As long as the compartments were small enough they usually showed up as a blotchy part of the ship that was disregarded. Fortunately, Armonia was rather petit and just fit into the compartment.

    The airlocks hissed as the doors both in front of and behind the ship slid open. Daleth's shoulder's dropped downward, his fist opened allowing the crystals to slide safely back into their pouch. He placed both his hands back on the steering pad and sped out of the checkpoint.

    After he had gotten far enough away from Circapto for his taste, he put the ship in neutral once more. He stared out at the emptiness beyond the system. *Is that, after all is said and done, where I truly belong?* The idea of just going straight ahead to the oblivion of deep space crept into his mind, as it frequently did. He could leave Iris far behind and give himself up to the silent void that those pinpricks of light inhabited. He concentrated on one such point and pictured himself floating around it. A home that seemed so close, yet so far. If he ever acted out his fantasies he would surely die out there in the blackness but he would surely die within the system as well. His life was probably a little over half done. There was not going to be a joyous Twin Flame ending for him, he was sure of that fact more than he was sure of anything else. His shoulders slumped forward as he let out a heavy sigh.

    He got up from the steering console and opened the secret compartment door on the floor of the bridge. The mass at the bottom didn't stir. Daleth carefully unwrapped Armonia who was indeed still unconscious and he donned his cloak once more. He found some cargo straps and used them to bind her hands together and fixed them to a pipe that ran along one of the sub-corridors. He checked her to ensure himself she was still alive and in good health, physically at least. He then returned to the bridge and set course for the Orbit of Baabcrest.

⟨ ⟩

EBJAN ORBIT

Zean dragged her feet up the stone steps to her modest home in Sector 321. She paused at the door. It had been a micro of a gremrev but still a trying journey to Iris and back. True it was a thrill to have laid her own eyes on The Spark and hear its commanding yet soothing voice. At the same time though she felt drained by the petty and shortsighted minds of others around her in that most auspicious conference. Indeed in Zean's opinion, it should have been the system's finest moment and a testament to the commitment all Orbits should have to The Way of The Light. Instead, it was a depressing reminder that even after all The Spark has shared with them Uprights are still irresponsible. *They remain committed to individual gain first and foremost. Didn't anyone besides me pay attention to their history lessons in their respective Prep Centers? Did they not heed the mistakes of the ancients? I will have to ensure my Light is all the brighter so as not to fall victim to the dark ignorance of these other supposed leaders.*

Zean tried to push these depressing thoughts out of her head. The familiar rustic buildings of her home sector gave her comfort. Ebjan was known for its quaint feel and it always rejuvenated her resolve. Now that business was finally done she desired most a hot bath and some restorative candle contemplation, her favorite ritual aside from dreaming. It would be just the thing to set her back at ease.

When Zean stepped over the threshold of her home a familiar voice met her ears, "My brightness, is that you?"

Zean's chest felt like it would burst when she heard the voice of her reflection. She saw Jamila's oval face with its bright green eyes. Her long dark hair swayed from side to side as she rushed to embrace Zean. They squeezed tight their flesh and felt as though it melted into one another's. Their flush cheeks nuzzled together and they couldn't help but make soft murmurs of delight. Zean's skin tingled at the physical contact, a sure sign of a reflection that would become a Twin Flame.

"I'm overjoyed to see you but what are you doing here? I thought you were doing a tour of Orogunu?"

They separated and a playful smile budded on Jamila's face. "I took a brief leave. Even we guardians need a little self-care sometimes. Happy Grevolios!" With a flourish of Jamila's arms, Zean took notice for the first time of the house full of decorations. Practically every wall had a mirror of some size while lights hung from the ceiling and lined every door frame. It illuminated the otherwise plain abode.

"It's perfect! You did all this?" Jamila nodded grinning from ear to ear at her reflection's exuberance. Zean's own brown eyes became wet as she gazed into Jamila's. "You are the best reflection one could ever hope for. I was happy enough to settle for a nice bath and some candle contemplation."

Jamila took Zean's hands in hers. "You can still do all of that but now you have company." They embraced once more before giddily skipping off to the washroom.

《 》

BAABCREST ORBIT

Corry scuttled through the awe-inspiring corridors of the headquarters for the School of Knowledge. The giant arched hallways echoed with her footsteps. The ornate stone and woodwork which she usually took time to admire were completely lost on her at the moment.

The three moons of Baabcrest are rather small and had no original life on them. They were uninhabited before the coming of The Spark, aside from military outposts. When The Spark arrived and deemed each Orbit design its form of government it proved to be a challenge for Baabcrest. The entire planet was sparsely populated with small diverse tribes that barely had any leadership. After many discussions amongst themselves, they realized that every individual needed and sought three things, prosperity, knowledge, and relationships. Thus centers were erected on the three moons to oversee and master just those items. Any resident of Baabcrest, if they ran into a problem in any one of those areas, could go to the moon that oversaw that aspect of life and have their issue addressed by masters. Likewise, the residents of those moons ensured the inhabitants of Baabcrest saw the very best possible of those three areas as they worked toward Twin Flame status.

Those centers grew and attracted Uprights from all over the system who wanted to learn more about the three subjects. Corry was one such example. She saw a lack in her Origin Orbit of Fimeger which was more interested in status than expanding their horizons. Corry decided to spend some time in the School of Knowledge to see what she could learn. That was when she met Ramek and they struck up a good rapport.

It still took a little time till Ramek informed Corry that he was part of the secret Order of Consciousness. Corry had become aware of the Order while studying at the school. Ramek had been crafty in dropping hints to Corry beforehand. Ramek had subtly influenced their conversations with tidbits of the Order's philosophy to test Corry. Corry was intrigued but she was a little hesitant to seek the Order outright. The Order made more sense to her than the Way ever did but joining it would have made her an outlaw. All her training in the Prep Center pushed against her doing it but something within her gut pulled her toward it regardless.

It surprisingly came as a relief to Corry when Ramek exposed himself and asked Corry to join. His confidence reinforced the feelings she had been having that this was the right path for her. She enthusiastically agreed and the two have posed as reflections ever since.

Now Corry found herself at the center of the most audacious undertaking the group has ever done. An experiment to try and stretch the boundaries of the mind of an Upright further than they had ever been stretched before. To do through science what was unable to be achieved through discipline. There were old dusty writings of ancient inhabitants of this star system receiving visions of strange creatures and worlds. Whether these were the lunatic ravings of Uprights losing their grip on reality or Uprights seeing a reality hidden from common sight was never definitively determined. The debate seemed null and void to the system at large when The Spark appeared. But there were a few who were not so easily able to discard these stories. They were intent on doggedly pursuing the truth at all costs. These pioneers were the founders of the Order of Consciousness.

They created the Order to free the mind of the physical world's constraints. They firmly held that the mind no longer caged could free themselves and perhaps all the inhabitants of the system from the overbearing grip of The Way of The Light. The discipline of the Order was to achieve just that end but no member to date had ever gotten to what was believed to be the full level of mastery of their mental facilities. When the overpopulation crisis caused whispers in the Orbits of handing full control to Twin Flames the Order knew it must take drastic action.

With the School of Knowledge being a covert hub for the Order Corry and Ramek found themselves at the center of the enterprise. But things quickly got out of hand. The Order strove to release themselves from all emotion but they let anxiety creep in and the results were disastrous. Corry was sent to try and get a handle on the situation and now she needed to report to her Cell.

Corry lifted the trim of her purple robe off the marble floor and increased her pace when she saw familiar faces. Her Cell was clustered in a crevice on the far side of the building. The slanted ceiling behind the ornate grand staircase made it an especially good place to hide.

Since the Order of Consciousness was deemed an Obstruction to the Light by The Spark, members had to develop safeguards to protect the organization. The Order was divided into Cells which usually consisted of eight to twelve members. Each Cell had one member who was called a transmitter that dealt exclusively with Cell intercommunication. In this way, if there was ever a turncoat in the Cell it would only take out one Cell. At worst if it was the transmitter who betrayed them then it may result in transmitters from other Cells being eliminated but it would stop there. Members were trained to overcome physical sensations and emotional attachments so interrogation of captured members would be worthless.

Corry's Cell was a small one. Aside from her and Ramek, there was Florian, Mareen, Xanjiv, Ava, and Evelyn. Tania filled out the Cell as their transmitter. Corry initiated the customary salutation of the Order and said, "Corruption in all that is holy and right."

Ramek responded, "Corruption is The Way of The Light."

Ava got right down to business. "Did you find Daleth?"

"Yes, my observation trek proved to be a successful guise." It was customary for Magistrates of Knowledge to take frequent tours of the system and observe the various cultures to enhance the comprehension of the system. Corry used the custom as a cover to search for Daleth.

"I still believe it unwise to involve the Follower of Vuhox," said Florian as his button nose crinkled. The Order was trained to not see things as good or bad. Instead, all were neutral and one need only decide how they wished to experience it. The use of the word unwise was the strongest language Florian could use to show his displeasure over the involvement of Daleth.

Tania, the most senior and disciplined member present, responded to the rebuke. "We were given this task and meditated heavily upon it. Your thoughts are acknowledged but we have already committed to this course of action."

Xanjiv tilted his bulbous head. He moved his gaze down to his robe and gently smoothed it with the back of his hand. "I believe our brother wished to remind us of the fact that we are involved in strained, one might even say, volatile times. We must keep our minds sharp so we can adjust to the events as they unfold."

"Indeed. Fortunately, the Orbits did not go so far as to turn over full control of this system to The Spark but it may very well still happen and perhaps sooner than we think." The group's faces turned grim at the words of their sister Evelyn.

"We have Cells working to stall that occurrence for as long as possible. We must focus on our part." Tania shifted her attention to Corry once more. "Speak to us, sister. How did it go?"

Corry was taken aback at how much her body fidgeted when she told of her encounter with the infamous Daleth. Tania seemed to take notice of this but did not announce her observations to interrupt Corry.

Florian's face twisted into a mask of disgust as Corry recounted the events. "When he brings us the experiment we should just end his existence. It would do the entire system a favor. The fact that The Way of The Light didn't put an end to him shows its true sinister nature. How dare they use the Order as a scapegoat for the Vuhox."

"You are letting emotional bias affect your judgment, brother", Tania reprimanded. She did so with the gentleness that she was known for after nearly three gremrevs. Her soft features and bright yellow eyes showed tempered wisdom beyond all the others. Still, she was starting to grow wrinkles under those deep eyes. Her time was growing short regardless of whatever happened to the Order.

Corry found it hard to believe a mind so expanded as hers was coming to its expiration. That was after all one of the hopes of the great experiment. To show that the mind could shape its destiny beyond all other forces.

"We must not complicate matters," Ava reminded the entire Cell as she tossed wisps of greasy blue hair out of her face.

"Matters are already complicated," Xanjiv said. "The experiment escaped after shorting out its tracking implant and now could be anywhere to say nothing of its mental state."

"Which is why we had to use the Vuhox," Ava stated in a matter of fact tone.

"Agreed it is a calculated risk but his talents prove to be our best hope for finding the experiment," Tania added almost to remind herself of the justifications for their extreme actions, as well as the group as a whole.

Evelyn's almond eyes closed and she shook her head slightly. She cut right to what was on everybody's mind. "We must stabilize the experiment. For it's our only antidote to the inevitable takeover of The Spark."

"This whole crisis of overpopulation was just cooked up to allow The Spark to tighten their grip of control throughout the system," said Xanjiv. "That derelict Upright we used must be brought under control before the people's minds get any more revved up with hysteria."

A thought that has always nagged at Corry popped into her head once more. She decided to finally give voice to it. "If The Spark wanted to dominate us, why give each Orbit the ability to choose their government in the first place?"

"Freedom is always best given up voluntarily. The mind must willingly decide for it to truly be subsumed," Xanjiv solemnly said.

Ramek put a hand on Corry's shoulder and looked deeply into her eyes. As he spoke Corry noticed his thick heavy brows crease with genuine concern. "Remember your teachings. Remember why you are here. The Spark exists to quell the spark of the mind." The heavy mask he wore on his dark features was so unlike the Ramek she usually knew. Everybody in her cell was faltering with their training under these strained circumstances.

"Rest assured The Spark will root out all of us once full control of this system is handed over. Our time is limited", said Xanjiv gravely.

"The experiment's mind cannot be defeated, it just needs to be managed properly", said Evelyn.

"Which is why Daleth is the key. Someone like him properly motivated will not fail." Tania then gazed at Corry. "So do you believe he was sincerely motivated?"

Corry concentrated for a moment to ensure all bias was removed before she answered, "I do."

"I just hope he finds the experiment quickly," added Mareen. Her head hung so low that her red curls obscured her freckled face.

Mareen's sentiments were echoed by all. Corry was taught, as was the rest of the members of the Order, to transcend emotion but she couldn't help feeling that the entire system was waiting to explode. Still, Daleth's reputation was renowned. She sensed raw power during their encounter. She had to trust it would be enough.

⟨ ⟩

EBJAN ORBIT

Armonia blinked her eyes open. Everything had a fuzzy haze around it but it looked like she was inside a ship. Her head throbbed. She tried to bring her hand to it but found she could not move either of them. A lump formed in her throat as she realized they were tethered to something above her head. "Help!" she instinctively screamed in a high-pitched voice. It did not surprise her when no one answered her cry.

It all flooded back to her brain at once. There was that creep in the alley who wanted her to come with him. He must be the one who held her captive. At least she had that much figured out. She still hadn't the faintest idea who she was or anything from her past. Only vague memories of stowing away on a cargo ship to get to Circapto. After that, her memories dropped off again until the guy in the alley showed up. Even those events were jumbled fragments in her tortured mind.

The thumps of her heart rang in her ears like an incessant drum. Then slowly but surely the dull colors in the scant light began to shift. It was happening again. Her eyes widened. She strained against the straps that held her in place. Suddenly like a piercing hot knife through her brain she saw a cavern with jagged rocky spears pointing down from the ceiling over a large teal lake. It felt like she was inside the cavern even though she knew from the pressure on her wrists she was still onboard the ship. The cavern was familiar even though she had no memory of it. There was movement in the shadows where there wasn't any before. Her hands were clammy and her mouth became parched. Her head felt like it was being pried apart. Her stomach was turned upside down. She began to kick her legs as the spiny creatures from the darkness emerged into full view. She knew so little but she did know in the debris of her mind that these crawling shapes didn't belong. Some had spindly legs while others had webbed claws. Some had diamond-shaped heads while others were triangular. They all had beady eyes but they varied in number. As they moved toward her she let out a scream from the deepest pit inside her.

Daleth was piloting his ship when the guttural scream slammed into his eardrums. He didn't have time to think about it for at the same moment the console before him began to overload. Arches of violet and green-colored electricity flew up in his face. He kept his hands firmly planted on the sensory pad. He wasn't sure if he could lift them even if he wanted to do so. A sucker punch to his gut let him know the inertia canceler had ceased to function. The bile and acid in his stomach projected out of his mouth and onto the console.

The yoke implanted above his right shoulder blade was being affected. Usually, he could barely feel it while using it to pilot. The yoke was so small and was engineered to fuse with the tissues of the body, even ones acquired on the darkness trade like his own. The yoke allowed him to connect with the ship when his hands were placed on the sensory pad so the ship became a seamless extension of his own body. Right now though it felt like it was being cut out of him with a jagged rusted blade.

He used all his training to keep himself conscious through the agony. The electrical jolts caused his muscles to convulse. The spasms would have made pulp of his internal organs if he had been unable to shield himself. The instruments appeared to be fried beyond repair. He knew they were passing over Ebjan before all this occurred. With the ship dead it would be pulled down toward the surface at the mercy of the planetary forces. *If my quarry and I are to survive the static shields would still need to be intact despite what just transpired.* There was nothing for Daleth to do but hope. For the first time in a very long time, he was utterly at the mercy of chance.

Chapter 3

EBJAN ORBIT

Peridot and Turako had been partnered guardians for almost a quarter of a gremrev. The two got along great. They had an ease of familiarity while working together on Ebjan to ensure everyone's safety and well-being.

Turako considered himself quite lucky Peridot was his first assigned partner after graduation from the academy. Because Peridot was a Twin Flame in development from two councilors of Ebjan, Turako was able to remain stationed in the Ebjan Orbit his entire career with Peridot. Ebjan was such an orderly Orbit that nothing ever too big came up. There were a lot of darkness traders in this Orbit who tried to take advantage of Ebjan's bureaucratic systems but they mostly existed under a "don't bother us and we won't bother you" policy. They didn't want any trouble and the ones who didn't know how to fly low were usually picked off by their kind. You didn't have the wild gangs trying to find excitement and danger that roved around Gremoilio and Circapto. The natural environment of Ebjan was also not very dangerous. No ravenous beasts like Fimeger or inhospitable cold like Comqwo. Yes, Ebjan was one of the more cushy tours that a guardian could do.

It was a good life but it would be coming to an end soon. Peridot's maturation was nearly complete. In a little more than the blink of an eye he would become a full-fledged Twin Flame. Peridot assured his friend that he would use his newfound influence to help him out. Set him up somewhere nice where he could leisurely look for his own reflection to join Peridot in Twin Flame status. Turako wanted to believe that was true but he still doubted he could be so fortunate in life.

Tonight Peridot and Turako decided to relax by the river that ran through section one hundred and eleven. "So you think you can give up food and water when you become a Twin Flame," Turako remarked as they gazed at the indigo sky.

"The winds seem to be blowing that way so don't have much of a choice. I'm sure it's only temporary, till everyone calms down. I'll still be venerated."

"Yeah. You're right. It's still got to be better than being a guardian."

"You'll get there one day as well and till then you got me to look out for you." Peridot turned his charming baby face toward Turako and flashed his pearly whites.

"Don't mock me. You will be living on Iris busy overseeing so many that I will be a distant memory to you."

"Twin Flames give out benefits to those they favor all the time. It's how it works. I will be no different. I promise."

A smile flashed across Turako's face. "Thanks, buddy."

"You still thinking of leaving the guardians after I become full Twin Flame?"

Turako shrugged. "Yea, probably. Why?"

"This whole Twin Flame fasting to preserve resources is all just a stall tactic. I think the guardians will be answering to Twin Flames before you know it. You might want to stick around. It will make it even easier for me to take care of you."

"You think it will happen that soon? I mean I just can't see Orbits like Circapto or Fimeger giving up their power so easily. I think they will just try to downplay the whole crisis."

"All the Orbits are just working behind the scenes so their rulers will get fast-tracked to Twin Flame status or make sure Twin Flames from their Orbits take over. Like I said Twin Flames look out for where they came from."

Turako shrugged. "I suppose you know better than me."

"Once all that maneuvering gets taken care of you will see another conference and they will easily hand power over. It benefits them in the long run. The current governments don't want to be responsible if things get worse. It will just make it harder for them to hold any kind of prestige."

Turako pulled a laxal flower from the ground and began absentmindedly pulling its coral and red petals one by one. "I know I asked this before but what does it feel like being a Twin Flame?"

Peridot jutted his lips out as he considered the oft-asked question. "I would imagine it feels just as you feel. I don't have anything to compare it to, after all."

"Do you have like two minds inside your head?"

"Kinda. At first, it felt like I had two people inside my head, then it eventually felt like they are both me but like sometimes they disagree. Now it just feels like it's all me."

"Sure, that makes sense."

"Come on we better get back on patrol before the higher-ups get all bent out of shape."

Peridot and Turako got up off the ground and brushed off their gold jumpsuits. Suddenly Turako pointed to the sky. "Will you look at that!"

Peridot followed his gaze and saw a streaking bright light coming across the sky. "Is that a comet?"

"Too small and we would have seen it sooner." The object continued to plummet in altitude till it landed with a giant splash only a mile away from them up the river. Water vapor erupted like a volcano from the spot. "Come on we better get over there and check it out. I'll drive, you radio for backup just in case."

"What do you think it is?"

"Probably just some orbital scrap but these days you can't be too sure." They got in their patrol skimmer and headed off along the bank of the river to investigate. The cool night air whipped in their faces as they rode the sleek gold vehicle.

⟨ ⟩

EBJAN ORBIT

Daleth emerged from the muddy waters. He gasped for air as Armonia's arms wrapped around his neck. She rode half-conscious on his back to the riverbank. He laid her down on the ground and took stock of himself. Aside from some bruises and mild burns he was unscathed. He assessed Armonia next. Her clothes were torn up something fierce and she had some scratches but nothing appeared too serious. This surprised him since she did not have his assets. As he pondered this she groaned and rolled over and scrunched into a fetal position. Daleth noticed two large scars on each of her shoulder blades. He ran a hand over his scars as his mind wandered into the past. He was snapped back to the present moment by the shouts of two voices.

Peridot and Turako scurried down the steep embankment. "Halt! Identify yourselves!" yelled Peridot.

"We crash-landed our ship but we're fine. There's nothing more to worry about," Daleth snarled.

"He's trying to abduct me!" came Armonia's shrill voice. She attempted in vain to get to her feet.

Daleth stepped in front of Armonia to conceal her with his own body. "Don't listen to her. She's a prisoner. I'm escorting her to a Light Bearing Center for rehabilitation."

"Can we see your documents?" Turako asked.

"Be my guest, they're at the bottom of the river."

Armonia stumbled out from behind Daleth and fell into Turako. "He won't kill me so maybe you can or are you scared like him?"

Peridot who had a flicker of recognition from the moment he laid eyes on Daleth suddenly unclipped his laser from his hip and trained it on him. "Wait! You're the Follower of Vuhox! Don't move!"

"Don't you dare presume to tell me what to do." His voice was steady now without a trace of emotion. He had depleted all his reserves to save himself back on the ship but now this fool was recharging him. He felt it surge even stronger than normal. He wasn't sure why, he was just grateful for its taste. Armonia took the laser gun off the clip on Turako's hip. Turako lunged for it and tried to wrest it from her but was taken aback by her strength. Daleth used this momentary distraction to reach for his crystals.

"I swear I'll fire!" yelled Peridot, his voice shaky.

"Just walk away and let me handle this. I'm a mercenary, it's what I do." Daleth made a move toward Turako and Armonia who were still locked in a struggle over the weapon.

DREAMING

Peridot fired a shot from his laser. Daleth's instincts allowed him to step back in enough time to avoid the blast. Peridot seemed to be unfazed by the fact that his target so easily avoided his shot. "Don't move or the next one won't miss!"

Daleth stood there, his muscles tense. He tried to consider if this ridiculous mission was worth him taking out two guardians. Just then the laser gun Armonia and Turako were both in a struggle over went off, striking Turako. He grunted and hit the ground hard, along with the gun. Peridot redirected his weapon toward Armonia and fired. Daleth's crystals flew out of his hand and deflected the energy beam. Another flew off and went right through Peridot's chin and exited out of his eye socket. He dropped to the ground with a sickening thud.

"Whoa, ya need to teach me that trick," said Armonia. He angrily dragged her away from the two fallen bodies but froze when he spied vapors coming off of Peridot's body.

"Space dust," he murmured. The vapors increased till it formed a thick fog that poured out of Peridot's body and wafted into the night air.

"Are ya, like, doing that?"

"No, don't be stupid. He was obviously a Twin Flame in progress." Armonia gave Daleth a quizzical look. "A special body which two reflections pour their essence into so they can be immortal once they have cast out all darkness and obstructions to the Light within themselves. How do you not know this?"

"I told ya. I hardly remember anything. That guy didn't look like anything special to me."

"There is no real difference until the transfer is complete, which usually takes about a third of a gremrev. I just made two bitter enemies."

Armonia scrunched up her face. "Gremrev?"

"The time it takes for Gremoilio to circle Iris. What is wrong with you?"

They were interrupted before Armonia could answer by the shout of voices. More guardians were starting to appear over the crest of the hill so he quickly grabbed Armonia and against her protests dragged her into the shadows.

CIRCAPTO ORBIT

Leon wetted his mouth with a sip from the glass of water on the table next to him. He then cleared his scratchy throat and continued his presentation. "So in conclusion this specimen, although not an Upright, will prove to be the perfect foil for Uprights, physically speaking." The faces before him in the cramped sterile room looked blankly back at him. Leon's stomach churned as he had to connect the dots for the small crowd. "Being the perfect foil, they will quickly reduce the population of Uprights which will lead to the necessity of the hatcheries once more."

The group of Uprights broke into loud whispers as they conferred amongst themselves around the massive stainless steel table. One of the voices rose above the others. "I don't see how these things are going to stand up to our technological forces."

Leon pinched the bridge of his nose and took a slow deliberate breath. "As I explained their skin is nearly impervious."

"That means nothing when it comes to lasers."

"Their skin is specially designed to disperse most forms of energy including heat."

"Then they can't be killed?" a high-pitched voice asked.

"Sonic weapons will be fairly effective. They will permeate the skin and disrupt the internal systems."

"There are already contracts in place," Leon's boss reassured. "If everyone feels comfortable with this solution we will start to reach out to various smugglers, through the proper channels of course, so they can start delivering these creatures to various Orbits."

"I thought you told us these organisms hatch in the vacuum of space?"

Leon couldn't help but heave a heavy sigh at having to explain the life cycle of his creation once more. "These creatures lay eggs which do need a period of being in an airless environment to mature. They hatch upon exposure to the elements in a standard atmosphere, then mature rapidly upon hatching. This life cycle was used to offer a plausible means for their arrival in the system."

"Will they be delivered to Circapto?" An Upright in the corner asked.

"Of course", responded another in the crowd. "You want people to start asking the wrong questions?"

Leon rolled his eyes. *How did this group ever get to be at the top of their respective trades? These were the best and brightest of Circapto's industry?* It made him smirk. The gathering in the room began to discuss the logistics of propagation. Leon had little interest. These were messy details that had nothing to do with his genetic labors. He caught bits and pieces as he tried to gather his things and make a tactful exit. Something about shipping fully sedated ones in crates timed to wake up and devour the criminals transporting them. It was all so crass, unlike his creation which was a work of art.

Perhaps that's the reason why this group finds themselves so desperate to reclaim their notary within the system, Leon thought to himself. *They build their self-worth on the fickle foundation of the whims of the populace. True art, something you create by pouring yourself freely into, is what lasts forever. It stands indifferent to the opinion of others.* Leon was bemused by his insight.

After all, he did not make his creation to impress anybody or to win any prize. He made it simply because he knew he could. It was as natural as taking a breath. The system will now take notice of something born of him. Not because they asked for it. They will take notice simply because it exists and demands to be noticed. This gave comfort to Leon.

⟨ ⟩

EBJAN ORBIT

Daleth opened the window to Lorelei's place and roughly shoved Armonia through. He then followed suit. "Would ya quit pushing me around, already?" Armonia took in the disheveled abode. Blankets and clothes were strewn on the floor haphazardly. A couple of crates and a worn mattress served as the only furnishings. Some empty bottles and chipped plates were stacked on top of one of the crates opposite the mattress. The only source of light seemed to be what trickled in from the neon sign of the theater across the street and the roadway lamps. The scent of musk and stale sweat hit Armonia's nose and she cringed. "What are we doing in this dump?"

"Just keep quiet till I can figure something out."

"Why should I listen to ya? You're a meany."

Daleth ignored Armonia and began to pace back and forth. The city was currently swarming with guardians and he could sense palpable anxiety on the way over. Even if no one had seen him on the riverbank they would surely stop to question him on the streets, especially with Armonia in tow. He was just about to abandon the whole ordeal and lay low when he heard the door open. He instinctually reached for his crystals but stopped when he saw the pock-marked face of Lorelei.

"I thought you would be here!" She exclaimed. "There are guardians everywhere looking for you. I had to ditch an unauthorized dreaming session. What did you do?"

Before Daleth could answer Armonia collapsed to her knees and clutched her head. She uttered unrecognizable words and her eyes rolled back in her head. The vision of the cavern with the lake tried to creep into her mind once more and she clenched her teeth to fight it back. Daleth's jaw stiffened as he moved toward Armonia but he stopped in his tracks when Lorelei held out her arm. "Who is this?"

"An annoyance," grumbled Daleth. "It is because of her that I killed a guardian who was a Twin Flame in progress."

Lorelei moved her intense gaze from Armonia to Daleth, her eyes seemed like they were ready to pop out of her head. "Not Peridot?"

"How should I know what his name was?"

"You better hope that wasn't his name. His Origin Flames are both influential councilors here. But again I ask who is this Upright?" Armonia exhausted and soaked with perspiration lowered her hands. She began to scream. Daleth pounced on her in a heartbeat and stifled her cries with his hand. "What is her problem?"

"That's what I'd like to know. I was given a job to find her and deliver her to the School of Knowledge moon. She's been acting this way ever since I found her on Circapto. I think she shorted out my ship and now she's trying to bite me." Daleth pushed Armonia away from him. Out of his clutches, she scrambled over to Lorelei.

"What's this place? Who are ya two?"

"Again with this? That's it I'm done with you!" snapped Daleth. Daleth moved with ferocity toward Armonia who hid behind Lorelei. It was only Lorelei's severe expression that halted Daleth in his rage. "That Upright is an unwieldy dagger at my throat!"

"I don't even know ya!"

"You lie and not well. I abducted you only microns of a gremrev ago."

Lorelei slowly knelt to face Armonia. "Perhaps the better question is who are you and what was that language you were speaking?"

"Who cares?"

Lorelei's head whipped around to Daleth. "Shhh!" She then returned her focus to the bewildered person thumping her head with the heel of her hand.

"Language? I don't know what ya talking about. I speak the same as you do. My name's Armonia though."

"It is not! You told me you had no name. You saw the word you call yourself on a slip of paper I had."

Lorelei glanced up at Daleth with a smirk. "So you did consider dreaming?"

"I forgot it was there," he said through gritted teeth.

Armonia's head swiveled between the two strangers. "What's dreaming?"

Lorelei peered deeply into Armonia's eyes. Armonia noticed a gentle strength in those violet eyes which studied her. A strength that her red ones seemed to lack. Even Daleth's dark eyes while intimidating lacked the purpose of these violet ones.

In a soothing voice, Lorelei answered Armonia. "If you trust me I can show you."

"I don't know ya both. How should I trust either of ya?"

"We don't have time for this."

Lorelei rolled her eyes up to meet Daleth's. "Bright out."

"What exactly about this situation should cause me to bright out?"

Lorelei ignored him and turned her attention back to Armonia who was hunched over on the floor and now held her arms tightly against her as she softly whimpered. Lorelei gently guided Armonia to get off the floor and sit on the edge of the mattress with her. Daleth protested but Lorelei snapped, "loodeev" and he relented.

"I am Lorelei a darkness dealer and Daleth over there is a mercenary. I believe dreaming will help you feel better and answer a lot of questions."

"It can take away the pain?"

Lorelei offered her hand. She stared down at it and then met those welcoming violet eyes. With a distinct quiver, she put her hand in Lorelei's. She was guided to lay back on the bedding.

"You're really going to do an unauthorized dreaming session with her?"

"Neither you nor I give a care for the Way," replied Lorelei dismissively. Daleth grumbled and made his way toward the window but just stared out it.

"Unauthorized?" Armonia's voice raised an octave.

Lorelei fluffed the pillow behind Armonia's head. "You asked if dreaming would remove your pain. It removes all discomfort both physical and mental. But it does so much more than just get rid of the pain."

Lorelei carefully pulled off the tattered damp rags which clung to Armonia's body. She then proceeded to casually remove her dress. "Dreaming discharges stored energy that has built up so we can act and think clearer."

Lorelei caressed Armonia's face and began to slowly move downward. She languished at her breasts, grazing her areola and nipples before moving to her abdomen, which she peppered with pecks of her lips. She felt Armonia's core muscles flex underneath the soft flesh. "Just relax. Dreaming lets us release the world, the demands we and others put on ourselves so we can be our true selves."

Lorelei continued her journey and began to give tender smacks with her lips to Armonia's inner thighs. "It allows us to focus on our bodies and be fully present in the sensations which are the gift of life." Lorelei gave a wet slow lick to Armonia's vulva. She heard her breath get caught in her throat and felt the body beneath her shudder.

"It lets us play with different energies so we can learn what we are capable of." She then gave another slow lick with a broad tongue. Armonia let out a steady groan in response. Lorelei then placed the heel of her hand on Armonia's mound, her fingers draped over her vulva. She curled her middle finger and stroked. She could feel the moist tissue grow hotter and wetter after each stroke. "Dreaming allows us to be free."

Armonia reached up and gripped Lorelei's bicep. She squeezed and dug her impressive nails into Lorelei's skin, nearly piercing it. Daleth saw this out of the corner of his eye and snapped his attention back to the room. He moved toward them but Lorelei held up her non-occupied hand. He abated and went back to the window.

Lorelei brought her hand down and started to massage her vulva with it. Her voice became a hushed whisper as she spoke. "Dreaming is how we find our rhythm with the world." Lorelei felt Armonia press against her palm, her clitoris throbbing. They both rocked their hips back and forth in a smooth rhythm with one another. "It lets us roll with the cycles of life."

Lorelei gave a momentary pause to her stimulation and handed a pillow to Armonia, whose moans increased in volume and frequency. Armonia's mind took a brief pause from the waves of pleasure and suddenly remembered the discussion about this dreaming being unauthorized. She instinctively used it to muffle herself.

"Dreaming allows us to connect with someone on a fundamental but profound level. Two momentarily cry out to the universe as one."

Both were breathing heavily and swayed in unison now. Lorelei closed her eyelids but continued, her voice now choppy amidst heaving gasps for air. "It allows us to see our role in the bigger picture. With dreaming, we commune with something which can't be comprehended. But we still get to glimpse the beauty of the oneness of life. With that glimpse, we see more than we ever could with our eyes."

Lorelei felt the tremendous contractions and heard the muffled cries under the pillow. Only then did she fully let herself go. Like the unrelenting waves of the oceans, she let her own sensations crash over her entire body. Her feet curled and flexed as her chest heaved. Though her eyes were still shut she saw a brain in front of her with invisible hands tearing it asunder. Scenes of life poured out of the remnants. Moments of destruction, violence, and suffering entered her vision. She couldn't tell if they were events of what will be or events that already passed. She then saw an explosion of white which quickly transformed into the deepest blackness she had ever known. Oddly it was only at this point that she felt a tremendous calm come over her.

Lorelei's eyelids fluttered open as the sounds of Armonia's orgasm abated. She glanced over at Daleth who turned from the window to meet her gaze. The two locked eyes for a moment which seemed to freeze time itself as an eternity passed through the space between them. Finally, Daleth arched his brow, "So did you fix her?"

"Her mind is a force unlike any I have encountered. It is as untamed as nature and as powerful too."

"Nothing I can't handle," said Daleth. He once more shifted his eyes to the window.

Armonia swept the pillow from her face to reveal a grin from ear to ear. "I like dreaming."

"Are you still a wild freak?" Daleth asked leaving his station by the window.

"I think I'm better. The pain is gone at least."

"Look her wounds are gone too," Lorelei's mouth fell open in awe. "I've never seen dreaming do that before."

Daleth snapped his attention back to the room and with a chill in his voice said, "Impressive dreaming." He hoisted Armonia over his shoulder. "We'll steal a ship and be on our way then."

Lorelei scrambled to get in between them and the door. She thrust her arms out and said, "Have you lost your mind now? You can't just walk through the streets with her."

"I suppose you're right." Daleth snatched a blanket from the mattress and tossed it over Armonia.

"Hey!" Armonia cried yanking the blanket off. "I can walk you know."

"Good, then let's move." Daleth plopped Armonia down.

"You don't understand. Armonia might be the key to toppling The Spark."

"I couldn't care less. All I want is to collect my payment and be done with this mess."

"You said you think she shorted out your ship. After our session, I have no doubt she's capable of such a thing. Did she also damage your yoke?"

"I'll figure it out."

Lorelei cocked her head. "Get real. Even if you managed to avoid all the heightened security you can't get far in a ship with a damaged yoke. Not to mention if you are supposed to deliver her to the School of Knowledge then it was the Order that hired you."

"I'm aware."

Lorelei's voice rose. "They'll kill you for what you are, a stain on their organization."

"I'd like to see them try," Daleth's voice was a low rumble.

Armonia broke the awkward silence. "Do you two always fight?"

Lorelei walked to a closet in the far corner of the apartment. "Come I'll give you some of my clothes. We're almost the same size, you're just a bit more substantial so I'll find loose-fitting stuff."

"Then we're going," said Daleth.

"It would be the end for both of you if you do."

Daleth jutted his chin out. "I'm not scared of the Order."

"What's the Order anyway?" Armonia asked.

"A group of heretics that believe all sensations are a distraction for the mind's true potential." Lorelei tossed Armonia some clothes and then turned to Daleth. "Someone of her potency should be brought to the House of Yowgn."

Armonia slipped her new tank top over her head. "What's that?"

It was Daleth who answered her this time. "The House of Yowgn is a heretical group that believes all things are part of and governed by an unseen innate life force. They use dreaming to gain insights into that life force so they may better experience it." His voice trailed off at the last sentence as he stared intensely at Lorelei who averted her eyes.

Armonia slipped an elastic skirt decorated with frills on her hips. "They sound more fun."

"I thought you were just an illicit dreamer in the darkness trade. Why didn't you tell me?" Daleth's voice cracked ever so slightly.

"We're not supposed to tell non-members." Lorelei paused and then finally looked up from the floor to face Daleth. "I'm telling you now aren't I?" Daleth made his way to the door ignoring her. "I need to take her to my Room. You don't understand what she is."

"I thought this was your room?" Armonia asked.

Daleth paused with his hand on the doorknob. "Rooms are what different groupings of the House of Yowgn call themselves. You know it's said the House of Yowgn gave the Book of Vuhox to the Order of Consciousness so the Followers would be created and destroy both their enemies, the Order, and The Spark."

"That's never been substantiated and even if it is true I had nothing to do with it."

Armonia shook her head. "I'm so lost when you two talk."

"I'm sure they will compensate you and help you get out of this Orbit. But I'm taking her with or without you. Sorry." Lorelei quickly slipped her dress back on then stood next to Armonia and grabbed her hand, her face a mask of defiance and fortitude. "You want compensation? You either kill me or come with us. But if you kill me and take her, you kill us all."

Daleth's eyes met Lorelei's and they stared at each other. The tension was palpable even to Armonia. Finally, Daleth blinked. He grabbed a blanket and tossed it to Armonia. "Disguise yourself." He took another blanket and wrapped his face with it. He opened the door and extended his arm to indicate for Lorelei to lead the way.

"He's right. Let's go." Lorelei dropped Armonia's hand and walked out the door.

Armonia clapped her hands together. "Yay, more dreaming." She followed Lorelei with Daleth bringing up the rear.

《 》

EBJAN ORBIT

Fawna and Osarian huddled together in their modest home. Iris had started to shine its light some time ago but it gave no comfort to either. The plush couch they sat upon offered no comfort, as well. Tissues were strewn all over the mahogany table in front of them. They sat close to one another in heavy silence vainly attempting to process the unfathomable turn of events. Each had glassy eyes that were red and swollen. They were transfixed at nothing in particular in front of them, just the emptiness of the moment.

Osarian blew his nose and having already broken the silent respite from sobs made a grasp for words. "At least we can still try again." He was a long-standing councilor of sector 254, well known for his pragmatism. Tonight it did little good. Fawna only offered a soft whimper in response. "I know it doesn't bring him back. The individual that was Peridot—". He choked on the next words and decided not to speak them. It was a fascinating peculiarity that each Twin Flame was a unique Upright. Not quite like the two who combined their essence. In the rare but tragic cases of Twin Flames dying before full maturation the second attempt was wholly unlike the previous attempt. So the entity that was Peridot truly was gone forever.

"He was one of the good ones," Fawna offered weakly.

A knock came from the front door. In the silence of the house, it sounded like explosions going off. "I will get it. Probably another friend offering condolences," said Osarian softly. Both Osarian and Fawna had been councilors for adjacent sectors for some time. They had many relations and well-wishers.

His feet shuffled along the finely finished wooden floor as he made his way to the entrance of his home. Everything he saw along the way was a reminder of Peridot. Of the home the three of them made together, of the life they shared. He reached for the door handle and paused before turning it.

His mind had been slowed ever since they heard the news, so it took him longer than usual to acknowledge the face staring back at his sunken expression. It did not help matters that the figure at the door was severely scarred. Burn marks crept up like vines from underneath his tight-knit navy blue shirt. They stopped below his chin but they were still jarring.

Aside from the scars, he was a pristine model of an Upright with wavy black hair parted to the right and a firm square jaw.

"Do you recognize me?"

The familiar voice jogged Osarian's memory. "Of course, Turako. How could I forget Peridot's dearest friend? I thought they said you were seriously injured when—well when it happened?"

"I was. I came here as soon as the healers let me go. May I come in for a moment?"

Osarian stepped aside to allow Turako to hobble in with a strained gait. Fawna came into the foyer. She gasped audibly. "Turako! I didn't realize."

"It went off right below my face. The blast affected my nervous system. Fortunately about half hit my harness shield, otherwise, I would be worse off." He then bowed his head for a moment before he addressed both of the councilors. "I just wanted both of you to know that I won't rest until I make Daleth pay."

"So it was the last Follower of Vuhox?"

Turako nodded gravely at Osarian's question. His eyes darted between the two councilors. "He had an accomplice with him. She's the one who shot me. They will both be apprehended. Guardians are already fanning out all over the system looking for them." Turako paused once more and took a long slow breath. "But I'm taking it even more seriously. Peridot was my best friend. You have my word he will be avenged."

"We only seek justice," Osarian said firmly.

Fawna quickly added, "But we both appreciate your devotion to Peridot. It means his life meant something to have affected you so. We take great comfort in that."

Turako gave a small nod to signify he understood. "I will keep you both informed of our hunt."

"We appreciate it very much," said Osarian as he walked Turako out. "I know from how Peridot spoke of you that you will not fail us."

Turako's spirits were lifted somewhat by the compliment. He was often in awe of Peridot's valor and to hear it was reciprocated, at least to some degree, made him feel the burden of loss slightly less. He bid the mourning couple goodbye. "May Light still shine on you both."

"May the Light shine on you too." As soon as Osarian closed the door he spun around to his reflection. His voice was now cold and deep. "So the reports were right. It was that rotten Daleth after all."

"He must be extinguished once and for all."

"You heard Turako. Guardians already look for him."

"Turako's a fool to think they will catch him. His intentions are admirable but Daleth will find some hole to crawl into and hide. Too many powerful Uprights rely on him to clean up their messes."

"I agree with your evaluation. So what do you propose we do?" Osarian asked gravely. "How do you catch a shadow like Daleth?"

"Same as you get rid of any shadow, flood it with light," hissed Fawna.

"We will have to get our Twin Flame coaches to support us of course. I think I know a High Councilor who may help us petition The Spark but it is not easy to get something declared an Obstruction, let alone someone."

"The Followers of Vuhox were declared and is he not one of them?"

Osarian blinked rapidly for a moment while his mind processed the case his reflection was making. "This is true but it was technically their teachings that were declared an Obstruction. Daleth swore to never spread their ways. To my knowledge, he has kept that oath. I don't think a single individual has ever been declared an Obstruction to the Light."

Fawna was stone-faced. "When there is a will there is a way."

⟨ ⟩

EBJAN ORBIT

Daleth leaned against the interior wall of the dilapidated building with his arms crossed. Only the bare skeleton of the structure remained but it was enough to conceal the activities that unfolded within. The scent of essential oil from the omnoberry made Daleth's nose twitch. He squeezed his crossed arms tighter as he watched the dancing rituals. Several Uprights writhed and gyrated their bodies against each other in a maelstrom of limbs. The sweat glistened in the dim candlelight as they moved in a synchronized rhythm with one another. Together they sang, "This world keeps a moving and I keep a dreaming in this beautiful world. This world keeps a moving but I keep a dreaming of a beautiful world." It made Daleth's stomach turn.

Armonia walked up to him wearing a carefree smirk. She leaned her back against the wall next to him and sighed. "Dreaming is the best. You should have joined us?"

"Be careful spouting that outside of here. It's not allowed to be done freely. Lorelei and other House of Yowgn members do it at frivolous risk."

"Why?"

"How should I know? I couldn't care less. It is a waste of time."

Armonia shrugged. "Get's rid of my pain and they seemed nice. Nicer than ya."

"It's not hard to be nicer than me."

"Ya can say that again. So I guess I'm no longer your prisoner, huh?"

"You realize they're just going to use you as a weapon in their wars, don't you? They have no regard for you beyond what you can achieve for their campaigns."

"If that's the case then I will just have to protect myself."

Daleth snorted. "You were a mess when I found you so I wouldn't hold my breath."

"I got free from ya, didn't I?"

Daleth rolled his eyes back and shook his head. "I delivered you to Lorelei. I can take you back whenever I wish."

"Like to see ya try."

"It would be quite humorous to see you try and stop me."

"Those crystals you used were something. I betcha if I had some of them I could hold my own."

"I thought you didn't remember anything?"

Armonia put a finger to her chin. "I do now that I dreamt, I think. But only stuff with ya. It's weird. Anyways come on ya gotta show me how I can do your neat trick."

Daleth narrowed his eyes. "First you become lost."

Armonia tilted her head to one side. "No problem there."

"Then you go through unimaginable pain."

"Check."

"Then you lose connection with everyone and everything."

Armonia nodded vigorously. "Uh-huh."

"Then you become reviled by all, even yourself."

"Alright, I did all those. So where's my crystal?"

"You're not hated."

"Hello, ya were sent to kill me."

"I was sent to abduct you, which means someone wanted you. There's a difference."

"You just don't want to show me."

"Yea, there's that too."

"You are so much less fun than Lorelei. I'm going to find someone else to dream with."

Daleth watched Armonia join the dancers for a moment before he turned his back on them and walked away. He was done waiting around. He was not going to waste any more time on a failed mission. He needed his yoke repaired and a new ship so he could put all this behind him.

Daleth used his heightened senses to search for Lorelei's voice amongst the moans and grunts which provided the soundtrack for the hallways he walked. His ears picked up her velvety speech behind one of the few rooms which still had a door attached. His feet made no sound on the molted carpet as he moved to enter but the lock on the door stopped him. He considered tearing it off its hinges which would prove to be fairly easy considering his strength and the shoddy state of the structure as a whole. The sound of his name on the other side of the door gave him pause, though.

On the opposite side of the door, Lorelei pleaded with the three leaders of the Ebjan Room of the House of Yowgn. Normally a planet the size of Ebjan would have one, maybe two, such overseers but due to Ebjan's bureaucratic nature it proved fertile ground for the House of Yowgn. It offered many abandoned buildings awaiting demolition or remodeling approval to rotate through as safe houses to hold ceremonies. All of the paperwork and stringent protocols also left gaping loopholes which the darkness trade exploited to its full advantage. Part of the strategy of the House of Yowgn was to promote what is considered darkness by the Way. In this manner, recruits were always flowing in.

The three leaders of Ebjan's Room were some of the most well-respected members of the House of Yowgn and had spent nearly their entire lives under its doctrines. Unak was the most senior though. He had come to the House of Yowgn almost right out of his Prep Center. He had been with them for more than two full gremrevs which meant his time with them was nearing an end. Of course thanks to the tireless efforts of the geneticist he showed nearly no wear and tear on his physical body. His pale face was lean and his shoulders broad, you couldn't see a single crease, scar, or evidence of waning muscular mass. He had curls of chestnut-colored hair which stopped just above his ears. He was by far the most handsome of the three.

The next most senior leader was Isadora. She was shrewd and analytical. Her eyes darted constantly about her environment, especially when she spoke. Her head seemed to come to a point under a short crop of wavy pink hair. She was known for her cunning throughout the House. It was this reputation that brought her to Ebjan to ensure her skills were utilized to their fullest. She was probably the most respected of the three within the organization.

The final leader was Benseog, who was arguably both the fiercest and the gentlest. His pendulum-like personality was attributed to his strict devotion to the core beliefs of the House of Yowgn. He claimed to have mastered riding the entire spectrum of his existence and could now easily shift from one state to its complete opposite if the situation called for it. At the moment Lorelei could not decipher where he was on the spectrum based on the impassive face that stared at her between those drapes of auburn hair.

"Didn't you see it?" There was a strain in Lorelei's voice.

Benseog continued his impassive gaze on Lorelei. "We saw her. A fractured individual but they are becoming more common."

"She is more than that. I know what I saw when I dreamed with her at my place. I saw her heal her own body. I saw her alter consciousness itself. I saw her potential. Her power could be unfathomable even to the Way. Think of the implications."

The three glanced at each other for a moment then Isadora spoke. "We are trying my dear. But your vision, although potent, does not bear the weight of scrutiny. We have no reason to consider her different than any other expression of Yowgn."

Benseog put a hand on Lorelei's shoulder. "Yowgn does not favor. We have dreamed with her and saw nothing extraordinary aside from her mind being torn asunder and in need of mending."

"Who knows what the foolish Order did to it," Unak interjected before allowing Benseog to continue.

"Precisely why she needs our help, not vice versa. We will calm her mind and try to put it back together. Perhaps afterward she will dream greatly but her time is not now."

"What about shorting out Daleth's ship and her claim of visions without dreaming?"

Lorelei saw the polarized shift before she heard it in Benseog's voice. "Delusions from a damaged mind and nothing more. The matter is closed."

Isadora rolled her gaze from Benseog to Lorelei. "But it does bring up another matter. We see you also brought Daleth here. Does that mean you have finally succeeded in your assignment to recruit him?"

Lorelei did not meet the gaze of the three but instead stared at a vacant corner of the room. "I—no." She turned back to them and saw three masks of confusion. "He simply needs safe passage off this Orbit."

Isadora bowed her head and pinched the bridge of her nose. "We thought you were up to this task."

Lorelei clenched her fists and threw them down at her side. "I am!"

"Then stick to the assignment at hand instead of bringing us strays that our rivals have chewed up and spit out," Benseog sternly said.

"But the Twin Flames are going to take over and they're not going to give it back. Trust me, their grip will just get tighter and tighter."

Unak spoke softly. "Most likely you correctly asses the political situation which is why you were to bring Daleth into our folds."

Lorelei narrowed her eyes. "His will is strong but it may be swayed by halos and a ship."

"We did not wish to bribe him," said Unak.

"He sought the teachings of Vuhox which means he seeks an alternative to the Way," added Benseog.

Isadora sighed and dropped her shoulders. "We had hoped you would show him the proper alternative."

Lorelei turned her head abruptly away from them once more. "I just need more time."

On the other side of the door, Daleth had heard enough. He stormed off, his boots falling heavy as the faded carpet gave way to a concrete slab. He didn't get far before a participant in the dancing rituals he had been observing blocked his path. "Out of my way," Daleth growled.

"I saw you watching. Are you interested in dreaming? It soothes mind and body."

"I haven't dreamed in a very long time and I have no intention of changing that anytime soon. Now leave my sight."

The dancer writhed seductively for a few moments. "Maybe you would be a little nicer if you dreamed."

Daleth unsheathed his trikilldo and put it to their throat. "I am being nice."

"Don't kill me!"

"Give me a reason."

The sound of his name hit his ears and he instinctively flinched. The dancing participant took the opportunity and made a hasty exit just as Lorelei jogged up to the scene.

"What in Iris are you doing?"

"Sorry to disappoint but I will not be joining your little club. You can tell your bosses to eat space dust for all I care."

The venomous tone of Daleth startled Lorelei. Though she was familiar with his reputation she had never before seen an indication of it. "What are you—?"

Daleth shoved the trikilldo back in its sheath. "Enhanced hearing. Or did they forget to include that in your dossier?"

Lorelei instantly realized the situation and took a precautious step back. "I'm sorry."

"You were doing your job. Just as I am doing mine. I'm taking Armonia to the School of Knowledge and collecting my fee."

"Just because you found out why we first came together does not change where we are now. You killed not only a guardian but the Twin Flame prospect of two influential councilors."

Daleth made a dismissive gesture. "Death is death. The life on the other end does not matter."

"It may not matter to you or me but it matters a lot on this Orbit. Not to mention, you probably have a busted yoke."

"I'll figure something out. I always do." Daleth went to walk away but Lorelei grabbed his shoulder. He snatched her wrist and she yanked it from his grip.

"For once will you just do things the easy way? The heads of the Room have agreed to get you an untraceable ship and set you up with a dark trade mechanic to fix your yoke." Lorelei paused and sighed. "You can even take Armonia with you if you want."

"I thought they wanted her here with them?"

Lorelei shrugged and cocked her head to one side. "They won't listen to me. They think you're more important. They believe helping you will persuade you to help them."

"And what do you think?"

Lorelei tightened her lips. "I think you'll do whatever you want."

"And you? You give up on your vision that easily."

Lorelei turned her palms up. "Guess I just got caught up in the dreaming. It wouldn't be the first time, especially with newbies."

Daleth studied Lorelei's face for a moment. He took notice of her pockmarks. He had always assumed they were leftovers from some past trauma. A mark of remembrance like his own. He had gotten lost in that fantasy of finding another like himself. Now he felt inclined to believe they were just a genetic defect.

"Where's the ship?"

"You got to wait till Iris goes away, too easy to be spotted right now. I'll take you and Armonia to it as soon as it gets dark. The mechanic will meet us at the ship." Daleth furrowed his brow. "Come on let me do this for you. I don't want there to be any hard feelings between us."

"A bit too late isn't it?"

"We always knew we were both Uprights who lived hard lives and had to do whatever we needed."

"When you're on your own you do what you have to survive. You at least have your posse. Apparently, I was just another target for you all."

"My target is The Spark."

"And the means matter not."

Lorelei looked away and inhaled deeply. "Like you said we survive whatever the costs. Don't let your pride get in the way of that."

He tasted bile at the thought that she was right. His yoke was damaged, he could feel it. The House of Yowgn was deep in the darkness trade so there was no reason to doubt they could provide such services. "I'll be in the northwest corner meditating till then." He left Lorelei with a huff. Even though he agreed he was going to be prepared for anything. It's how he had stayed alive for this long.

《 》

EBJAN ORBIT

High Councilor Zean sat in her plush office chair. It was fairly sparse as offices go. Just a large wooden desk with two high-backed chairs facing it for the occasional visitors. A coat rack stood in one corner and a floor lamp in the other. She did have a mirror placed on the far wall across from her desk in honor of Grevolios but she stopped there. This was a place of business and she did not want to overwhelm it. This was why she appreciated Jamila's decorating so much. At home, she could enjoy the event.

Her weary eyes started to droop. She had been pouring over the paperwork necessary to start emptying the Prep Centers. Of course nothing much would change right away. There were still infantile Uprights that needed preparations for society but with no new influx of Uprights, they had to make sure all the necessary steps were taken to close things out as the current residents matured. Staff would need to be removed. This proved the worst tangle. Some like Zean wanted to place them in other areas but there was a rather large contingent of councilors and even High Councilors who wished them to be supplemented by the tributes the government collected. They believed the hatcheries would open up sooner rather than later and this would keep the staff in a retainer, thereby avoiding a scramble to restaff when the inevitable happened.

Zean had poured over the figures and graphs for nearly half a cycle and was about to go home when her assistant came over the communication transmitter. "High Councilor Zean. I have councilor Fawna from sector 253 and councilor Osarian from sector 254 here. They have not filled out an appointment request but insist that you will see them regardless."

"Yes, please have them come to my office." Zean had heard about the loss of their Twin Flame in process and felt a twinge of guilt turning them away. They were in her territory after all. The door to her office opened and the two downtrodden councilors stepped in and closed the door behind them.

"Forgive the breach in protocol," began Osarian.

Zean shook her head. "Forget about it. If my reflection and I had lost our Twin Flame in process I would not worry about procedure either."

"So you have heard?" Fawna anxiously asked.

"Of course. Dreadful and senseless violence. You have my deepest condolences. I only wish the Light had penetrated this system further to prevent occurrences such as this."

Fawna remained by the door but Osarian drew nearer to Zean's desk. "That is actually what brings us here."

"Daleth is an Obstruction to the Light and it is high time he is treated as such," hissed Fawna.

Zean's eyes widened at the word "obstruction" being used. "I understand you're upset but an Upright can't be deemed an Obstruction. We are all vessels of the Light."

Osarian slammed his fist down on Zean's desk. "He killed our Twin Flame."

Fawna trained her eyes onto Zean's own. "An Obstruction is anything that prevents the flow of Light and needs to be removed. How can you honestly call Daleth anything else?"

Zean tried to compose herself. She was not fresh and did not expect this. She thought at most the two councilors were here to request her to fast-track a memorial into the Grevolios celebrations. "Daleth is a darkness. The darkness exists so we may better move to the Light. When we have moved to the Light then darkness will no longer be."

Fawna pointed a finger at Zean. "Don't quote the teachings of The Spark to us. We were about to become a Twin Flame ourselves remember? Daleth is not darkness because darkness eventually can become Light. Daleth will never be Light. We all know this, so let's not fool ourselves."

"Daleth exists to support the darkness trade and keep people in darkness. How many more Lights will he be allowed to snuff out before he is categorized correctly." Osarian slapped Zean's desk with the flat of his hand to emphasize his point.

"Allow me a moment." Zean stood with her hands behind her back. She began to pace in front of her office window as she often did to sort out a knotty problem. Zean's sympathies were with these two counselors. But her professional mind felt what they were asking was beyond comprehension. *Could a single Upright be declared an Obstruction?*

An Obstruction to the Light declaration was reserved for practices or institutions that disrupted people finding their path to the Light. Daleth certainly seemed to fit the description based on what Zean had heard of his exploits. Of course, The Way of The Light taught that all Uprights were redeemable to the Light.

Zean paused and parted the fuchsia drapes at her window. She looked out onto the bustling street. To her knowledge, Daleth was not part of one of the heretic cults that existed in the system. He was regarded as any other dark trader. Someone who had fallen into darkness and it was hoped would find their way back. But this recent development showed that unlike the pirates and darkness traders who had some kind of code of conduct Daleth acted without consideration for anyone but himself. In addition, Daleth was probably one of the most lethal Uprights in existence. Zean's responsibility was to her people and to follow the Light. The Way of The Light was very clear about your duty to your fellow Uprights. *What would she be if she let other innocent Light Walkers fall victim to a dark spot like Daleth?* She thought.

Besides an Obstruction could only be ruled as such by The Spark no matter what others felt. Zean would simply be bringing the entire matter to a higher source to decide upon. If Daleth was redeemable then The Spark would know. In The Spark's infinite wisdom it was deemed best for those who were learning the Light to realize for themselves what Obstructions were. *Perhaps these counselors in their grief had an insight that others had missed. After all, they were nearly Twin Flames themselves.*

Zean turned back to the anxious faces of the two councilors. "Alright. We must do this by the books but I will help you move it at the quickest pace it can be done." As Zean watched the two councilors embrace she felt resolved that she had made the right decision. The rest would be given to the Light.

《 》

EBJAN ORBIT

Iris had retired its light for a while and the barely standing structure that Daleth inhabited had grown quiet. He had not wavered from his meditation until he heard a hushed whisper. "Come on, let's go." Daleth slowly opened his eyes. He could make out the delicate frame of Lorelei who stood over him but it was not till his focus sharpened that he noticed the stern expression she wore. "I convinced Armonia to go along willingly with you. You're welcome by the way. We got to hurry before this door closes." Daleth rose to his feet.

His stiff muscles protested but he paid them little heed. He followed Lorelei through the labyrinth of empty rooms.

"Where is everyone?"

"We only congregate when Iris is gone. With all the guardian activity they didn't want to use the same place two nights in a row. I stayed behind to take care of you and Armonia."

Daleth bristled at the insinuation that he needed to be taken care of. He saw Armonia standing by a hole in one of the exterior walls. Her hair was tucked under a scarf and what appeared to be a quilt was wrapped around her just below her shoulders. Daleth pulled up his hood and tugged at it so it cast a deep shadow on his face.

"Follow me and both of you keep your head down. Try to stay clear of any mirror decorations."

"You don't have to tell me," Daleth grumbled. Lorelei ignored him and led them along the back alleyways.

The route was fairly deserted due to the Ebjan curfew but there were still a few dying embers of some approved Grevolios parties. Armonia was intrigued by the bright lights and laughter but remembered Lorelei's warning and only stole fleeting glimpses.

As they walked Lorelei asked, "Daleth, how much of a punch you got?"

"I still have a small amount leftover from those guardians. Plus I've been siphoning off the general anxiety which seems to be especially thick in the air." He paused and then added, "I could get us out of a jam."

"All I needed to hear."

《 》

THEY CAME TO AN EMPTY port on the outskirts of the town. Lorelei suddenly signaled for them to crouch down behind some containers. A dozen or so yards away a group of Uprights were gathered with grim faces.

One of them had a flushed red face. He was yelling in a hushed tone at an Upright with a black hood. "You cheating piece of space dust!" He then pulled a laser gun out of his belt and pointed it at the hooded individual. In a quick movement, the hooded Upright grabbed the gun and twisted the man's arm so he now pointed the gun at himself. The others all pulled out their guns pointing them at each other.

"Your crew may take out some of my crew but not before I get you to pull this trigger on yourself," the hooded Upright confidently declared. "Now you know me and my crew ain't afraid to die. So the only question that remains is, are you?"

The color in the Upright's face drained. "Let's go!" Several of the group put their guns back and began to walk away. The hooded Upright shoved the one he was holding roughly. He then tossed him his laser gun. The individual spat on the ground and then walked away with the others. All that was left was the hooded Upright, another one with long curly green-colored hair and a rotund figure with a shock of curly violet hair. This last figure wore uncharacteristically loose apparel so it was difficult to determine a gender one way or another. The other two Uprights wore the traditional leather thong and snug leather torso cover of pirates. However, the one with the green hair seemed to have cut a piece of his away to reveal his chiseled abs. They were certainly an odd-looking trio by any standard.

Lorelei walked out from behind the crate much to the surprise of Daleth and Armonia. "Hey there, Gimeld," Lorelei called out as she casually walked up to the three strangers.

The two retrained their guns on Lorelei and the hooded Upright also drew a gun. The confidence was now missing from his voice. "Lorelei? What are you doing here?"

"Can't someone take a stroll along the ports?"

"Not unless she's looking for trouble," replied Gimeld.

Lorelei let out an exasperated sigh. "Put the guns away already. We don't need violence."

"Give us a reason, darling," said the green-haired man.

Daleth then walked up behind Lorelei. The others seemed to lose their nerve upon the sight of him. Lorelei cocked her head back. "That a good enough one."

"You're Daleth the last Follower of Vuhox?" Daleth only nodded slowly in response to the question of the green-haired individual.

Gimeld put his gun away and the other two followed suit. "What do you want, Lorelei?"

"We need to hitch a ride off this rock."

"Good luck with that."

"You owe me."

"Like space dust I do."

Lorelei smirked. "I haven't told Sophia that you've been skimming Niorpyn off the shipments for your beau."

The green-haired Upright scrunched up his face. "You're just jealous."

Gimeld seemed to consider things for a moment. "Let's go," he finally said. Lorelei signaled for Armonia to come out of her hiding spot.

Daleth turned on Lorelei. "I thought you said the House of Yowgn arranged a ship and mechanic for me."

"I'll explain once we get onboard."

"Why should I trust you after everything?"

"There's no reason." She shrugged. "You just either get on or you don't. Use those famed instincts of yours. Am I out to get you?"

"You better start being straight with me."

"I will as soon as we're over the border." Daleth ground his teeth as the three followed the pirates aboard their ship.

The ship named The Wayward Star by the crew was your standard triangle freighter. Its magnetic propulsion thrusters were in the rear at the base of the triangles. It had four sides which were triangles themselves that came together to form the pointed front of the ship. A side that resembled a trapezoid made up the rear.

The interior was not brightly lit, nor was it dingy. It by no means looked small from the outside but due to the angle of the sides, it gave the impression of a more cramped interior. This was far from the case. In reality, the inside of the ship was filled with many spacious compartments lined with monitors and storage bins. It also featured wide corridors to move about and was even equipped with eight distinct rest quarters. The storage bins seemed well stocked with IO's. IO's being the general term for food and supplies meant to sustain life forms during inter-Orbit travel. Thanks to inertia-canceling technology ships moved extremely fast but travel between Orbits still usually required nourishment before reaching the intended destination.

Daleth thought it odd such a small crew had such a large ship. He did not voice this, however, for he felt it was none of his concern.

ONCE THEY REACHED THE bridge Gimeld gave curt introductions. "This is my first mate, Arjan."

"Only mate," corrected the green-haired man.

"Over there is Sil. Good in a pinch." The violet-haired individual gave an up turn of their chin in acknowledgment.

A clunky robot with boxy limbs and three rotating lenses in the center of what resembled its face walked in. "Are these three joining our crew?"

"Only temporary passengers." Gimeld stuck a thumb out at the robot. "This is our maintenance and technical overseer. Call him M.A.T.O for short."

Armonia approached Gimeld and gazed at the darkness under his hood. It looked like an endless chasm. She could not see any facial features. "How come I can't see ya face?"

"That's kind of the point," said Arjan.

M.A.T.O. then added, "His hood utilizes an ancient principle termed magic which is considered by many to be mere superstitious stories of the primitive people who once lived in this system long before The Spark. The only ones who can see his face are those he truly wishes to and trusts which at this point is only Arjan."

"Wow." Armonia reached for the hood but Gimeld grabbed her hand and threw it down.

"Weren't you taught manners at your Prep Center?" Armonia shrugged in response to Gimeld's rebuke.

"You'll have to excuse Armonia here. Her mind's been a bit all over the place lately," Lorelei said.

Daleth spoke his first words since getting aboard the ship. "Don't tell me I gotta get in a snuffer with her?"

Armonia shot Daleth a quizzical look. "Why not and what's a snuffer anyways?"

Gimeld chuckled. "Please that's amateur stuff." He walked over to the pilot's chair and placed his hands on the console. The ship began its ascent.

M.A.T.O.'s lenses rotated as he inspected Daleth. "I sense a damaged yoke in you. I can repair it if you would like me to."

"Wait till we get clear," Gimeld called back.

The ship stopped at the border of the Orbit. Ebjan was not as much of a trading hub as Circapto but they were a stickler for procedure and their borders were no exception. A booming voice blurred over the communication transmitter. "Please have someone bring your documents to your airlock for inspection."

"Jock! How you doing old buddy?" Gimeld's voice had lost its bitterness and now sounded cheerful.

The voice over the transmitter now also sounded more amicable. "Gimeld? Sorry I didn't realize this was your ship. Been a long day."

"Don't worry about it old friend. I'm sending M.A.T.O. out with our papers." Gimeld reached into a hidden compartment below the console. He took from it a tiny satchel that bulged with halos. He folded the transport documents around the satchel and handed them to M.A.T.O. M.A.T.O. dutifully strolled over to the airlock compartment used for inter-ship communication while in the vacuum of space.

A few moments later and Jock's voice even chipper than before sounded through the transmitter. "You have a bright Grevolios, Gimeld, you hear?"

"You as well." Gimeld cocked his head over to Daleth who stood impassive. As M.A.T.O. stepped onto the bridge Gimeld crossed The Wayward Star into inter-Orbit space.

It was only then that Lorelei piped up. "We need you to take us to Baabcrest."

"What do we look like chauffeurs? And even if we were our clientele would rate higher than you," teased Arjan.

"We have a pick up at Circapto. So that's where you're going." The harsh tone had returned to Gimeld's speech.

"Armonia's condition might get worse with their electromagnetic fields. Anywhere but there, please Gimeld," Lorelei pleaded.

The black void under Gimeld's hood stared at Lorelei then shifted to Armonia who made herself look especially demure. Gimeld then nodded to Arjan who brought up some maps on his view screen. "You're in luck.

Hanoweh is in alignment with Circapto. We can drop you there without losing time."

"Fine."

Daleth grabbed Lorelei's arm. "We need to talk." Lorelei motioned for Daleth to follow her to a different compartment of the ship.

⟨ ⟩

AS SOON AS THEY WERE alone Lorelei spun on Daleth. "Will you just bright out already?"

Daleth seethed. "You've been telling me to do so since I brought Armonia to your place. How do you expect me to bright out when all you've done is lie to me?"

"The House of Yowgn wasn't going to let you leave. They consider you too valuable at this critical time. I know you're too headstrong not to fight your way out so I did what I did to keep us all alive."

"Wish I could believe you," said Daleth with a bite in his tone.

"I'm being straight with you now."

"I can take care of myself. If your little group tried to stop me they would learn I'm not to be trifled with."

"The Ebjan room has been infiltrated, I'm not sure by who or for what reason. You can't risk fighting the unknown."

Daleth narrowed his eyes. "You're just saying that only to make yourself reflect better."

"One of the leaders compromised the dreaming with Armonia. Someone's trying to hide what she is? It's why I had to be deceptive to get her and you out. It was the only way."

Daleth folded his arms. "And what exactly is she? Just so you know I'm listening to your heartbeat now despite its drain on my reserves."

"You don't have to do that," hissed Lorelei.

"I do."

Lorelei huffed. "I'm not exactly sure what she is. She can reach places we can't and change consciousness itself. I think she's some sort of portal. She could be a way out for all of us."

The last sentence hung in Daleth's ears. He heard no telltale sign of insincerity when she spoke it but she was hiding something.

"I believe you but you're not telling me something. Out with it."

Lorelei averted her eyes and the corners of her mouth turned downward. "She's dying though. I was able to abate her symptoms when we dreamed but her mind, her body, it can't take whatever she is. It's literally tearing her apart. I think there is some way out for her and it may be the key to everything. Which is why I need to find someone who knows more about her."

Daleth felt the faintest twinge of empathy at this revelation but he dismissed it immediately. "You think you'll find what you're searching for on Hanoweh?"

Lorelei shook her head. "No. It's why I wanted to go to Baabcrest. It's where a lot of the teachings of the House of Yowgn came from. The name Yowgn was even stolen from a long-extinct tribe there."

"I can kill the crew and hijack this ship."

"No, you said your reserves are too low. Gimeld and Arjan may not have your powers but they're formidable. It's not worth the risk."

"I sense no fear from anyone on this craft. If you had coordinated this with me I could have fed off more fear before we boarded."

"I'm doing the best I can, alright. I don't believe Armonia will die for a while so we have time. When we get to Hanoweh we'll have to find a ship to take us to Baabcrest."

"Neither of you have yokes or did I also miss that fact about you, as well?"

Lorelei shot Daleth a piercing look in response and then said, "We'll get someone to give us a ride. You can go on your own way when we land."

"I never agreed to let you steal the price she is worth from me."

"I have access to Baabcrest account holders for the House on Baabcrest. I can afford you if you'll wait till then."

"I thought they didn't believe you about Armonia?"

"I'll explain to them the situation, hopefully, they aren't compromised as well." Lorelei feigned a mask of innocence. "If that doesn't work I can be duplicitous when I need to be."

Daleth detected no irregularity and so was fairly convinced Lorelei was being honest with him. "So I'm to take you two to Baabcrest and get handsomely rewarded?"

"Yes. Once there you can take your halos and I'll find a way to save Armonia so she can help the House of Yowgn end The Spark's reign."

"Ambitious goals."

"Fine line between ambition and desperation."

"Agreed. But if I'm to only take you to Baabcrest to empty the House of Yowgn's accounts I don't need to be either. What if she shorts out whatever vehicle we are using as she did to my last ship?"

"I'll keep dreaming with her. It keeps her stable."

They eyed each other for a moment. Lorelei sighed then averted her eyes to the ground. Daleth extended his hand and Lorelei raised her face to meet his as they shook.

⟨ ⟩

"WOULD YOU LIKE ME TO repair your yoke for you now?" M.A.T.O. asked as Lorelei and Daleth reentered the bridge.

"We don't owe them anything more than a ride," snapped Gimeld.

"I'm not offering out of any obligation, my captain. My A.I. programming ensures that I serve and take pleasure in fixing things."

"I don't let just anybody open me up, programming or no programming," Daleth interjected.

Sil piped up for the first time. "I can vouch for M.A.T.O's skills. I know we just met but I would highly recommend you take him up on the offer."

Daleth started to argue but Lorelei elbowed his ribs and whispered, "He's ship maintenance A.I. It's what he was built for. Let him do it so we gotta worry about one less thing when we land."

"Very well," grumbled Daleth uncomfortable at folding to Lorelei's logical reasoning once more.

"Wonderful! I'll get my tool attachments." M.A.T.O. scampered off.

"I need someone to dream with so I can astral project a message to some Uprights in the House of Yowgn," Lorelei announced.

"What kind of message?" Gimeld asked suspiciously.

"Don't worry it won't include anything about your crew. If you don't let me give this message I fear others may come looking for us. It may cause more trouble for you in the long run."

"Is that a threat?" Arjan snapped.

"No malice. Just the situation."

Arjan looked toward Sil who gave a discreet handle signal which was part of their secret code. It appeased Arjan's concerns that Sil detected no menace from Lorelei.

Daleth yanked Lorelei's arm and said in a hushed but severe tone, "I thought you told me they were compromised?"

"Exactly why I need to throw them off the trail. I told them I was going to rendezvous with them at Iris' descent and bring you both along. They'll have operatives looking for us."

"Sorry dear even if you are on the up and up I only dream with one Upright. Besides your anatomy doesn't tend to take me places." Arjan stroked Gimeld's bare bicep. He then turned his sights to Daleth and flicked his serpentine tongue. "You on the other hand may be a different story." Daleth narrowed his eyes in response to Arjan's remark.

"I'll dream with ya again," exclaimed Armonia as she shimmied out of the quilt. She then pulled the scarf off. "I like it."

"I think it's best I don't dream with you for this particular communication. Your dreaming is unique. They might be able to trace it easily."

"Oh, gotcha." Armonia dragged her booted foot across the floor in disappointment. "How about Daleth then?"

"I don't dream," he growled in answer to Armonia's proposition.

Lorelei rolled her eyes and walked over to Sil. "Guess that leaves you. How about it?"

The usually stoic-faced Sil could not hide their astonishment. "Me? I—I have a disability, my toes are fused."

Lorelei shrugged and gave a warm-hearted smile to Sil. "Doesn't matter to me if it doesn't matter to you." She held out her hand for Sil who hesitantly took it. They both strode out of the bridge.

Armonia then spied movement on the floor under the pilot's chair. She began to crawl on her hands and knees, pulled like a magnet by her curiosity.

A greenish-blue column of muscle not much longer than a foot or so slithered out from under the chair and along the wall. It had a diamond-shaped head which it held in the air as it moved. The top of the head was adorned with two orbs that had thick filaments radiating from them and then around the head was a ring of small needle-like spines.

Armonia reached out her hand to touch the odd-looking organism. "You're neat looking." The Non-upright slid up her outstretched arm and when it reached her shoulder let out a short high-pitched squeak. Armonia giggled at her new friend.

She then heard a low hiss emanate from the Non-upright. Armonia rotated her head and saw Daleth standing over her holding his trikilldo. He swiped at the life form coiled around Armonia's arm. At the last second, Armonia flung her arm away and shielded her new companion with her body narrowly missing the blade herself.

"What are you doing?"

Daleth prepared for another swing. "Trying to kill that vermin."

"Don't! She's my friend."

"Ridiculous." Daleth swung again and Armonia leaped away from him.

"I'll fight ya if I have to."

Daleth snorted. "Don't be absurd." The Non-upright hissed at Daleth as he raised his arm. He was about to bring his weapon down but was stopped by another blade held by Gimeld. "What do you think you're doing?"

"That's a serposa. You don't kill ones you find on ships."

"Don't give me those silly old stories."

Gimeld stood steadfast. Daleth looked into the void under the hood. Neither seemed intimidated by the other. When Arjan got up though and took out his laser Daleth relented and re-sheathed his trikilldo. Armonia triumphantly stuck a forked tongue out at Daleth.

M.A.T.O. re-entered the chamber. "Are we ready to begin?"

"Come on sweetie let's have a little us time. M.A.T.O. can monitor the auto-pilot trajectory and our stowaways," said Arjan.

M.A.T.O. rotated his lenses. "Of course."

"I don't trust him," said Gimeld.

"He's done it for us before plenty of times and hasn't screwed it up."

"Not him. The other one." Daleth narrowed his eyes at Gimeld's remark.

"He could always join us." Arjan winked at Daleth.

Daleth stepped close to Gimeld. "If you got a problem with me, get in line."

Gimeld eyed the stowaway for a moment before he moved back to Arjan. "Just remember whose ship this is. You wouldn't be the first thug I had to throw off it." Gimeld then grabbed Arjan's hand and they walked out of the bridge together.

⟨ ⟩

IN A REST QUARTER, Sil sat on the edge of a bed. It wasn't especially plush but the foam mattress was soft enough compared to what Sil was used to on their Origin Orbit of Dooga. A single pillow lay askew at one end of the bed. Aside from the bedding the room was rather stark with plain stainless steel walls. Iridescent light fixtures were embedded in the ceiling but only a third of them were presently turned on to dimly light the room. Sil crossed their legs and then uncrossed them just as quickly.

Lorelei removed her boots. "You okay with this?"

Sil smiled weakly. "Uh sure, it's just kind of the—I'm not used to this."

Lorelei slipped off her dress and tossed it aside. "You are not the first newbie I've dreamed with so don't worry." Lorelei sat next to Sil on the bed. "Do you have a preference for feminine or masculine?"

Sil slowly shook their head. "Is that a problem?"

Lorelei stuck her lower lip out. "Not at all." She ran her hand over Sil and began to remove the loose-fitting garments. "It just means I get to play with both energies."

⟨ ⟩

DALETH SAT WITH HIS eyes closed in meditation as M.A.T.O. worked on his yoke. Groans, shrieks, and grunts emanated from the adjacent rest quarters echoing throughout the bridge. Armonia sat on the floor across from Daleth and M.A.T.O. transfixed with her new companion. She watched with wonder as the Non-upright slithered around her body and tickled her. "What did Gimeld call you again?"

M.A.T.O. without being prompted answered Armonia's musing. "That is called a serposa. Serposas are a type of Non-upright that originated in the Orbit of Orogunu. Because of their adaptivity, they have become prolific throughout the system. Their most notable attributes are the ring of spines around their neck which are tipped with a mild poison and the ability to regenerate as long as the head remains intact."

"Wait they're poisonous?"

"Do you not know that all Uprights were rendered immune to poison by geneticists post-Spark?"

"I don't know much but it sounds like ya do?"

"I have the collective knowledge of the system at the time of my assembly stored in my central processing unit," M.A.T.O. answered straightening himself up.

"I think I will name this serposa Kristal since Daleth won't tell me how to get crystals like his."

"Ah yes, the infamous primary weapon of the Followers of Vuhox, an extinct fanatical cult that grew out of the Order of Consciousness. They believed in dominance and absolute freedom of the individual even at the expense of other individuals."

Armonia leaned forward. "Ooo can ya tell me how to get his kind of crystals that fly around?"

"The crystals that the Followers of Vuhox carry are found by a disciple during their training. Each one is then linked to one of the individual's senses by overcoming all sensations of both pain and fear attached to that particular sense. Only then can they wield them by feeding off the fear and pain that other individuals experience through the five senses. Feeding off the energy of fear and pain also allows them to energetically shield themselves and enhance their senses."

Armonia's eyes grew wide. "Wow. That all sounds good to me. How do ya—ya know overcome the sensations?"

"The trikilldo is usually a favored method. One is created specifically for each inductee and then given to that disciple upon the completion of their training."

"What is a trikilldo?"

"The trikilldo and its special sheath which sharpens the weapon upon insertion and extraction are unique throughout the system. The secrets to the construction of both are only known to Followers of Vuhox, although it was said the Book of Vuhox contained detailed instructions but the book was lost with the cult. It is rumored Daleth himself burned it. The trikilldo is a weapon designed to inflict maximum damage and pain. The central blade is sharpened to a fine point to penetrate deep upon insertion. Its curved sides hook organs and muscle tissue upon retraction." Armonia cringed as M.A.T.O. continued. "It is also very effective at flaying flesh due to the curved blades being sharpened to a razor edge that is nearly microscopic in measurement. A disciple endures maximum torture just short of death at the hands of the implement so they can master their senses and mind. Although many of the torture methods are kept secret, some are known. One such example is the nerve exposure technique which consists of a small section of the body being skinned so the exposed nerves can be prodded."

Armonia looked at Daleth with her mouth agape. She hadn't realized where all Daleth's scars came from until now. Daleth's eyes opened to slits and met Armonia's unblinking ones. He closed them again slowly. Armonia decided she no longer wanted his crystals and she also decided to take a break from questions for a little while.

Chapter 4

HANOWEH ORBIT

Daleth, Lorelei, and Armonia started to make their way along the streets. The pirates had at least dropped them off on the side facing away from Iris so there were only a sparse number of Uprights to contend with at the moment.

Daleth carried a large sack on his back and kept himself bent over. His face was concealed in shadows cast by the hood of his cloak.

"Do I have to wear this heavy dress again?" Armonia whined. She was covered up once more by the quilt which hid the shape of her body. Her hair was also obscured by the scarf again.

"Yes, for the moment. All guardians are still searching for you two."

Lorelei was correct for patrol skimmers flew by often. Their white sleek outline stood in stark contrast to the grey dim industrial city they were making their way through. Fortunately for the group, Daleth's senses were still keen enough to give them ample warning so they could duck into a corner or alley. The view screens on the sides of the warehouses and factories played news coverage of Daleth interspersed with coverage of Grevolios and reaction to the hatchery closure throughout the system.

"We should have had them drop us at a moon," grumbled Daleth.

"There are Uprights on the moons here too but don't worry I have an idea." Lorelei clumsily collided with a well-dressed Upright who stood on the street.

"Watch it, dimwad!" She angrily scolded.

Lorelei hunched over and kept her head low. "So sorry."

Daleth shook his head as they kept on walking. "Smooth."

Lorelei turned and winked at him. "Smoother than you know."

They entered a large park designed to offer an oasis from the cement and metal structures that proliferated in this part of the city. Once concealed behind some shrubs and trees Lorelei revealed a cosmetic kit hidden under the top of her dress.

"Where did ya get that and what is it?"

Lorelei couldn't help but smirk at Armonia's naivety. "Just a little something I borrowed to give you two a makeover."

Daleth dropped the sack and nodded his head slowly. "Impressive thievery skills. I'm learning a lot about you."

Lorelei gave another wink to Daleth. "Just be glad I'm on your side."

Daleth cocked his head. "Are you?"

Lorelei didn't answer but instead went about using the tools in the kit to darken Armonia's hair. She also put black rings around her eyes and gave her a pair of dark brown contact lenses which subdued the amber fire of her normal eye color. Armonia peered at her reflection in the nearby pond. She made a sour face in the faint light that the returning Iris was beginning to shine. "I like me better the other way."

"Relax. It'll all wash out. Just keep it on till we get to a ship." Lorelei next made Daleth's normally pale facial skin a pinkish hue. She then had him turn his cloak inside out and made a sash for him out of the quilt Armonia no longer needed. She outlined his normally meaty lips in a ruby-red color which made them look even larger and fuller. Lorelei stood back and admired her work. "Now we just need a wig for you."

Daleth who looked miserable protested. "What do I need a wig for? This is plenty."

"Please. The braids are a dead giveaway."

Daleth crossed his arms and pointed his nose up in the air. "I'm not the only one with braids."

Lorelei's expression lit up and she jogged a few paces to a pink bush dotted with green and white berries. Its branches appeared covered in ice despite the mild air temperature. She entreated the others to come over. "Look!" She waved her hands excitedly pointing at the bush. Daleth sighed and walked over with Armonia in tow.

Daleth was unimpressed with Lorelei's find. "You've never seen an omnoberry bush before?"

"It's frosting which means it's good luck." Lorelei drew a branch into her mouth. "Go ahead, for luck. It tastes great."

Armonia tentatively licked the branch. She smacked her lips and smiled. "Delicious!" She then voraciously licked several other branches.

"Omnoberries are the sweetest berry. Sometimes the bush has an excess of sugar. When that happens it expresses the natural sugars through the leaves and it mixes with the sap," explained Lorelei. She invited Daleth to partake before Armonia slurped every last branch.

Daleth rolled his eyes and took a branch and slid it across his mouth. "Satisfied?"

Lorelei nodded. She instructed them to stay put while she went into the market to purchase a wig. "While I'm gone eat some of the IO's M.A.T.O. gave us. I'm sure you're both hungry."

"Hope they're as good as that plant," said Armonia.

"Don't you need to eat?"

"I'll get something at the market," said Lorelei as she left them.

⟨ ⟩

EBJAN ORBIT

High Councilor Zean had just finished meeting with several other High Councilors and was making her way back to the office. Her feet fell heavy on the cobblestone sidewalk. The chorus of townspeople going about their business filled her ears like white noise. Her mind was still at the meeting. She had called it to try and garner backing for the request of The Spark to declare Daleth an Obstruction. Although several High Councilors did throw in their support, attention was still mainly focused on the Prep Centers.

Everyone had their reaction to the murder of a guardian and a Twin Flame in process at that. Murder was rather uncommon since The Spark's arrival. Even guardian's rarely fell in the line of duty. A guardian's role was mostly to ensure order and keep disputes from escalating. Darkness traders knew it was bad business to kill them so they just stayed out of their way and deferred to them if there was a confrontation. Those who had degenerated to a point of becoming a chaotic nuisance were brought to Light Bearing Centers for rehabilitation. They were usually too far gone to be much of a threat. Their mental facilities were too frayed to carry out any lucid actions. The Light Bearing Centers provide the necessary therapy to reintegrate Light into the individual.

This occurrence was fairly unprecedented and many felt overwhelmed dealing with it in addition to the unprecedented closure of the hatcheries. There were more and more economical concerns piling up about the suspension of the Prep Centers so a prudent decision was made by certain High Councilors to simply focus on that issue. In Zean's opinion, however, occurrences in the system couldn't be ignored just because procreation had stopped.

It also did not help that Grevolios was almost upon the system. Many did not want to deal with such grim matters at such a festive time. Truth be told Zean also wanted to relax and enjoy the celebration. Past Grevolioses held some of her favorite memories. She found it hard to retrieve and cherish those memories let alone make new ones with the darkness that seemed ever looming. With all guardians throughout the entire system taking on extra shifts in search of Daleth she did not hold out much hope of seeing Jamila either. The impromptu visit when Zean returned from the conference on Iris would have to be their Grevolios celebration together.

Despite her best efforts to focus on more productive matters, Zean kept being called back to the pit of loneliness in her. She missed Jamila so much. They saw so little of each other it's a wonder that they reflect at all. The sensible thing would be for one or both of them to step down from their demanding post. Alas, Zean knew in her heart of hearts that is the very reason why they were so good for each other. As much as they were devoted to one another they were equally devoted to the system, to the Uprights they were responsible for. The thought brought a warm smile to her. It would have to serve as a replacement for Jamila's physical presence for now.

As Zean entered her reception lobby she saw a Magistrate of Knowledge seated on the bench. "High Councilor Zean, Magistrate Ramek has been wanting to speak with you," said Zean's assistant. "No formal request was filed."

Zean pulled her facial muscles tight and slowly shook her head. "I'm sorry but I'm much too busy right now for an impromptu inquiry. You'll have to try another High Councilor or fill out the proper paperwork and wait."

It was Ramek's turn now to shake his head. "Although I am on an inquiry that is not what brought me here." It was the kind of statement the Order was known for, the kind that is technically true but phrased in such a way as to conceal certain things. Since Corry had used an inquiry as a guise to find Daleth and elicit his services she could not leave the moon of Baabcrest once more so soon. So when word reached her Cell of Daleth and an unknown Upright killing a guardian on Ebjan it was decided Ramek would go on an inquiry so he could investigate for the Cell. Not long after he arrived on Ebjan he learned of Zean's campaign to declare Daleth an Obstruction and decided to utilize it.

Zean was not sure of the intentions of this stranger. Something about his cockeyed smile felt off. "Whatever brought you here can wait for the proper procedures. It's been a long cycle and Grevolios is almost here."

Ramek stood and smoothed his purple robe. "Of course. I wouldn't want to intrude on your festivities. My apologies, I merely wished to aid your presentation of Obstruction to The Spark." Zean's ears perked up. Her stance shifted so she now faced Ramek head-on. The sudden shift in Zean's posture was not lost on the observant Ramek but he gave no hint of it. "I will just continue along with my inquiry trip. All the best with your endeavor and may your Grevolios be bright."

Ramek went to leave but Zean grabbed his arm as he walked by. "Wait!" Ramek paused and turned to Zean wearing a passive expression. "You can get support for my Obstruction presentation?"

Ramek jutted out his lower lip. "I believe the Schools of Baabcrest would be interested."

Zean extended her arm to entreat Ramek to come into her office. "Hold my communications," she said to her assistant as they left the lobby.

Once inside her office, Zean closed the door behind them. "Would you like to see the presentation?" Although she tried to remain professional she could not hide the enthusiasm in her voice. With another Orbit's support, she could potentially have this wrapped up much quicker than she initially feared it would take. She would not need unanimous support from her fellow High Councilors, for with governing officials from two Orbits signing off on it that would suffice. Since the incident happened on Ebjan and the proposal was so unprecedented she hadn't considered asking another Orbit to join. The weight was already lifting off her shoulders. *To have one less matter to contend with is worth the breach in the protocol.*

"There's no need for me to see it. I've researched you and believe the presentation is as good as it can be." Zean couldn't help but blush at the compliment. "In addition, Magistrate Molomew of the School of Prosperity speaks highly of you."

Ava had been one of the Magistrates in attendance at the Conference on Iris. When Ramek reported Zean's activities to his Cell Ava immediately went to work on the Magistrate she had observed conversing with Zean. Molomew was made to understand that his support, as well as the rest of the School of Prosperity, would mean the tempering of Zean's push for Iris to have a firmer hand in the governing of Orbits.

Zean hesitated at first to confirm what Ramek seemed to be implying. "Are you saying both Schools are behind this presentation?"

"The School of Relations will follow suit with the other two so you have Baabcrest unanimously behind it and can thank Molomew for it. He knows you won't forget it."

Zean didn't acknowledge the implication of political leverage for the time being but filed it in the back of her mind for consideration later. Getting the Obstruction proposal was paramount. Molomew's desire to avoid complete Twin Flame control will be an issue she will take up with him directly later after she has properly weighed the costs. Perhaps there would be another token she could swap if needed.

"It will be hard to get other support, especially with all that's going on right now throughout the system. I've gotten some Councilors and High Councilors here on board but the Panel of Judgement won't touch it. However, with the full support of Baabcrest, I think the number that would agree here on Ebjan will be enough."

"It's a minimum. It is better to have a larger exterior Orbit on board to balance it. Fimeger will never support one who originated there being named an Obstruction. Circapto will not risk the fragile trifecta the current political situation has forged. However, I highly doubt Gremoilio would be able to resist the jab at their rival Fimeger."

Zean furrowed her brow. "Won't they also not want to upset their current ally?"

"Gremoilio and Fimeger will never be true allies. They are simply coerced to work together in the present time. Fimeger will be forced to look the other way as Gremoilio will claim it as a legitimate concern. I happen to know there was a recent altercation between several of Gremoilio's populace and Daleth which will give them the proper reason."

Zean grabbed a pen and pad of paper. "Do you know the exact location of this incident?"

"The city of Cemia, I believe."

The sparkly feathery end of the pen danced in the air as Zean frantically moved it along the pad. "I will make some communications."

Ramek gave a stiff nod of his head. "I think it prudent."

They stood in awkward silence for a moment. "Well then, I won't take up any more of your time," said Ramek. He moved quickly to the door.

His task was done here and he wished to continue the search for Daleth. He suspected he was no longer on Ebjan but hopefully being ruled an Obstruction would either force him to come to the School of Knowledge looking for help or result in his capture. If the experiment was still with him then the School of Knowledge could surely claim to help her and she would end up in their possession regardless of whatever folly Daleth was trying to pull.

"Thank you for your help and support with this," Zean said.

"I think we both believe in justice."

"Justice is of the Light. The Light is what keeps us from becoming lost in darkness."

Ramek gave a polite smile in response to the utterance of one of the creeds the Way drilled into society. "May you have a bright Grevolios."

"May it reflect to you," replied Zean in the traditional formal custom.

After Ramek left the thought occurred to Zean that he may be a part of the Order of Consciousness and supporting the request for vindictive motives. She quickly dismissed them though. It was not right to assume all Magistrates of Knowledge were members of the Order. Besides, the Order would have bigger concerns than Daleth with all the talk of Twin Flames taking over the administration of the Orbits. On the off chance she had just met with an Order member with a grudge then the darkness would serve the Light as all things eventually did.

With any doubt within her now resolved Zean reveled in her good fortune unburdened. The Light was truly shining brightly within her. She had fulfilled her wish of seeing The Spark with her own eyes and had nearly succeeded in a dicey spot of shadow on her home Orbit. *My works are obviously of Light if things are coming together this well and this quickly. Perhaps all this means my Twin Flame union with Jamila has almost arrived.* She would have to bring it up at their next Path Finder session. She walked home with a lightness in her step.

⟨ ⟩

HANOWEH ORBIT

Before they had departed Ebjan Lorelei had made sure to gather as many halos as she could from her place. She had gone while Iris shone after the Room had dispersed. It was a calculated risk that any traitors would not make such a hasty move as returning to the building to confront Armonia and Daleth. She had stuffed all she could find in a satchel that she had slipped into her boot and then quickly returned to the hideout to make sure Daleth and Armonia were still there. The gamble had fortunately paid off.

Now she walked the markets of Hanoweh which were already busy with eager Grevolios shoppers. Her legs were prickly with goosebumps from the cool gusts of morning air that swept through the aisles but she ignored her chills. She found a pretty emerald green wig that would fall nicely at Daleth's shoulders. The maker used to be an actor and set designer on the live story circuit. He now made costumes for performers and aspiring performers. He asked Lorelei what live stories she had been in. Lorelei rattled off a few names and dodged precisely locating any.

"I can't recall seeing you around. Are you new to this Orbit?" the artisan inquired.

"Just here to see the Grevolios celebration. Heard Hanoweh has the best in the whole system."

The artisan nodded smugly. "We do."

She quickly paid the Upright and added in a few extra halos. She told him it was to honor his fine craftsmanship but in reality, it was to give him a favorable impression so no suspicion arose in his mind. Of course, it was not a completely dishonest act. The wig was of very nice quality but Lorelei had learned prudence paid greater dividends than halos.

"How fortunate I was able to find you." Lorelei turned and saw Unak amongst the throngs of Uprights. She reeled back as her mind raced. Her eyes went wide and her throat constricted. Almost in response to this Unak leaned in close to Lorelei's ear and whispered, "I was on my way here after our last meeting. It is by the grace of Yowgn that we find each other once more." He then leaned slightly back and looked into Lorelei's eyes. They appeared to be studying hers. "How were you able to escape Daleth?"

Lorelei had almost forgotten she had sent an astral message during her dreaming session with Sil to the Room leaders indicating Daleth took her and Armonia hostage. She moved away from the others in the market so she could not be overheard. Unak followed. Lorelei looked around her to buy time and then said, "I lost them in the crowds. I was purchasing this wig to help my discretion as I searched for Room members here on Hanoweh to dream with and hopefully recapture both of them." *It is fortunate time could be inconsistent in dreaming messages, the memory appears but how long it was there for is always hazy. Because of this odd feature, Unak may buy that I was on Hanoweh when the message was sent.* Lorelei comforted herself with this thought.

"What about the individual you dreamed with here to let us know Daleth turned hostile?"

It had worked. She still wasn't sure how Unak made it here so quickly or knew they were on Hanoweh, to begin with. *Had I unknowingly let something slip into my message?* "Only a one trick degenerate. They wanted only to use me for an unauthorized dream not to benefit our cause. I need friends."

"You have fortunately found one. We must dream together immediately and find them. Daleth is considered of the utmost importance throughout the House. We need to find a spot where we will not be disturbed. Once we have their whereabouts I will keep surveillance on them while you alert the room of Hanoweh."

Lorelei nodded obediently. "I observed a damaged factory awaiting to be repaired a few blocks from here." Lorelei hadn't actually passed by it but heard others talking about it. A bad storm struck it with lightning and they were waiting till after Grevolios to begin repairs and reopen. She suggested it because according to what she heard it was in the opposite direction of Armonia and Daleth.

Unak smiled approvingly. "It sounds like it will do just fine. Lead the way then."

Lorelei complied. She tried to keep herself composed and her face impassive but she could feel her palms becoming clammy. She walked in the direction the gossiping Uprights had indicated for the factory and soon saw evidence of natural destruction. She tried to make it look like she knew where she was going and hide the sway in her knees. Eventually, she saw what had to be the factory. Unak used a discarded metal rod to force open the door. While he was distracted Lorelei slipped a couple of pieces of broken glass against her skin and the top of her dress.

"Shall we begin?" Unak asked once they entered the warehouse and closed the door behind them.

"Why wait?" Lorelei tried to keep her voice steady. She undressed Unak and began to suck on his neck. He in turn began hiking the hem of her dress up. As he reached for her breasts she quickly pulled out one of the pieces of glass and put it to his neck. Lorelei then tilted her head back and saw an amused smile on Unak's face.

"How pointless, my dear, since neither of us can die."

Suddenly it all clicked for Lorelei. A Twin Flame would be able to tamper with dreaming and block what Armonia truly was. A Twin Flame would also be able to pull whispers from the inner psyche of the sender of a dream message. Ones the sender had no intention to share. *How could I have been so naive to think a Twin Flame couldn't infiltrate the House of Yowgn? He saw through my ruse so easily when I couldn't see his.* She let the sting of regret pass. She pressed the glass into Unak's neck so a thin line of red began to form around its edge. "True but we can still feel pain." Lorelei's eyes moved downward and Unak's followed. His smile faded when he saw another piece of glass held to his genitals.

"Why did you think you could hide? I may not have your dream journal to give me a roadmap but when you sent your message I pulled what I could. Using that along with our past dreaming experiences I was able to locate you. Fortunately right after we last met I went directly to acquire the fastest ship I could. I was already in inter-Orbit space when you sent your message."

"Clever." She did not attempt to hide the derision in her voice.

"Tell me, Lorelei," he said slowly. "How did you get rid of your tattoos?"

"I carved them out."

Unak's brow scrunched up in confusion. "But we regenerate?"

"I kept the point in my skin so it healed around the instrument and scarred."

"So that's how those pockmarks came to be. Clever yourself."

"I endured excruciating pain to be free of the Light, unlike you." Lorelei took the back of the hand which held the glass to Unak's throat and wiped it along one of his cheeks. It revealed a flame tattoo under a skin tone paste.

"My dear, I am all Light." Unak tore away from Lorelei who only managed to gash his thigh. Unak grabbed a metal rod from the ground and took a mighty swing. Lorelei couldn't move fast enough to avoid the blow but was able to turn her body so the rod landed on her back. A cracking sound filled the stale air of the warehouse. A fiery jolt ran up Lorelei's spine. She stumbled to the ground. Her hands landed in the warm blood which pooled on the floor from Unak's wound.

"Tell me where she is and I'll forget all about you as well as your deceit," sneered Unak. At that moment Lorelei realized she was right about Armonia, she was the key to tearing down The Way of The Light. She had to find a way back to her. Lorelei flung a piece of glass at Unak which caught him in his bare abdomen. He doubled over in pain and dropped the rod.

Lorelei got back to her feet and tried to run but she had trouble feeling her legs and they faltered. The damage to her spine had not yet healed. Unak pulled out the glass and pounced on Lorelei. He stabbed her furiously. She managed to spin herself and do the same to Unak with her piece of glass.

Panting and saturated in blood, they stopped. Unak remained on top of Lorelei. "Stop making this so difficult."

"I will never give you any information about her. And we both know dreaming doesn't work if it's forced. You'll get nothing from me," Lorelei managed to say between labored breaths.

"Very well then. I will find another way. The Light always finds a way." He slashed her wrist and she was forced to drop the piece of glass. The loss of blood began to make her woozy. The assault on her body was taking its toll. Lorelei used what remained of her strength to kick him in the pelvis. She pushed his stunned body off of hers and then scrambled to grab the piece of broken glass she dropped. With a vicious quickness, she turned on Unak and stabbed his genitals before he regained his senses. Unak let out a blood-curdling screech and clutched a piece of wood that he used to bash Lorelei in the head.

This was pointless. They could beat each other senseless till the next Grevolios. Lorelei lifted her head up and through her blurry vision saw a thresher with its grinding wheels exposed. She ran to it hoping it still had a power source attached. Unak got to his feet and pursued her. He grabbed her neck and slammed her head into the metal feeding tray.

Unak then snatched a nearby coil of rope and wrapped it around Lorelei's throat crushing her trachea. He then grabbed her arms in a vice-like grip. Lorelei surmised he was going to attempt to tie her up and decided to let him start to throw him off while she meanwhile conserved her energy. He pinned her wrists behind her back and began to secure them. Before he could finish the knot she kicked out her leg and wrapped it around Unak's. Using her full weight she threw Unak off balance and leveraged him head-first into the grinding mechanism of the thresher. She thrust her shoulder into the power switch and it started up. Unak's head and neck were reduced to pulp and his body fell limp to the floor. An end of the rope got caught in the spinning wheel pulling one of her arms in, and tearing it to shreds before she was able to stop the machine.

Lorelei searched the place and found some tarps. She wrapped the stump of her arm in them to contain what little blood she had left to bleed. Her legs buckled as she wrapped another tarp around herself to conceal her blood-drenched body. She removed her saturated boots so she wouldn't leave a trail of blood. She abandoned the wig and satchel of halos, as well. It would take a while for Unak to regenerate but she had to use all that time to get far away and find a safe spot for her own body to recoup. She weakly stumbled out into the streets. A Grevolios parade was going on so most Uprights were focused on that and not her. She made her way slowly and stealthily along the parade route behind the frenzied crowds.

Eventually, her legs no longer felt like they could support her weight. She could go no further. She hoped she had put enough distance between her and Unak. She found a storage warehouse that was closed for Grevolios. She couldn't break in lest she tipped off Unak if he searched for her but fortunately this building must have also been hit by the storm. It had a boarded-up window, as well. Lorelei was grateful Grevolios had slowed the usual zealous workforce of Hanoweh. She used her last strength to pry one of the boards off and shoved it into the narrow slot. She then followed suit. She let consciousness slip away. Before it was gone completely she had one last thought which comforted her, *Daleth is strong enough to protect Armonia.*

⟨ ⟩

HANOWEH ORBIT

Armonia knelt on the grass sampling all the IO's M.A.T.O. had given them. She hadn't expected much from the multi-colored mush. She was pleasantly surprised, however, to find they held an exciting array of tastes. The green one had a mixture of sweet and sour that danced on her tongue. The red one made her mouth tingle in a way that fondly reminded her of dreaming.

"These are pretty good." She turned to Daleth who sat a few feet away with his brow tightly knit. "Though not as good as the omnoberry. Sure ya don't want anymore?"

"Be quiet!" Daleth snapped. Armonia shrugged and continued to eat.

Daleth was deep in contemplation trying to plot out the best course of action. Lorelei should have been back by now which meant something had gone amiss. He wasn't sure how to address it since he didn't know exactly what had occurred.

Lorelei's deceptive behavior made him wary of a potential trap. Strangely he found he regretted their relationship had come to such a state.

Another option was that Lorelei was correct and her Room was compromised. As unlikely as it was, somebody could have found her and she could be captured or dead. If that was the case then he had nothing more to do here. He had no compulsion for vengeance or obligation of honor since the affront was not directed at him.

Either way, it seemed Lorelei's promise of payment was null now. Which meant he should go back to the original mission and bring Armonia to the School of Knowledge to redeem his payment. He was a wanted fugitive now so he needed the halos all the more to lay low till the guardians lost their zest for justice.

He was low on energy so he needed to feed on fear before stealing a ship just in case he was walking into another trap with this troublesome Upright he was saddled with. Hanoweh was a proud Orbit. They reveled in the highest graduation rate to Twin Flame status. Now with Grevolios almost upon the system, they would be all the more self-assured. It would take time to access the appropriate target. Perhaps that was simply what was holding him up, the labor of torture that laid before him as well as the theft of a ship. On an Orbit such as Hanoweh, he must plan everything precisely out if this was to succeed. The noise from the nearby parade did not help his mental facilities. He glanced over at Armonia who appeared to still be stuffing her face. He shook his head back and forth. She proved herself to be an invalid where serious affairs were concerned. *At least it keeps her from bothering me,* he thought.

Armonia yawned and blinked her eyes suddenly feeling tired. She looked up to the rust-colored sky and squinted from the light of Iris. Suddenly Iris grew black. The only light it gave off was from a reddish-purple ring on its edge. Armonia looked around and saw the landscape change from a green and yellow meadow to a grey swamp. The trees and shrubs around her became black with red thorns on their branches. She no longer saw Daleth. The only Upright she spied was a lone figure wrapped in tattered robes making its way toward her. As the figure neared Armonia she could make out that although it was an Upright it had no mouth, ears, or nose. Just a red slit in the lower portion of a smooth round head. The skin was blotchy with various colors that seemed to glow brightly in different patterns before fading away. Suddenly they were both standing in the cavern with the teal lake. She let out a scream.

Daleth pounced on Armonia and threw his hand over her mouth. "What are you trying to do, sabotage me?" Daleth noticed Armonia's terrified eyes begin to roll back in her head. She stopped screaming. Daleth cautiously removed his hand. Armonia tilted her head up at the golden clouds and began to say strange words. Daleth quickly put his hand back. "Not this again," he muttered. Armonia stopped her babble and began instead to whimper softly. She pulled at her hair. Daleth removed his hand slowly. "You going to stay quiet now?"

"The pain's back. Feels like my head's splitting open. Dream with me!"

"No."

Armonia leaped onto Daleth and they began to wrestle around on the soft dewy ground. Daleth was caught off guard by how strong Armonia seemed. However, he was more powerful and eventually pinned her to the ground. As they faced each other, Daleth felt a strange magnetic pull toward this damaged being under him. He felt her chest heave against his. He noted the softness of her breasts. Her legs were wrapped around his own flexed thighs. She raised her pelvis toward him.

She then did something which completely caught Daleth off guard. She brought her moistened lips toward his plump ones. The touch of their mouths was as light as a feather but the force it sent through their bodies was a seismic wave. Both of them wore faces of surprise and confusion. They stared into each other's eyes for a moment groping for an answer.

Armonia's arms were still being held to the ground but she twisted them so she could grip Daleth's forearms with her own hands. She flicked her tongue along Daleth's lips and the tip of his nose. "Dream with me," she whispered. With gentle but firm force she brought one of Daleth's hands to her wet vulva. She moved his hand in circles over her. Almost involuntarily Daleth used his other hand to sweep his tunic to one side and with a great thrust he entered her. Armonia moaned in response and clenched his rear pulling him into her deeper. He felt her vaginal walls undulate and flex around his member.

They pushed against one another and then separated every so slightly. Again and again, they repeated this rhythmic rolling of their pelvis in perfect unspoken synchronization. Each time they came back together it was just a little bit more strenuous and held for just a second longer. Armonia was rubbing her mound with her free hand as the intensity built for both of them.

Daleth tried to fight against it but it was like he was possessed by some unnamed force that was attempting to merge him and Armonia. He was helpless in a way he had never recalled being.

With their bodies on fire and locked together it felt almost unbearable but neither could pull away. They both just pressed against each other tighter until there was a silence of all thought and all sensation.

《 》

DALETH LOOKED AROUND him. He was in a location he had never been to. Everything seemed to be of light around him only differing in degrees of brightness. Even more peculiar was that the light did not hurt his eyes. He could see easily and clearly.

"Where are we?" Daleth spun around at the sound of Armonia's voice. She stood before him but differently as well. For she now had two leathery red wings. It took but a moment to realize that the scars he had seen over Armonia's shoulder blades were from removing the genetic mutation of wings. It was rumored Uprights occasionally sprouted wings like Non-uprights but they were always surgically eliminated upon the first detection.

"You have wings," he said matter-of-factly. He was struck by how it completed Armonia's physical structure.

"Weird right? This must be how we're supposed to look. See, ya scars are gone." Daleth glanced down and realized Armonia was correct. "This didn't happen the other times I dreamed."

"Nor is it supposed to. Dreaming gives visions and insights into one's self and the world. It does not transport the dreamers to some other world altogether."

"So we're not in the system anymore?"

"This is no known Orbit."

DREAMING

"So then where are we?"

"I don't know but we will not find out standing around." Daleth began to march.

"How do ya know that's the right direction?"

"I don't," stated Daleth.

Armonia flew after him surprised at how easily flight came to her. They only got a few paces before both froze. Before them, appeared to be a thin wall of light. On the other side of the wall stood robed figures who appeared to be made entirely of light like The Spark but unlike The Spark, they had deep black orbs where faces should be and their light was all different shades of colors. There were many of them.

"Who are they?" Armonia asked.

Suddenly a voice answered. It seemed to come from everyone standing on the other side of the wall but it spoke as one voice not with sound but within the mind. "We have come before you. We are pleased you two have found each other again although we regret it was not till after you both suffered so much damage."

"How do you know us?"

"Wait, we knew each other before I lost my memories?"

The voice once more answered Armonia's question. "Not in your current lifetime but you two spirits know each other very well. You both volunteered to free the others together. Time and again you have tried but have always met challenges that prevented you."

"Current lifetime? We have but only one miserable lifetime," snarled Daleth.

"We volunteered to free who?" The beings responded by silently raising an arm and extending a finger of translucent light.

Armonia and Daleth both looked in the direction they pointed. They froze unable to comprehend what they viewed. Stretching on endlessly were images of the different Orbits but every upright seemed gaunt and withered. Their skin appeared worn and cracked. Their eyes were sunken in and their bodies were hunched over.

"What happened to them?" Armonia was eventually able to ask.

"Their energy is being drained off so they walk depleted of their full potential. You both do as well. Most probably this is what keeps leading you astray from your mission lifetime after lifetime."

Daleth sagged and whipped his head back to the crowd. "There's that talk again. Don't mock me with the idea that I must endure more than one cruel life."

"Oh Diocess, you have grown so weary," the voice stated.

"Who is Diocess?" Snapped Daleth.

"You call yourself Daleth in this life but your true name is Diocess. Just as she recalled her true name Armonia."

Daleth threw his hands up. "This is ridiculous!"

Armonia stepped forward. "What is draining them?"

"Much."

"This is all some trick." Daleth turned on Armonia. "You play so innocently but I always saw through you. What ends are you scheming for?"

"Huh?" Armonia drew back.

Daleth unsheathed his trikilldo and brandished it at Armonia. "Don't. It will only make me angry."

"Aren't ya always angry?"

"You will know when I'm angry and I am very close."

"Diocess," the voice called out.

"Shut up! That's not my name!"

"You always were headstrong, Diocess," the voice said soothingly.

Daleth charged the crowd. "I told you to stop calling me that!"

As he reached the wispy wall of light he felt like he hit instead a wall of solid stone. A tremendous force pushed him back. At the same time, a wave of emotions washed over him. His chest felt like it was expanding, growing into such a monumental thing it would break apart bones and skin to reach beyond him. All things at once seemed possible and connected. It lasted only the briefest moment but so intense was the moment that Daleth noticed a tear drop fall from his face for the first time in an entire gremrev.

Armonia's voice brought Daleth's mind back to him. "Ya don't think I'm scared, confused, and upset. Ya can't just act all crazy."

"Why not? You do," sneered Daleth.

Armonia stomped her foot. "I can't help it, ya big—meany!"

The voice entered their minds once again. "You two can both come home and rest."

"Home?", an unmistakable note of disdain and disbelief lingered on the word as Daleth spoke it.

"I thought ya said we're on a mission?" asked Armonia.

"You can always come home and try again. Of course, it does get harder each time."

"I—I don't understand," Armonia stammered.

"We know. It is better to forget others while currently in a life. It allows you to focus on the role." The voice paused before it added, "We will be watching over you like always."

With that everything began to swirl together as if Armonia, Daleth, and all the light went down a huge bottomless black drain.

《 》

INTER-ORBIT SPACE

"You dimwad! Why did you give them our IOs?" Gimeld yelled at M.A.T.O.

"I only gave them rations enough to last a cycle or two. I am programmed to serve."

"I don't care what you're programmed to do. You follow my orders or so help me I will disassemble you and you'll be nothing but space debris. You got it?"

"It is logged in my memory banks."

"And keep it there. Now serve me by decrypting whatever you can about our recent pick up from Circapto." Gimeld jutted out his arm and pointed his index finger at the shiny metallic box to add emphasis to his command.

"I have already tried captain. There seems to be nothing there."

"Hmmm, then it must be high-priced dark trade to not even have an encrypted docket. To not even risk decryption means they don't want the contents known. This means I can leverage more halos from our recipient upon delivery. This almost makes up for the loss of IOs, almost." With that Gimeld left the gallery.

As he entered the bridge Arjan asked "I heard shouting."

Gimeld sat down in the pilot's chair next to Arjan. "The pile of junk gave Lorelei and her companions some of our IOs."

"Did you throw him out the airlock?" Arjan asked with a good-humored smile.

"I should have along with Lorelei and those other two."

"I disagree." Gimeld and Arjan turned to see Sil standing behind them.

With the same smile, Arjan said, "That's just because Lorelei showed you a good dream."

"I don't care whether you agree or disagree or has everyone on this ship forgotten whose captain," said Gimeld.

Arjan stroked Gimeld's leg and then gently gripped his member. "You will always be my captain."

"You included me on this crew because you valued my foresight and guidance. Did you not?" Asked Sil.

Arjan got up and put a hand on Sil's shoulder and made a pouty face. "We brought you on board because you're such a sorry specimen."

"Are you saying you saw something with those three?"

Sil nodded. "I know they seemed gruff but I think they are meant to do something important and we are meant to help. We should dump the cargo we picked up into inter-Orbit space and turn around to find them."

Arjan began to laugh overly loud. He bent over clutching his stomach in dramatic hysterics. "Now that's the real reason we keep you around, Sil. You always entertain." He went to go sit back down.

"Your recommendation is heard. Anything else?" It was a dismissal from Gimeld. Sil turned around and left the bridge.

Sil sat in one of the rest quarters and stroked the air beside them. In a soft gentle tone, Sil said, "I know you haven't left me or lead me wrong as you promised. I just hope Gimeld hasn't led us too far astray. I know you can't always save us." Sil flipped on a view screen on the wall and gazed at the pinpricks of light that flickered on it. As Sil watched the tiny dots of white glimmer, memories flooded into their mind. Sil retraced the path which led them to this crew.

DOOGA ORBIT

Sil was placed in a Prep Center on the wild Orbit of Dooga and upon graduation found herself part of a powerful mountain tribe. As was the case with the majority of tribes on Dooga, Sil's tribe was rather primitive and took their cues from nature. Sil's fused toes did not sit well with them. They came to see Sil as a weak individual and therefore a bad omen. Sil was shunned by most of the tribe. The seniors in the tribe felt it would be pointless to train Sil in hunting or fighting. Likewise, anything Sil constructed or sewed could potentially become faulty since from the maker flows the creation.

Due to the lack of companionship, Sil spent much time on the outskirts of the village with the Non-upright inhabitants of Dooga. Sil grew especially close to one particular Waheeyun. The pair would sit together under the dark sky silently staring up at the twinkling lights above. No words needed to be spoken. The sound of their breathing was the only communication needed, to let them know they were by each other's side. The two formed such a strong bond that Sil gave the Waheeyun a name, Arratup. Arratup was a colloquial greeting on Dooga amongst friendly relations. It seemed fitting to Sil.

A Waheeyun was a fanged beast with pointy ears that preyed on the smaller game that roamed the Dooga landscape. It was not uncommon for Waheeyuns to hang around villages to hunt the scavengers the settlements attracted. They were usually welcomed since they helped preserve the tribe's food stockpile. But none in the village could remember any Upright becoming so connected with a Non-upright. They felt Sil put Arratup above the rest of the tribe.

SO WHEN IT BECAME TIME for, Dawba, the ritual done every time the night sky had moved through its cycle of different combinations of lights, Arratup was selected to be the honored sacrifice. The ritual called for the members of the tribe to gather in a circle and for the selected honoree to be placed in the center of the circle. The warriors would then hold up special clubs made of rock and wood while they chanted a special song about the hardships of life. After the song, the warriors would take turns clubbing the honoree. It would not take many blows for the sacrifice to succumb but each warrior needed to take a swing. Afterward, the body was roasted and the meat was distributed to the tribe.

Sil could not bear the thought of this fate befalling Arratup. Arratup was taken to a special tent the night before to be washed and anointed with oils. Sil was not allowed to be a part of this. Sil did though approach the keeper of the sacrifice, Vitbito, an Upright who, although a stern leader in the tribe, probably took the most pity on Sil.

"May you allow me entry to the tent so I may wish Arratup courage and peace in Dawba when Iris awakes?"

Vitbito smiled at Sil's humbleness and devotion. "You make it harder for yourself by naming that Waheeyun and acting like it knows what is coming. Non-uprights are not blessed with the Light like us they live in a world blinded to anything deeper than survival. We learn how to survive from them and learn how to bear life with dignity from The Spark."

Sil never held The Spark in any high regard for The Spark had not offered any assistance in Sil's memories to Sil. Sil bowed their head and with a meek voice said, "I know this but it gives me the courage to think that Arratup needs courage." Vitbito shook his head and then waved his hand toward the tent. Sil hurried in before Vitbito could change his mind.

Inside the aromas from the fragrant oils were so overwhelming they made Sil's nose scrunch up. Arratup was tethered to a stake in the ground but did not seem the least bit concerned. He simply was laying on the ground calmly. Likewise, Arratup didn't seem surprised to see Sil. Sil always believed they had a special understanding and the thought occurred that maybe Arratup knew Sil would rescue him. Sil hugged Arratup and then got to work. Sil removed the loop of rope from Arratup's neck and covered him with a blanket. "Stay under there my friend. I don't want your sensitive nose to be affected." Sil used a knife they carried and made a slit in the back wall of the tent then wrapped the cloak they wore around their face making sure to cover their nose and mouth.

Sil next took out a small reddish clay jar that they had concealed under their cloak. Sil popped open the cork near the opening of the tent. Sil had very little time to gather the ingredients and let them ferment but still believed it to be enough. Before knowing Arratup, Sil had watched with keen eyes the other members of the tribe go about their tasks. They thought Sil knew nothing of the ways of hunting or any other skill for that matter but it was untrue. Sil knew many things including how to gather the right ingredients to make a confuser, the special potion sometimes used to disorient difficult prey to make them easier to take down. Sil fanned the gasses coming from the jar out of the entrance of the tent. After a moment Sil with all the might they could muster gathered Arratup up in their arms blanket and all. Quickly they exited the tent through the back flap Sil had created. Vitbito stumbled after them but thanks to the mixture in the jar could not call out or see where he was going in the darkened sky. Sil did not turn back to see any of this but instead kept running. Their lungs fought against the thin dry air. Again Sil counted on the tribe to underestimate them. They thought Sil feeble but Sil and Arratup had traveled great distances together while enjoying each other's company.

After they were out of sight of the tribe Sil let Arratup down but quickly snatched him back up again due to him being somewhat affected by the vapors of the confuser. It wasn't till they were nearly halfway down the mountain that Arratup regained his composer. Together they reached the base of the mountain range just as Iris re-entered the sky. They decided it was a sign to keep going for fear of pursuit by the others.

Not much later they came upon a tromophon hive. Tromophons were dangerous insects nearly the size of an Upright's head. They had venomous fangs and fast-beating wings. It was not safe to go near one of their hives but Arratup turned toward it for some reason. Even though Sil hadn't seen a tromophon, unease slowed their feet. It was the confidence of Arratup that gave Sil courage. Sure enough, as they both entered the hive Sil realized that it was, in fact, empty of any tromophons. "We can hide out here. If the tribe comes this far I don't think they will come looking for us inside it for fear of a tromophon attack. Good, find my friend."

Even though all Uprights were now immune from the venom of a tromophon, Doogans still kept a healthy fear of them from their ancestors. It was probably for the best. Even though their venom was not deadly anymore, a single tromophon was still fierce enough to do considerable damage let alone an entire swarm.

Inside the compartments, the tromophons once lived in, was a jelly-like substance with a savory aroma. Arratup began to lick it up and Sil followed their friend's lead. It tasted sour at first but with a sweet finish. It sustained them that first cycle as they rested after their descent off the mountain.

⟨ ⟩

SIL LEARNED FROM ARRATUP how to live alone in the wilderness. The tufts of dark fur on Arratup's ears would tremble and his nose would stick straight up in the air when there was something new afoot. Arratup led Sil to food and led Sil away from danger. Their bond grew closer as countless cycles passed. Sil never saw another member of the tribe during those times. They had most likely not been all that distraught over Sil leaving. Sil was fine with that for all seemed happier in this new arrangement.

Sil lost track of how long it had been since they ran off with Arratup but after one cycle Sil took notice that Arratup seemed to be moving slower. Sil ignored it as simply just imagination but it got more and more severe. One cycle when Iris re-entered the sky Arratup did not get up. Arratup's golden bands around his midsection rose and fell in rapid bursts. Sil put Arratup's head gently in their lap. They stroked his brown fur as they dripped water into his mouth. Sil whispered over and over, "It's okay my friend. I will be alright. I know you have to go. I promise I will go on." By the time Iris left the sky, Arratup stopped breathing altogether. Sil sobbed bitterly in the dark, afraid to rest knowing that they would have to wake and for one brief moment they would forget their friend was no longer by their side. Then it would all rush back on them. Sil just couldn't bear it, didn't know if they could survive it.

Sil did nod off for a brief rest and sure enough when they woke their chest felt like it had caved in on itself. It was at that moment that Sil considered ending their existence. *What life can be lived alone now?* Sil suddenly heard a voice shout. Sil had learned to hone their senses from

Arratup. Sil also noticed that the winds had picked up and felt a minor tremble in the ground beneath them. Sil didn't want to leave Arratup's body but also did not want to deal with anyone at the current time, Upright or Non-upright. Sil picked up the now stiff body of Arratup and began to walk away from where the voice had rung out.

As Sil walked the ground continued to tremble more vigorously and more frequently. The winds picked up as well. Sil squinted off at the horizon and thought they saw a faint bend to the landscape. Almost like the ground itself was being pulled inward. Sil wondered if a polar shift was happening. The elders of the tribe had told legends about such an event. That every so often the sky changes. Before the change, the coasts get pulled into the oceans and winds blew fiercely. During the change, tremendous jolts hit all the lands like someone was swinging Dooga around like you beat your cloaks on the rocks to clean them. *If such an event is occurring then it would be just as well,* Sil thought. For it would surely end Sil's life and take away the burden of bearing life without Arratup.

Suddenly a voice rose above the screeching air that stung Sil's face. "I've spied someone." Sil reflexively turned toward it and saw a robot with three optical lenses on his face pointing a mechanical finger toward them.

A second figure appeared on top of the dune next to the robot. This one was an organic Upright with green-colored hair. "We already told you we're just going to hide in the ship until the storm passes." *Fools,* Sil thought. If it was a polar shift in the works the magnetic pulses that would radiate up from the ground would end up frying them inside the ship.

"Then we should at least offer them shelter as well," the android replied. "Hey! You there! Do you need to take shelter in our ship?"

Sil was about to keep on walking without answering but then got an idea. The jolt would kill all of them. *If these dimwads wish to die why shouldn't I accompany them? Surely I can't go on without Arratup.*

Sil faced the two figures. "Yes, please."

"Excellent!" the robot exclaimed. "I am called M.A.T.O. and this is Arjan. We will take you to our captain Gimeld. What is your name?"

"Sil."

Arjan looked down and pinched the bridge of his nose. "You and your soft heart. Don't you know you're part of a bloodthirsty pirate crew?"

"I will not hesitate to destroy enemies for you but I am programmed to serve and I sense no threat from this individual. Of course, my sensors have been somewhat off since we crash-landed."

"You can explain all that to Gimeld 'cause I ain't sticking up for you." Arjan began to walk down the dune. Sil followed along with M.A.T.O.

M.A.T.O. rotated his lenses and peered at the body Sil carried. "Why do you carry a dead Waheeyun with you? Were you looking to gain sustenance from it for we have many IOs?"

Arjan whirled around on them. "Don't give away our IOs!"

"I do not need your IOs," Sil said softly.

"Good, you're not getting any."

The Wayward Star came into view half buried in the sandy soil. "It looks worse than it is," assured M.A.T.O.

Gimeld walked up to them. "We better get inside the storm's picking up. Who's this?"

"A traveler in need of shelter. They bring their own food," said M.A.T.O.

"I don't care. We're not guardians. Tell them to find their own shelter." Gimeld waved Sil off and went to head back to the ship but stopped and unsheathed his gun when he saw a large group of Uprights heading toward them.

Sil's eyes widened when their faces came into view. They were Sil's tribe. Most likely they had come down off the mountains to try and find a suitable sanctuary.

"Oh great more freeloaders," growled Gimeld. "Get ready to fight them off."

Arjan took out both a laser gun and a short blade. He got into a fighting stance.

M.A.T.O. elevated both arms and small laser canons rose out of them. "I assess that their numbers may be too great for us to fight them off without suffering loss ourselves."

Gimeld snorted. "You underestimate me, robot."

The tribe stopped a few feet in front of them. Vitbito was at the front. He locked eyes with Sil but neither made any sign of recognition. "Don't think you're seeking shelter from this storm in our ship," bellowed Gimeld.

Vitbito cocked his head. "You must be strangers to Dooga. Don't you know a polar shift when one is upon you? A ship is the last place you want to hide unless you want your brains cooked out. We are searching for a trench to hide in and hopefully, most of us survive."

"What's a polar shift?" Arjan asked still holding his weapons up.

"Ah, that would explain the disturbance to my sensors as well as the crash itself. A polar shift is an event Dooga suffers from occasionally where the magnetic poles shift position. It causes extreme weather conditions as well as electromagnetic pulses."

"You're robot knows well. Too bad he won't survive." With that Vitbito pushed past the pirates and Sil. No one outrightly acknowledged Sil as they passed but Sil saw flickers of recognition in their averted eyes.

M.A.T.O.'s lenses rotated. "I recommend we follow them. They know the terrain better than us and a trench or ditch would be the best location to try and survive the shift."

"Now you tell me, dimwad," Gimeld said as he followed the group.

"My apologies but my sensors were affected by electromagnetic disturbance."

"What did he mean you won't survive?" Arjan asked.

"The shift will short-circuit me I'm afraid but I will try to stay online for as long as I can to aid you."

Sil's eyes grew wet despite the harsh wind. Something about the robot reminded them of Arratup. *The diligent loyalty maybe or was it just the fact that the robot was the only one who showed me kindness just as Arratup did?*

They had only traveled a short distance when Sil froze. To Sil's left staring in earnest was Arratup. Sil for a moment thought they were imagining things. No one else seemed to pay any heed to the Waheeyun and Sil still felt the weight of Arratup's body. Then Arratup pointed his long snout up in the air and turned it to his left. It was the same manner he communicated with Sil in life when he wanted Sil to follow him.

"Wait!" Sil called out not sure why. Sil had cried louder than they meant to and all now focused their attention on them. "We need to go to the left. That is where safety lies."

"What makes you so sure all of sudden? You were ready to hide in a ship and die just a little bit ago," said Arjan.

Sil looked at the faces of the tribe they once knew. They looked at M.A.T.O. and then turned back to Arratup who once again made the same twist of the head toward the left. "I just know. I've survived these lands by myself for countless cycles. It's true, I wanted to die before but you all wish to live so let me show you how."

Gimeld and Arjan looked at one another while nearly the entire tribe looked at Vitbito. Vitbito stared back at Sil who kept turning back to the specter of Arratup who kept his snout to the left. Vitbito for the briefest moment followed Sil's gaze before returning it to Sil. Without a word, Vitbito walked in the direction of Sil's stare. Gimeld and Arjan watched them. "Let's go," said Gimeld in a low harsh tone.

Arratup stayed in front, shifting slightly in trajectory, always with a turn of the nose It was just as Sil and Arratup used to travel. Sil directed the group based on Arratup's guidance. The ground quaked violently. The polar shift was nearing and they were running out of time to find shelter. Just when Sil started to wonder if Arratup was a hallucination a giant mound came into view.

"What is that up ahead?" someone from the tribe cried out.

As they got closer they could see the mound was not just dirt but stone and other materials. On the sides were carvings of an Upright taking on great beasts and waging valiant battles.

Sil recognized the figure but it was Vitbito who spoke so all could hear. "It is the tomb of Ravi, the great hero of Dooga. It has been lost since before the arrival of The Spark. The shaking must have knocked the dirt away to reveal it once more. Surely this is a sign."

Sil continued to follow Arratup around the perimeter as the others gawked at the monument. Sil saw their old friend walk into a narrow split in the rear of the stone structure. Sil yelled for the others. "In the back is a crack! We can enter here! We'll be safe inside!" The others came up to see if Sil spoke the truth.

Gimeld took out his laser gun. "Worth a try I suppose." He aimed it at the hole to enlarge it but before he could fire Vitbito pushed his arm up in the air.

"I will not let you desecrate the tomb of the great Ravi."

"Touch me again and there's going to be a need for another tomb."

Vitbito and Gimeld stared each other down while some tribe members used walking sticks and tools they carried to chip away the dirt caked along the sides of the opening to allow them to enter. Vitbito followed his people in. Gimeld and his crew also entered. Last was Sil and only because of the sight of Arratup at the entranceway. The others barricaded the opening behind Sil with their supplies. M.A.T.O. turned on his illuminators so they could descend the stone stairs safely into the main part of the tomb.

"What makes this place any safer than our ship?" asked Arjan.

"It is said the tomb of Ravi was built to be indestructible," said Vitbito.

"Not very reassuring when it's been lost for so long and had a hole in it," quipped Arjan.

"Lost and destroyed are two different things," sneered Vitbito.

M.A.T.O. scanned the walls. "It does appear to be a very sound structure. Better than many modern buildings I would even venture to say. The dome shape with the triangular support beams allows for maximum strength. The adhesive used to seal the stones that make up the walls has Gabinip in it. The properties of that mineral should diffuse the electromagnetic pulses."

Sil piped up for the first time. "Does that mean you will survive?"

"Indeed. I believe we will all survive and the laser guns we carry should also remain functional. We just need to brace—"

Before M.A.T.O. could finish the ground felt like it slid out from under them. Everyone toppled over. The polar shift was commencing. The magnetic fields had built up enough energy that they had slowed the rotation of the ball of rock and gas to a full stop. Now the forces were locking up against each other in rapid jolts that sent shockwaves throughout the entire orb. Each shockwave was accompanied by an electromagnetic burst. Eventually, the poles migrated to a new point thus creating a new axis for rotation. Slowly but surely Dooga began to spin once more. The ground became still and no longer bent inward.

The group huddled closely in the tomb of Ravi unsure whether or not to venture out. M.A.T.O. said, "My sensors have returned to peak functionality and indicate no electromagnetic surges remain."

Sil who had clutched the body of Arratup the whole time now glanced over to the stairwell leading to the entrance of the tomb and saw Arratup once more standing there. "I agree it is now safe for us once more outside."

Vitbito stared at Sil and then nodded his head. Some members of the tribe opened up the hole once more and everyone filed out. Sil was the only one left in the tomb. Sil saw in a sliver of light from Iris the stone box that held the body of the legendary hero known as Ravi. Ravi was said to be the protector of Dooga when he lived. Sil took the body of Arratup and wrapped him in their cloak. They then placed it on top of the sarcophagus. Sil kissed the palm of their hand and placed it on the wrapped body. They then turned to exit the tomb with the others.

After Sil emerged stones were placed to cover up the hole out of an obligation of respect. Ravi had protected them but only Sil knew it was Arratup who led the way.

Iris radiated warmth which seemed to comfort all but Sil. Arjan and Gimeld embraced. Arjan pulled away and asked, "Do you think you can repair the ship?"

"Now that the electromagnetic storm has passed it should be a simple repair job," M.A.T.O. interjected. "Rewiring of the central interface board will be the most complex."

"Given the right tools and parts there's not a ship in the whole system I can't get to work," Gimeld said.

"I can show you the way to a port so you can get parts. It will probably take a cycle to get there and back. Who knows what state it will be in of course."

Gimeld eyed Sil up and down. The blackness under the hood unnerved Sil but they did not waver. "You are a strange one. Tell me how did you know where the tomb was?"

"You would think I was stranger if I told you."

"Try me."

"I have a sense of things beyond what most have."

"What's that supposed to mean? Don't confuse us with your superstitious nonsense," commanded Arjan.

Sil did not feel an explanation was owed. Gimeld seemed to agree for he held up his hand to silence the discussion. "Can you do other things besides find lost tombs, such as sense danger or escape routes?"

"Probably."

"Do you still wish to die?"

Gimeld's question caught Sil off guard. It seemed to Sil since Arratup saved Sil's life it would dishonor their friendship to end their life now. "I don't know."

Gimeld touched the void under his hood with his hand. "I see. You are welcome to join our crew if you wish." Arjan and M.A.T.O. seemed genuinely surprised by this development.

Sil looked off and caught the gaze of Vitbito. They hung there for several moments. Vitbito then gave a nod of his head and turned back to his tribe. Sil turned back to the pirates and surprisingly saw Arratup sitting next to Gimeld. Sil couldn't stifle the surprise.

"What is it?" Gimeld inquired.

"I will join your crew."

"Good. Take M.A.T.O. to the port. You two will gather the necessary parts and then meet Arjan and me back at the ship."

Sil nodded and started off with M.A.T.O. "So may I inquire as to the type of extra sense you have? I have many sensory components such as infrared and sonar."

"It's nothing like that."

"Then I am confused. What is it?"

Sil looked ahead of them and saw Arratup leading the way. "Just something an old friend taught me."

Chapter 5

HANOWEH ORBIT

Daleth drug Armonia through the streets of Hanoweh as the parade finished up. The crowds which milled around different illuminating light displays as darkness slowly crept across the sky paid them little heed. The frenzy of Grevolios had too much of a hold on them.

Armonia winced at the vice-like grip Daleth had on her wrist. "Lorelei told us to stay put. How's she supposed to find us now?"

"Not my problem."

"What are we going to do anyway? Won't people recognize ya? I don't have my quilt. Ya never put on a wig."

"I got my hood up. We just need to make it to the port."

"Oh, we stealing a ship?"

"Yes."

Armonia yanked her wrist and Daleth jerked. "Then ya can let go of me. I'm all for stealing a ship and getting outta here. I don't like this place. Everyone looks at me weird."

"If you try to run off I will hunt you down. I have very little reserves left but I have enough to make you regret running."

Armonia rolled her eyes. "Sheesh, I get it. So after we steal the ship we gonna talk about what happened?"

Daleth kept moving through the crowds. "No."

Armonia tried to keep up with his brisk pace. "Well, when are we gonna talk about it."

"Never."

"Don't ya think we need to talk about it?"

Daleth gritted his teeth. "What I need is a ship and to feed."

"I told ya to eat more."

"Not that kind of feed." Daleth spied a small circular ship in the port. It had a ring of lights on its outer edge. Inside the ring was a trapezoid-shaped structure, attached to the ring with cylindrical posts that extended out. "Ah, here's what I need, a luxury vessel from Fimeger."

"We're traveling in style now? I didn't know ya knew how to enjoy life."

"I don't care about the type of ship."

"Then why did you get excited it was a luxury one?"

The corners of Daleth's mouth curled up in a malicious grin. "The more you have to lose, the less dangerous you are."

Daleth approached the side of the craft where there was a small door. He slammed the flat of his hand against the door several times in rapid succession.

From inside came the distinct din of clatter and muffled obscenity. "What in all light do you think you're doing?" came a harsh voice on the other side of the door. When it opened an Upright with an athletic build and a round clean-shaven head stood there. He wore a simple vest with long sleeves which fit snuggly over his toned arms. His pants were equally snug atop but flared out below the knee. The grimace on his face quickly dropped upon setting sights on Daleth. The whites of his eyes grew and his body stiffened.

"You'll do nicely," Daleth said in a low monotone as he pushed the Upright inside the ship. Armonia followed with tentative curiosity.

The ship itself was small but cozy. It had warm yellow lighting fixtures and mahogany trim along the edges of the orange-colored walls. There was a red cushioned seat that looked like it could seat two comfortably across from a view screen. Overall, it was the opposite of the spacious but sterile environment on The Wayward Star. The stark contrast was not lost on Armonia. "Ooo I like this one better than the last one."

An Upright with blonde wavy hair that barely grazed her shoulders stepped out of the adjacent room into the entryway of the ship. "What is the meaning of this?" Her face was one of indignation and her pointy nose seemed to curl up further into the air. The formal black dress she wore not only accentuated all the curves of her body but also suggested the couple had important Grevolios plans.

"Close the door." Armonia dutifully obeyed Daleth's order and pressed the button marked 'door'.

"You're the fanatic who murdered that guardian on Ebjan." The vest-wearing Upright mumbled the words as though he had to force them out of his mouth. He backed away so he stood next to his companion.

"We are not giving you any help. We're calling the authorities." The Upright in the dress moved to the communication transmitter on the wall next to the view screen. Daleth unsheathed his trikilldo and threw it with a deadly aim at the transmitter. The point went straight into the control panel with authority, cracking it. She stopped in her tracks and scowled at Daleth. "You're paying for a new one."

The Upright with the vest stepped in front of her. "Please we just want to see the light show. Hanoweh is supposed to have the best in the system."

Daleth already felt this Upright's fear flowing into him but he wanted more. He grabbed his face. "I assure you this show will get your heart racing." Daleth pressed one of his claws into his flushed cheeks. He then drew his finger down slowly. He felt the Upright's jaw clench in his hand and saw a red line form on his face. Daleth threw him on the floor in front of his companion.

Daleth's next movements were quick. He yanked the trikilldo out of the screen and strode over to the couple. He grabbed the blonde locks of the standing one with ferocity. She let out the first start of a scream but stifled it. He could feel the fear starting to build in her, as well. It was always sweetest when they pushed back against it. Still firmly holding her hair he jerked her head back. Her gasp only urged him on. He drew the point of the trikilldo up to her neck just under her jawbone.

"You say you want me to pay for the communicator but I am sure you don't know how to truly earn something, even a useless trinket such as that. If you want to earn something you must suffer for it. You must understand the weight of it. You think me cruel for feeding off your pain but I know the weight of pain. Did you feel the cold pointed steel violate your most sensitive and sacred flesh?" Daleth paused but she just stiffened and didn't give an answer. "You ever bite your tongue? Imagine how much worse it is when it's cut out from underneath. Maybe when you have only half a tongue you would be a little more careful with your speech." Daleth pressed the point of the trikilldo into her skin and saw blood begin to run down her neck. He heard her whimpers and drank in her suffering and fear. "Somehow though I doubt it. You are nothing like me." He pulled away the blade and slammed the front of her body against the wall. "You disgust me," he whispered in her ear.

Daleth then grabbed the other Upright who was paralyzed by fear and yanked him to his feet. He roughly shoved him against the wall next to her. "If neither of you moves, maybe I will make this quick." Daleth saw beads of sweat forming on that round clean-shaven scalp. "The curves of the trikilldo are different." He put one edge of the trikilldo against the Upright's neck. "One curve is wedged and tapers to a fine edge which is ideal for cutting deep into soft tissue." Daleth moved the blade up to the gentleman's ear and stopped only when he heard his stifled moan. Small drops of blood dribbled down the blade. Daleth wiped his weapon on the form-fitting white sleeve his victim wore and then slid the trikilldo over to his companion's bare shoulder.

"The other curved edge is slanted on an angle which makes it ideal to slice away layer by layer." He pressed it into her skin lifting only the thinnest piece. Blood pooled underneath. "The choice I will leave up to you two."

"Wait. You're not gonna hurt them, are you? You're just trying to scare them, right? So they don't tell on us?" Armonia asked.

"If you're squeamish cover your eyes."

"They didn't do anything to us. We can't just hurt and kill them."

"Don't lecture me on foolish morals."

"Did ya already forget what just happened? What we saw and learned?"

"I said we're never going to talk about it."

"We're here to save not hurt." Armonia touched Daleth's hand which held the trikilldo. It began to quiver. "I don't want my life to be about hurt anymore."

Daleth closed his eyes. Her words and soft touch made him remember the feeling he felt when he hit the wall of light. But he quickly pushed it out of his mind and his eyes flew open once more. "These two are worth nothing."

The dignitary spoke up. "I am Keeper of the Seal of Fimeger and she is the Seneschal."

"Which means nothing to me," said Daleth his voice now not as controlled as it was.

"It should." Everyone turned and saw Lorelei at the galley entrance to the ship. She looked prim as she stood there erect wearing what appeared to be the one-piece white jumper of a healer. She held a small bag in one hand which she casually tossed aside.

"Lorelei! How did you find us?" Armonia stammered.

"I didn't. We just thought alike." Lorelei addressed Daleth. "Did you get enough?"

Daleth narrowed his eyes. "You know it's never enough."

"And you know what I mean. You don't want to add more officials to your body count. We already have enough problems. Let's just get to where we're going." Lorelei opened a nearby closet and pulled out a bundle of rope. "Work on breaking the pilot lock so you can fly the ship. Armonia and I will tie them up outside. Everyone's waiting for the Grevolios light show so they won't notice them until it's over."

"We promise we won't turn you in, as a favor from one Fimegerian to another."

Armonia cocked her head. "Is Fimeger your home, Daleth?"

Daleth grabbed both hostages by the nape and thrust them toward Lorelei and Armonia. "I have no home." He then walked off toward the bridge of the ship.

"Can you make sure we still have a good view of the light spectacular?"

"Shut up." Lorelei shoved the two out the door. "Come on Armonia."

⟨⟩

DALETH WAS EASILY ABLE to disable the pilot locks. The ships hadn't changed much at all from his Prep Center days. He caused enough mischief back then by changing the locks of unguarded ships to still do it by rote memory. He wiped the smears of make-up off his face with the underside of his cloak then sat in the pilot's chair with his arms crossed. There was no limit to how much energy he could store. He was gifted in that respect. He could have siphoned more off those two if Lorelei hadn't shown up. He still had enough to tangle with anything this system brought his way. It was only because of that and Lorelei's sound logic that caused him to relent. Still, he questioned his decision now. Those two tried to hide their fear and it is always more potent when that happens. The energy somehow flows more.

Daleth moved his hands to the control panel. He felt the slightest tingle above his right shoulder. *The A.I. did good work.* His sensitized skin picked up the sudden rush of air which indicated the entrance door had opened.

Daleth removed his hands from the control panel and recrossed his arms just as Lorelei and Armonia strode onto the bridge. Lorelei once more had her small bag with her.

"Were you really gonna do what ya said ya were gonna do?" Armonia asked Daleth.

Daleth gave a nonchalant shrug of his shoulders. "There was no reason not to."

"You can't hurt Uprights like that."

Daleth's cold eyes met Armonia's. "Life is full of hurt."

"Would you hurt me like that?"

Lorelei chimed in. "Daleth feeds off fear and pain. It gives him special powers. For some reason, he can't feed off you so there would be no reason for him to hurt you."

"Would he hurt you?"

Lorelei looked at Daleth who looked away. "No." She reached into the bag she held. "I have Grevelios' gifts for each of you." She pulled out an automated blood pressure band. She tossed it to Armonia who fumbled with it. "It's a pressure cuff. I took out the electronics and opened them up. I thought Kristal could use it."

Armonia's face lit up. She quickly secured it to her left bicep. Armonia then moved her left hand to her left thigh. Kristal slithered out from under her skirt, up her arm, and into the band. A high-pitched squeak rang out. Armonia smiled at Lorelei. "She likes it. Thanks! I know she'll keep me safe."

Lorelei approached Daleth. Daleth squeezed himself tighter and stiffened his back. "I thought you and I didn't pay any heed to the Light?"

Lorelei shrugged. "Some rituals are nice." She took a stethoscope out of the bag.

Daleth looked at it and then turned his hard gaze back to Lorelei. "I thought you were getting me a wig."

The smile faded from Lorelei. "I couldn't find any I liked."

Daleth took the stethoscope and tucked it into his belt. Lorelei's smile partially returned.

"What took you so long to return?"

"Yea. Daleth and I dreamed while ya were gone."

Lorelei's eyes flew open wide. With her mouth agape, her head swiveled between Daleth and Armonia.

"I had to keep her quiet somehow. It's over. Drop it."

"But what we saw? It was different than when you and I did it. There was this place and they said me and Daleth have lived other lives. Then everyone was gross. They called it Daleth Diocess."

"I said drop it!" growled Daleth as he rose from his seat. Lorelei put up her hand and stepped in between them.

"Ya don't get to tell me to drop the most special thing that happened to me. Ya don't know what's it like! Being in a world that's so confusing and mixed up, in constant pain."

"You know nothing of pain," roared Daleth.

"It's the only thing I know! Everything is strange to me. I mine as well be walking upside down and backward. Ya don't care though, nobody cares." Armonia put her face in her hands and ran off.

"I'll take care of her just get us out of here when they start the show. Think you can handle that?" Daleth didn't answer and just turned back to the console. "Daleth?" Lorelei said with more force.

"I'll do it." Lorelei walked off after Armonia.

The light show outside began. Every possible pattern of light with every possible color combination filled every square inch of the sky. Again and again more and more brilliant explosions of illumination made it seem like Iris had returned. Through this dizzying array of light, Daleth flew the ship with ease. His enhanced senses told him exactly where to go and before long Hanoweh was just another object in the endless blackness along with them.

GREMOILIO ORBIT

Gimeld and Arjan stood outside The Wayward Star just by the bay door. The Grevolios celebration was in full swing. Various lit designs appeared in the sky overhead punctuated by flashes of bright white light. All along the port throngs of Uprights shouted and cheered enthralled by the celebration unfolding.

Arjan crinkled up his face as a flash of light went off nearby. "Circapto's show is better. I so detest Grevolios."

"Everyone on this ship does. It's a tool The Way of The Light uses to manipulate Uprights into falling in line with them."

"The whole system is in complete disarray and yet these dimwads all around us only care about some stupid shiny things."

"It's the world we live in."

Arjan shook his head and rolled his eyes. "So aggravating. Speaking of aggravation where is our buyer for this dumb cargo they had us haul up here?"

"I don't know but if they don't show soon we're heading back to Circapto and fencing it."

"Why don't we just dump it here and move on? With the whole system distracted by shiny lights, I'm sure we can have some fun and make a decent profit out of this run-around."

Gimeld shook his head. "Our cargo is too important to just dump. I've been in this game too long not to know that." He touched the shadow under his hood. "They want us to dump it because they don't want us to know the buyer. We'll blackmail them to get it back and make double, maybe even triple, the halos."

Arjan let out a seductive sigh and placed his hand on Gimeld's chest. "When you talk extortion it gets me erect."

Gimeld caressed Arjan's cheek. "We'll get M.A.T.O. to monitor the ship till the show is over so I can make full use of that fact."

"These lights up in the sky are nothing compared to the lights I'm gonna make you see." Arjan took Gimeld's hand as they ran back onto the ship.

《 》

BAABCREST ORBIT

Tania and Corry walked together along the garden path in the courtyard of the botanical center of the School of Knowledge. The garden was maintained and kept with the express intention of observing the plant life on the moon of Baabcrest. Still, it was objectively beautiful. Drones drew brilliant designs with luminescent smoke in the sky above them to celebrate Grevolios. It gave the vibrant shades of green, yellow, and cyan in the plant life a surreal look. The usual sharp edges of the colors seemed to blur and bleed into each other. The open flowers with their tinges of violet and orange looked like tiny lanterns in the light given off from the night sky above. The whole thing seemed to Corry like the grand oil paintings from ancient times she saw on Gremoilio while she searched for Daleth. She wished Daleth was less present on her mind so she could enjoy the garden stroll she was taking with Tania but her interaction with him still weighed on her.

It had been a significant amount of time since she had sent Daleth after the experiment. They knew he had an altercation on Ebjan with some guardians. The reports of him being accompanied by another Upright suggested he had found the experiment. But he still had not contacted Corry and it unsettled her as well as the rest of her Cell. Hence, why Ramek took an inquiry so he could search for the elusive pair.

The Order of Consciousness was under heavy pressure all over the system. It was inevitable, based on their analysis, that the Twin Flames would soon take over. Once that happened they would surely root out Corry's organization. They needed the experiment to have any hope of staving off disaster and even then their chances may be slim. Still, it was her memories of her encounter with Daleth that seemed to nag at her more.

"Tania, may I ask you a question?"

"That's an odd thing to ask on the School of Knowledge." She said this with such good-natured humor that it encouraged Corry to go on.

"I still feel a residue from my interaction with Daleth."

Tania nodded her head thoughtfully. "That is to be expected. He has many mental misgivings which cause his presence to be quite disturbing."

"Yes. I can sense he is capable of much malicious action. I must admit I questioned the validity of him having supposedly killed the entirety of the Followers of Vuhox. After our meeting, I no longer do."

Tania clasped her hands behind her back. "I know you're rather new so you weren't around but I saw the gruesome images myself. He butchered all of them. The various administrations passed it off as a heroic feat. Of course, they were influenced by the Way which saw the Followers as their greatest threat."

"Were they truly that dangerous?"

Tania turned to Corry with a grave expression. It was not an expression in line with her usual tranquil nature. "You felt the menace of Daleth for yourself. They were a group that felt they had nothing above them and could do no wrong. A group such as that, with no accountability, was always going to self-destruct. The entire system knew it. The mind perceives what one sows even if it loathes to admit it."

Corry paused at Tania's last statement. It was one of the mantras of the Order which drew her into the organization. She had always felt she perceived things but too easily let them pass by without examination. *What is the point of life if it is so casually considered?* She remembered the words Ramek spoke when he admitted to being part of the Order, they had sealed her decision to risk everything and become a member of the Order of Consciousness herself. Now she must not waver from the same mantra.

"Tania, although I certainly felt Daleth's heaviness, I have meditated on it further."

Tania interrupted Corry's train of thought, "There is no need. One's challenges are for that individual alone." She then added as almost an afterthought, "We have no hope or desire to recruit Daleth to our ranks."

"It is not his reaction or behaviors which I examine but my own. I thought it was simply as you said his hindrance of the mind that clung to me. His reputation being what it is, that conclusion made logical sense. However, when I delved further it felt as though our meeting was somehow prearranged."

"Well, it was. We intended for you to find him so he could recapture the experiment."

"Beyond our plans I mean," said Corry with some trepidation.

"You believe Daleth has already been compromised by another group?"

Corry shook her head. "I am certain he operates of his own accord. What I felt was something beyond the plans of Uprights. As if Daleth and I knew each other before and had agreed to have the conversation we had."

Tania relaxed her countenance. "A simple short circuit of mind. Perhaps a coping mechanism you have yet to fully exorcise which you used to instill courage in yourself for your mission. Control your thoughts as you have been taught."

Corry shrugged. "I have tried. When I confront it I feel it is a grand thing I was supposed to accomplish though I can't say what exactly I did accomplish."

"You accomplished much if Daleth brings us the experiment. Most probably our cause can continue and may even save the System."

"That's just it. I feel like it's already been saved. That a chain of events is already in process."

Tania stopped walking and put a hand gently on Corry's shoulder. "Chain of events are for inanimate objects, with the mind there are infinite possibilities, or have you forgotten your learnings so easily?"

"I have not. Just seeing them to their ends."

Tania sighed and turned to continue her stroll. "You fall into the trap of seeing more than there is. We are in uncertain times. Mind your mind."

Corry paused to look down at the ground for a moment and ponder. Corry realized only time would tell who was right. *It would make for a fascinating experiment.* She then jogged to catch up to Tania so they may continue their stroll together.

⟨ ⟩

OROGUNU ORBIT

Zean sat in the backseat of the hovercraft. Its grey interior was in stark contrast to her jubilant mood. She wiped her sweaty palms discreetly on the soft seats. Her head faced out the partially opened window as the driver zipped over the fields of crops. The pungent odor of jumquia along with the earthy aroma of plump arp beans was much preferred over the acrid smell which clung to the inside of the small craft, most likely the remnant of

Grevolios debauchery. *Shame how some use such a celebration of Light as an excuse to dabble in darkness.*

Zean's heart skipped a beat when she saw the glass point of the Temple breach the horizon. Dreaming always made Zean's heart flutter but to do it on Grevolios added an extra layer of intensity. She had not expected to see her reflection for quite some time. So when she got a communication from Jamila that her superiors were giving guardians leave for Grevolios Zean chartered the fastest ship to Orogunu. While in route she managed to get a hold of their Twin Flame Lantern who agreed to oversee a dreaming session.

Zean stepped out of the vehicle after she paid the driver. She was compelled to take pause and admire the Temple even though she had seen the awe-inspiring pyramids many times. Like all Temples of Light, columns of colors ran down the sides of the pyramid. A luminous red and warm orange were on one side. Vibrant yellow and a rich green adorned the second side. Then shimmering indigo and deep purple rounded out the pyramid. The top third of the pyramid was made of glass stained in a myriad of colors.

Zean like all non-Twin Flames couldn't enter the main part of the Temple. She never could help peering in from the vestibule though.

As the hovercraft came to a stop at the main entrance of the Temple, Zean programmed a standard Grevolios tip into the meter and then got out. She smoothed her suit with her hands nervously before she opened the exterior doors of the Temple. She took a deep breath before entering. Four Twin Flames stood as exalted sentries in the main foyer. Above the interior doors in flowery font read the words, All is Light, Light is All.

"I just wanted to peer in and watch till my reflection arrives," Zean stated in answer to the stares of the Twin Flames. They smiled and parted for her. She took a step forward with a slight tremble and put a hand over her brow as she bent toward the glass.

Inside was a rounded atrium despite the angular exterior. The beams of Iris which shone through the glass top of the structure bathed the entire room in light of every possible color imaginable and even some beyond imagination. The different shades swirled and blended into one another like a magnificent living piece of art.

Gathered around the atrium in a loose circle were dozens of Twin Flames dressed in their shimmering white robes which now took on different tones of color thanks to the light pouring in from above. Their heads were bowed and their eyes softly closed. They held their hands clasped together and pulled tightly to their midsection. They hummed together. This was a popular practice of Twin Flames. It was believed if they could harmonize themselves they may be able to influence harmony within the system.

"Illuminated Grevolios, my reflection!" Jamila's greeting pulled Zean out of her trance. Jamila stood there decked out in a floral print dress with pink frills along the short sleeves. Zean had never thought she looked more beautiful. She tore herself away from the glass and sprinted into Jamila's open arms. They pressed each other's flesh and savored the feel of skin touching skin. The warmth of their bodies seemed to coalesce and become a greater fire that filled the entire foyer.

"Look deeper. Are you ready?" Zean opened up her eyes and saw Shilo standing at the exterior doors. "I saw Jamila run up the steps," he explained. "Are you two ready or should I give you a few more moments?"

Jamila and Zean chuckled. It had become an additional ritual amongst them for Shilo to always ask this question. Jamila and Zean saw so little of each other they were often caught up in just being together rather than learning how to live in The Way of The Light.

"No, we are ready." Jamila took Zean's hand and squeezed it. Together they followed Shilo as he led them to another entrance at the base of the pyramid.

They walked a long corridor lined with different colored doors. Behind each was most likely a pair of reflections with one or more Twin Flames. It was in these rooms that reflections examined themselves under the supervision of a Twin Flame Lantern who was assigned to guide them. Occasionally other Twin Flames helped or were being trained to become Lanterns themselves. Eventually, they stopped at a bright crimson door. Shilo opened it and the trio walked inside.

The white walls of the room along with the warm colors of the sparse furniture gave a minimalist but still inviting appeal to the space. Zean and Jamila sat down on the soft orange couch. The desk across from the couch was small and gilded with gold. Shilo perched himself behind the desk on an ornate wooden chair with a tall back that was stained a deep reddish brown. The walls were bare aside from a gold-framed painting that hung behind

Shilo. It had swirls and blotches of pink, red and purple. Zean could tell it was obviously from the early classical period of Gremoilio when people partook in such activities to grope for an understanding of existence. This was of course before The Spark came to enlighten the system.

Shilo took a quilled pen from the desk's holster and opened the huge tome in front of him with the white cover and gold etched lettering which spelled out the names of Jamila and Zean. He flipped through the gold-leafed pages for a moment till he exclaimed, "Ah here we go. So how have you two been doing on your path since last we met?"

Jamila and Zean exchanged a glance, one common among reflections. A glance that in an instant said what it would take a hundred times longer to say in words. Zean could tell Jamila wanted her to tell it for both of them, that she knew Zean needed to speak it out loud more than Jamila did. "It has been hard, especially on me but for both of us. With everything going on right now we hardly have time to talk and when we do connect our other worries and thoughts seem to intrude."

Shilo nodded his head as he wrote some notes down. He then looked up from the book to the two reflections before him. "This is both the gift and the curse of the reflection. Uprights believe having a reflection brings more Light and it does but with the addition of that Light you see more shadows. You both reflect the darkness in each of you."

"But I've removed so much darkness. How much more is there?" Zean almost wailed. Jamila rubbed the palm of her hand in circles between Zean's shoulder blades to offer support.

Shilo closed his eyes and took a deliberate and slow breath. "The Way of The Light is not an easy one."

"I know that," Zean blurted out. "I just don't know what else I can do."

"We thought a dreaming session would allow us to strengthen our bonds and offer insights into what we are lacking," Jamila calmly added.

Shilo rubbed his eyes for a moment. "Dreaming can do those things but it is an activity that invites in a multitude of energies. You must be cautious with it. You could end up coming out worse than when you went in."

"Do you think we should hold off on dreaming in this session?" Jamila inquired keeping a stiff upper lip.

Shilo let out a heavy sigh. "Professionally yes but my instinct says no. One must learn to follow one's instinct. I think both of you would benefit from that lesson. So tell me what does your instinct tell you?"

"My instinct tells me that Zean and I will be alright. That we are just going through a rough patch but if we stay focused on what's important, on the Light that is, then we will make it."

Zean took Jamila's hand in hers. "That was beautiful."

"And what does your instinct tell you?" Shilo asked.

Zean shook her head slowly from side to side. "I don't know what my instincts tell me. They are on mute right now."

Shilo got up from his desk and crouched in front of Zean putting a comforting hand on her knee. He placed his other hand on her upper arm. "The same neurotransmitters in your brain are in your intestines. The brain solves puzzles and it often creates puzzles to solve when it doesn't have enough. The gut tells us what the finished puzzle will be. Don't worry about solving the puzzle. Just listen to what your gut tells you it will be after it is solved."

Zean looked between Shilo and Jamila. She wiped away the liquid pooling in her eyes. "It says we'll be happy."

Shilo nodded. "The Light will illuminate a way for you both. You just have to trust that it will be there."

Zean and Jamila stood facing each other in the room Shilo lead them to for dreaming. It was a small room with barely enough space for the two of them to stand there next to the soft mattress. Jamila and Zean undressed and hung their garments on the hooks that lined one wall. They stared at each other's naked bodies taking it in and summoning the courage to partake in a dream. They both enjoyed their dreaming sessions immensely but there was still so much trepidation too. Shilo went over all preparation beforehand as always and of course, there would be a detailed review afterward but still, they were cautious. Jamila made the first move. She put her hand on Zean's cheek and whispered, "You ready?" Zean nodded and then they pressed their bodies together. They tasted each other's flesh as they ran their tongues over each other. They felt the warmth of blood rising to the surface of the skin under their fingertips. Their nerves were on fire as passion began to overtake their thoughts. They were dreaming.

⟪ ⟫

IRIS ORBIT

"The Light always prevails over darkness."

Intense light flooded the Room of Enlightenment at The Spark's proclamation. The gathered Twin Flames rose and shouted in unison, "Look Deeper!" With that, the closing speech was over and another Grevolios had come and gone. The address which had been broadcast to the entire system was especially noteworthy this Grevolios. For the system had not been on edge like this since The Spark's arrival.

The Spark walked away from the gold podium and left the riser to retire to more private chambers. As The Spark entered the inner sanctum of the Iris station Unak came running up somewhat out of breath. "Spark!" Unak cried out. "I must speak with you."

The glowing figure of The Spark turned to Unak. The harmonious voice spoke through the light. "What troubles you Twin Flame? We have presided over another successful Grevolios."

"And if we're to see another you need to act immediately."

"Few things require such haste in this world when all is set right."

Unak waved his arm in an exaggerated gesture. "Things are definitely not set right!"

The Spark motioned him into the inner sanctum. Inside was a raised altar with four marble columns that looked like giant towers of petrified cream. Each was adorned with a lit golden oil lamp atop. "I seek to harmonize my Light after the ceremonies but what requires my attention first?"

"Senior Twin Flames assigned me to go undercover on Ebjan within the House of Yowgn. I have been living that role for more than two gremrevs to monitor their activities."

The Spark seemed to nod. "Impressive deception."

Unak unsure whether the words were meant as a compliment or not decided to continue nonetheless. "But an even greater threat has crossed my path." Unak waited for The Spark to react but there was no discernible change in the radiance of the light or shape. Instead, The Spark seemed to become even more serene if anything. "I do not know how but an Upright, who I believe is the one who helped Daleth murder that guardian, is capable of leaving this system while dreaming." Again The Spark seemed to offer no reaction. "I don't know how it's possible but I dreamed with her and sensed it."

Finally, The Spark spoke. "All can leave the system while dreaming that is why dreaming is done with the utmost care and supervision. For there are dangerous energies beyond the boundaries."

"I know this, your eminence, but there is something different with her. Her dreams are not like any I have encountered. She can see deeper into things than should be possible, maybe even change consciousness itself."

The Spark stood there seemingly motionless. "What is it you fear?"

"In the hands of the House of Yowgn, she could be used as a lure to their ways. To bolster their abilities so they could pose a threat to everything we have built. They will make people doubt the Way."

"Why would they do such a thing simply because of a dream?"

Unak ran his hand through the curls which adorned the top of his head. "It's hard for me to put into words. I'm afraid she will make them see alternatives that aren't there. It will confuse the masses."

"There is only one alternative to the Light. Your ancestors knew it well. It was a way of death and darkness. Do you believe they will choose to go back to it?"

Unak threw his head back in exasperation. "That's why I came right to you. You know how easily Uprights can be seduced away from the Light. This is why we must do things such as go undercover to keep them from straying off the path."

"They stray but most do not stray far."

"I believe based on what I was told she was created by the Order of Consciousness. That's enough of a reason we need to bring her here for scrutiny."

"But I do not see her here."

"I pursued them in the fastest ship I could find. By the sheer grace of my Light, I was able to locate them again on Hanoweh. She is with a Twin Flame who defected to the House of Yowgn named Lorelei. I was able to follow her energy signature for some time but have since lost it. I believe Lorelei is purposefully trying to keep this mysterious Upright for her own ends."

"So this Lorelei defeated you then? You have lost the trail and now come here for guidance."

Unak bowed his head. "Yes."

The Spark stood there. The silence between the two grew thick and uncomfortable. Finally, The Spark spoke, "Do you know all you speak of beyond doubt?"

"I'm pretty sure."

"It is always best to stick to what you know absolutely. You are dismissed."

"Shouldn't we make plans?"

"I will address with my Light. Trust in it. Thank you though for bringing it to my attention. That is all for now."

Unak bowed to The Spark. "Yes, your brightness shines on me." With that Unak left the inner sanctum.

After a few steps, he paused and clenched his fists. *The Spark doesn't realize the danger.* It was not altogether surprising. Unak himself would not have appreciated the gravity of it had he not experienced dreaming with Armonia himself. *She could be the fulcrum that shifts the entire system, as impossible as it seems. It has to be prevented at all costs.*

The Spark had many powers but the omniscient sight of everything that occurred in the system was not listed as one of them to Unak's knowledge. He decided he would have to bring her to The Spark himself so the threat she posed could be fully appreciated.

⟨ ⟩

INTER-ORBIT SPACE

Armonia buried her head in the red quilt and sobbed quietly. The faux wood paneling and plush bedding offered her little comfort though. Her body ached and there was the occasional shooting pain from her head down her back. She had washed out the make-up Lorelei had put on her back on Hanoweh to try and make herself feel better but it didn't work. She was sick of it, of it all.

Lorelei entered the room carrying a mug the same color as the quilt. Wisps of steam wafted above it. Lorelei reached out and touched Armonia's shoulder. Her head lifted from the silky fibers of the quilt in response.

"Here, sip on this. It will calm you." Lorelei offered the mug.

Armonia tossed the unwieldy strands of her hair back and took the mug. She put it under her nose. "What is it?"

Lorelei arched her thin almost transparent eyebrows. "No one's ever offered you omnoberry and jotoon root tea to comfort you?"

Armonia shrugged. "No memories, least not till I met ya and Daleth."

"Right. Well drink it, it will make you feel better. Just be careful because it's hot."

"Nothing makes me feel better, except dreaming."

"What do you see when you dream?"

"Nothing. Well, aside from pretty colors. But it was different the third time when Daleth and I did it. We were someplace I'd never been."

Lorelei's eyelids flared. "We?"

"Yeah. Me and Daleth." Armonia blew on the mug. "I had wings and his scars were all gone."

"He was with you or you just saw him?"

"He was with me. You could ask him if he wasn't so grouchy. We saw this place made entirely of light." Armonia slurped the liquid in the mug. "Say this is good."

"Light you say?" Lorelei's body was tense.

Armonia nodded her head vigorously. "Uh-huh. And everyone wore robes."

"You mean Twin Flames? So you were on Iris?"

"What's that? Oh, and they told us we have lived many other lives and are also supposed to free Uprights."

"Free them from what?"

Armonia smacked her lips after she took a big gulp of her drink. "Do we got more of this stuff?"

Lorelei repeated her question. "What were you and Daleth supposed to free them from?"

"It doesn't matter," came Daleth's gruff voice. He stood at the doorway to the room. "It was just a delusion caused by a foolish act."

"How can ya say that!" cried Armonia. "Ya were there! Ya saw the place. It was beautiful! They said we were important and we had a mission to finish." Armonia suddenly began to seethe and put down her mug. She started thudding her forehead with her fist.

"Your head?" Lorelei asked. Armonia nodded and began to massage her temples. "Dreaming always means something. Many of the ancient Pupils refer to the significance of dreaming. It's why the Way couldn't fully eradicate it, just try to control it."

"This was not dreaming, it was her deceptions," Daleth coldly stated.

"I don't do deceptions. Why are ya being so difficult with this?"

"She has a point," said Lorelei.

Daleth glared. "Because this isn't important. What we need to focus on is bringing her to Baabcrest so you can pay me, now that we have a ship."

Armonia's head shot up. "Why ya bringing me to Baabcrest?"

"I think we should all dream together first," Lorelei stated.

"I'm not dreaming with him again. I don't care how beautiful the place is or how nice it feels to fly."

Daleth crossed his arms. "One of the few things we have agreed on since we met."

"Fine. But we should probably wait a bit before going to Baabcrest. The two that had this ship will report us, despite their empty promises. Hanoweh and Fimeger are strict Orbits with persistent guardians. We should lay low for a time to throw them off."

"That's why you should have let me kill them."

"Why are we going to Baabcrest?" repeated Armonia more forcefully this time.

Lorelei and Daleth exchanged a glance. "It is where there used to be a lot of dreaming ceremonies held by the ancient inhabitants." Lorelei took a pause. "I think we may find something to help you there."

"If it involves dreaming I'm for it." Armonia stuck her forked tongue out at Daleth. "Except with him." Kristal popped her head out of the arm cuff and hissed at Daleth.

"Would you be willing to dream with me? To show me the place you and Daleth went to."

"Sure," said Armonia enthusiastically. "But I'm not sure how we got there."

"While you two goof off I'll take care of what needs to be done."

Lorelei smirked. "It's why I hired you." Daleth shot her a glare before leaving the room.

⟨ ⟩

CIRCAPTO ORBIT

M.A.T.O.'s ocular lenses rotated as he bent over the metal cube. It seemed simple enough, your standard inter-Orbit cargo container. Despite the container's seemingly regularity, the decryption algorithms of M.A.T.O.'s programming were still perplexing.

The doors behind M.A.T.O. slid open and Sil walked into the storage bay. "We entered the Orbit of Circapto. Gimeld wants to know if you have figured out how to open the package."

"I am sorry, despite my sophisticated programming, I have not. I have, however, determined that there's a built-in timed opening mechanism. I managed to somehow delay it when I was attempting to search for a dossier."

Sil's lips pursed. "Guess they didn't trust us with this thing. I suppose that was smart of them. So when's it supposed to open?" M.A.T.O. did not respond but continued to peer at the crate. He then straightened up and took a step back to join Sil. "I said when will it open up?"

"Now."

A hiss screamed out of the box as its four outer walls fell to the floor. The top of the crate flew into the air and Sil instinctively ducked. Neither could comprehend what was in front of them. An organism of some sort but one unlike any Sil or M.A.T.O. had ever seen. The imposing figure was twice the size of an Upright with velvety black skin that eerily reflected the light in the room. Curved barbs sprung from the front part of the four clawed limbs. The monstrous being reared up and stood on its back two legs which appeared thick with sinewy muscles. The face had two yellow bulbous compound eyes, the only color on the creature. The skull was flat and broad, and horns of various sizes lined the entire head, some straight, others curved. No snout or nose was visible just a large jaw lined with serrated black teeth which appeared sharpened into fine points. The strange being seemed to eye Sil and M.A.T.O. silently. Smooth black covers slid up over the eyes for a moment then dropped again.

Sil's voice was caught in their throat. "I do not find any catalog of this Non-upright in my database but I deduce that the Non-upright wishes to consume us."

The beast lunged without warning at Sil. M.A.T.O. pulled Sil, who was frozen in place, out of the way not a fraction too soon. M.A.T.O. raised his arms and fired his built-in laser cannons. The energy blasts hit the creature's skin, turned it a muted pink color for a moment, and then quickly faded. The creature made another lunge at them. This time both sprung out of the way but the barb caught Sil's arm making a deep gash as it tore the skin. Sil clutched the wound and stifled a cry of pain using the conditioning they had received on Dooga.

"It appears invulnerable to energy projection weapons," M.A.T.O. stated in his usual monotone voice.

"Run!" Sil screamed as the monster made a third lunge at them. They both ran to the cargo bay doors and sealed the creature on the other side. "Blow the airlock!"

"What if the other cargo inside is not secure?"

"I'll explain it to Gimeld, just do it!"

"Keep in mind you informed me we are in Circapto's Orbit so if we breeched the atmosphere there will not be as significant of a vacuum present."

"It's Circapto's atmosphere. It will do enough!"

M.A.T.O. complied by opening the electronic panel next to them. He inserted an antenna that emerged from one of his fingers. With it, he accessed the control for the airlock and opened the cargo bay doors to the outside elements. "It is done."

As Sil tried to catch their breath, Arjan entered. "What are you two dimwads doing? We got a sensor alert that said an airlock was open in the cargo bay."

"It would appear the mystery package was a new life form," answered M.A.T.O.

"What a wire come loose on you?"

"No, he's right," said Sil. "A terrible Non-upright that could stand like an Upright attacked us. We had to send it out the airlock."

Arjan put his hands on his hips. "Really? The two of you couldn't handle a Non-upright." Before either could respond they were all startled by a thunderous bang heard on the other side of the cargo bay door. "What in all of Iris' sight was that?"

The sound came again even louder and this time pointed claws protruded through the doors. "It would seem the organism is still with us," declared M.A.T.O.

Arjan's eyes widened and his usual smirk left his face. "You blew an airlock in Circapto's upper atmosphere. No one can survive that."

Sil started to back away from the doors. "This is what I was trying to tell you."

Another tremendous noise erupted and a piece of the door tore away. The creature's mouth could be seen with its endless rows of teeth. A high-pitched roar slammed into Arjan and Sil's eardrums. They clasped their hands over their ears.

"Based on my analysis of the situation I advise we flee and regroup." All three sprinted away. The sound of scraping metal chased them.

⟨ ⟩

ALTHOUGH GIMELD WAS concentrating on piloting the ship through the tricky atmospheric routes of Circapto he still registered the hiss of the doors to the bridge sliding open and then closing again. He expected his first mate to return to his side but was surprised to hear heavy breathing and panting coming from behind him. He turned and laid eyes on an unusual scene, his crew huddled together in fright.

"What is wrong with all of you? We've traversed Circapto's atmosphere countless times. It just sounds worse than it is. Besides we're almost to the surface."

"Good! Cause we need to abandon ship," Sil cried.

Unseen to everyone but Arjan Gimeld narrowed his eyes. "Never. I would die first."

M.A.T.O. rotated his lenses. "Yes. Those would most likely be our two options."

"What are you prattling on about, A.I.?"

Arjan rushed over to Gimeld and grabbed his shoulders. "There is something awful on board our ship."

"It was the package. It contained some deadly new form of life and now it is trying to kill us." Arjan nodded in agreement to Sil's words.

Gimeld sighed and got up from his seat. He removed a long chrome cylinder with three pin-like needles at one end from under the steering console.

"Lasers don't do anything," Sil said.

"Yes, it seems to have an outer membrane that disperses energy to nil effect."

Gimeld placed the laser rifle cannon back under the console and instead removed an ax with a long point opposite the main blade. "There's more than one way to kill someone. M.A.T.O. you think you can keep us from crashing?"

"Yes, it should be a fairly straightforward task now that we are below the electromagnetic field." M.A.T.O. placed a hand on the control panel.

"Then do it." Gimeld strode to the doors of the bridge but halted when they rattled. He steadied himself and raised the axe above his head, his hands twisted ever so slightly around the reinforced steel handle. "Arjan, open the doors."

Arjan complied with a tremble. As soon as the doors parted the sleek black mass sprang through them to pounce on Gimeld. The others stood rooted to the spot and unable to move. Gimeld swung his axe but the creature sliced through the handle with the serrated claws on its right forearm. The blade somersaulted through the air till it embedded itself into the wall less than a meter from where Sil stood. The beast was now on top of Gimeld who writhed and strained to stay away from its snapping jaws.

Arjan leaped on top of the monster and unsheathed a long dagger from his belt and plunged it towards the head of the creature but he only felt a jolt run up his arms as the smooth skin of the organism refused to give in to the blade. The beast raised a claw and slashed the stunned Arjan across the chest. He let out a gasp and tumbled to the floor. Gimeld let out a roar of hatred for the creature and used the distraction to unsheathe a small sword which he drove upward with all his might. The creature squealed but the wound was superficial at best. The creature slammed a clawed hand down on Gimeld who strained to keep from being crushed.

"M.A.T.O., turn the ship upside down," Sill yelled.

"Those were not the captain's orders."

"Just do it," Gimeld choked out.

M.A.T.O.'s processor gave the electro impulse so the ship became inverted. This tossed everyone about inside. The creature crashed into the control panel which in turn destroyed the navigation system. The ship weaved around erratically taking out several control satellites which hovered in the air to monitor the comings and goings of crafts such as The Wayward Star. The Wayward Star itself eventually came to a rather violent stop when it smashed into a smaller building near one of the more industrial sectors.

Gimeld felt the weight of brick and aluminum on his back. The inside of his right boot felt wet and sticky. He assumed he was bleeding from somewhere but his whole body ached so he couldn't tell from where. He pressed his palms into the rubble beneath him and pushed himself up. He hadn't been hit this hard in a long time but he still knew how to get back up. His ship was lost, that was obvious, but he knew that when he had M.A.T.O. turn it. Right now his mind was on only one thing.

"Arjan!" There was no answer to his cry. He scanned the area and realized he was outside the ship on the ground of Circapto. He saw that his ship had a gash along its right side. "Arjan!" Uprights were starting to mill around the outskirts of the crash site.

Gimeld was about to call out a third time when he heard Sil cry, "I got him over here! Help us out!" It came from inside the ship. Gimeld scrambled over pieces of debris and climbed up the remains of his craft. He knelt over the precipice of the gash and peered into what was left of The Wayward Star.

Sil stood there with traces of blood zig-zagged on their face. Propped up by Sil was an unconscious Arjan. His leather chest covering was torn and shiny with wetness. "He's still alive but he's lost a lot of blood."

Gimeld let his breath out upon hearing Sil's words. He cupped a hand to his mouth. "Hold on I'll find something to toss down to hoist him up with."

"No need." M.A.T.O. crawled out of the twisted metal inside the ship carrying a small server. "I am equipped with a retractable winch. Just find something to attach it to." A compartment in M.A.T.O.'s chest opened and there was a pop as a winch fired up in the air. Gimeld caught it and searched for a spot to attach it to. Everything in the area was damaged. He didn't have the luxury of being choosy though. He wrapped the steel coil around a bent-up fin of the ship. It was a lifetime ago that he believed in anything above himself. Now he wished he still did and that it knew only mercy.

"I got it!"

At Gimeld's call, M.A.T.O. handed the server over to Sil. "Please hold onto this and me. I will take Arjan." Sil nodded. In another moment they were in the air hurtling towards Gimeld. When they got to the top of the ship M.A.T.O. handed Arjan to Gimeld. "My sensors indicate he's not in the best shape but I will cauterize the wound which should prevent any further blood loss. I can do the same for both of you."

A screech echoed from the remnants of The Wayward Star and filled the crew's ears. The group turned toward its source and their feet became fixed on the spot. Below them was the creature clawing up the interior walls of the ship toward them. Gimeld yanked his laser blaster from its holster on his belt and began to fire wildly. "Just die already you scum!" The blasts which hit the organism seemed to have no effect aside from a momentary discoloration of the skin.

"I suggest we instead try to evade the Non-upright."

"M.A.T.O.'s right. We gotta move. Come on. I'll help you with Arjan." Sil handed the server back to M.A.T.O. Sil and Gimeld each draped an arm of their fallen comrade over their shoulders and made a hasty retreat from the ship. M.A.T.O. followed.

The crowd which had grown thick and close let out a unified gasp after seeing the creature emerge from the wreckage. Gimeld unsheathed his knife from his belt and began to slash at the distracted onlookers. "Turn hard right", he commanded. As he had hoped the creature drew toward the scent of blood and descended on the crowd leaving the pirate crew to escape. The sounds of flesh tearing, bones cracking, and screams of horror were heard behind them as they disappeared into the immense city of Circapto.

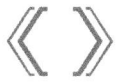

INTER-ORBIT SPACE

Daleth sat at the control panel. The familiar tingle of the yoke ran over his hands and up his arms. He kept away from the normal courses that most inter-Orbit ships utilized. He was several leagues below the system itself, far below the ability of any guardians. Being this much out of visual contact with Iris was only done by the most skilled pilots. This was due to the ease with which one could become disoriented without any frame of reference aside from the far-off points of light. Daleth felt no such confusion, he did this often enough that he could almost navigate purely on instinct this far below the system.

The more difficult challenge he faced was ignoring Lorelei and Armonia. He had only just now finally managed to tune out the dreaming noises from the adjacent room, either that or Lorelei and Armonia had finally called it quits. Daleth doubted it though. They were both stubborn fools who would waste the entire trip on folly.

Lorelei shuffled onto the bridge and plopped down in the seat next to Daleth. Neither acknowledged the other. They just sat and stared at the view screen.

Daleth's monotone bass broke the silence. "We are nearing Baabcrest."

"You have to dream with us."

"I don't have to do anything."

"Then please dream with us. You must be the key to unlocking her potential. I'm not sure why but maybe between whatever they did to her and your training with the Vuhox, the dreaming is different."

"I have no concerns with that. Find one of your housemates to help you when we reach Baabcrest. I have no idea why you're so obsessed with all this."

"You don't know why I want to get back at the Light? It cut me, both of us, out of life. You should understand that after all those conversations we had laying next to each other in the dark."

"It's a little hard to trust those conversations when stuff was being withheld."

The bitterness in Daleth's voice was pungent. It stung. She had trampled many in her driven crusade. She never wanted Daleth to be one of them. Lorelei leaned back and continued to gaze at the view screen, her eyes looked like porcelain as they watched the emptiness pass them by. "I calmed her down. She was pretty upset by watching you torture those diplomats."

"You stopped me from torturing them, as I recall."

"She's more innocent than you and I, even though she's been hurt just as badly. Maybe it would be easier for all three of us to just hide out here for a while you know, on this ship I mean."

Daleth's attention did not waiver from the screen in front of him. "You contracted my services and I always deliver. So just worry about getting me paid. I can find plenty of places to hide." Daleth paused for a moment then added, "Besides we are nearly out of food on here."

Lorelei pivoted her head toward Daleth and furrowed her brow. "What? These Fimegerians didn't have IO's stocked on here?"

Daleth shrugged. "Not much. Guess they intended to dine locally."

"What about the IO's from those pirates?"

"Armonia ate it all."

"All of it?" Lorelei's eyes fluttered and then bulged.

"I suppose dreaming works up quite an appetite."

Lorelei crossed her arms and sat back in the chair. "Not like you would know. For someone so adamant against dreaming how did you even end up doing it with Armonia in the first place."

"I did it to shut her up. She was having one of her weird states and about to give away our position."

Lorelei's eyes became slits as she glared at Daleth. "Dreaming can't be forced. Even you know that." A cold silence was Daleth's only answer. Lorelei sighed and gazed at the vacant view monitor. "You know, in this emptiness, no one will know and you will satisfy me that it was nothing significant."

"I don't need to satisfy you in any regard."

"As a favor to me then?"

"Our relation is not of that nature."

Lorelei's face dropped. There was an icy pause between them. "Just because you were part of an assignment does not mean it was the sole reason for our relation."

"Why is she so important to you?"

Lorelei's eyes blinked slowly and softly. She stared at the floor. "She's something to hold onto. I thought you would understand." She debated in her mind whether to add anything else. "It's why I volunteered for the assignment to recruit you."

There was another long pause between them.

Daleth shifted uncomfortably in his seat and seemed to tilt his gaze even further away from Lorelei. "If you want to hold onto Armonia then you should forget this dreaming nonsense and go to Baabcrest to find a way to prevent her from dying."

A shrill voice was heard from behind them. "I'm dying?" Both Lorelei and Daleth turned to see Armonia. She stood on the bridge, her entire body trembling, her eyes glassy and wide as saucers. "How do ya know? Do ya know who I am?"

Lorelei shook her head gently. "I see it when we dream." Armonia spun around and ran off the bridge.

Daleth returned his attention to the view screen. Lorelei slowly stood and started to walk off the bridge. She stopped abruptly. "You know if what you saw was real, maybe it would show us how to save her."

"It wasn't. You die and that's all. There's no saving anyone."

"What if all the Pupils and The Spark were wrong? What if death wasn't the end?" Lorelei closed her eyes and let out a heavy sigh. "What if we all had a chance to start over." She opened her eyes and looked toward Daleth but his face remained impassive. She turned away to find Armonia.

Chapter 6

CIRCAPTO ORBIT

Gimeld and his crew had not gotten far. They could still hear the screams and cries of the crowd several blocks away in the maze of buildings that served as Circapto. Arjan was still unconscious and the usual cool confidence had left Gimeld's voice as he ordered everyone to stop. "Can you patch him up?"

"I believe so. Set him down and hold this for me." M.A.T.O. handed Gimeld the server he had recovered from the ship's wreckage.

"What's this? Why are you carrying around this junk? The ship is gone. Can't your A.I. chips process that fact?"

M.A.T.O. began to examine Arjan. "It is not a necessary component for the ship but it does hold value."

"I'll take it," Sil offered.

Gimeld tossed the server to Sil. "Just save Arjan," he barked.

"That is precisely what I am preparing to accomplish at the moment. Will someone please hold him still while I cauterize the wound?" Gimeld held Arjan in his muscular arms and put his hooded head against his. He fought back tears as Arjan began to buck and writhe as M.A.T.O. used his arsenal of tools to seal up the gaping wound which ran across Arjan's chest. "Considering the creature seemed to be capable of cutting through metal Arjan is fortunate that it only grazed him."

"You call this fortunate," snapped Gimeld.

"It is an objective assessment of the situation." M.A.T.O. finished up and declared, "That is all I can do without the use of a Healing Center. The rest is left up to his body at this point."

"Do you think we should try to find a Healing Center?" Sil asked.

Gimeld stroked the top of Arjan's head. "Pirates don't go to Healing Centers without also going to a Light Bearing Center."

Sil pulled a small pouch out of their cloak. "These are Acoda flower petals I picked the last time we were in Dooga. They have healing properties that are quite potent." Sil pressed the dried pink petals into Arjan's wound. Sil also put a pinch under Arjan's tongue. "They will take a bit to dissolve."

"Then we'll wait here before moving out," said Gimeld.

"I can cauterize your wounds as well while we wait," M.A.T.O. stated.

"First tell me what exactly happened."

"The cargo we picked up contained that creature inside. The lock had a timer on it which I had delayed while I tried to decrypt its contents. So it went off later than intended," stated M.A.T.O.

"When was it set to go off originally?"

"Based on my analysis it was set to go off during the rendezvous time for the pick up on Gremoilio. If I had known what was inside of the container I would have attempted to disarm the mechanism entirely."

Gimeld touched the dark void that served as his face for the others with one hand and held it there for a moment. "We will find those which supplied that crate. When we do they will wish they were facing the creature which was inside it instead of us."

《 》

HANOWEH ORBIT

High Councilor Zean walked with Oland, one of the Esteems of Hanoweh, through the halls of the capitol building. Their voices as they conversed echoed softly in the marble vaulted corridors.

"I thank you and the other Esteems for backing this presentation."

Oland clasped his hands behind his back and leaned ever so slightly forward. He glanced down at the crimson carpet they traversed. "I was present at the recent convention on Iris which resulted in the closing of the hatcheries. I heard your impassioned statements and was moved by them. I knew if you had something to say it should be taken seriously."

Zean welled with pride. "I appreciate your generous words. I do sincerely believe we have looked the other way for too long with Daleth."

"Indeed. This is why I and the other Esteems have given Hanoweh's full support to your endeavor. Closing the hatcheries was an emergency measure. We must redouble our efforts on focusing on the Light to truly repair this crisis."

"I couldn't agree more and it pleases me a great deal to hear someone else state the obvious."

They had reached the exterior glass doors which reached several meters above the two politicians. Oland pressed a button to the side so they would open for them. He extended his arm to allow Zean to walk outside into the crisp air as a show of courtesy. Iris's light had nearly faded. "It is always good to converse with like-minded individuals. Are you in process with a Twin Flame?"

Zean hung her head. "No, but I do have a reflection to hopefully begin with soon. How about yourself?"

"Yes, our Twin Flame has just reached full physical maturity. It will not be long now till my reflection and I have fully transcended death."

Zean gave a weak smile. "You must be thrilled. Congratulations."

Oland acknowledged the praise with a slight tilt of his head toward Zean. "I wish you the best in getting there as well. Be careful getting back home. There are more and more reports of those dreadful creatures every cycle."

"Like this system doesn't have enough troubles right now. We are truly being tested."

Oland nodded. "The stronger we stay fixed to the Light the more the darkness beckons us. Those things seem to congregate around spaceports so do be cautious on your journey."

"It's because the dark trade was allowed to go unchecked that we have all these woes now. But I always stay in the Light. It is how one rises to my heights. Still, I appreciate your concern."

"No matter how high we go there is always something to bring us down. Hopefully, one less if your presentation convinces The Spark to declare Daleth an Obstruction to the Light."

"Indeed. Thank you again. May bright Light shine on you."

"May the Light shine on you as well." Esteem Oland returned to the capitol chambers while Zean boarded a waiting hovercraft to take her to the port. Zean felt confident that her trip to Hanoweh was successful but something still nagged at her. When one spends as much time as her in politics one grows a sense apart from the other five. This sixth sense told her there was something amiss in the air. *What trials does the darkness hold for me?* She contemplated the question and tried to summon the strength of the Light on her journey home. She wished Jamila was with her.

《 》

CIRCAPTO ORBIT

The three assassins walked with their heads down amidst the crowded streets of Circapto. They buried their faces in the turned-up collars of their woolen vests. These precautions against identification were a force of habit rather than necessity, for the throngs of Uprights paid little heed to them. Instead, they were transfixed on view screens covering the vicious attacks by unknown creatures occurring throughout the system. Many already had the fear seared into their brain and darted their eyes to and fro in an attempt to see if monsters lurked in the alleyways and shadows. Three figures walking briskly through the city were simply not of their concern.

The three assassins moved with determined swiftness to their intended target. Each walked with a gait different than their natural one. Once more this was out of habit to obscure their identities. The nameless organization they were a part of had drilled all these precautions too thoroughly in their head for them not to act them out. Clients paid the nameless organization handsomely to ensure someone's Light could be snuffed out and the body disposed of quickly and cleanly. The actual taking of another's living flame more often than not proved to be the easiest part of the process of assassination. Much more difficult was ensuring it was done without interference from other parties. An Orbit such as Circapto's usually made it easy to obscure the taking of life from any kind of scrutiny. Uprights here were consumed by distractions all around them. They were also very competitive so if a misfortune fell upon someone most steered clear. If someone was no longer around it was seen as one less adversary to climb over.

Their current target lived alone in a dwelling on the border of one of the rare gardens that existed on the Orbit of Circapto. The abode was not accessible through an interior lobby like most dwellings on Circapto. Instead, it had a private entryway on the side of the building up a small stone staircase. This fact provided discreet access to his home.

The trio made their way through the screened-in landing after they ensured no neighbors were around. Unlike the door to the tiny porch, the interior door was locked which they expected. One of them knelt and silently picked the lock. The other two obscured the action from Uprights who were passing by. While the lock was being worked on one took out a stunner and prepared it. Meanwhile, the other member of the trio slipped on insulated gloves and unfolded a small insulated blanket they pulled out of a special pocket in the interior of their vest.

In ancient times, members of their organization were masters of different poisons. Some acted so quickly that it was over before the target could even blink. But now that all Uprights were made immune to even the deadliest of poisons they had to use other methods. Fortunately, the stunner was developed by an ingenious mind. It delivered a counter-current to the natural electrical impulses of the nervous system and rendered an Upright completely immobile and non-vocal. It eventually wore off but it provided plenty of time for one to find the main artery on the body and deliver a sonic concussive shock to rupture it. The insulated blanket was used to safely hold the target in place so it didn't cause a disturbance.

This particular target was tagged to disappear which always was the easiest route. You just had to wrap them up and deposit them in a ship marked for a meltdown at the scrap yard. Usually, no one got inquisitive at the scrap yard and even if someone did threats were seldom necessary. Just a few halos usually sufficed to send them on their merry way.

To make matters even easier the target followed a very rigid routine. It was a simple matter to pinpoint an ideal time and place for execution. Assignments don't get any more effortless than this one so the three assassins were completely thrown to find the domicile vacant. The target was under the strict control of one of the major firms here on Circapto. His every movement was scheduled out by the firm and the target was observed to follow it to the letter. He was always scheduled for rest at this time.

"No matter. We'll just wait for him to return from whatever errand he is on," one of them announced.

"Over here!" another called out holding up a yellow slip of paper. On it in black ink were scrawled the words: Sorry to disappoint - Leon.

《 》

COMQWO ORBIT

Leon sat in the tavern nursing his drink, a mixture of puree fruits imported from Baabcrest. It was premium stuff that Leon had never tasted before. The place had a tropical theme with faux trees and flowers. There was even a recording of waves rolling onto a beach that played in a constant loop. None of this seemed very convincing to Leon since the entire establishment was entirely made of ice. Leon wondered if the irony was intentional or not, after all the majority of structures on Comqwo were made of ice. The cold air on his face kept him alert and invigorated despite the weariness that remained in his bones from his long trip. But that was all behind him now and he was ready to settle into his new home.

He watched the view screens which were filled with coverage of his creation. They were the perfect balancing mechanism. Uprights had no natural predator. That's why they turned on each other so viciously. But all the wars and plagues were removed when The Spark arrived which is why they are now in an overpopulation crisis. Further proof in Leon's opinion that The Spark was a fraud. If The Spark were true then there should have been a better understanding that nature works in foils. Leon held his head high as he took in the images of carnage. He had delivered the proper answer to the equation of Uprights.

The name which was coined for his creation was the Breathless. Partly because they already determined their eggs incubate on the outside of inter-Orbit ships and partly because the sight of them is said to take your breath away. His former employers did well with their publicity. Leon approved of the name.

When he heard the one analyst state the Breathless are believed to have no sense of smell since no snout is visible he ground his teeth. Didn't they know anything about anything? The nose is usually the quickest route to the olfactory bulb. Some are designed with specialized features to enhance one's sense of smell but they are also an access point to the interior of the body. So it can prove to be a liability as well as an asset. The fernal, for example, is an organism with a snout but to truly examine a scent in minute detail it will open its mouth over the specimen to allow molecules to make contact directly with the olfactory bulb which is located in the back of a fernal's throat. Leon had used the same principle for the Breathless to ensure as few weaknesses as possible. Even their susceptibility to sonic attacks was overstated by Leon to his former employers. In turn, he underemphasized their ability to procreate.

Leon smirked. The thought of his former bosses being delivered his little note amused him to no end. *Did they think he was new to the methods of power?* He had studied competitiveness from the best, Non-uprights. It was they who taught Leon the ways of survival, and the laws of self-preservation.

Comqwo was the perfect spot for him. Its highly militarized populace would surely be called on soon by the rest of the system to address his creation. This would throw the Orbit into a chaotic state. As his teachers in the uncivilized sections of the system taught Leon, chaos is a wonderful camouflage. It's doubtful his old employers would track him in this distant inhospitable world anyway but always best to add extra layers of precaution. He would give himself over to the tundra. Although these drinks were so good he was tempted to return once in a while and indulge.

While here Leon planned to study the ecosystem which was unlike any other Orbit. Comqwo was ice to its core. The name Comqwo came from an ancient Gremoilion dialect. It meant comet. Leon believed this Orbit may originally have been a comet that was trapped in the pull of Iris. Not much life existed on Comqwo. Outside of Uprights, there were only small Non-uprights that scurried about on flat squat legs. They had thick layers of fur and blubber. They fed on each other or the fungus that grew throughout the ball of ice.

This fungus was what piqued Leon's interest most. He theorized the fungus originated from somewhere else outside the system. This theory was considered nonsense by the general scientific community. Leon felt they were swayed by the general fear of anything outside the system. This irrational thought process went back even beyond The Spark. The idea of something outside the light of Iris being bad existed since the first writings of the system.

Leon was not going to let instilled bias stop him though. Shivers of excitement ran down his spine at merely the thought of studying the organism. The fungus was the linchpin to the ecosystem on Comqwo. The fungus fed on the decomposing organic matter throughout the orbit. In turn, life on Comqwo fed on it. Even Uprights on Comqwo used it regularly in their diets. It seemed like a fairly closed and confined loop of energy but for some reason, it worked. Leon intended to find the fungus' origin. How it all started and why it persisted may teach new lessons on how to sustain oneself in an inhospitable environment.

And Leon knew things in the larger system of Iris were about to get very inhospitable. He did not delude himself like the useless rulers and his haughty former employers. No, it was all changing, there was no going back. Change was, after all, the natural way of things. He had observed it well in the past which is why he knew he needed to change too.

Who knew what wonderful discoveries awaited him here on this peculiar Orbit? Perhaps his lust for discovery over finding purity made him a member of the heretical Order but he cared little for any of those organized thought groups. They were much too limiting. Life held more possibility and force than could ever be confined by Uprights.

Leon finished his drink and felt the tangy tartness wash over his tongue. He put an extra couple of halos down to foster the goodwill of the server. Leon put on his furry outer coat and ice boots to distribute his body weight, the ice was solid but life was always full of surprises. Leon then trudged through the arctic tundra to his campsite. He looked forward to beginning his research into the fungus while society came unglued.

《 》

BAABCREST ORBIT

Magistrate Corry closed the door behind her and stepped out onto one of the many observation decks which decorated the School of Knowledge's main campus. This particular one overlooked a peculiar mountain range on the moon. Peculiar because of the sparkle it seemed to have in the light of Iris and because of the shape its peaks took. The peaks were all bowed in. It was suspected that volcanic activity was to blame but since there have been no traces of magma found it remained up for speculation.

Ramek, who had just returned from his inquiry, had come with Corry to the observation deck. It never arose suspicion for Corry and Ramek to spend so much time together since they posed as reflections. Already on the observation deck were Tania and Florian who also posed as reflections. To anyone else, it would simply seem like two reflections happened to meet on an observation deck. The reality of what was to transpire was an emergency meeting to try and disperse information into Corry's Cell.

"Corruption in all that is holy and right," Ramek said in a low voice.

Florian responded, "Corruption is The Way of The Light."

Tania hung her head. "I see little evidence to suggest that control of all Orbits will not be granted to the Twin Flames after this new convention on Iris wraps up."

"Agreed," said Ramek solemnly. "The panic I witnessed on my travels dwarfs the overpopulation situation. No one thought twice about me cutting my inquiry short. I wouldn't be surprised if those Breathless were planted by the Twin Flames themselves when the first convention didn't hand them the control they wanted."

"That may be so," said Tania, "but whatever their origin we must prepare for the changes they have ushered in. The other Cells are observing and modifying accordingly. I will keep you abreast. That being said if Daleth brings us the experiment we proceed as planned unless new orders are given."

Corry raised her head in surprise. "Do you still think Daleth will deliver her?"

Florian gave a disdainful laugh. "That scourge has ruined us as he ruins all he touches. He will burrow deep down into the lowest echelons of this system if he doesn't get himself caught. I told you we should never have utilized him."

"Regret will get us nowhere," chastised Tania.

Ramek sighed. "If the presentation of that High Councilor goes through and Daleth is declared an Obstruction to the Light he may still show himself out of desperation. He has to have figured out it was the Order who hired him. Desperate times call for unusual friends. Isn't that why we sought him to begin with?"

"The Twin Flames will not care about him now that control of the entire system has been achieved," Florian sneered.

"The Twin Flames will still need to use The Spark as a mask of righteous justification. I believe Daleth may show up here which is why I want Corry to still keep the beacon on her at all times." Tania turned and looked so intensely into Corry's eyes that she straightened her posture reflexively. Corry gave an affirmative nod. "Now more than ever the experiment may be the only hope we and this entire system have. If Daleth shows himself we do all we can to secure the experiment, no matter the risk." The grave determination in Tania's eyes sent chills down Corry's spine.

⟨ ⟩

INTER-ORBIT SPACE

Armonia sobbed softly as she held her legs close to her chest. It wasn't so much dying that upset her, it was dying without ever living that caused her tears. She didn't know who she was and had only a few memories, mostly of dreaming and the amazing colors she saw while doing it. Kristal slithered around her arm in rhythmic contractions but it offered none of the usual comforts. She didn't even raise her head when she heard the bedroom door slide open and Lorelei's footsteps.

Lorelei placed a hand on Armonia's back and made slow circles with it. "I'm sorry. I should have told you after our first dream together. Whatever I sense when we dream, your body and mind can't handle it. It's wearing them down."

Armonia raised her head and shouted, "Then get rid of it!"

"I don't know what it is to get rid of. I was hoping it would become clearer as we dreamed but it hasn't."

Armonia's body sank. "What if we dream with Daleth?"

"I thought you both didn't want to do that?"

"I just wanna be not me." Armonia plunged her face back into the soft pillow.

Lorelei folded her hands in her lap. She stared down at them, the corners of her lips raised for a brief moment. "Believe it or not all of us on this ship want to not be us. So at least you're in good company." She laid down and nestled close to Armonia. "In ancient times Baabcrest was known for its bizarre dreaming rituals. Maybe we'll stumble upon some remnants that will help."

Armonia threw the pillow across the room. "I must've been a really bad Upright to deserve this," she huffed.

"The House of Yowgn teaches there is no bad or good. We are all just parts of Yowgn."

"What's Yowgn?"

"Everything." Lorelei tilted her head up and seemed to look past the ceiling. "Yowgn is the intelligence that drives life and it can never be destroyed." She turned her head back to Armonia. "That's why when roommates leave each other we remind one another of that fact by touching our abdomen and saying 'body', then touching our head and saying 'mind' and then our chest and saying 'Yowgn.'"

Armonia sat up and gave a puzzled expression.

Lorelei propped herself up with her arm and continued softly. "The mind is the interface between Yowgn and the body. Together they make us who we are. The ritual was supposed to have originated from a tribe on Baabcrest." Lorelei reached out and touched Armonia's stomach, head, and chest while she whispered, "Body, mind, Yowgn."

They both paused and looked into each other's eyes. Each revealed deep trauma that neither themselves nor the other could touch. Armonia finally sighed. "Thanks but it doesn't help."

"We can dream." The two women spun their heads to see Daleth's massive frame filling the doorway. Somehow they had not heard him enter their moment.

"I'm tired of dreaming", Armonia sneered, "and even if I wasn't, ya suck." Kristal gave a drawn-out hiss toward Daleth before Armonia added, "And not in a good way."

"You're actually willing?" Lorelei arched her brow in surprise.

"Only to prove that what happened between Armonia and I was of no meaning or consequence."

Lorelei placed her hand on top of Armonia's. "Dreaming can't be forced so if you don't want to we won't but if Daleth's wrong it may provide answers for how to help you."

"Well," Armonia turned away and crossed her arms. "Only to show he's wrong."

"I'm not wrong and you will see that it was just a delusion from dreaming with someone such as you." Armonia stuck her forked tongue out in response.

《 》

LORELEI RECLINED NAKED on the soft mattress. Her breaths were heavy. She was just about ready. As she reached down and felt Armonia's swollen clitoris at her fingertips she knew Armonia was too.

Armonia ceased the tantalizing strokes of her tongue and pressed it into Lorelei's vulva. She was getting to be quite adept at dreaming, at feeling the rhythms of the body.

Lorelei glanced over at Daleth who propped himself up in the corner of the room observing the two with an expression chiseled in stone. She signaled him to join.

He came up behind Armonia and squeezed the warm flesh of her rear, running his hands along her rounded hips. As he entered her, she let out an involuntary moan.

A shudder of pleasure ran along Armonia's spine. She squeezed her vaginal walls around his engorged penis to entice him further into her.

Daleth felt the same magnetic pull he recalled from the previous time. He tried to resist but the tension only made the pull stronger. He braced himself against the curve of Armonia's hips as their pelvis' fell into a rhythm. His thrusts were gentler this time so as not to injure her or Lorelei but somehow the sensations that coursed through his body were all the more savage. He slid in and out of her vaginal lips as Armonia kept her tongue pressed against Lorelei's hot throbbing clitoris. His glance unexpectedly met Lorelei's eyes for a moment before a pulsating ecstasy lashed his body. He squeezed his eyes shut.

⟨ ⟩

DALETH OPENED HIS EYES again and saw a brilliant shade of indigo. He seemed to be alone and enveloped by the vivid color. Confusion crept upon him.

"Ha! Ya were wrong, this never happens when Lorelei dreams with me." Daleth craned his neck upward toward the voice and saw Armonia, wings intact, descend to him.

Daleth checked his body and saw his skin was once more pristine. "Space dust," he muttered under his breath.

"This wasn't the place we were last time though." Armonia fluttered around in a topsy-turvy manner and then suddenly jerked to a stop. She trained her gaze below her. "Oh, what's that?" She reached out and grabbed Daleth gliding them both downward, Daleth's mind was too busy attempting to process everything to thwart her.

They both approached a thick cord that seemed to glow different shades of yellow and was without a beginning or end. Armonia went to touch it. Daleth tried to prevent her but was still too dazed to succeed. Instead, he grabbed her forearm just as her fingertips made contact with the unbroken line of light. Spontaneously both saw the entire history of the system flash through their mind.

"The Spark?" Armonia whispered when it was all over.

"Why did you show me that?" Daleth snapped.

"It wasn't me! Why do you keep thinking it's me?"

"We have to find a way out of here." Daleth began to look around wildly.

"Why, so we can go back to that world?" Armonia pointed to the golden tube in front of them. "Ya saw it too and don't even pretend ya didn't."

"I don't know what I saw."

"Please, let's just stay here."

Daleth thrust his face before Armonia's and glared into her eyes. "First off, we don't even know where here is, that's why we can't trust what we saw. Second off, we hate each other so why would we want to stay stuck together."

"You hate me?"

Daleth stood erect and narrowed his eyes. "Don't you hate me?"

"I said you're mean not that I hate ya. Why do ya hate me?"

"Because I hate everybody."

"Liar. You don't hate Lorelei."

"How would you know?"

"I'm not stupid just cause I don't remember nothing."

"I'm finding a way out of here. You can do what you want." Daleth began to march away.

"If we go back ya gonna do anything bout what we saw?"

Daleth froze and sighed deeply. "No."

"They're probably doing it to both of us too, ya know."

"It doesn't matter. I don't care."

Armonia fluttered over to Daleth so he had to look at her. "Don't give me that, ya do."

Daleth's eyes blazed. "No one's ever cared about me and I don't care about anyone either!"

"Lorelei cares about ya. She told me what happened with ya."

Daleth seethed. "She should not have done that."

Armonia lost her composure. "Ya think you're the only one with a miserable life? I can't even remember mine but I'm sure it stunk! Hasn't been great from what I can remember. At least here no one's gonna hurt us more! But no you just want to go back so ya can torture and yell at everyone."

Daleth averted his gaze from Armonia and mumbled. "It's the only way I feel something."

Armonia plopped down and hugged her knees into her chest. "When I dream it feels great and beautiful. But when we dream...is the only time I feel safe."

They stayed rooted to the spot neither knew how to move from it. They avoided each other's gaze for what seemed like an eternity. Then the yellow hue of the cord began to fade till the whole thing disappeared. They had both almost forgotten it was there.

"What's happening?" Armonia whined.

Daleth looked around as the indigo aura grew darker. "I think we are going back whether we want to or not."

⟨ ⟩

THEY WERE BOTH SUDDENLY back in the bedroom. Lorelei sat on the bed, her back toward them. Armonia and Daleth glanced at each other. Armonia with a timid voice asked, "Lorelei, where were you?"

She turned toward them, her eyes glassy and wet. The path of tears could still be seen on her scarred face. Daleth and Armonia were both startled by the emotion she wore. "I saw what I needed. Tell me everything you saw."

Armonia shook her head. "I don't want to." Lorelei's eyes pleaded to grasp some purpose or meaning in existence. Something to assuage long-buried regret. Armonia seeing those eyes felt a sudden pang of guilt hit her gut. She averted her own eyes away.

"Please", Lorelei's voice cracked. "I've chased what you two can see for too long. Don't deny me now, don't be that cruel."

Daleth and Armonia exchanged a long look. "Be cautious about what you ask," warned Daleth. "Advice from one who knows that some doors should not be opened."

Lorelei nodded gravely, "I know but I've knocked on this door till my hands are raw. I have nothing left but a thirst that I know you two can quench."

Daleth looked at Armonia who bowed her head once more staring through the mattress. Daleth's gaze then met Lorelei's. Her eyes begged for mercy. He remembered his own pleas for mercy during his training with the Followers of Vuhox. A scream from his entire essence to put out the burning fire that raged. He saw the same scream within Lorelei now. *How similar Lorelei and I are, how lost and desperate we both became. We are both destined to be the end of ourselves.* He swallowed a lump in his throat. "So be it."

⟨ ⟩

EBJAN ORBIT

It was late by the time Zean and her assistant left. "May the Light shine bright on you," Zean weakly said to her assistant as they parted ways.

"You as well," he replied just as weakly.

It had been an exhausting cycle, actually for the past several cycles. The so-called Breathless were attacking more and more frequently all across the system. All Orbits were now in a state of panic. A new convention on Iris had been called for to address the matter. Zean was unsure how to calm the populace of her sector. She tried to talk Light to them but found herself faltering in her trust in it. Things throughout the system had become so chaotic in such a short span. There was no way around it. Control of all the Orbits must be handed over to the Twin Flames. Zean was already working on her speech to convince the other Orbits that they are the only ones bright enough to guide the system through this terrible ordeal. This was certainly the worst she could remember in her existence and in her opinion, nothing had even come close to this since The Spark arrived.

Zean tried to massage her tense shoulders but they were like boulders. She wished Jamila was here to do it but with everything going on there was little chance of that any time soon. Zean was so in her own morose that she was startled to hear Fawna's voice call her name. She saw both her and Osarian cross the busy intersection to join her.

Zean managed to force a smile. "Fawna, Osarian, so nice to see you both. How are you doing? Did you begin with another Twin Flame yet?"

"No, they state we have to do some internal healing before we can recommence," answered Fawna.

"How goes the proposal?"

Zean didn't have the strength left in her to hide her surprise at Osarian's question. "It was going well but with all the Breathless commotion I have had to put it aside." Zean could not mistake the flare in both their eyes.

Fawna's voice was steady as she said, "You mustn't do such a thing. It is because of dark renegades such as Daleth that those things found us."

"You're referring to the theory that their eggs traveled through space from another planet and attached themselves to inter-Orbit ships that went outside the standardized flight routes?"

Fawna gave a flippant gesture. "Of course, what other possibility is there?"

"We must not waver from the Light in this dark time." Osarian put a hand on Zean's shoulder and gave her a quick smile. "We trust you won't let us down."

Zean nodded in an almost absent-minded manner. "I am your champion of Light."

⟨⟩

BAABCREST ORBIT

Daleth, Lorelei, and Armonia walked along the boards of wood that served as the major travel artery for the Great Band on Baabcrest. Small, non-obtrusive crafts skillfully weaved in and out of the groups of people that milled around in the last fleeting rays of Iris. Armonia lagged behind the other two distracted by the myriad of artists, musicians, and crafters who lined both sides of the walkway. She was dressed in a violet frock and her plumes of hair were in a severe braid wrapped around her head.

"This wig irritates my scalp," grumbled Daleth as he scratched the blue locks that fell from his crown every which way, obscuring his face. He was not in his normal cloak but instead dressed in more tight-fitting formal wear with gold piping down his legs and arms accenting the black uniform.

"Just be grateful there was stuff in their closet to disguise you two with," hissed Lorelei. She also had donned a red wig and put dark circles around her eyes to alter her appearance. She no longer wore the healer's uniform but instead wore silver shorts and a pink tube top.

"I don't understand why you insist on walking?"

"What do you want to do? Rent a wheeler? You seem to be having a tough time getting it through your head that you're a fugitive."

"I'm not afraid of any guardians," muttered Daleth.

Lorelei rolled her eyes. "I'm not saying you can't take them. I'm just saying let's do this the easy way."

"As soon as you get me my halos I am out of here."

"I can't believe after everything you told me you're still just concerned about halos."

"What can I say? A deal's a deal."

"You'll get them as soon as the Room here has all the information. You may need to dream with Armonia again if it's decided more details are needed."

"What more could you possibly want?"

"I don't know just try to stay flexible. I know it's not your strong suit."

"I do not struggle with that. What I do struggle with is why we are going to a Room at all when you said the House of Yowgn is compromised."

"I said the Room of Ebjan was. Rooms do not confide in each other all that much under normal circumstances. It's a practice done just for that reason, to ensure safety if one is compromised. Someone needs to hear what you and Armonia found out. It's why I joined the House of Yowgn in the first place. I felt they were the best hope this system had."

Daleth gave a mocking grunt of disapproval. "And what then? Do you expect to blow up Iris? The Twin Flames are still immortal you know."

Lorelei's voice raised an octave. "I don't know but everyone should know what is happening to them."

"Uprights won't care. They prefer nothing disrupts their meaningless existence."

Lorelei looked down at the ground as they continued to walk. "It's why you joined the Followers of Vuhox right? To give meaning to your existence?"

Daleth answered with icy silence.

They walked along not saying another word to each other until Daleth stopped suddenly and thrust his arm out in front of Lorelei. Armonia who was not paying attention collided with Daleth's back. "What gives?"

Daleth pointed to guardians several meters away loading people into a small ship. "Is that not our destination?"

"Space dust!" Lorelei cried. "Unak must have known we would head here and somehow got them busted up."

Daleth reached for his pouch concealed under the waist of his pants. "The fear is thick in the air for some reason. I can take them if you want."

"Not without creating a scene, you can't. We'll have to think of something else."

"Ya two have to save me. I wanna be done with all this," whined Armonia.

Daleth pointed at Lorelei. "That's all her."

"Come on, let's get out of here before they spot you two." The group turned and saw Turako standing in their path.

"So Daleth, I knew you would eventually show up here. Running out of places to hide, are we?"

"Do I know you?"

Turako snorted and unclipped his laser gun. "That offends me. Peridot was going to be one of the greatest Twin Flames before you snuffed out his Light. It's time for you to be held accountable."

Lorelei lunged toward Daleth. "No!" But she was too late the crystal flew out and went through Turako's left eye. It exited out of his right eye. As his limp body fell to the ground the crystal returned to Daleth's waiting hand. Lorelei quickly grabbed Armonia's arm and ran. Armonia dragged behind at first not understanding but soon kept pace.

Meanwhile, Daleth swerved to face the on-rushing guardians. He casually tossed all five of his crystals in the air. They hung there for a moment seemingly frozen in time and space. Daleth removed his wig and narrowed his eyes at the guardians who were nearly upon him. He then commanded his crystals to commence with their terrible onslaught. They weaved in and out of the guardians, barely seen due to their speed. The only marker of their path was the miniature spurts of blood when they entered or left flesh. The guardian's laser blasts were all in vain due to Daleth's shielding. The last guardian collapsed, his hand smacked Daleth's boot as it fell. The energy he had drank in from those Fimegerians served him nicely. He still had much left over.

Daleth gathered his crystals in his palm once more. He heard the patrol skimmer approach from behind but he could tell it was traveling at such a high speed his best bet was to divert energy to increasing the strength of his shield. He barely felt the impact and was instead scooped up by the craft. He maneuvered to face the guardian driving it and having redeposited his crystals back in their pouch moved for his trikilldo. The driver saw Daleth reach under his pants to take out the concealed blade. She turned the patrol skimmer hard upward so they climbed high in the air. It did little to jostle Daleth and he punched through the windshield and opened her jugular all the same. In her death throes, she managed to dislodge him from the patrol skimmer as it went tumbling. Daleth glanced below him and saw a Temple of Light. *Perhaps that last guardian wasn't as foolish as I had taken her for*, he thought to himself as he crashed through the multi-colored stained glass.

⟨ ⟩

ARMONIA KEPT LOOKING behind them. Since she didn't see anyone pursuing them she wondered why they were still moving at such a rapid pace. She glanced up at the pale blue sky as Lorelei continued to pull her along. She saw a patrol skimmer and an Upright both plummeting downward. "Do ya think that's Daleth falling?"

"He'll be alright. He can shield himself from a fall."

"He just crashed into that pointy glass ceiling with all the pretty colors."

Lorelei halted immediately and her head whipped behind her. "That's a Temple of Light. It will be full of Twin Flames."

"I thought Daleth said Twin Flames are immortal. How's he gonna defeat them if they can't die?"

Lorelei didn't look at Armonia who waited for an answer or the people who dashed about in a panic. Instead, she just stared at the shattered glass pinnacle in the distance which loomed over the skyline and herself equally. Out of the corner of her eye, she spotted a surf skimmer. It had a net on a long pole sticking out of the back, most likely a local coming back from a day skimming the shores for wave walkers. She snatched the net from the vehicle. The driver made a sharp U-turn and shouted, "Hey! What's the big idea?"

Lorelei smashed him with the net knocking him off the surf skimmer. She jumped on board. "Hurry and get on," she called back to Armonia who promptly followed her command. They sped off toward the Temple.

⟨ ⟩

DALETH PICKED HIMSELF off the floor. He rotated his limbs to make sure he still had full mobility. A circle of robed individuals formed around him. He knew that although they were not guardians, they would not let him leave without a struggle. There was no fear or pain in this Temple so he would have to use his reserves carefully.

"You are Daleth are you not?" The face of the Twin Flame who asked this question was stern.

"Must have me confused with somebody else," he grumbled. He moved to the exit.

"Halt! You will not leave here unless it's to go to a Light Bearing Center," another voice echoed within the chamber. "Your Light needs to be brightened. You took a life without just cause."

"Says who?"

Daleth's path was blocked by a wall of steadfast Twin Flames with severe expressions. "It was a guardian whose life you took." The small flames tattooed on either side of their nose made it seem as though double the eyes glared at him.

Daleth reached for his crystals and began to shield himself. "I am responsible for no one but myself. I take care of my own affairs just fine. They should have minded their own business. Just like you."

The crystals flew out of his hand as bodies piled on top of him. It was impossible to discern which came first. Some had grabbed shards of glass and Daleth felt them poke at his shield. His crystals flew to his command but they had little effect. He tried to reach for his trikilldo to sever their heads but they were holding his arms. He realized their strategy was to restrain him and use the pieces of glass to empty his reserves. It would take some time but overall was a good strategy. He was at a loss about how to counter. There were just too many.

The crystals whipped and lashed at the skin of the Twin Flames but they seemed ignorant of them. Daleth still strained and battled with determination. He was not going to their brainwashing center without fighting tooth and nail.

At some point, the Twin Flames seemed to be struggling with something besides himself. He was surprised to see the face of Lorelei. His astonishment was replaced by an even greater shock when he noticed Twin Flames slashing her with their glass weapons and her gashes healing almost instantaneously.

As Lorelei and Daleth struggled with the mound of Twin Flames Armonia watched unsure of what to do. Kristal slithered out of her cubby hole on Armonia's bicep and moved her way down Armonia's leg. Kristal then made her way over to something lying on the floor. It was Daleth's crystals. He must have abandoned them and they coalesced away from the melee. Kristal let out a squeak and Armonia walked over to investigate. She reached down to pick them up and examined them. Kristal ran up her body and squeaked in her ear. "What do ya expect me to do with these? I'm no follower of whatever. I can't zip them all around." She saw Lorelei and Daleth being overcome in the writhing mass of bodies. She knew it was all over. She squeezed her fist around the crystals. "I wish everyone would just leave us alone."

A shadow fell over Armonia. Her head pivoted as she saw two robed individuals approaching her with arms outstretched. She put her hands up instinctively to resist them. Suddenly they seemed to jerk and falter. Light radiated from them and expanded out on either side. The light seemed to cleave their bodies, it then dissipated like water vapor escaping hot coals. The bodies hit the floor with a sickening thud. Armonia reeling from what she just witnessed moved her line of sight to the cluster of robed individuals who had piled on Daleth and Lorelei. To her horror, she saw the same thing happen to the Twin Flames there.

Daleth clawed his way to the top of the heap of corpses. He slid down and helped Lorelei emerge as well.

"What happened?" Armonia's voice was shaky.

Daleth felt for a pulse on one of the empty husks but it was only to confirm the unfathomable truth he already knew. "They're dead." He and Lorelei both stared at Armonia.

Her mouth gaped open as she groped for words. "I—I just wanted them to go away."

Lorelei slid her eyes to Daleth. "I told you."

Before anyone could say anything they heard a thunderous pounding coming from outside. Daleth ran to the vestibule. The others quickly joined him. Their eyes bulged as they saw a gushing tower of water falling from the sky. The column of unrelenting liquid was moving over the ocean toward them.

"A waterfall!" Lorelei cried. "We won't make it in here. You compromised the integrity of the structure when you crashed through the ceiling."

"Then we head back to the ship."

"But your reserves are depleted, what if we run into more guardians?"

"There is a waterfall coming they need to run for cover, as well. Besides the fear that thing inspires will fuel me plenty. Give me my crystals!" Daleth snatched them from Armonia.

"Wait, what's a waterfall?" Armonia asked.

Lorelei grabbed her hand. "We willexplain later just run and don't look back!" The trio dashed out of the Temple.

"Here!" Lorelei yelled to get Daleth to notice the surf skimmer.

"I'll drive," Daleth said as hopped on. Lorelei threw Armonia on and then slid on behind her. The two held on as Daleth sped away.

Armonia heard a terrible crash behind her and craned her neck just in time to see the last remnants of the Temple splinter under the tremendous pressure of the water which seemed to pour endlessly from the black clouds in the sky.

"It's turning towards us you're not gonna outrun it," screamed Lorelei.

Daleth saw the crest of a nearby hill with a small opening in it, not big enough for the skimmer but it might just fit the three of them. He hopped off and ran to the crevice in the rock. The sound was deafening and they could all feel it reverberate through their chest.

"You two get in, I'll shield myself!"

"Are you crazy? Your lungs will fill with water and you'll drown! I'm the only one who can survive, so I'll stay out here!"

"You're not staying out here alone! You'll lose consciousness and get swept away with the water!"

The waterfall was nearly upon them. They both turned their heads to the opening and saw Armonia huddled in the fetal position within the fissure. Although she was soaked to the bone from the moisture in the air, the path of tears remained visible on her face.

"Go! I'll cover the exit!" Daleth shouted.

Lorelei climbed in and took Armonia in her arms. She pressed her head close to her chest and stroked her hair. Daleth stood at the entrance shielding himself to provide some type of door to hopefully prevent them all from drowning. *Even my powers are not enough against the full unrelenting force of a waterfall*, he thought. So he kept himself well within the tiny nook but in front of Lorelei and Armonia. He muted his ears to the sound of the crashing water. A natural ability he was genetically granted which allowed him to vary his sensitivity to certain frequencies. Lorelei's cooing high-pitched tones still could be heard saying, "I'm here with you. Just listen to the beat of my heart."

Chapter 7

CIRCAPTO ORBIT

The president of Genetical Illumination rapped his fingers on the desk while he rocked back and forth in his leather chair. His section of the Orbit had rotated away from Iris a while ago and wouldn't face it again for some time. Not that it ever mattered on Circapto. Outside the window was still abuzz with activity. On Circapto there was always something going on. For some reason, the old mantra from some forgotten period of history popped into his head. If his memory served him right it went, *The darkness comes so we never lose faith in Iris.* He remembered being taught it in his Prep Center, obviously well before he took over the company that ran those very centers.

The voice communicator buzzed and his dark-shift assistant informed him he had visitors. He feigned surprise but was expecting them. He quickly popped a jolt pill to keep himself awake and alert. He probably didn't need it since his nerves were so on edge but it was still prudent.

Two Uprights walked into his spacious office. One was short and thick-bodied with his brown hair neatly combed in a part. The other was tall with an athletic build and her pink hair kept very short. Without turning from the window he spoke to them. "Has everything been arranged before our senators leave for Iris?"

The short one answered, "Yes the presentation is complete and the senators have been briefed. They confirm that Gremoilio and Fimeger have both agreed to sign onto it. Orogunu as we expected has also agreed to sign on. They are still waiting to hear from Hanoweh."

The president of Genetical Illumination spun his chair around to face his visitors. "Those Hanowehs believe too much in the Light and too little in themselves sometimes. But we have enough of the larger Orbits as it is."

He was, after all, speaking to the head of the largest freight company and the head of the largest security firm in the system. He didn't have to spell things out for them.

The tall one now spoke. "I have a feeling they will sign once we reach Iris. My greater concern is our inability to locate our old friend."

"Running the leading security provider for as long as you have, it's understandable you would have security concerns. That being said, I honestly don't think we will hear from him. In the event we do, our media people have already made preparations. He would be a raving lunatic at best and a lone mass murderer at worst. We have little risk."

The one who coordinated cargo all over the system added, "I still would feel better if he had been removed."

"We all would and we are still searching for him, as you know. But we must focus on the other gears in motion just as much if not more so."

The one who kept the system safe voiced her mind. "Although those abominations are more deadly and prolific than anticipated I do believe we can avert disaster."

"We all didn't get where we are by chance. We are all victors and we will conquer this as well." The president of Genetical Illumination leaned back in his soft leather recliner and swiveled it once more to gaze out the window at the masses below him.

《 》

INTER-ORBIT SPACE

Lorelei and Armonia lay together spooning on the bed. They had changed out of their wet clothes and had put new dry ones on. Armonia had undone the braid so her hair could dry better. She was back in the top and skirt Lorelei gave her when they first met. It was familiar and although it was a minor comfort she clung to it with all her might. "So ya were one of those Twin Flames things? Daleth told me they were some kind of special combo thingy but, I mean ya are Lorelei too, right? Like ya weren't pretending with us?"

"Sometimes you believe in something so much you give yourself over to it. Eventually, you realize it took all of you and you fight to reclaim yourself. Lorelei is what's truly left of me."

"I'm not a murderer," Armonia whispered.

Lorelei stroked her hair. "I know."

Both sat up in a flash when they heard Daleth enter. He stood at the doorway wearing a hard scowl on his face. He was dressed once more in his normal tunic and cloak. "I shook any pursuers and we're well below the system. I don't know of any pilots other than me that go this far down."

Lorelei fidgeted with the cuffs of her tightly knit blouse. "That's good."

Daleth glared at Lorelei. "Is there anything else I should know about you?"

Lorelei smoothed her skirt and avoided eye contact. "No."

"Who were you loyal to when I met you?" Lorelei's eyes darted up at Daleth's question but she remained silent. "How long ago did you defect or have you been a spy for the Way all along?"

Lorelei's eyes narrowed into venomous slits. "Don't ever accuse me of being a part of the Way."

"You were."

"Not for over a gremrev."

Daleth averted his eyes so he stared at the empty wall. Lorelei heard the hardened shell of Daleth's voice crack. For a razor-thin moment, a wounded child's voice peeked through. "It doesn't matter. We have only ourselves to be loyal toward. It's a teaching of The Followers of Vuhox that I still agree with. To that end, I'm taking Armonia to the School of Knowledge."

Lorelei's face morphed to one of concern but she held her tongue and instead joined Daleth in staring at the blank wall. She wanted to say something but found no words to use. She had so many regrets which she had already learned to live with and fight through. This would have to just be another to add to the pile.

Armonia noticed the expression on Lorelei's face and her own grew worried. "Wait what's the School of Knowledge? They don't have more of those waterfall thingies do they?"

"They are the ones who hired me to find you? I'm fulfilling my contract."

"You can't. She can kill Twin Flames."

"Which means they underbid me. I intend to get a fairer price from them and then disappear. Nobody will see me for quite some time. I'm going to live on this ship down here and only venture back to the system when I need supplies."

Lorelei's jaw clenched. "That's not what you want."

"Don't presume to know what I want."

"Wait," Armonia interjected, "what's gonna happen to me?"

"It doesn't matter. You, Lorelei, and the Order can bring the entire system crashing down for all I care." With that, he turned and left.

"What does that mean?" Armonia's head swiveled between the door Daleth exited from and Lorelei.

Lorelei squeezed Armonia's hand and made her look her in the eyes. " You'll be alright. We'll be alright. I'm not leaving your side. These are probably the people who caused whatever makes you different. And we'll make them fix everything. I promise."

Armonia buried her head in her hands. "No more," she whimpered.

《 》

IRIS ORBIT

Zean shuffled her feet along the crimson carpet of the corridors of Iris. Media staff and dignitaries swarmed around her in a frenzy. The cacophony of chatter that echoed through the arches was an oppressive beating of drums hanging over her slumped shoulders, much worse than the aftermath of the first conference she attended.

It felt like she had been at Iris for a quarter of a gremrev. Of course, it hadn't been anywhere near that long but she did fly in early before the convention.

After running into Fawna and Osarian, she had reached out to Iris to see if she should still make her presentation. She was told she should, which surprised her. She was even more taken aback when she arrived and found out there was a second presentation as well originating from Circapto senators. One to get all pirates and smugglers declared an Obstruction to the Light. Her palms were sweaty and her mouth parched when they called her in to present to The Spark. It was a surreal experience. Zean had little recollection of it now. The next concrete memory she had was being told it had been approved. Actually, both presentations were approved.

Now that the convention was over all Zean wanted to do was curl up under the covers of her soft warm bed and take a long rest. It would be wonderful if Jamila was there to surprise her again but after all that had transpired, she knew there was no chance of that.

She happened to glance up and spotted Esteemed Oland and Magistrate Molomew huddled in a corner in deep discussion. She averted her face and tried to alter her path but it was too late they had spotted her. She forced a smile and walked over to them.

"I suppose I must concede to your wisdom. You were right we should have given control over to the Twin Flames the first time we convened and saved us all a trip," said Molomew with a wry grin. "Congratulations on getting your presentation passed. I know how much effort you put into it."

Zean bowed her head to accept the praise graciously. "Thank you but it was the Light shining through me and through all of us here which allowed these events to transpire. The Spark simply wanted us to realize the Light more fully before acting."

Molomew stroked his bearded chin absent mindlessly. "Indeed. I believe this convention will go down in the records of the system as a turning point. Hopefully, the Twin Flames set the system right in short order so we can go back to normal."

Esteemed Oland nodded vigorously. "Yes, we have reached the point when we, at last, shed the final vestiges of darkness and fully embrace what The Spark has revealed to us through the Light. All be well soon enough."

"We'll find out in a quarter of a gremrev when we're all back here to reassess. Thank you, Zean, by the way for your support of that measure."

"We all agreed on it." Zean tasted bile at the thought that Molomew felt her backing a reassessment was a quid pro quo action for his support of her proposal. It was the prudent thing to do and nothing more. "If you will excuse me even though Iris rotates artificially it has been a trying few cycles."

Esteemed Oland straightened his posture and jutted his chin out. "Of course, may the Light shine brightly on you."

Zean parted her lips but there wasn't much she could muster behind it. "And on you both as well."

Zean quickly boarded a chartered ship. She could have ridden back with her colleagues but she felt even less like waiting around for them than she did the last time. Since she traveled to Iris on a chartered ship it would not necessarily seem like a breach in the protocol for her to take one back to Ebjan.

Zean settled into her seat and rested her head back. It was not the most comfortable position to rest in but she was so tired it probably wouldn't matter. She closed her eyes as the pilot made the departure announcement.

Soon she would no longer be High Councilor Zean. She would be just Zean. *Would I even know herself in that identity?* The change wouldn't be immediate of course. Power doesn't transfer seamlessly all by itself. It may even take as long as point zero one gremrev till all was said and done. But however long it took it would usher in new. Perhaps Jamila and she could intensify their reflection of one another. Zean could feel the change afoot to the marrow in her bones as she nodded off.

《 》

IRIS ORBIT

Unak approached the chambers of The Spark. He put his hand on the panel that controlled the door and took in a deep breath. He exhaled in a controlled and purposefully slow manner to better center his mind. He then opened the door and walked in. The Spark was alone in meditation as usual.

"Unak, I take it you are pleased with the outcomes which just transpired."

"Your Light shines brightly as always to show us the Way. We are moving in the right direction."

"Yet you are still troubled?"

Unak bowed his head. "As you know the waterfall swept away the evidence but it does not change what happened. I witnessed it, thankfully the Light kept me from the fray or I would not be here to discuss this with you.

How long till our enemies get a hold of this Upright or she herself turns into an enemy."

"You mentioned the waterfall sweeping away the evidence and you staying clear of danger. Tell me, do you think these were chance occurrences?"

Unak raised his eyes to The Spark with hopeful awe. "Are you saying you had a hand in them?"

"Not directly. But when the course of life is set properly, occurrences such as the one you mentioned work themselves to a proper resolution."

"What about the Twin Flames on Baabcrest who are no more?"

"Their choice for believing they were invincible. I hope those who know of their unfortunate fate will be more prudent."

"When you made us a Twin Flame you promised us immortality."

"Which is different than invincibility. I trust you now understand the difference."

"I warned you about her before this happened. Even her very existence could shake the faith of this system in you. Even the faith of other Twin Flames. She could bring us all down!"

The Spark seemed to somehow shift but Unak couldn't put his finger on exactly how. "Unlikely but that is the price of free will."

"We must destroy her and the darkness that she brings."

"And what does that bring us? One less Upright? Do you think she is the only danger that has ever threatened the Light?"

Unak bowed his head. "No. But she may be the most dangerous."

"The darkness grows darker so the Light can grow brighter."

Unak abruptly raised his head. "Then you say she serves a purpose?"

"I say her purpose remains to be decided by the Light."

"I didn't mean to presume on your radiance."

"I know this."

"May your Light forever shine on all of us." Unak took a deep bow and left.

《 》

UNAK RETURNED TO HIS quarters on Iris. Sitting on his silken rug in meditation he tried to suppress the questions that raced through his mind, as he had been taught even before he became a Twin Flame all those gremrevs ago. For the first time, he could remember, it was not working. *Was The Spark being foolish? Was The Spark even capable of foolishness?*

It then suddenly hit Unak as if he had smacked into a stone wall. Just as The Spark allowed the various Orbits to realize it was better for the Light to lead, so too did The Spark want Unak to realize his purpose within the Light. Unak now felt relieved. The Spark could not directly act to extract this Upright and calm the quivers she sent through the Light of the system for Unak now realized it would not be enough to simply take or destroy her. She is far too powerful. She must be wiped from any desire of the seditious elements. *I'm an instrument in the cleansing. The Spark saw too much Light but I have known darkness for over two gremrevs, while I was undercover, so I can move amongst it better. It's up to me to find a way to make sure the dark forces coalescing around this Upright remain neutralized. That was, after all, my original assignment. To ensure the darkness which still resides in this system never threatens the Light. Why should I assume my mission is over?* He arose and strode out of his chamber with renewed determination in his step. He had found he still had lessons in Light to learn but he would not shirk those lessons any longer. His unique abilities were just what was called for in this unique situation.

《 》

OROGUNU ORBIT

Micah followed the crowd along the gravel path. The anxiety was palpable in the air as the Uprights around him whispered to each other. They swapped harrowing stories of attacks from the Breathless with one another as they walked. He only heard bits and pieces but hoped those parts which were heard were exaggerated. He was glad to be on Orogunu where Uprights lived in communal homes. The camaraderie of this Orbit which he was told about in the Prep Center held true. It helped one feel less alone even though nobody knew exactly what was going on or what to do. That's why they were having this open forum.

He entered the plain building painted all white which served as an all-purpose center for the surrounding community. There was a long table at the back with a sign-in sheet and some recently picked produce from the farms, as well as some freshly pressed juice. He fixed a small plate in the hopes of using the food to calm the nerves.

He spotted some Uprights from home. One of them was waving his hand wildly to call attention to himself. "Hey, over here we saved you a seat!"

He hurried over to join them. Not a moment too soon either. As soon as his buttocks made contact with the chair an Upright strolled onto the raised platform in the center of the room and made her way to the podium. She had much makeup on but Micah could still tell it was a plain oval face underneath it all. Her black hair was pulled tightly back in a bun and she wore a fine navy suit with modest frills at the shoulders.

"Thank you all for coming," she began. You could hear the shuffles and squeaks as the last Uprights settled in for the discussion.

"We have a lot to talk about so let's get started," continued the speaker. "As I am sure all of you are now aware a new life form has become prolific throughout the system." The screen behind her suddenly became illuminated with a picture of Leon's creation. Audible gasps erupted amongst the gathered assembly. To many, including Micah, no matter how many times they had seen them the sight of a Breathless still inspired terror.

The speaker paused for a moment to allow the room to resettle before she continued. "Our top scientists have determined that these Non-upright's most likely traveled as eggs from somewhere beyond the system and attached themselves to ships. When these ships reached atmospheric conditions the eggs hatched and they preyed on the occupants of that Orbit, both Uprights and Nons."

Murmurs erupted again. It was hard to believe life forms existed outside the system. However, if this was a sampling of what existed outside the sight of Iris it was a good thing no one ventured there. An Upright who stood by the table of food shouted, "I thought Comqwo monitored what came into the system to ensure we were never threatened?"

The speaker smoothed her coarse black hair. "They can't be expected to pick up everything that comes from beyond the system." The image changed behind her to a diagram showing a graphic of the entire system with a thick bright red line through it. "However, as I am sure we are all aware here, all freight travels on specified routes within tight boundaries of the system. Only dark market smugglers and pirates travel outside the area you see here outlined in red. It is strongly believed for this reason that pirates and smugglers brought the Breathless to our system. Considering how many Breathless there are, many ships must have traveled through a cluster of their eggs. Normal commerce would have detected this and notified the proper authorities." A hushed murmur crept into the gathered crowd once more. "In response Circapto, along with several other Orbits, made a presentation to The Spark to show that we in the system now understand piracy and smuggling is not just a distracting vice but an Obstruction to the Light. The Spark agreed and all resources including the Twin Flames are now being utilized to route out this Obstruction."

The crowd flashed their pocket lights in support of this announcement. Micah joined with enthusiasm. Since Orogunu was one of the hardest hit Orbits by piracy this was especially welcomed news for them. It was a relief to know that there would be limited cycles left with piracy and smuggling in this system. He remembered from history lessons how quickly something disappears when deemed an Obstruction. Nobody wants even an indirect connection with an Obstruction and the work of the Twin Flames is without failure when they unite in an effort.

The speaker waited passively for the excited murmurs to die down before she continued. "The freight companies, as well as leisure travel businesses, have been working with Twin Flames to ensure all inter-Orbit ships are thoroughly inspected and meet stringent guidelines. This will ensure they carry no Breathless. Comqwo's warriors have been tapped by the largest security firm on Circapto to capture or eliminate every last pirate and smuggler in the system. A significant decline has already been seen."

A stout Upright in the front row stood up. Micah noticed her face appeared tired and flushed. "This is all bright news but what of the creatures already out and about? I just heard of a sighting two cycles ago and not more than 50 kilometers from the northern edge of my farm."

"Twin Flames due to their immortality will be hunting these things down. They have been equipped with the latest weaponry being developed on Circapto."

"Lasers don't work on these abominations!" Micah couldn't see where the owner of the voice came from who yelled this.

"That's been found to be the case. Sonic weaponry does seem to have some effect. Fortunately, since Circapto uses sonic scanners they have been able to adapt this technology. That being said, it only works when aimed at certain locations and is only lethal when right on top of them. This is why it has been ordered that you do not engage them. If you think one is close by you are to get away and contact the guardians so they can cordon off the area for the Twin Flames."

An Upright in the back called out, "But what if it escapes?"

"No one will know if it's there if you are dead, dear."

A tall hairless Upright stood up in Micah's row. "I heard that renegade cultist is also being hunted by the Twin Flames. Aren't the Breathless the more pressing issue?"

"It is their number one concern but Daleth is also dangerous darkness. Consider him on par with the Breathless."

Shivers ran down Micah's spine at the name Daleth. He remembered the Prep Center lesson on The Followers of Vuhox. A bloodthirsty religious sect whose aim was to not only overthrow all the governments of the system but also The Spark as well. It was based on the ancient ravings of some self-appointed Pupil from Washa. The most ruthless member they produced was Daleth who slaughtered the whole lot of them. He was said to be a hero for removing them but nobody ever trusted him fully.

Micah wanted to ask if they could organize a watch party or something such as that to keep each other safe. Being so fresh out of the Prep Center it still felt weird to speak up at these kinds of gatherings. But no one else seemed to be bringing it up and it seemed like such an obvious idea to him. *Why shouldn't we look out for one another?*

His stomach churned with nerves and in another moment he stood amongst the crowd. But blood-curdling screams drowned out Micah's words. He saw Breathless coming through every access point. They slashed and chomped the panic-stricken Uprights who were running every which way.

Micah's brain seemed to shut down as the creatures grew closer. It didn't seem quite real for some reason. Their carnage was unlike anything Micah had witnessed before. Even more so than the grainy stock footage of the great wars before The Spark, which was shown in the Prep Center. A passing Breathless seemed to almost absent mindlessly slash Micah's abdomen with their dreaded claws.

Micah felt no pain as he lay on the floor bleeding out. No wetness, cold, or warmth was felt either. Emotionally speaking he did not feel fearful or sad. The only sensation Micah could detect was resentment. An intense resentment for having lived such a short life with no memories made of anything talked about in the Prep Center.

⟨ ⟩

EBJAN ORBIT

Both of Ebjan's moons were full. They cast what light they could into the darkness of Sophia's office. Sophia, a slender Upright with black patterns tattooed all over her skin, sat at her desk looking over her ledger's latest entries. The profits of her business had been increasing recently. The growing chaos from the population issues caused more Uprights to seek out her services. It always made her smile how much Uprights talked of the Light while running to the darkness when things got a little rough. Her illicit services are what comforted them, not the Light. However, recently her business was running into problems finding people to move merchandise. She needed to find the cause and fast.

The study of her recent losses was interrupted by one of her employees knocking at her door. "Come in." Her voice was velvety but measured as she always made sure it was when dealing with her subordinates. It made them unsure of where they stood with her. Exactly how she wanted them to feel.

A burly Upright with thin lips and thick jowls entered her office. "Speak," she commanded him.

"The majority of our freelance distribution associates have not responded to our attempts at contact."

"That's been the situation since Grevolios. Why do you come here if you don't bring me new information?"

"I do have something new."

"Then don't waste my time. Out with it."

"Although Gimeld has not made contact directly we have reliable information that his ship crashed on Circapto and a Breathless emerged from the wreckage."

Sophia leaned back in her chair. "So my theory was correct. The disappearance of the pirates has to do with the appearance of the Breathless."

"It would seem."

Sophia turned her chair to gaze at the dual moons outside her window. "So these Non-uprights show up while my freelance smugglers disappear. In the blink of an eye, pirates are declared an Obstruction." Sophia turned herself back to face her underling. "It fits too nicely to be an accident. Someone targeted us."

"You think it was The Spark."

"Doubtful. Most likely it was either the Order or the House playing some desperate game and using us as pawns to get at The Spark."

Sophia's employee furrowed his brow. "You think so? I mean the House uses us often enough. Why strike against us?"

"You question my judgment?"

He bowed his head and tried to steady his voice as he responded, "Of course not."

"This is why I lead. Because it takes a certain mind to understand the ways of power. You don't need to know the specifics just see the patterns. Someone or some group is always in power. Other individuals or groups seek to topple whoever that be. But only fools make frontal assaults, for those are easily deflected. Tell me have we heard from our friend Lorelei?"

The subordinate shook his head. "We have tried to locate her but she seems to have disappeared without a trace."

"That is no accident. That fits into all of this." Sophia stood. "I believe it's time we paid a little visit to her home."

《 》

BAABCREST ORBIT

Corry felt like she had swallowed rocks when she saw the beacon light up. She left the agreed-upon signal for the others and forced her legs to carry her to the rendezvous point. Corry had heard about an altercation between Daleth and guardians on the Great Band. She had hoped Daleth had attempted to reach her but fled due to the guardians. The thought of him stirred something deep within her that she found unsettling even though he would most likely bring salvation with him. Still, something about him shook her to her core. Her inability to pinpoint why Daleth had this effect on her made it sharper somehow.

Corry reached the designated meeting spot she and the others in her Cell agreed upon if Daleth showed. Since it was tucked in a crevice of one building and the flat wall of another it cast long deep shadows. Even though such a secluded spot was necessary for discretion it made Corry more uneasy. She waited using her training to keep her patience. What seemed like an entire gremrev passed but there was no sign of him or a ship for that matter. She tapped her foot on the ground as she tried to determine how long to wait. She turned around to leave and find Tania when she suddenly felt a vice grip around the upper portion of her throat. Only the tips of her feet touched the ground. She found her face centimeters away from Daleth.

"So," he snarled. "It was a setup after all."

"No set up," Corry stammered. "The payment is yours just give me the target."

"Then why was I attacked when I arrived here? I had to ditch the ship in the middle of nowhere on this forsaken rock."

Armonia appeared out of the shadows and said, "Yeah ya made me kill more people. I don't like killing people but they were gonna kill us."

Daleth whipped his head toward Armonia. "Shut up! Didn't I tell you to stay out of sight!"

Armonia rolled her eyes. "Like I listen to anything ya tell me."

Lorelei walked out of the shadows. "Sorry, she's quick. You mine as well lay it all out."

"It was a setup. There's nothing to lay out or do but gut this backstabber and leave.

Corry raised her hands. "There was no deceit on my part. You were attacked because The Spark declared you an Obstruction."

Lorelei's mouth went dry. "What?"

"They know," murmured Armonia.

Daleth lowered Corry to the ground and released her throat. "Obstructions aren't individuals. At least die bravely instead of with the cowardice of deception."

"I do not fear death but I do admit I fear you for some reason."

"I know. I'm feeding off it. It's the only reason you still breathe."

"They declared all pirates and smugglers an Obstruction but they singled you out for the murder of that guardian on Ebjan."

"Why did they declare all pirates and smugglers an Obstruction?" Lorelei asked.

"On account of the Breathless. Haven't you three seen any media coverage of the system in the past several cycles? Those ravenous creatures are terrorizing every Orbit. All the Orbits just gave over all their authority to The Spark and Twin Flames." Corry pointed at Armonia. "That's why the experiment is our only hope now."

Lorelei felt her body cinch up at this latest piece of news. "Because of what she can dream," Lorelei stated almost to herself. "But even so if all has been given to The Spark it may not matter."

"What are you talking about dreaming for? Do you think the Order cares about that old barbaric ritual? Her mind can see into other dimensions. She can use it to navigate trans-dimensional travel."

"I have fed plenty and had enough of this foolish talk." Daleth unsheathed his trikilldo. He was about to bring it down on Corry who stood her ground but Lorelei halted his arm.

"Wait I wanna hear more," Daleth grunted in disapproval and lowered his arm. Lorelei turned to Corry. "Trans-dimensional travel doesn't exist."

"That's what we are told but it's not true. The Order managed to uncover secret files that detail the creation of a trans-dimensional drive and its testing shortly after The Spark's arrival."

"The Spark got rid of it, right?" Armonia interjected.

Corry nodded. "It was declared other dimensions are much too far from the light of Iris to be safe. The Spark pointed toward the fact the tests showed although travel could be done navigation was unreliable. A firm on Circapto managed to construct and save two such drives in case they held other technological benefits. They store them secretly that's how the information was first discovered. The Order's founders determined navigation problems were because no computer could match the mind so it was up to the mind to navigate. That is its unfettered potential. We planned to develop our minds to reach that potential, it's the whole point of the Order."

"That's why those that started the Followers of Vuhox came from the Order they had decided to not flee but stand their ground."

Corry's face soured at Lorelei bringing up the Followers. "They were impatient disgraceful space dust who understood nothing. Good riddance to them."

"Agreed and the same could be said for you." Daleth raised his trikilldo once more but Armonia came between him and Corry.

"Does that mean I was a member of this Order you're going on about?"

"No. When the riots started we knew we had to speed things up with unconventional methods. You were a nobody on Circapto who was strung out on Niorpyn. The perfect test subject."

"Indeed, until you left us and disappeared." Everyone turned to see Tania appear on the scene with Ramek and Florian in tow.

"You were worthless gutter trash so we made something worthwhile out of you," Florian added.

Lorelei and Daleth noticed Armonia's body slump at this revelation. Florian then shifted his eyes to meet Daleth's. "I suppose it fitting it took one useless piece of trash to find another."

Daleth drove the trikilldo straight through Florian's throat. Blood gushed everywhere. It happened so quickly and brutally no one could react for several moments. Daleth pulled the trikilldo out taking Florian's tongue with it. Corry looked down at the blood pooling around Florian's corpse and to her surprise felt no great loss. Her training was so complete and so thorough that she felt nothing but a slight twinge of regret for not feeling more. *Why then do I react to Daleth?* Corry wondered.

Tania and Ramek produced laser guns which they trained on Daleth. "I'm not leaving without compensation. Give me what I'm owed or I'll scoop those brains that are so precious to you right out of your skulls. Do you honestly think those lasers intimidate one such as me?"

"Probably not but they intimidate your companions I'm sure." They moved their laser's aim to Lorelei and Armonia. Lorelei stepped in front of Armonia who was in a state of shock from the sudden carnage Daleth had unleashed.

"Touching," Ramek mocked.

"This isn't necessary," Corry protested. "Just give him the money and he'll go."

"She's right they mean nothing to me."

"Don't bluff an Order member. Why else would you have dallied with them for so long before coming here."

"Ship complications. You'd do better to pay me off."

"We can give him some of the ship-building funds and just steal the drive," Corry pleaded.

"This is simpler and the simplest way is always the best," Tania admonished.

"Plus it's the principle of the matter," added Ramek.

"Now Daleth make your choice. I suggest it's to walk away.

"You won't shoot Armonia. You need her. Wasn't that what this was all about?"

"Your other companion did us the favor of shielding her for us. She, however, will lose her life. The shock of loss will interfere with your shielding allowing us to end your life as well."

"I'm warning you that your assessment of our relation is incorrect."

"And I warned you not to bluff. We Order members are adept at nonverbal cues."

Daleth reached for his pouch of crystals at the same time Tania and Ramek fired their lasers. The beams struck Lorelei who fell to the ground as the concentrated energy went through her skin and ruptured organs as well as burned away muscle tissue and nerves. The lasers were certainly a deadlier brand than the ones carried by the guardians, probably purchased off the dark trade. At the same time, two of Daleth's crystals flew out of his hand past Tania and Ramek, they then came to an abrupt stop in midair and reversed direction. They flew right through the napes of their necks and up into the cerebellum of Tania and Ramek before returning to Daleth. With their exalted brains jolted at the most crucial point the rest of their body could not get off a second shot. It wouldn't have mattered anyway for Daleth shielded himself in precaution. The two Order members fell to the ground unable to make any movement before Daleth drove his trikilldo into the underside of each of their skulls to ensure their lives were ended.

Corry stared at their now lifeless bodies and once again took note of her detachment even to Ramek. Her training was very sound. *Why then does Daleth evoke such a sensation?* It surely was not some sentimental attachment, she knew that much.

Corry's pondering gave way to an incomprehension as Lorelei rose, wounds closed up underneath the remains of her blouse. "You're a Twin?"

"Yes. I defected over a gremrev ago."

Daleth nudged one of the bodies with his boot and muttered, "Dimwads." He turned to Corry. "The only way you're going to avoid joining them is with a substantial amount of halos."

"Have you not been listening?" Lorelei shrieked. "There's a trans-dimensional drive out there! You can steal it and finally escape."

"I thought you were intent on destroying The Spark."

Lorelei looked away. "How is that possible anymore?"

Daleth's eyes narrowed. "Oh no. You're not tricking me into joining you on any more of your crusade. This is where I get off." Daleth glared at Corry. "Halos now or your death."

"I don't have any. I wasn't the Cell leader. That was Tania who you just killed. For security reasons such as this she was the only one with access."

The vein in Daleth's neck bulged, and his eyes grew wide and menacing. He moved toward Corry with trikilldo gripped tightly but was prevented by Lorelei once again. "She knows where the trans-dimensional drives are. You don't need halos anymore. You know what a smart move is and getting her to take us to the drive is a smart move. With Armonia's ability to defeat Twin Flames and your talents we can get it easily."

"Did I discern your words correctly? You claim the experiment can kill Twin Flames."

"I have a name ya know. Armonia. And yea. When I hold his crystals for some reason I do. But I'm not like him," muttered Armonia as she stared at the corpses.

"If this is a truth you speak then you will not have to make me do anything. I will gladly bring you to the secret location of the drives for this new revelation makes all things possible."

"I just killed your brethren, why would you aid us?"

"Emotions can cloud good judgment. We Order members must follow rational thought at all times. Although I will miss them, circumstances both grand and small call for us to work together against a common enemy who is far more powerful than us."

Armonia looked far off at the ground and her head swayed. "You have no idea."

"Shut up!" Daleth snapped.

"Take ya dagger and shove it somewhere!" Kristal punctuated Armonia's retort by sticking her head out of the armband and giving a hiss."

Corry's countenance became perplexed. "What did the experiment mean by insinuating I have underestimated the Twin Flames and The Spark?"

"Never mind that," said Lorelei. "Just get us to those drives and I'll make sure Daleth doesn't make you join the rest of your Cell."

"You can't control me."

"No, but I know you looked for a way out all your life. You killing her will just leave you a fugitive with nothing. If you took us to Circapto you'd be a fugitive with a way out. Think about it."

Daleth narrowed his eyes. "Don't presume to know me."

"But I do."

He turned with such gusto that his cloak flared up. "Let's go."

⟨ ⟩

EBJAN ORBIT

Lorelei's tiny squatter den sat empty in the dark. It had grown slightly dustier but otherwise unchanged since that faithful night Daleth and Armonia climbed through her window. The tranquil atmosphere was shattered by the door being kicked open and two gruff hulking Uprights barging inside. They quickly began to toss the place, the mattress was flipped, and the crates Lorelei used as tables were smashed. The chaotic destruction then ceased just as quickly as it began. Sophia strolled into the room from her perch at the doorway where she had observed the melee with an intense eye. "No trace of her, Sophia," said one of her underlings.

Sophia flashed a wicked smile. "She hasn't been here for some time, the clever trickster. You two would know that if you were anything besides brawn."

"Then why did you have us wreck the place?"

"To send a message to anyone who associated with her."

"Are you sure she had something to do with pirates and smugglers being declared an Obstruction, Sophia? I mean wasn't it on account of the Breathless?" The other underling asked.

Sophia shoved one of her artificially serrated fingernails up his nostril. He yelped in pain. "Are you questioning me?" As Sophia asked this she twisted her finger and the stream of blood dribbling from the nostril increased.

The Upright winced. "I'm just trying to understand."

Sophia pulled her finger down and out of the man's nose. He cupped his hands over his face to catch the blood. Sophia walked around the apartment as she talked. "There's no need for you to understand since I'm the one in charge. One of the many reasons I'm in charge is that I don't believe in coincidences. The fact she disappeared so soon before the declaration means something."

Sophia peered down at the mattress and noticed a slit on the underside. Another wicked smile flashed across her face. She plunged a hand into the slit. She pulled out a bag of Niorpyn, no doubt from one of her shipments but not enough to be worth cheating her for. She tossed the bag to one of her underlings. "Hold this." She then shoved her hand back in. It curled around something cylindrical and she yanked it out. It appeared to be an ordinary candle but from the scent, Sophia could tell it was made from the secretions of Asikis, a type of insect found on Baabcrest. The candle answered Sophia's question about the Niorpyn. Both items were commonly used to enhance dreaming states. Sophia knew Lorelei dabbled in darkness market dreaming in addition to her jobs for Sophia but giving people unauthorized dreaming and taking it so seriously as to use these tools were two completely different matters.

The candle now released from Sophia's grip made a dull bang on the floor. Once more she reached inside the mattress this time fairly certain what she would find. She felt a glass vial, no doubt containing essential oil from the omnoberry bush. She didn't bother to pull it out but continued to rifle through the contents of the mattress. Her hands next felt straps. All of this left no doubt that Lorelei did more than dabble in illicit dreaming for extra halos. When her finger grazed the edge of paper, she knew she found what would confirm Lorelei's true allegiance. She pulled out a leather-bound journal. She ran her lethal fingernails over the etching of two humps intertwined with a circular curl in the middle. A dream journal, the calling card of the House of Yowgn.

Sophia didn't need to probe through the other dreaming paraphernalia she was sure to find in that mattress, she had what she needed. She knew now who had crossed her in their attempt to topple The Spark. Luckily, she was no stranger to the practices of the House of Yowgn herself. Sophia was prudent enough to search out any edge she may be able to utilize no matter how fringe. Those who were highly skilled members of the House could send messages through their dream. She knew how to do an almost reverse of that procedure. It would be difficult but with Lorelei's dreaming journal she should eventually be able to pick up her dreaming signature whether she was still dreaming or not.

"I knew there was always something off about that one," she whispered. "Let's go," she barked at her underlings.

Chapter 8

EBJAN ORBIT

Zean looked out the window of her office which was several meters above the ground. She was about midway up one of the taller buildings on Ebjan. The structures on Ebjan always had such care put into them. Great polished stone walls and large window panes. Modest buildings but still impressive. Of course, no building on Ebjan could compare to the towering hollow mountains which filled Circapto. Still, Zean found herself high enough to see the many people going about their various activities on the streets below as a kaleidoscope in constant motion. She had always adored that toy during her Prep Center days. To see how things shifted about in seeming chaos only to snap into place to form something beautiful. Perhaps it was why she went into government. So she could ensure the chaos snapped into place.

The system was certainly in chaos right now. Even though her duties were diminishing as the Twin Flames assumed control, it is the greatest testament of a leader to know when to defer to one who knows better. She will not let down those people in the streets below.

Zean's assistant poked his head into the office. "There's a Twin Flame here to see you but he is without an appointment."

"If he's a Twin Flame he needs no appointment. Send him in without delay."

Zean's assistant opened the door wide. Unak fully decked out in the glistening white ceremonial robes of the Twin Flame stepped across the threshold confidently. "Look deeper," he greeted. Zean's assistant left the two alone and closed the door behind him.

"It's an honor. Why do you grace me with your presence?" Zean couldn't help but lower her head when she addressed him.

"I am called Unak. I was unable to attend the first convention you spoke at but heard many great things from my colleagues. I was in attendance at the second convention you spoke at and was thoroughly impressed. I also sat in on your presentation for Obstruction and admired it."

"You flatter me but I'm afraid I'm not worthy of your praise."

Unak strolled around the office and picked up a picture of Jamila and Zean on a shelf. "Modesty is a sign of the Light. You must be nearing a Union. Tell me is this you with your reflection?"

"Yes. She helps me see more of me, I help her see more of her."

"You will make a potent Twin Flame when the time comes."

"If it ever comes."

Unak put the picture back and came to Zean's desk. He leaned over it propping himself up on his massive arms. "We are both entities of the Light. Have faith in the Light. Darkness does not squelch out Light, instead, Light seeks out the darkness to overcome it."

Zean fully lowered her head now and squeezed her eyes shut. "Thank you for reminding me of that teaching from The Spark."

"Do you believe it?"

Zean's eyes flew open and her head snapped back up. "Of course. With every fiber of my being."

Unak gave a quick tight nod of his chin as he stood erect once more. "Good. Because some darkness needs Light shone on it and I think the two of us are just the ones to do it.

"Surely another Twin Flame rather than I is better suited."

"Alas, we Twin Flames have grown somewhat distant from the darkness of this system, what with us spending all our time on Iris or in Temples. But you, on the other hand, have not turned a blind eye to it. Isn't that why you dared to acknowledge, that despite being given a chance to seek Light, Daleth still wallows and abuses the ways of the misguided cult which was known as The Followers of Vuhox?"

"I did what I thought was right."

"You saw darkness others ignored and you took action," Unak said with a flourish of his hands. "Are you still prepared to take action even if the darkness is worse than you could imagine?" A crease of concern formed on Zean's forehead. Unak took note of it and continued. "Daleth is conspiring with the House of Yowgn to wreak havoc on this system. The roots of this plan are right here in this Orbit."

"The Spark must be made aware of this," said Zean with haste.

"The Spark is aware and hence I am here to thwart Daleth and his schemes. The proclamation that you spurred on was very timely indeed."

"What is Daleth's plan? What can I do to help you stop him?"

"His plan is complex. We haven't been able to parse it all out as of yet but we do believe he will eventually end up on Circapto in a violent attempt to gain control of some very sensitive technology."

"If he's after something on Circapto then why do you need me."

"I need you to help me locate two citizens of Ebjan who are co-conspirators of his. I was undercover with them for a time to bring them to the Light. Unfortunately, Daleth not only deterred me, but he also exposed me. I can no longer approach them for they know the Light I pose but a High Councilor may have more luck." Unak paused here. He placed a hand on Zean's arm and looked deeply into her eyes. "The Light is calling you to action."

Zean glanced out her window at the Uprights who passed by depending on leaders like her to keep them safe and show the path to the Light. She would be a disgrace to her office if she refused to help a Twin Flame. She would never be able to look Jamila in the eyes again. She shifted her attention back to Unak with a mask of determination and courage on her face. "You can count on me to see this to the end no matter what lays ahead." Unak smiled.

《 》

INTER-ORBIT SPACE

Lorelei, now wearing a new intact top that hung loosely above her midsection, walked onto the bridge of the ship Corry had gotten them onto. "Good thing the last Magistrate of Knowledge who used this inquiry ship forgot to take all their wardrobe. And they had good taste underneath that robe."

"What are you doing here?" Daleth barked from the pilot's seat.

"I came to check up on you!"

"Don't leave Armonia alone with that Order stooge."

"What's she gonna do? Besides Armonia can take care of herself."

"Please. She has the mind of a child." Daleth sprung up from his seat. "Do I have to do everything?" He slammed his fist on the console and stormed off the bridge. Lorelei rolled her eyes and followed.

⟨ ⟩

CORRY SAT ACROSS FROM Armonia on one of the benches which lined the open interior of the ship. She stared at her so intensely Armonia couldn't tell if she was attempting to see the wall behind her. She slid down the bench but Corry's eye's followed. Kristal stuck her head out of the band on Armonia's arm and hissed.

"Is that a serposa?" Corry inquired.

"Yeah. And she doesn't like ya staring at us."

"I'm trying to figure out how one such as you is capable of terminating Twin Flames."

"When ya figure it out be sure and let me know, ya hear."

The buzz of a door sliding open was quickly followed by the stomp of Daleth's boots. Lorelei scrambled to get in front of him. "Don't kill her. We still need her."

"You still need her. I don't need anybody. And I wasn't going to kill her. But she needs to know I don't trust her."

"Then listen to her heartbeat as you do with me."

"Order members are difficult to detect because of our level of control over ourselves."

Daleth lowered his face in front of Corry's. "If I get even the tiniest inclination you are trying anything I will open up your skull and scoop out that organ your kind likes to worship."

"Did you shake our pursuers?" Corry asked seemingly unbothered.

"Of course I did." Daleth straightened himself once more but continued to train his gaze on Corry.

"Will you be able to evade the security on Circapto?"

"Of course, but it's going to get rocky."

"I don't wanna go back to Circapto," Armonia whined.

Lorelei sat next to Armonia and made her lie down with her head in her lap. "I know darling but this drive might be the best way to fix you and it's the only way to escape The Spark."

"You're right about the latter but not about the former," Corry began. "There's no fixing her. Her brain development was too aggressive, her mind too simple. The advancements are all that keep her body intact as it is. Why do you think we resorted to such drastic measures as Daleth? She will not exist for all that much longer."

"Shut up!" Shouted the other three in unison.

Lorelei ran her hand through Armonia's hair. "Don't listen to her. If the drive is being kept on Circapto they will have full specs on it. One of my Origin Flames was a scientist. We'll use the information about the drive to save you once we're clear of the system. The answer is out there. And we'll dream together before we reach Circapto so you don't freak out."

Corry rolled her eyes so far backer pupils nearly disappeared. She shook her head and turned to look at the view screen with a disgusted grunt. "Oh, will you look at the view of Ebjan? I believe it's the most beautiful Orbit with all its varied seas and terrestrial terrain. Certainly much better than my Origin Orbit of Fimeger."

"Didn't I tell you to stop talking?" Daleth's voice was like ice and his hand moved toward his trikilldo.

"I wouldn't mention the F Orbit around him," Lorelei warned. "At least not till we reach the drives."

"Bad experience there?" With a wry smile, Corry added, "Forgive me but it's part of my nature to inquire."

"Lorelei told me it's his Origin Orbit and he hates it."

"You should all stop talking. Now."

Armonia raised her head slightly from Lorelei's lap. "If you don't like it, go back to flying the ship."

The room grew tense as Armonia and Daleth stared each other down. Daleth eventually broke the stare and left. As he sat down at the control panel his mind wandered back to Fimeger, despite his efforts.

⟨ ⟩

FIMEGER ORBIT

Daleth had been out of the Prep Center for almost a fifth of a gremrev already. He worked maintaining the grounds at one of the community gardens. Although there were others who he worked with, he preferred the company of the plants. He certainly felt society's pressure to find a reflection and begin his path toward Twin Flame status but it irritated him rather than motivated him. The Light had never felt right to him. The more time he spent living the less anything felt right.

He wasn't sure whether he avoided Uprights because they avoided him or vice versa but whatever the start of it was, he now found himself a loner. Those rarities who did speak to him conjured a strong repugnance in him. The reason Daleth could never put his finger on but the lack of identifiable cause made it no less forceful.

Often he would take what meager halos were left after paying for necessities in life down to the local tavern. He despised the taste of the drinks they served. They grated his tongue. He remembered learning in the Prep Center they used to be somewhat poisonous and would act similar to Niorpyn.

Niorpyn was a synthetic mix of poisons that simulated the experience of dying and temporarily heightened your other senses. Officially Niorpyn was only supposed to be used in the final Twin Flame ceremony under the direct supervision of The Spark. But since the effect of other intoxicants once used by Uprights before The Spark became null, Niorpyn became prolific in the darkness trade.

The drinks were not as potent as Niorpyn. Uprights before The Spark would drink these toxic drinks often to feel good or drown their woes. Now he wasn't sure why people still drank them, seeing as how every Upright was immune to poison. Maybe they secretly sprinkled Niorpyn in them. Maybe it was just habit. He wasn't even sure why he drank them. Maybe the bitter shock to his taste buds made him feel more alive, maybe it was just an excuse to silently sit unnoticed amongst others, or maybe he needed habit too.

Often during these times at the tavern, Daleth would hear tales of hunts in the Outlands, the uncivilized places of Fimeger where ancient beasts still roamed. Before Uprights came to Fimeger it was full of some of the nastiest and most vicious Non-uprights ever encountered. For Fimeger to be settled by the civilized, brave Uprights had to hunt down and kill the creatures. It was a war between Upright and Non-upright. The Uprights of course won. The Gremoilion Empire even eventually moved their seat of power to Fimeger as a show of dominance. This of course backfired and Gremoilio split from the Empire. Still, Fimeger liked to brag even after all this time. There were many lessons in the Prep Center recounting tales of Fimeger's history and the heroic pioneers who allowed the Orbit to be settled.

Citizens of Fimeger still went into the few untamed sections to prove their valor and worth by killing one of the surviving beasts who remained. The tales were most likely embellished but Daleth couldn't help but notice the gleam of confidence in the eyes of those who told these tales of heroism. They surely no longer doubted themselves or their place in life.

Daleth always returned to the dingy basement he called home with the recounted tales on a loop in his mind. One restless night he lay in the dark thinking long and hard about those who hunted in the Outlands. He wanted to be like those in the tavern, someone who knew who he was. Daleth decided to skip the tavern for a while and saved up his halos for what he needed to hunt in the Outlands.

He bought a fanger, an essential weapon for the Outlands. Fangers consisted of a hollowed-out metal shaft with three sharp curved blades coming off one end. There was another straight blade inside the shaft which was serrated on both sides. By twisting the handle the interior blade sprung out in the middle of the other blades. The three curved blades were meant to trap and hold a Non-upright while the middle blade sprung out to pierce the Non-upright so it would bleed out. The instrument of death was inspired by the jaws of certain Non-upright predators, which like the fanger served two purposes as well, to hold and to kill.

Daleth practiced with it in the dim light of his basement abode. He was surprised at how natural it felt to use. He took it as a sign that he was on the right track.

Eventually, the cycle came when he hired some guides and set out into the Outlands. The guides were there simply to aid him in navigating the rugged landscape and help him locate a Non-upright. The actual confrontation would be his alone.

It did not take long for them to stumble onto the tracks of a bimbleboar. They followed the trail until they spotted the Non-upright digging in the dirt, no doubt creating a burrow. When the beast caught wind of them he spun to face them, a sharp gurgle rose in the creature's throat. His hair stood up and he scratched his front hoof across the ground. He lowered his head to point his curled horns at them. His bushy tail gave a flick before he charged. The guides moved away. This life-and-death contest would purely be between Daleth and the bimbleboar.

Daleth jabbed his fanger at the bimbleboar and he skittered on his squatty legs to avoid it. He then turned his elongated neck and clamped down on the weapon with his jaw. Daleth gripped the shaft with a hand on either side of the beast's mouth and wrenched the weapon so hard one of the bimbleboar's tusks caught his hand and it bled. Daleth unfazed by his opponent drawing first blood drove the fanger toward the creature which lay stunned on the ground. A squeal rose in the air as the curved blades pressed into the bimbleboar's torso. Daleth stared down at the trapped creature. This beast was no true threat just an outsider trying to make a life out of what he could on the fringes of civilization. He looked into the dilated pupils of the bimbleboar and saw a desperation that was all too familiar. The guides waited for him to twist the handle and shouted, "loodeev". Daleth lifted the fanger. The bimbleboar wasted no time scampering off to lick his wounds. The guides yelled and complained as Daleth silently walked by them. There was nothing to be said, nothing left for him on Fimeger, maybe even the entire system. He envied the bimbleboar, for at least the bimbleboar still had a chance.

《 》

CIRCAPTO ORBIT

Gimeld and his crew made their way slowly along, zigzagging in-between buildings and sticking to the shadows where they could find them. Many of the giant view screens which hung on the artificial towers broadcast the news that their kind were now Obstructions. The crew's entire life had changed. Piracy was of course outlawed by all the Orbital governments but each had different regulations with various cracks. With the right lubricant, you could slide through those cracks. There was a necessity for temptation which the rulers knew all too well. Now they no longer had a say. Those cracks would be filled. Gimeld and those who lived their lives in those cracks would have to change how they operated if they even could still operate.

Gimeld knew all this well, but his mind was more focused on Arjan and vengeance. "How are you feeling? Why are you shaking?"

"I can't help it," Arjan weakly answered through the spasms of his muscles.

"It's from the Niorpyn withdrawal," Sil said.

Gimeld unsheathed his long dagger. "Then let's kill one of these dimwads that walk these streets. I'm sure they have some on them."

M.A.T.O. rotated his lenses. "My scanners have picked up a heightened quantity of guardian patrol skimmers in the area. Such behavior may not be prudent at this time."

"I didn't ask for an analysis."

Sil pulled a tiny pouch out of their cloak. "But he's right. Here this will help with the withdrawal." Sil tossed the tiny pouch to Arjan.

"He doesn't need more of your herbs," growled Gimeld.

"Niorpyn!" Arjan exclaimed as he greedily stuffed his nose into the small sack and snorted.

Gimeld now turned his weapon on Sil. "You skimming our shipments?"

Sil's face remained placid. "Why do you care? Your lover has been doing it forever. But no. I steal it off rival crews or purchase it when we're in port. The House and the Order use it for ceremonies. By light, even the Way uses it for the Twin Flame process. It's not hard to come by in small amounts."

"Why didn't you give it to him sooner?"

"It would have interfered with the herbs I gave him. They needed time to work, that's why he's even up and about."

"Hey!" Arjan cried. "This smells and feels different!"

"It's cut with rotav leaves from Dooga. It helps me commune with Arratup. It will still help you with your withdrawal symptoms."

"Speaking of your friend, are you sure we are heading in the right direction?"

"I know as much as you do about the ones who set us up. Arratup is leading me to something. I trust him, you don't have to."

Arjan cocked his shoulders to one side. "My someone has certainly grown a backbone since that dark trader dreamed with you."

"You brought me on board because I led you to safety during a polar shift. I told you I felt we should have stayed with Daleth and his companions. Now our ship is gone. What do you want me to say?"

Gimeld drove his dagger back into its sheath. "I wouldn't be that confident. Daleth was declared an Obstruction."

"So were we in case you missed it. There's an old Dooga sang, the mountain is lighter, the more who carry it."

"That's absurd no one can carry a mountain," said M.A.T.O.

"Whatever. Arjan, are you able to keep moving?"

"Yea, that stuff Sil gave me did help."

"Good." Gimeld touched the shadow that served as his face. "My blood lust runs deep. Lead on Sil but know whoever you lead us to will taste my wrath."

《 》

CIRCAPTO ORBIT

Circapto nearly took up the entire view screen. Daleth heard the communicator chirp something about surrender but he turned it off. His ears then picked up the whoosh of air as the door behind him slid open. Lorelei, Corry, and Armonia entered the bridge.

"What are you three doing here? I can take care of this by myself."

"Like space dust, you can. Give Armonia your crystals so she can take out any Twin Flames."

"Do I have to? I don't like killing people."

"They're gonna kill us if you don't. It's not murder, it's self-defense."

"What's the difference? I'm gonna die anyway."

"We're all gonna die eventually but if we get to that trans-dimensional drive it won't be meaningless and we might even save you. Besides, what you and Daleth saw means we're all trapped right now but we never die. You're just freeing them so they can try again."

"You're not gonna die. You're a Twin Flame," Daleth grumbled.

"Just shut up and give her your crystals."

Armonia cocked her head in consideration of Lorelie's words. "Well, alright. But can we not crash this time?"

"I don't know what strange things you are trying to tell her but if the experiment is truly capable of destroying Twin Flames what are the plans for storming Iris?"

"There aren't any. Ya can't kill The Spark anyways," said Armonia.

"The Spark is just merely an illusion used by the Twin Flames to exert their will on the dull masses."

"No, they ain't. Ya can't kill someone who's in another dimension."

"What is that supposed to mean?" asked Corry.

"Drop it the both of you!" Daleth sneered.

Lorelei quickly scrambled to a rear seat and began securing herself to it. "Buckle up everyone. Here they come. Daleth stop stalling, quickly give Armonia your crystals!"

Daleth shoved his hand into his pouch and slapped the crystals into Armonia's outstretched palm. Daleth slammed his palms on the control panel and accelerated the fusion drive. He weaved around the interceptor ships with ease. Their triangular flat shape should have allowed them to outmaneuver the oblong craft Daleth piloted but he always had sharp reflexes and Corry's unease around him gave him enough of a boost to comfortably use his reserves to raise his senses to their limits.

"I don't think those ships are piloted by Twin Flames," Armonia said as she strapped herself into the seat next to Daleth.

"Or your claims are false as I suspect them to be."

Armonia stomped her foot. "I wasn't lying!"

"Relax, I told you I can handle this. It's just too bad this ship doesn't have any weapons so I have to do this the hard way."

As Daleth weaved to and fro, he steered toward a rock about triple the size of their ship. It sat right on the edge of Circapto's volatile atmosphere. This rock served as the smallest of Circapto's sixty-seven moons.

"Uh, that's looking awfully close in the view screen and we are traveling at quite a high speed," remarked Corry.

"If I wasn't preoccupied at the moment I'd be cutting your tongue out." Daleth dodged the laser fire behind him till he practically collided the ship with the moon. At the last moment, he sharply spun the entire ship leftward into the clouds of Circapto. He did not need to glance at the rearview screen to know the ships were no longer in pursuit. The smart ones veered away while the cocky ones were destroyed by either the moon or the atmosphere. Corry, being the only one who hadn't strapped into a seat, picked herself off the floor.

"I told you to buckle up." Lorelei turned to Armonia. "Just keep trying to do whatever you do. Who knows how many Twin Flames are in this Orbital area and we won't see them coming till we get to the electromagnetic barrier."

In the dense clouds, which engulfed Circapto, visibility was low. Daleth traversed it with uncanny ease. The throttle implanted in Daleth allowed him to become one with the ship as it does for any pilot who has one. He was able to extend his keen senses to the vessel. Radar sensors were unreliable in the gas cloud due to atmospheric storms. This is why Circapto was usually entered through specific channels which were artificially kept free of storms. This was unnecessary for Daleth who could sense the storms and navigate on their fringes. This was precisely what he did so all pursuant crafts would be lost to the natural forces of Circapto.

"This is all very impressive but may I ask how we are going to land? As soon as we cross the magnetic field they will be on us. Even someone such as Daleth can't maneuver the skyline."

Lorelei motioned to the back of the ship. "We'll use the emergency pod and then disappear into the crowd."

Corry pursed her lips. "Sounds risky but it may just work. With the advent of the Breathless, Daleth should be able to feed off the crowd if we get into trouble."

"They're that scary?" Armonia asked. Corry only nodded gravely in response.

CIRCAPTO ORBIT

Gimeld and company reached a plaza that flew three flags. One had a green 'V' with a red background which symbolized the region they were in, another had a turquoise triangle and a black inverted triangle against an orange background which was the flag for Circapto, and the highest flag was black with a large ten pointed gold star emblazoned in its center. This stood for the Light shone on the system by The Spark. Behind the flags were four massive buildings, even by Circapto's standards. They were interconnected by a series of glass bridges. Each structure seemed to spiral at the top and then come to a point. Even the callous Gimeld had to give pause as they stared up at it from a darkened spot under a ledge.

"This is where Arratup wanted us to come," Sil whispered.

M.A.T.O. rotated his lenses. "By my calculations, this structure can hold approximately fifty-thousand Uprights. How will we find who is responsible for the crate which contained the deadly Non-upright?"

Gimeld took his laser in one hand and his dagger in the other. "Guess we'll just have to kill them all."

"Even I would have difficulty with that." The pirates turned and found Daleth emerging from the shadows followed by Corry, Lorelei, and Armonia. "But by all means go ahead. Whatever the outcome you will make it easier on us."

Gimeld stepped in front of his crew. "What are you doing here?"

"We're getting a trans-dimensional something or other and burning outta this prison system."

Daleth spoke out of the corner of his mouth to Lorelei. "You would have thought with all the time you two have spent together she would have learned discretion."

Gimeld gave a cold chuckle. "Your group has been played worst than us. There's no such thing as other dimensions let alone traveling them."

"There is too! That's where The Spark comes from."

"Enough Armonia," growled Daleth. "We don't need to explain ourselves to them."

But Gimeld wouldn't let it go so easily. "You knew nothing about the Orbits or The Way of The Light last time I saw you. How do you know where The Spark comes from all of a sudden?"

Armonia blurted out, "Because the last time I dreamed Daleth and I saw the entire timeline and how those beings came into our dimension and posed as The Spark so they could—mmmm." Daleth clamped his hand over Armonia's mouth.

"What did she say?" Corry's eyes were wide. Gimeld's crew all exchanged odd looks.

"We mine as well tell them everything," said Lorelei.

"We're wasting time."

"They might be able to help us," Lorelei argued.

Daleth sighed heavily and released his hand from Armonia's face. She stuck her tongue out at him and then turned to the others. "The Spark is a bunch of somebodies from another dimension. They're projecting their, I don't know, energy into ours so they can like feed off our life force or something. Anyways, it makes them stronger and us way weaker. Like you should see what we all look like on the inside."

"You can't seriously expect us to believe this?" Arjan looked to Gimeld who was surprisingly still.

"I believe it," announced Sil.

"It would explain why The Spark buried inter-dimensional travel but why make us immortal?" Corry asked.

"I'm not sure why but the special ones give them even more to feed on somehow."

Arjan pointed a finger at Corry. "Who's this new recruit of yours?"

"A member of the Order. Daleth killed her Cell so now she's coming with us," Lorelei answered.

Gimeld touched the darkness which was his face. "What you say may be true but it does not change my vengeance."

"Vengeance is a cycle, all cycles keep us imprisoned," said Daleth solemnly as he stared down at the ground. All present turned to look at him with varying degrees of surprise and confusion on their face. Daleth glanced upward to meet their stares. "Little known teaching of Vuhox."

"The one who massacred the Followers preaching their teachings makes it carry less weight," Corry stated. Armonia expected Daleth to stab Corry with his trikilldo or fling a crystal through her head. Instead, she saw a mask of frustration and hurt on Daleth's face. She remembered she had seen the same look before the first time they dreamed together.

"What exactly are you looking to avenge? Perhaps our enemies are aligned?" Lorelei asked.

Arjan put his hands on his hips. "Was a monster placed on your ship too?"

Sil explained what had happened. Gimeld punctuated the story by adding, "That monster nearly killed Arjan and destroyed my ship."

"Wait, aren't they talking about those breath thingys?"

"Indeed. It seems this little meeting is full of revelations. If what they speak is the truth then the Breathless, as they are called, weren't a mere accident but a purposeful plan."

"But by who?" Lorelei inquired. "Who was your contact?"

"We have no idea. You should know that's the standard operating procedure."

"Then why are you here ready to blow apart this building?"

Arjan nodded toward Sil. "Sil here says their old animal friend lead them here."

Corry once more spoke up. "It would stand to reason the culprit is The Spark. It did spur power being given over to the Twin Flames."

"Why would The Spark do that?" asked Armonia. "They have everything they want. They don't need to be in control."

"All seek to be in control."

"The Order would know that well," said Daleth dryly.

"Then your enemy is our enemy," Lorelei quickly chimed in.

"The Spark is not my enemy," Daleth corrected.

"Sure they are. When we dreamed that first time—."

"Silence!" Daleth bellowed with such ferocity it was one of the few times Armonia felt compelled to comply.

"Regardless, we are all here to use the trans-dimensional drive to leave the system. It's the only way to hurt The Spark. There's no life for us here anyway now that we're all Obstructions."

"According to you, they will make others to feed them," Gimeld said.

"But they won't have us to feed on anymore. What's your other option? Go in there slicing and blasting Uprights who don't even know what The Spark is doing? Daleth's right, even he wouldn't last for very long in there. You'll just die a meaningless death."

Arjan propped his laser cannon on his shoulder. "You just convincing us because you need more muscle besides Daleth."

"We got plenty of muscle. I can kill Twin Flames and she is a Twin Flame. So ha."

The pirate crew was shocked into silence by this statement.

"The drives are in that building way down below. There are even two of them if you want to split up afterward. We can do this," Lorelei pleaded. "We can leave this all behind and start over."

Arjan cocked an eyebrow. "You're really a Twin Flame? And we're supposed to trust you?"

Gimeld reached up to touch the shadow underneath his hood. He held it there for a long moment. "What's the plan?"

《 》

CIRCAPTO ORBIT

The group rode the elevator to the basement floor. Lasers and crystals had taken care of the security guards upstairs in quick order. The elevator stopped at the bottom floor, and the doors opened with Daleth and Lorelei at the front. As they expected laser blasts greeted them but Daleth's crystals and laser fire from the pirates shot out from the elevator. Armonia and Corry braced against Lorelei until it was over.

"Ya okay?"

"I'm gonna need another change of wardrobe but I'm fine. You remain the only thing which can kill a Twin Flame."

"Maybe if you dropped that stupid box you could shoot better," Gimeld sneered at M.A.T.O.

"It is important that I hold onto it."

Arjan gave an exaggerated snort. "Never knew you to be the sentimental type."

"This is not sentimentality but good sense."

Gimeld stepped out of the elevator into a bland hallway with offices and conference rooms on either side. "So we made it to the bottom floor. Where are these engines or whatever?"

"This is only the bottom floor which is public knowledge. The drives are kept at the bottom floor of the classified section."

"This thing goes deeper? Ya gotta be joking."

Lorelei's head was on a swivel. "How do we get there?"

Corry began sliding her hands along the wall at the back of the hallway which seemed oddly empty compared to the rest. "There should be a secret elevator somewhere here."

"No need to do that I will just use my infrared scanners." M.A.T.O.'s lenses rotated. A red beam shot out of the center of them. It traveled along the walls for a few moments before coming to a stop at the midway point of the back corner. "I believe it is there."

Corry ran over to where M.A.T.O. indicated. "There's a panel here but I can't get it open." Before Corry could do anything else a sharp blade pierced the wall. On the other end of the dagger was Gimeld who twisted his wrist and pried the panel open.

Corry peered at what was beyond the panel. "Looks like we need a key to open it."

"Allow me." M.A.T.O. stepped forward and extended his hand. A small section on the flat of his hand slid open and a key-like instrument popped out. "It will just take a moment for me to configure the mechanism." M.A.T.O. inserted the device and a whirring sound could be heard as he manipulated the lock plates to give him access to the control panel.

Arjan folded his arms over his chest and wore a proud smirk on his face. "Knew we kept him around for a reason." Suddenly the wall next to the panel slid open to reveal a secondary elevator shaft. "Going down again I believe."

WHEN THE DOORS SLID apart they were in a large room with a high ceiling and open floor space. Along the wall were raised platforms covered in grey tarps.

"Where are we now?" Arjan asked.

"The Ofu Corporation has its headquarters in this tower. Here is where they keep their classified abandoned projects. We have to take these tarps off to find the drives." They all began removing covers to reveal various technological specimens that no one recognized.

Arjan struggled with his wound and winced in pain. "How will we know if we find it? None of us has seen a trans-dimensional drive?"

"It should be labeled and have a holographic dossier."

"I don't know what that is and I can't read but is this it?" Armonia pointed to two rectangular prisms about the size of her.

Corry jogged over to her and when she saw the symbols etched onto the bronze plate she stopped in her tracks. Her voice caught in her throat for a moment. "Those are indeed them."

"Great!" Lorelei exclaimed. "Now we just find something else about that size to use as the decoy and we can get out of here."

"No, I don't think you will be leaving." Lorelei recognized the voice as Unak's even before she turned around with the others. "At least not in the way you thought." Unak stood at the elevator shaft holding Benseog who was bound and gagged. Next to him was Zean who held Isadora who was also trussed up. Behind them stood a large group of guardians with lasers at the ready.

Daleth reached for his crystals at the same time Gimeld raised his gun. Lorelei held up her hands and cried, "Stop! He's a Twin Flame." They both hadn't noticed the tattoos under his eyes.

"So?" Arjan jerked his head toward Armonia. "I thought you said she can kill Twin Flames."

"That is true. I was there watching when she massacred the Temple on Baabcrest." Zean glanced at Unak with confusion. He ignored her and went on. "But you see she can't kill Twin Flames without Daleth's crystals which means Daleth can't stop these guardians, who by the way have lethal laser cannons, from killing all of you."

"Surrender now!" Zean cried.

"You'll find we're difficult to kill," Gimeld said.

"Also we're criminals. So we don't surrender because you got innocent hostages," added Arjan.

"I don't wish you all to surrender and these two are far from innocent." Unak produced a large knife from his robe. He used it to cut Benseog's bonds and shoved him toward the others. He then grabbed Isadora from a bewildered Zean and did the same.

"What are you doing?" Zean whispered. Before Unak could answer the elevator doors behind them opened. The remaining members of Corry's Cell emerged roughly corralled toward the others by even more guardians.

"What's going on here? Who are these people?"

"Ask your new friend, Lorelei?"

They turned to Corry who looked around her and then at the ground. "They're here to steal the drives. We had to change our plans when the Breathless showed up. We no longer had time to use the experiment to unlock the secrets of trans-dimensional travel. Matters became more urgent once the Twin Flames took over. We just needed the experiment to help us escape, what few of us could that is. We deduced the best way to get past security was with Daleth. Some of my Cell sacrificed themselves so the others could follow. While security forces and Daleth battled we would gain possession of the drives."

"What made you think I would give more than space dust about those drives?"

"Like Tania said we are masters at picking up subliminal cues. You've always been searching for some way out as Lorelei said."

"Lorelei, what is the meaning of all this?" asked Isadora.

Lorelei didn't answer her old leader but instead clenched her fists and addressed Unak. "So now you're going to massacre everyone."

"No. You're all heretics and criminals but you are all free to go. Even you Daleth. You can take the drives with you or anything else in this room for that matter. All I want is her." Unak pointed his knife at Armonia.

"Me?" Armonia looked around frightened.

"Yes. You will all be pardoned as long as you give me her."

"In case you didn't hear, many of us were declared Obstructions." Gimeld shifted his shoulder toward Daleth. "Some of us by name."

Zean's voice trembled. "You said you respected my proposal?"

"The Light can be quite forceful as well as adaptable. I can assure you that even if a zealous guardian nabs any of you, they will promptly release you. You can have the freedom to do whatever you want as long as you give up her."

Benseog motioned to Zean. "What about the High Councilor?"

"She is tenuous but she is of the Light and trusts in it, I assure you. She is well respected by other government officials who also have a large faith in the Light. Her words will carry a lot of weight to make all of your lives easier. You can go on battling or take the gift I'm giving you and coast your way to Twin Flame status. Your choice. The Spark always talks of free will."

"You can't do this. All of them should be brought to a Light Bearing Center for rehabilitation," Zean pleaded with a shaky voice.

Unak finally moved his eyes toward Zean. "When you spend enough time with the Light you see down avenues that are obscured with shadow. I know how Uprights think and react. That red-headed Upright may seem just like all the others but mark my words she will grow into a symbol. Symbols are more powerful than darkness. That being said, properly used they can also intensify the Light. This is for the greater good. The mercy of the Light will shine on everyone here and they will spread it so we may all continue as we have."

Daleth glanced at Armonia who stood bewildered in the center of everyone. He then shifted his focus back to Unak.

"What are we waiting for? Grab the experiment and give her to them," Ava cried.

"How would we navigate?" Corry asked.

"We'll have the drives we'll figure out something. The mind always finds a way." They moved toward Armonia.

"Don't touch me!" Armonia yelled.

"Yeah, leave her alone!"

"Lorelei, what are you doing? You cannot risk yourself and your roommates for an outsider," Isadora cooly reminded her.

"Is she not still Yowgn?"

"Yes and Yowgn knows best where we must go and what we must do. Leave her to her fate so we may continue to liberate Yowgn in others," instructed Benseog.

"You swore an oath to live in unity with Yowgn. Let her walk her path and you walk yours. Do not let resentment from your past cloud your mind."

"You knew?" They nodded.

Arjan whispered to Gimeld. "We always said worry about no one but us right?" Gimeld touched his face but said nothing.

The pirates stood transfixed.

"I don't have all cycle while you think about this," Unak said.

"There's nothing to think about. He's offering us clemency so we can fight another day," said Isadora.

"But you are giving up a powerful weapon to defeat The Spark with," Lorelei protested.

Benseog smiled and shook his head slowly from side to side. "You were the one with the vendetta and projected it onto us. We simply seek to free the Yowgn. It will be freed in its own time, in its own way."

Lorelei grappled with the teachings of Yowgn. They had made so much sense to her only a small portion of a Gremrev ago. *Why do I find myself fighting my teachers? Is my bitterness toward the Light truly pulling me astray?* "The freedom is now and with her. You are not valuing yourself above the greater good of Yowgn."

"It is you who have your values askew," said Isadora. Lorelei was struck dumb by the words of her once co-conspirators. Had she once more been betrayed by something she believed in or did she betray herself?

Isadora, Benseog, and the Order members advanced on Armonia who looked frantic.

"Please don't do this to me. I'm not bad. I know I'm not." A piercing pain shot through her head and down her spine. She fell to her knees and gripped her head.

Unak smiled. *It is working just as I planned. They had to all choose to give her up. By giving her up they will open themselves to the Light ever so slightly. Light needs but a sliver to get through.*

"Now while she's in a weakened state," Evelyn shouted.

Kristal popped out of her armband and hissed loudly and began snapping. "Don't worry it can't kill us," Mareen assured everyone.

"I don't want to die, please I don't want to die alone."

"Do not fear. Death just means a reunion with Yowgn," said Benseog in a soothing tone.

"No. When you die you—"

"Armonia!" Daleth suddenly shouted.

Armonia slapped the ground with her palms in frustration. "I know, shut up!"

"Yes and just do it!"

Everything happened in the blink of an eye after that. The crystals flew out of Daleth's hand. One of them shot directly into Armonia's hand which due to some innate instinct she instantly used to kill Unak. The guardians fired on Armonia but the crystals whizzed around her deflecting their blasts. It only struck and killed Isadora, Benseog, and the Order members. Corry who had hung back from the rest of her Cell flung herself away from the laser fire and into a tarp that had something glass underneath that shattered.

Zean witnessed the demise of Unak with a mixture of disbelief and horror. She ducked into a crevice to try and contemplate what to do. She wasn't entirely sure what was going on or why Unak had said what he said but he was of the Light. She had to have faith in him. She had always trusted in the Light just as the populace of Ebjan put their faith in her. She would not let them down. She was a servant of the Light, after all. *Daleth and that other Upright somehow figured out how to kill Twin Flames. This makes the danger severe and I must find a way to act.* Zean tried to think what Jamila would do in this situation and muster the same courage she had always admired in her reflection.

Daleth had raced over to Armonia and shielded her so his crystals could begin taking out the army of guardians. The one he had given Armonia left her and joined the others as they zipped through the air. As the guardians opened fire Lorelei raced over to shield Sil as the pirates also opened fire in turn on the guardians.

"Why are you shielding me?" Sil asked as Lorelei winced from the lasers.

"When we dreamed together I was asked to protect you by some entity. They said you had a lot to offer this system and to promise them." A tear rolled down Sil's cheek.

M.A.T.O. had stepped in front of Arjan to protect him but suffered severe damage.

Gimeld was struck in the shoulder and fell to the ground. It only grazed him and opened up a superficial wound. He saw more laser fire coming for him but one of Daleth's crystals deflected it. He glanced at Daleth who was still focused on the battle.

Daleth's shield left him as he used up the last of his reserves. The last guardian managed to strike Daleth on the leg before a crystal ruptured his neck. Fortunately for Daleth the energy beam only nicked him. He had pushed through worse pain. His one hand put pressure on it while the other received his returning crystals. He returned them to his pouch. It was over. The pirates gathered around the fallen M.A.T.O.

Daleth turned around to face Armonia. She stood on wobbly feet behind the nearly depleted Daleth and looked around "Why did ya—?" Suddenly Armonia's eyes grew wide. She pointed behind him. "Look out!" Daleth spun around only to see a blur of motion as Corry ran in between an on-rushing Zean and himself. Zean unable to stop herself plunged Unak's knife deep into Corry's gut.

Zean looked bewildered. "Why did you save someone like him?"

Blood began to fill Corry's mouth. "Because he's something wholly indiscernible and that's what terrifies you and me both." Corry swung her arm across Zean in such a quick motion it took Daleth and Armonia a moment to realize Zean's throat had been slashed by the piece of glass in Corry's hand. Both fell to the floor dead. Daleth and Armonia stared at the two corpses as the blood pooled around them. "Come on," Daleth finally said. He took Armonia's arm and limped with her to the others.

M.A.T.O. lay on the floor with Arjan kneeling over him. His circuits sparked. The laser fire had practically ripped him asunder.

"You stupid robot why did you have to go and get killed."

"I am meant to serve and you required protection, being injured as you are.

Gimeld knelt on the other side of M.A.T.O. and placed his hand on him. "Well done. Thank you."

"Just please take the server with you and connect it to the ship when you locate a replacement."

"You and that stupid box." Arjan's voice was choked up. Gimeld nodded to M.A.T.O. as he permanently shut down. "Why didn't we just hand her in?"

Gimeld looked up at Arjan. "Nothing good comes from The Way of The Light."

"Can't someone fix him?" Armonia asked her voice choked with a thousand feelings and thoughts whirling through her mind. Gimeld shook his head and stood. Sil walked away from the group.

Lorelei looked around at everyone whose faces showed mixed emotions about everything that had just transpired. "So where do we all go from here?" she finally asked.

"We find a ship and get as far away from here as possible," said Gimeld. "This mess will bring more guardians, maybe worse."

Daleth glared at Gimeld. "Do you know how far down we are? What kind of ship can you fly from way down here?"

"We're in a storage room filled with experimental technology. We'll find something."

"What about this?" Sil called out. They walked over to join Sil who stood in front of a holographic file. "It says this ship has EMF weaponry that bores through anything but its destructive potential was considered too broad so it was shelved."

"Wait if it uses EMF will it be able to get through the magnetic barrier?", Lorelei inquired.

Sil shrugged. "I would have to read further but I doubt Circapto would build a ship they couldn't get off their Orbit."

Gimeld yanked the tarp down off a large cone-shaped craft with its point sticking straight up. He surveyed the vehicle. "Perfect."

"Let's hope this works," Lorelei remarked.

"Arjan can get anything running. Get on board and fire her up. Sil help me load the drives."

"Armonia and I will get the other one." Armonia followed Lorelei's lead but as soon as she touched the drive it felt like a needle driven between her eyes. Her vision showed her a bright flash and then two white cones on their sides touching points. When she came back to the room she saw Lorelei's concerned face. "What's wrong?"

Armonia started to answer but stopped herself. Her eyes moved to Daleth who looked pensive. "I'll tell ya later."

Gimeld sat in the pilot seat looking at the control panels. Everyone was onboard and the two trans-dimensional drives were loaded. "Since we don't have M.A.T.O. did anyone read up on this thing?"

Daleth approached Gimeld and handed him a server. "Speaking of your old crew mate."

"We'll hook it up later. We don't have time."

"Agreed which is why you should let me pilot us out of here."

"No, one takes control of my ship. Besides your powers are all used up and you're injured."

"I do not have enough reserves to control the crystals or shield myself from lasers but it takes very little to heighten my already acute senses. We both know I'm the best chance we got to get out of Circapto alive."

"Where are we even going?" Sil asked.

"Washa. We need to go to Washa," Armonia said almost absent mindfully.

"Look at you finally knowing the Orbit's names," Arjan quipped.

Lorelei pleaded with her eyes. "Please. Let him pilot us out of here and then it's yours."

Gimeld looked at the rest of his crew who wouldn't look him in the eyes. He got up and growled, "Don't ding it."

Daleth sat at the control panel and placed his hand on the sensors.

"Oh no! It's too late," Lorelei said staring at one of the view screens which displayed soldiers and guardians running toward them firing lasers.

"Those look like Comqwo soldiers. They must be gunning for us now," remarked Arjan.

"To Gimeld's original question I did read the complete dossier. The entire skin of this vessel is the engine which when in use emits an EMF shield making it very hard to damage. The craft is an excavator as well as an inter-Orbit ship. It emits a concentrated dose of EMF radiation, enough to break down the molecular structure of anything it bores through," Sil explained.

"Good to know," said Daleth.

"Uh, we aren't going to cook ourselves are we?" Arjan asked.

"The interior has cancellers to protect us." Sil glanced at the view screen. "Those soldiers may be a different story though."

"Wait!" Arjan suddenly cried. "Lorelei might have a point. If this ship has its own electromagnetic field generator and cancellers what happens when it hits the field that surrounds Circapto? They grounded this thing for a reason, didn't they? Gimeld, maybe you should stop him, we might have better luck with the soldiers out there."

Gimeld took a step forward but one look at the intensity in Daleth's eyes stopped him in his tracks. It wasn't fear that held his hand but empathy. "We'll be fine." Even though Gimeld's instincts acknowledged Daleth was the one to get them all out of this it nevertheless made his skin crawl.

Without further delay, Daleth started the engines up. The ship seemed to come alive. The outside of the craft pulsated and the entire room began to crumble. Just as Sil stated it blasted through rock, steel, and concrete seemingly without effort.

《 》

ABOVE ON THE SURFACE of Circapto, a giant sinkhole formed much to the terror of those in the area. Out of it, a metallic blue and black cone-shaped vessel made its way high above the horrified citizens and the steel towers. When it hit the boundary of the magnetic shield a brilliant flash erupted and lightning streaked across the sky as far as the eye could see. Any interceptors in pursuit were fried by the brilliant energy surge as the cone disappeared into the violent atmosphere of Circapto.

Chapter 9

INTER-ORBIT SPACE

In the far recesses of the ship, Armonia toggled through the view screen attached to the far wall. There was of course the empty blackness with tiny hints of light. But images of the intimidating outer Orbits being left behind flashed up, as well. The shrinking magnificence of Circapto as they sped away from it. There was the multi-colored landscape of Orogunu which looked like a patchwork quilt. Gremoilio with its thick moist atmosphere looked like a small cloud floating far off in the vast reaches of space.

Armonia stopped on an image of the ball of light known as Iris. Unlike the outer Orbits, it grew ever so slightly larger and brighter as they headed toward it. She stared at it for a long time, it pulled her as it did to the system. For her, the pull was both terrifying and liberating. She wondered if it was the same for the rest of the system it held. So transfixed was she, that she did not hear Daleth approach behind her until he slammed his fist against the wall.

Armonia jumped out of her skin. "Space dust! You could've just tapped me on the shoulder or called my name, ya know?"

"We need to talk."

"Why did ya give me your crystal back there?"

"So you could kill the Twin Flame. Are you that dense?"

"I mean why me? And why did it work? I thought Lorelei said I could only do it when I had all of them."

"Followers of Vuhox connected each crystal to one of the five senses. It was believed therefore the crystals became an extension of them when all together. Lorelei and that other Twin Flame deduced it was the connection between you and me that allowed you to destroy Twin Flames much like the connection between the senses of two individuals invokes dreaming."

"So it's like when we dream? But I only had one crystal?"

Daleth studied the cold metal floor. "They didn't read the Book of Vuhox as I did. Even the founders of that cult failed to read between the lines. We're not the compilation of our senses. All of me is in each crystal." Daleth's head moved sharply up to look at Armonia. "But that's done with. I want to know what you saw when you touched the drive."

"I didn't see anything."

"My reserves may be nearly gone but I can still tell you're lying."

"So torture me for the truth. Isn't torture what ya Vuhox people were taught?"

"No. Torture was used to have us overcome our fears, doubts, and pain."

Armonia tightened her lips and rolled her eyes around. "That's some way to do it."

"It was effective. I am now free in life."

Armonia gestured around the compartment where they stood. "This is what you wanted your life to be?"

"Don't change the subject."

Daleth glared at Armonia and she glared back until finally she let out a heavy sigh and turned back to the view screen. "How's your leg?"

Daleth crossed his arms. "Fine. Sil's herbs did wonders. I'm still waiting for an answer to my question."

"I think I saw a way to stop The Spark and free everyone from whatever they do."

Daleth let out an exaggerated snort. "Is that it? Who cares about everyone? We'll get away and the rest is what it is." Daleth went to leave.

"It's why I didn't want to say anything, ya dimwad. To space dust with everyone else. I'm gonna be dead soon anyways. I mean I know ya and I are supposed to defeat The Spark or whatever but who cares. Nobody else cares about me."

Daleth whipped around. "Who says we're supposed to defeat The Spark?"

"Ya remember? Those light people from the first time we dreamed."

"They were beings of light. The more I think about it our dreaming was probably all a hoax concocted by The Twin Flames for some unknown purpose."

Armonia threw up her hands in an exasperated flourish. "Welcome to my life! Nothing ever makes sense. It probably didn't even make sense when I was an addict. Maybe if those dreams were real I would be special but whatever. I'm just a waste. Or even worse, a villain like you." Armonia hung her head for a moment then went back to the view screen to flip through the images.

"You either fall in line or become a villain. It's the way of this life." Daleth went to leave but stopped at the door. He looked back at Armonia. "You still didn't answer me. What did you see exactly when you touched the drive?"

Armonia didn't take her eyes off the view screen. "If the drive was flown into Iris and activated it will create like a portal and suck the entire system into a different dimension."

Daleth spun around fully, his face aghast. "You're talking about creating a black hole?"

Armonia turned her face away from the view screen and scrunched up her brow. "What's a black hole?"

"It's supposed to be a point in space so dense and large nothing can escape it. Anything that comes across it gets sucked in never to come out."

"I think this is different. I think they will come out and just maybe not remember stuff like me."

"It's still absurd."

"Why I didn't want to tell ya." Armonia went back to the view screen.

"Even if what you say will happen occurs, The Spark will just find the system again. It would be pointless."

Armonia shrugged her shoulders. "Probably."

"And who gonna fly the thing into Iris?"

"I don't know but whoever does I'm pretty sure will be dead. I think it's gonna create this explosion thingy."

"You and I are the only ones who can get past Iris' defenses. Are you suggesting we sacrifice ourselves to save the entire system?"

"No, I'm not."

"Good."

Armonia threw up her hands and cocked her head to one side. "Why would you even get that in your head?" They both stood there with nothing but the low hum of the ship filling the room.

"I'm done being a group member. As soon as we get a hold of another ship I'm installing the drive and going off on my own. You and Lorelei can stay with Gimeld's crew."

"You always say that."

"What's that supposed to mean?" Daleth snapped.

"It means you don't like being alone any more than I do."

"Your plan has us dying. It doesn't get more alone than that." Daleth crossed his arms and scowled. "We are nothing alike you know?"

"We have crazy visions when we dream together—and we both have scars."

"Apparently you have crazy visions even when not dreaming with me."

Armonia smirked. "Guess I'm getting worse. Maybe I'm getting closer to dying. Maybe that's why I wanna blow myself up, to take control of my life."

Daleth still wore a scowl but he turned away from Armonia and looked at the nearby wall so intensely he looked like he was trying to see what was on the other side. After a while he said in a hushed whisper, "We all die, death is a part of life, and life is a part of death."

"Is that another little-known piece of wisdom from Vuhox?" Daleth nodded slowly. His mind seemed far away. "If you believe our first dreaming we die over and over again."

"They were wrong." The venom in his voice was unmistakable.

Armonia gave a little grunt. "Guess I'll know soon enough." She looked at the view monitor for a moment then whipped her head back to Daleth. "Why did ya hate that first dreaming so much? I mean the second time I kinda get but the first one, wouldn't it be nice if we were immortal."

"So we can live multiple despicable lives."

"Was it because you're supposed to be on a mission with me?" Armonia stared keenly at Daleth. "It's something about what ya read in that book isn't it?"

Daleth's head jerked toward Armonia. "We should dream one last time."

Armonia couldn't help her eyes from bulging out. "What? You hate dreaming with me. Now all of a sudden you want to do it?"

"I need to know something." Daleth locked his gaze with Armonia's. She saw in his eyes something buried deep and closely guarded. It wasn't the first time she saw this flicker in those coal-black eyes.

"I knew it. It's something having to do with those Vuhox people?" Daleth didn't answer but just averted his eyes. "Everyone says you killed them because of some power struggle but it was something more wasn't it? Something in our dreams reminds ya of why."

"The past deserves to be buried. Forget I said anything." Daleth went to leave.

"Let's dream. It helps my pain and if it's all space dust we should know."

Daleth stopped in his tracks and slowly began to turn his body. He was startled when Armonia sprung at him. He instinctually held her up and she wrapped her legs around his waist. She began to suck on the side of his neck. Daleth felt the surge rise from deep inside him once more and it quickly overtook him. He didn't fight it this time, he was too weary. It was something so foreign yet so familiar when he made contact with this strange Upright.

She whispered in his ear. "This working for ya?" She then reached down under his tunic and grasped his engorged member. "Never mind."

Daleth shuffled over to the wall. He held out one of his hands to support himself, his other arm flexed as it supported Armonia. She undid his belt and let it fall to the floor. She looked at his face to make sure he wasn't upset she let it drop. She sensed Daleth was softer and less resistant this time. Their faces drew close until their lips touched. They both pressed their mouths into one another's and closed their eyes. This was something completely unheard of in dreaming. They only grazed their lips together the first time they dreamed. This time they opened their mouths and fit them together with an intense passion. Their tongues and breath intermingled. This was different for Armonia than any other instance of dreaming she could recall. Something about this simple act brought back memories. There were no sounds or images associated with these memories, just feelings. She cradled his face in her hands to hold it in place to ensure it didn't stop. Somehow she knew he was experiencing the same. These feelings attached to memories lost in a haze stirred new purpose in each of them.

She slid onto him and rocked her hips back and forth slowly, rhythmically. Her body shuddered and then she felt Daleth tremble. A savage spasm erupted throughout her entire being.

⟨ ⟩

ARMONIA OPENED HER eyes and found herself enveloped in quietude and blackness. She looked around. She saw she had her wings once more so she knew she was dreaming.

"Daleth!" she cried out.

"I am here." He stepped out of the darkness although Armonia couldn't say from exactly where. "We seem to be where we were last time but I don't see the timeline anywhere."

"No. It's not like last time. Something's off." Armonia's voice was panic-stricken. "I don't feel right! We need to leave!"

"We intercepted you two." The Spark stood before them.

"Get behind me!" Daleth moved in-between Armonia and The Spark. He unsheathed his trikilldo and crouched in a fighting pose ready to spring.

"Oh no, that's that Spark thingy isn't it? They know about us! They've come to kill us!"

"We do know about you but it serves no purpose for us to kill you. That trinket you hold is pointless against pure energy, you know?"

"Maybe but until I know what you want with us I'm not putting it away."

"We thought the time had come for us to have a dialogue."

Armonia stepped out from behind Daleth. "There's nothing to talk about! We're leaving your system. Just go away!"

"Neither of you intends to do that."

Daleth narrowed his eyes. "You don't know us and we don't know you."

"Besides how do ya know what we're planning?"

"We are not in a physical body so we do not have the amnesia that comes with it, unlike yourselves. You will be pulled to try and change things. That is the nature of your core despite your shortcomings. It's what you two do when you come together. We recommend you break this cycle for all our ease."

In a low voice, Daleth said, "It's a trick. You're afraid we'll stop you."

"What is it you are trying to stop exactly? Shall we examine it for a moment?" Daleth and Armonia didn't say anything so The Spark continued. "This system was rife with plagues and war before we arrived. We cured both those disorders of your kind. We made your kind stronger both physically and mentally, your immunity to poison and technological leaps attest to that fact. We have granted you eternal life."

"Actually while you're here," Armonia interrupted, "Why did you create Twin Flames and why can I kill them?"

"Your question attests to the ignorance of your kind. When two or more are joined they have a stronger connection to the source of all life."

"What ya feed on?"

"Yes, for lack of a better term. You seem to have acquired the ability to discern the connection and render it inert. This results in their returning to the source individually."

"So the whole light thingy was just so ya could get a bigger meal outta us?"

"There are other purposes which we do not need to go into."

"Seems like a lotta work to just get food?"

"It is hard for such lowly life forms to grasp the reason for such matters."

"Try us," growled Daleth.

"You used to work in groundskeeping. You know to get the most out of one's garden it must be tended to meticulously."

"It's wrong what ya do! Feeding off others! Plus ya released those monsters."

"The Breathless, as they are called, are the same as the dark trade and even the overpopulation problem. A result of the ignorance of this dimension and those who inhabit it. Even with all we have offered, this system has spiraled into the same destructive paths that it has always tread. All we can do is simply offer aid and more time for all of you to correct it. If you think it's so wrong go ahead then and stop us. But you would be no better than us then, choosing for all Uprights. What do you think the inhabitants of your system desire? Death or the possibility of eternal life?"

Daleth got a faraway look in his eyes. "Death is a part of life. Life is a part of death."

Armonia and The Spark turned their attention toward Daleth who remained staring off into nothingness like it was a portal to another time and place. The Spark seemed to dim for a moment then returned to normal. "I think you will see it is an easy choice." The Spark appeared more at ease after this rebuke. "Regardless of your decision, know we are not the villain you think we are. We just see how much the villain—you—all—are."

Daleth stood erect. Armonia could feel his muscles stiffen. An intense scowl permeated his entire face as he addressed The Spark. "I've never gotten what I wanted. I've been a villain all my life. Why stop now?"

"Spoken like a true villain." The Spark seemed to flicker and then disappeared altogether.

《 》

OROGUNU ORBIT

Jamila was on full alert with her fellow guardians. They had managed to corral several Breathless in the gokhano field on the local co-op farm. Twin Flames had responded and gone into the rows of tall spiny stalks of unripened gokhano. They were accompanied by a squadron of Comqwo warriors who would assist with the execution of the creatures. Now Jamila and her team would just have to hold the perimeter and wait.

Comqwo soldiers were the best fighters in the system due to the culture of that particular Orbit. Jamila was glad they were here to lend support to the Twin Flames so she didn't have to tangle with the Breathless directly. Comqwo was an Orbit that still kept strictly to the old war-like ways from before The Spark. Perhaps it was because they were in the outermost Orbit or maybe they just never knew what else to do in their icy world when the wars came to an end. For whatever reason, they stayed in a highly trained and rigid warrior caste system. *Who knew it would be so needed eventually*, Jamila thought.

Even though this mission was going well so far, everything still seemed to be unraveling. The Breathless seemed unstoppable. Add to it that attacks from pirates and smugglers were on the rise thanks to what happened on Circapto. According to the reports Jamila heard, a crew of pirates destroyed a major structure on that Orbit and emboldened all other black market traders to make a stance against the new Obstruction decree. Jamila just hoped Zean stepped down quickly. Her being a political figure made her a target for the pirates. It would be safer to stay out of the public eye right now. Things were just too unstable throughout the system for Jamila to feel comfortable with her reflection in such a prominent role. She acknowledged the hypocrisy but it didn't change how Jamila thought. *Zean always regards her as the stronger one but she needs Zean just as much as Zean leans on her.*

A fellow guardian named Baswa ran up to Jamila. "Baswa, what's wrong? Are they breaking through the perimeter?"

"No, I—I don't know how to tell you this but that attack on Circapto, at the Plaza of Commerce and Light." Baswa paused and took a deep breath. "Forensics confirm High Councilor Zean from Ebjan amongst the dead."

Jamila felt a crack somewhere inside the pit of her stomach, like the dirt cracking when a firmly entrenched plant is pulled out by the root. The crack traveled up her torso and along the back of her neck till it reached the crown of her head. Only then did Baswa's words coalesce into a piece of information.

Jamila stumbled and Baswa caught her. "I'm so sorry." The words seemed to come from far away to Jamila. "Come sit." Baswa tried to lead her to the command tent but Jamila's feet wouldn't move.

"What was she doing there?" she whispered. *Was she there for some meeting? Did the pirates abduct her? Does it even matter?* These questions entered her mind just as quickly as they left. Then all that remained was a vast nothingness that seemed to go on forever.

Screams bounced around her ears, again off in the distance. She didn't flinch. She felt liquid warmth on her shoulder but again gave it no heed. She then felt a sharp jolt and burning erupted in her chest. She thought it was her broken heart but when she saw the command tent pull away from her she realized it was a Breathless. She thought it strange how calm she was being. *Nothing matters anymore so what is there to get excited about?* Her body became as numb as her mind and then nothing.

INTER-ORBIT SPACE

On what served as the bridge for the experimental craft sat what passed for the crew. They all stood still in a loose circle with their heads hung low. The quietude was taught. Only Kristal slithered about exploring.

Finally, Arjan raised his head and tossed back his green locks. "So that's it? Just blow up the whole system. That's your plan?"

"It won't get blown up. Just go somewhere else. And I think everyone will kinda be like me and not know anything."

"Oh well never mind, that's a perfectly reasonable plan then."

Gimeld who stood as a statue with arms crossed in front of his chest finally spoke. "But those who go into Iris will not survive?"

Armonia moved her mouth side to side and looked up at the ceiling. "Hmmm, maybe, maybe not."

"It's an unknown. Whatever does happen though doesn't concern any of you." Daleth's voice held a mask of command in it.

Arjan threw his hands up. "You're going to destroy the system, I think it has a bit to do with us."

"There are two drives. Armonia and I will use one—"

"I'm coming with you," interrupted Lorelei. To replace her most recent destroyed outfit she now wore a makeshift dress fashioned out of the tarp that covered the drives, complete with a belt using one of the cargo straps.

Daleth and Lorelei stared into each other's eyes. It was a conversation between two individuals who knew the language of silence fluently.

"Fine. The rest of you can take the other drive and leave here before we go into Iris. Just drop us off as close to Washa as possible."

"Why Washa?" Sil inquired.

Gimeld answered for Daleth. "They will need a flare hopper to get that close to Iris."

"Exactly. They are only found on Washa and Iris."

"How do you even know what something we just found out existed, will do?" Arjan blurted.

"We just know."

Sil glanced at Arratup who had suddenly appeared in the room wearing a familiar knowing expression. Sil couldn't help but let a faint smile creep onto their face.

"I'll take you to Washa." The others looked surprised by Gimeld's proclamation. Gimeld looked square at Daleth. "I owe you a debt."

"Don't insult me or yourself," Daleth's voice was cold. "To be in someone's debt is the most egregious form of giving up one's freedom, for it is laced with hypocrisy. Take us to Washa or drop us off at the nearest Orbit but don't give me that space dust of being in our debt." With that Daleth walked out of the bridge.

The rest waited awkwardly to see what Gimeld would do or say but he seemed to be somewhere else inside that hood. He just stood motionless. Finally, Armonia broke the tension and walked up to Sil holding out her armband where Kristal made her home. "I want you to take care of Kristal. She took good care of me and I don't want anything to happen to her."

"Why me?"

"Lorelei told me what she saw when she dreamed with ya. She was my first friend and I know you'll understand."

Sil gave a knowing nod and took the band from Armonia. Armonia then walked up to Kristal and held out her arm for her to slither up. She said in a cooing voice. "I have to go soon but Sil's a real nice Upright so I am leaving ya in good hands. Be friends with each other, okay?" Kristal squeaked in reply and Armonia wiped a tear from her eye. Gimeld watched the scene with a tear hidden by his hood.

⟨ ⟩

GREMOILIO ORBIT

Gimeld walked into the bake shop. He had accepted his sweet tooth. It was a fault of his to be ruled by such a physical craving but his tutelage under the Way had shown him how to let his faults flow through him, rather than resist them. Only then could he purge his faults. He hadn't been to a bake shop in hundreds of cycles. It was part of his regiment to purge his sweet tooth. To set realistic goals of how long he could go before indulging. Sure enough each time he partook of the sweets it had less power over him.

Still, the aroma titillated his nose. The fragrance of all the goodies on display reminded him of a newly blooming jungle on Gremoilio. He deliberated carefully before he made his selection. The Upright at the counter gave a seductive smile as she handed him his purchase. Gimeld was used to it. He was a strikingly handsome Upright by any reasonable standard. His skin was smooth and richly bronzed. His eyes were like emeralds and his lips full. His muscular body was toned without being bulky. All of this sat underneath voluminous waves of sandy brown hair which just reached his ears.

Gimeld gave a friendly smile to the clerk in return. It was a well-rehearsed polite refusal for he already had a reflection. They were making final preparations to begin the Twin Flame process. Gimeld always felt a twinge of empathy when he had to dismiss someone's advances. So many Uprights were desperately trying to find what he and Jonah had.

Gimeld's partner, Harper, drove the patrol skimmer so he could eat his treat. They had been partners for only a relatively short time but Harper had learned Gimeld's rituals well. In fact, she was a fast learner all around. Ever since his old partner became a Twin Flame he had taken extra care to show Harper what it meant to be a guardian. She proved to be a sponge that soaked up all the wisdom Gimeld had learned from his journey along the Way. "We are one of the pillars of this society," he would often remind her. "The Uprights look to guardians for protection. We are the first ones they reach out to when they are in trouble. We prove to them the Light does always show the Way out of any situation." Gimeld loved talking Light and teaching others.

《 》

ONE NIGHT, AFTER HE got off duty, Gimeld waited on the balmy streets of Gremoilio for Jonah in front of their favorite eatery. They were celebrating. Their lives were about to enter a new phase. In one cycle they would be traveling to Iris to start the Twin Flame ritual. A body would be created that they would pour their thoughts, emotions, and Light into. They would guide this being as it grew. Through their Light, Gimeld and Jonah would teach it how to live, just as their Twin Flame guides did for them. Jonah and Gimeld would put their entire essence into this entity till they were joined inside of it. It was the final test to ensure the two of them knew the Light well enough to be a flaming torch to illuminate the Way for others.

Gimeld spotted a jeweler across the street and diagonal from the eatery. He was still a bit early and knew how much Jonah loved decorating himself with different colored crystals so he decided to pop into the store real quick and get a gift to surprise him. As he got across the street and was about to enter the store he heard strange noises which sounded like they came from behind the establishment. His guardian instincts kicked in and he walked around to the back to investigate. He found a group of hoodlums in the shadows. There appeared to be three of them and they stood around someone on the ground.

"Next time just give us the crystals if we ask for them," one of them sneered.

"Yeah we want to be like those Vuhox Uprights," another added with a giggle.

"Cease and desist right now," Gimeld shouted.

The three thugs turned to Gimeld seemingly without fright. When they did so Gimeld could see the face of the unfortunate Upright who lay curled up on his side. Even in the shadows and even with the blood and bruising Gimeld recognized the face. "Jonah." His voice was barely audible.

Gimeld suddenly sprang on the three hoodlums. His mind was nothing but blind rage. His body moved on nothing more than countless cycles of training and conditioning. The one who seemed to be the leader swung at him. He dodged the blow and grabbed the thug's arm. Using his assailant's momentum he hurled him into one of his buddies. The third Upright took out a knife and tried to stab Gimeld. Once more, he moved too quickly for the gang member and grabbed his arm. He twisted the arm behind the Upright's back with one hand. Gimeld drove his knee into the punk's backside. The sound of cracking ligaments bounced off the concrete and brick around them as the shoulder dislocated. The Upright dropped to his knees as his leader made another attempt on Gimeld. In the blink of an eye, Gimeld punched him in his jaw and the leader fell to the ground as teeth flew through the air. The third and final thug was just getting to his feet when Gimeld punched him in the stomach and he doubled over. Still hunched he was then tossed into the wall. Gimeld didn't know if the impact killed the brute or simply knocked him out but he didn't care. All he cared about right now was his reflection.

Gimeld ran over to Jonah. He wasn't conscious but he was still breathing. He picked him up and ran out into the street to his hovercraft. He placed Jonah in the passenger seat. "Hang on! I'm getting you to a Healing Center!" He vaulted into the driver's seat and zoomed off. He wished he was in his guardian patrol skimmer so others would move out of the way but he was a skilled enough pilot to weave in between the other vehicles, even in the clunky hovercraft. He always drove while on patrol, aside from when he had one of his indulgences. He had helped so many nameless Uprights in his life he would not fail the Upright who meant the most to him.

Suddenly another hovercraft outside of the main traffic stream turned a bend sharply. Gimeld was traveling too fast to avoid it. He heard the impact but after that things went black.

《 》

HE AWOKE IN A HEALING Center confused. It felt like something was on his face and he reached up for it. He realized his head was wrapped in bandages. As soon as he touched his face everything came flooding back to him. They had to have taken Jonah to the Healing Center too. Gimeld sprung up from his bed. "Where is he? Where's the one I was with?"

A healer came running in. She had short dark hair and dark skin but Gimeld was in such agitation that was all he allowed to register about her. "You need to calm down."

Her soothing tone was wasted on Gimeld who thrashed against her. "Where is he? I want to see him now!"

"I'm sorry but the one you were with, his injuries were too severe. We lost him, he's gone."

The words didn't make sense to Gimeld. "What do you mean you lost him? How do you lose an entire Upright?"

She made Gimeld look into her dark satiny eyes. "He died. I'm sorry." Gimeld's knees buckled. He tore the bandages from his face, threw his head back, and screamed.

THE NEXT FEW CYCLES were a blur. There were a few scraps of fuzzy memories of being questioned by guardians and some Twin Flames. Healers came to see him but he did not recall anything they said. When he left the Healing Center he went directly to Melia his Twin Flame Lantern. He had hoped to find some comfort or peace from her but was sorely disappointed.

"I lost Jonah!" Gimeld pounded his fist on the desk Melia sat behind. "Don't you understand?"

"Yes, I have acknowledged you have suffered a loss." Melia looked down at her lap and smoothed her robe. "I would watch the temper. Obviously, there's still much Light work to be done. You clearly weren't ready to become a Twin Flame. So although the circumstances were certainly unfortunate, what happened has served the Light." Gimeld stared at Melia with mouth agape. Tears welled in his eyes and dribbled down his cheek soaking into the bandages which still covered his face. They stared at each other, Melia's face tranquil and Gimeld's a mask of pain.

"I am not unsympathetic," she finally said. "I would just expect someone who was about to embark on a Twin Flame birth to better understand the Light. The Light exists to purge the darkness. If you were truly full of Light you would have expelled the darkness you encountered not take it on, as what you did to those Uprights in back of that shop surely attests to."

Through gritted teeth, Gimeld said, "They hurt Jonah."

"You're a guardian. You know full well the pain darkness causes. The Light allows us to see it for what it is, unnecessary. You instead chose to propagate more of it. Isn't that the cause of your suspension after all?"

"I—I tried to save the Upright I love."

"And you did not succeed because you were not utilizing the Light. You were behaving like the Non-uprights who rely solely on instinct. Your rash behavior caused Jonah further injury when you crashed which resulted in his Light being extinguished. If you channeled the Light it would have shown you the proper course and you could have avoided all this pain." Gimeld didn't say anything but just stared at Melia as she continued. "Do not beat yourself up. The Light shines on all of us, it illuminates our path but we still can have trouble seeing it. Uprights still bare the darkness from before The Spark. Like a nocturnal Non-upright who lives their life in the dark and then cowers or runs away when light is shone on them, so too do Uprights try to resist the Light for its brightness throws them since they are not fully accustomed to it. You just need to grow more accustomed so it becomes as natural as breathing to turn toward the Light for guidance. Now, why don't you take a couple of cycles of solo reflection and then go out and find yourself a new individual who you can reflect with and then come back to me so we can start fresh."

"Don't you see my face? How am I supposed to attract a new reflection like this?"

Melia got up from her desk and walked over to the door. "There's always reconstructive and corrective procedures for something such as that. Although I would recommend during your solo reflection you consider the value of looking beneath the surface. If you have difficulty let me know and perhaps we could do a very mild Niorpyn session under close supervision to get you over the hump." Melia turned the gaily carved door knob and held the door open for Gimeld. "Look deeper and may the Light shine bright on you."

"You as well," was all Gimeld could mutter in response.

《 》

WHEN GIMELD GOT HOME from the Temple he sat transfixed at nothing in particular on the wall. The plain beige seemed to stare back at him with mockery. He wasn't sure how long he sat there but a desperate rage built up in him. He slammed his fist through the wall. He took all his books on The Way of The Light and tore them to pieces. While he was doing this he happened to glance up at a mirror. He saw the ugly wounds weeping underneath the bandages. They made him look as ugly as he felt. He took the mirror and slammed it to the ground.

《 》

GIMELD RARELY LEFT his home after that. He gorged on his vice of sweets but soon found they gave him no comfort. So he began to delve into the darkness trade. He tried anything he could find on the market to numb himself. Niorpyn and dreaming illicitly seemed to be all that helped. It was easy for him to find access because of his experiences breaking up these activities while he was a guardian. Gimeld had always stayed clear of darkness. Upon leaving his Prep Center he became a frequent visitor to the Temples trying to soak up as much Light as he could. *A lot of good it did me now,* he thought to himself bitterly. With newfound clarity, he understood why so many Uprights became obsessed with the darkness trade.

Harper stopped over at one point. "Look at you," she cried. Her eyes were wide and her mouth twisted in disbelief and disgust.

"Yeah look at me. Take a good long look," Gimeld said with a sardonic smile.

"When are you coming back to the League of Guardians?"

"Never. Why guard anybody? It's all pointless."

Harper's body shrank at the words of her mentor. "Do you mean that?"

"Go. There's nothing for you here."

"Maybe you can talk to some Twin Flames."

"The Light is all illusion. Life is miserable."

"The Light is all we have," pleaded Harper. "We must not waver from it or we will lose our way. You were the one who taught me that."

"Spare me your space dust and just leave already."

Harper slowly made her way to the door and opened it. She stood at the threshold and hesitated. She turned back to Gimeld with tears welling in her eyes. "I must say your new face now matches your new heart." She slammed the door behind her.

Shortly after that Gimeld heard a knock. When he opened the door he saw a very old Upright standing there. The bodies of Uprights only withered when they were very near to natural death. So Gimeld assumed the one who stood before him was at least three gremrevs old, if not much older. One who obviously would not taste immortality, much like Gimeld.

"Can I help you?" Gimeld's voice was harsh and loud.

"I'm glad I've finally found you. I wanted to try and make amends," the Upright's voice was coarse.

This one must be cycles away from the end, Gimeld thought to himself. "I don't know you, nor have any interest to." Gimeld went to close the door but a wrinkled hand reached out and stopped the door. *He is surprisingly strong for such a decrepit exterior.*

"Please, my time is short, and when I do leave I wish to have nothing left undone."

"I told you I don't know you."

"Because you were unconscious not because our paths have not crossed."

"What?" He had caught Gimeld's attention.

"I was the one driving the craft you crashed into."

Gimeld's eyes flared. He grabbed the Upright and yanked him inside roughly. "Do you know what you cost me? I would kill you if you weren't so close to death already! I ought to cut your face up at the very least!"

"This is why I'm here to make amends."

"There's no fixing what happened."

The stranger wet his papery lips. "Perhaps but I am very old and know of things even more ancient."

Gimeld glared at him. "What are you getting at you crazy Upright?" As though it was a response he reached into a pocket and pulled out a black hood. He held it up as if he were presenting something of great value. "How in all of Iris' is that supposed to fix everything?"

A sly smile crept onto the old wrinkled face. "You can't change what has occurred but you can hide it. This hood uses ancient techniques that were referred to as magic. Long before The Spark certain Uprights knew how to get around in a tough life. Your life has turned tough so I am giving one of their tricks to you so I may be absolved of my part in your misfortune."

Gimeld snatched the hood and tossed it aside. He brought his face close to the old Upright's. "You think this is all I care about? You think this is all I lost?" Gimeld roughly shoved him out the door. "Get out! Don't come back with any more of your craziness or you'll regret it!" Gimeld slammed the door shut.

He let out a grunt and picked up the hood. He turned it over in his hand and then held it up for further examination. He shrugged and slipped it on, although he couldn't pinpoint the exact reason for doing so. He shook his head when nothing happened even though it was exactly what he expected.

He was about to yank it off when his eye caught one of the mirror shards that still lay on the ground. He rushed over to it and picked it up. He peered at it in disbelief. He dropped it to the floor in order to pick up another to make sure. His face was gone, all which remained was a black void. He pulled the hood off and his face returned. He studied his reflection, as he turned the mirror shard this way and that to get a better view. "Ouch!" he yelped as the glass shard cut into his hand. It fell to the floor, and blood dripped onto it from his wound. He watched the blood splatter onto his marred reflection. He stomped the shard with his boot and slipped the hood back on.

⟨ ⟩

OROGUNU ORBIT

Gimeld went through his reserves of halos quickly and soon began to do odd jobs for the darkness trade to still get his Niorpyn and dreaming in. His ferocity and naturally quick reflexes earned him quite the reputation. The fact that he had no face also added an intimidating mystique. It wasn't long till he was recruited by a band of pirates.

Well after Gimeld settled into a life of piracy the crew commandeered a cargo ship leaving Orogunu. In typical fashion, they lined the staff of the ship up along a wall in the loading bay. Gimeld was one of the pirates assigned to guard the workers, while his fellow pirates transferred the cargo of produce to their ship.

One of the shipping crew members, who seemed to separate himself from the others, caught Gimeld's eye. It was the first time anyone drew any special attention since Jonah's death. "What's your name?" Gimeld grunted.

"Arjan. So I take it a life of piracy is more exciting than a farmer's life?"

"I wouldn't know I've never been a farmer."

"Well, I've never been a pirate but I'm fairly certain I know the answer. So you accepting any new applicants?"

"You would have to take that up with the captain."

Arjan gave Gimeld a cockeyed smile. "That's not you with those broad shoulders and firm biceps."

"I have no interest in being a captain."

"Such a shame. What's your name?"

"You don't need to know it."

"Hmmm. I guess you're right. Still, we could have fun together if I did. Even your scars wouldn't put a damper on it."

"What did you say?" Gimeld's mind bristled.

"Oh don't take offense. I think they're very distinguished. Gives your face character. It's hard to find someone with character on Orogunu." Arjan gave a dismissive wave of his hand. "Believe me, I've tried."

Gimeld at first thought the spell wore off. He jogged over to the shiny metallic loading bay doors to look at his reflection. His face was still shrouded in shadow. "What's the problem?" One of his crewmates called out.

Gimeld rushed over to her. "Can you see my face?"

The crewmate creased her brow. "No. I thought that was your whole deal. Just get back to your post."

Gimeld left her and walked back over to Arjan. "Why can you see my face?"

Arjan gave a little dismissive snort. "It's a hood, not a mask, sweets."

"What did you call me?"

"Sweets, 'cause you look scrumptious and you won't tell me your name."

Gimeld hadn't thought about his baked goods in a while. Not since he binged on them right after Jonah's death. His mind recalled an illicit dreaming session where he had seen himself flying a ship with someone sitting next to him but could not see their face. This was long before he joined the pirate crew. The Upright who dreamed with him was most likely a member of the House of Yowgn. He told Gimeld that life will show us where we are supposed to go and who needs to join us. It sounded too similar to the rhetoric of the Way for Gimeld's liking so he very harshly told the illicit dreamer to get out. His mind couldn't forget those words though, despite his efforts.

He looked at Arjan whose smile melted him. There was a pull there unlike Jonah's pull but maybe good enough to pass the time. The Niorpyn was losing its potency and the illicit dreaming experience was growing stale. Perhaps this Arjan was just the vice he needed to reinvigorate his existence. Arjan's green hair did remind him of the Limone tarts that used to be his favorite at the local bakery. *How could I live with any more regret?* Gimeld thought to himself. That simple fact made his decision clear.

"My name's Gimeld. What would you do if I was starting my own crew?"

Arjan grinned. "Ride with you anywhere, sweets."

Gimeld opened fire on the other staff members of the ship. He rapidly slaughtered them all.

"What are you doing?" cried one of his crewmates.

He shot his fellow pirates before they had time to react. He had always been subdued and obedient. His sudden unprecedented actions threw them so off, they failed to counter in enough time. He took their weapons and gave a laser and a sword to Arjan. "Follow me."

"You don't have to ask me twice."

While on their way to the bridge they ran into an A.I. "How can I serve you?"

Gimeld raised his gun to destroy the android but Arjan stopped him. "That's a highly developed maintenance and technical overseer, a M.A.T.O., they exist only to serve the crew of a ship. It's experimental and was on loan for us to try out. It may come in handy."

"Why didn't it protect you and your shipmates?"

"I have no weapons otherwise I would have. I was told the best way to help was to stay put."

"They can do pretty much anything with a ship. Override locks, even fly them," said Arjan.

Gimeld lowered his gun. "You come with us then."

"I don't recall you being a member of the crew."

"You remember me don't you?"

"Yes. Arjan, produce quality control registered C72."

"Right. And I'm telling you Gimeld here is now our captain. We're getting rid of these pirates so you need to listen to whatever he says and help us."

"As you wish."

They soon entered the bridge. "M.A.T.O., I need you to disable the pilot locks and blow the airlock in the loading bay?" Gimeld barked.

"But there's a ship attached. It would cause a vacuum that would suck out the contents of the whole loading bay as well as the contents of the other ship."

"Exactly. Do it."

"As you request."

M.A.T.O. extended his right hand and a compartment in the palm slid open. With his left hand, he pulled out a cable and plugged it into a jack on the console. Within moments a thunderous explosion echoed through the corridors of the ship.

"Good job, M.A.T.O.," said Gimeld as he stepped up to the control panel. "Welcome to the crew of The Wayward Star. Now break the locks so I can fly this ship."

"Yes sir."

Arjan rubbed Gimeld's shoulders. "Since we're all outlaws now how about some elicit dreaming to celebrate our new freedom?"

Gimeld ran his finger softly down Arjan's hair. "There'll be plenty of time for that. But first, let's arm ourselves. I'm not going to risk losing you."

Arjan smiled. "I have no plans to go anywhere, sweets."

"Good." Gimeld turned back to the console. "I'm your new captain, M.A.T.O. Understand?"

"I do."

"We're getting you some weapons too so next time someone boards this ship you can defend the crew."

"Affirmative."

Gimeld piloted the ship to the nearest darkness mechanic he knew of to begin his new life.

Chapter 10

WASHA ORBIT

The cone-shaped ship had burrowed its pointed nose so far into the rust-colored clay dirt of Washa that the back of the ship was nearly level with the ground. Since it was dark it was almost impossible to see it through the hazy air. Fortunately, the inhabitable parts of the ship were on a gyroscope which always kept the interior level.

Gimeld had exited the ship through a hatch in the back. He stood and looked out at the bleak landscape. Washa was sparsely populated. Its nomadic people set up dome tents when they settled in a spot for any stretch of time and there were none around. Arjan crawled out of the hatch and joined Gimeld to take stock of their surroundings in the dim light of Washa's solitary moon.

"How's your wound?"

"It will heal." Gimeld brought his hand to his face. "Do you believe what Sil says? That life has a pattern or rhythm that speaks to us?"

Arjan gave a dismissive grunt. "Ridiculous inner Orbit superstitions."

"Perhaps."

"This is stupid. We should just leave now. They have no IO's and they're crossing the Washa desert carrying a trans-dimensional drive. Even without the heat of Iris, they're all goners, well except Lorelei, I guess."

"We said we'll give them till Iris is directly overhead and we will."

"Why are you helping them? I thought we agreed to only do what's best for us."

"Call it honor amongst thieves. And anyway maybe this is best for us too."

Arjan crossed his arms and drew them tightly against his body. "I doubt it. I mean sure we were lucky this experimental ship can create a hole to hide in and had working hydrogen and oxygen tanks to dispense water but we're still on Washa in the dark without MATO to scan the horizon. Plus we don't have any IO's."

"Sil will find something."

"I'm not holding my breath. Who knows if we're even able to survive inter-dimensional travel? You heard the Order member, they made Armonia to do it."

"They made Armonia to try and control where they go. The Order is all about control. We have no such reservations. Wherever the drive takes us is better than here. Our kind can't survive in this system much longer, even Daleth can't."

"Is that why he's killing himself?" Arjan asked with no attempt to hide the derision in his voice.

Gimeld touched his face once more. "He's at an end either way. He's just decided what he wants his life to mean."

《 》

DALETH AND LORELEI plopped the trans-dimensional drive down into the parched dirt with a unified grunt.

"I'm hungry and tired," whined Armonia.

"Shut up. You're not the one carrying this thing," grumbled Daleth.

"I offered."

"Iris will be in the sky soon. We're running out of time," Lorelei said through labored breaths.

"If I had my wings I would search for ya. Not that I really know what we're looking for."

"A settlement," snapped Daleth.

"There's nothing here! It's all just flat dirt aside from that dome thingy over there."

Lorelei sprang to life. "A dome! Where?"

Armonia pointed to her left. "Over there a little ways but I think it's just a hill."

"Washa is completely flat," explained Lorelei. "A dome is exactly what we are looking for. It's how the tribes here protect themselves from the elements."

"Don't tell me, after all this time, she can see in the dark."

"Better late than never." Lorelei stooped down and grabbed the drive. "Come on, Daleth, get the other end. Armonia, show us the way."

⟨ ⟩

THEY REACHED THE DOME just as the first rays of light from Iris were peering over the horizon. The sky was now peppered with auburn and red. The white dome stood in stark contrast. A gigantic porcelain marble half buried in the dry clay of Washa. The canvas material that made up the structure was torn on a lower section. Armonia peered into the hole and found the inside a disheveled mess. "I don't see nobody but the place looks destroyed."

Lorelei and Daleth put the drive down and joined Armonia at the opening.

"Whoa," exclaimed Lorelei as she surveyed the damage. She touched her hand to one of the several smears of blood. "Do you think one of those Breathless creatures did this?"

"Who cares," Daleth said. He pointed to the far side of the dome. "There's a flare hopper and a beam catcher. Exactly what we needed and we don't have to contend with anyone for them. They both appear unscathed so let's get to work."

"Look!" Armonia held up a container in each hand. "Whoever was here left behind food and water!"

Daleth grunted. "Help me get the drive in, Lorelei."

Armonia made a face and pursed her lips. "Fine more for me."

⟨ ⟩

IRIS HAD FULLY REVEALED itself over the horizon now as Gimeld kept his vigil. Arjan paced behind him. "I say we just leave. I have a bad feeling about all of this."

Gimeld gently took Arjan into his arms. They gazed into one another's eyes. "Don't you trust me to protect you?" Gimeld softly asked.

Arjan looked out into the desolate seemingly endless landscape. "It's not that. I just think we're in over our heads."

"We are but it doesn't mean I won't get us out." Gimeld stroked Arjan's cheek. "We swore to take care of each other and that's the one thing which will never change." They embraced.

Arjan suddenly spotted a group heading their way over the horizon. "Look! We've been found!"

Gimeld stared at the mass of Uprights coming toward them. "It could just be a tribe on the move but get a weapon just in case."

"You think I was out here without one? If they're guardians we can't fight them all. Let's just cut our losses and go." Arjan tried to pull Gimeld by the arm but he wouldn't budge.

Instead, Gimeld took a scope out of his belt and peered through it. "Sil is at the front of them."

"They captured Sil?"

"I don't think they're guardians. They look like Washans."

Sil led the group of Uprights toward the mostly buried ship. Gimeld was correct. Behind Sil were about fifty Washans who were caked in dirt. Many of them carried bundles wrapped in linens.

Arjan could hardly compose himself. "Sil what in Iris's light is this? We sent you out for food, not as a recruiter."

Sil remained composed and stated matter of factly, "I have done so. Although Washa and Dooga both have challenging terrains they are very different. It is difficult for me to learn how to forage here in such a short time. These Washans were attacked by the same creature that attacked us. Their tribe has suffered heavy losses. They feel because of this creature's appearance this system is no longer an appropriate home for them. They saw the fact that I carry a serposa with me as a good sign. They wish to barter passage with us in exchange for food."

Arjan crossed his arms defiantly. "There isn't room. This ship isn't as big as The Wayward Star."

"It's big enough," Sil said

"Gimeld?" Arjan implored. Sil also turned to him for a verdict.

"They are your responsibility Sil. They are to follow all orders to the letter and we reserve the right to expel them at any point."

Sil nodded. "I will make sure they understand."

Arjan stared at Gimeld with his jaw dropped. "We should have just killed them and taken their food."

"In a different place and time, yes, but we are going to the unknown. Washans are simplistic survivors. I know you think I've changed from the Upright I was but I'm doing everything still for us."

Sil reached into their cloak and pulled out a small bundle of cloth. Sil tossed it up to Arjan. "Here. This might calm you."

Arjan sniffed the bundle and the bitter scent stung his nostrils. "Niorpyn!" He untied the fabric and took a pinch of the powder between his fingers. He drew in his breath and savored the burn that ran up his sinuses. Arjan felt the familiar warmth spread from his chest all over his body right down to his tingling fingers and toes. He fought against it for a moment. The resistance used to be greater, more painful, now it lasted but an instant, so used to it was he. The core of himself longed for it, all of it. The sweet death of releasing all he was. Gimeld snatched the bundle from him.

"You want some too?"

"No. I haven't taken it since we met. I told you that you're all I need."

"Then give it back. It's pure. I can tell."

"You have to find something else to hold onto as I did. I know a thing or two about addiction. About needing something in life so you won't get washed away by it. It doesn't work. Sooner or later life washes you away unless you become strong enough to stand against the current."

"You never gave me a hard time before about this."

"I've been there. I empathized. But we're no longer adventurers, we're pioneers and we need to be fully here for it."

"So you're not going to let me have that?"

"Aren't you listening to me?" Arjan turned his head away but Gimeld went on. "There isn't going to be this stuff where we're going. You need to use what we have to ween yourself off it. You either change or you die."

"You're the strong partner. That was our deal."

It's time we both be strong. It's why we have to go somewhere new and use different methods than we have been."

"You still haven't explained why we're helping those three out there who want to blow everything up."

Gimeld turned back to the horizon and touched his face. "I can't explain either. It's a recognition of a sort. But even though I can't make sense of it, I ask that you still trust me. I will not betray our bond, even if my sticking to it angers you."

Arjan dropped his arms and let out a heavy sigh. He squeezed his eyes shut. Pools of moisture began to collect in them. He forced them open again. "I don't know much of anything anymore." He reached for Gimeld's hand and squeezed it, "Except it's you and me till the end." Gimeld squeezed Arjan's hand back.

《 》

DALETH PUT THE CASING back into place and tightened the bolts. He then slammed the outer haul door of the flare hopper shut. "It's done."

Lorelei finished folding the last garment in the tent and placed it in the pile she made. "You could still go with the pirates. You would just need to give Armonia your crystals."

"You wouldn't last long piloting through Iris. You're the one who doesn't need to go."

"Trust me I do. I don't know if The Spark always knew this was coming or what but you have no clue how fortified Iris is."

Armonia sprung up from a chest she was rummaging through. "Did ya two hear that? It sounds like a ship."

"It's just the wind. Stop thinking your hearing stuff because you're not," said Daleth.

"You're just not used to the climate here in Washa. Few are. No ships land here except at designated trading posts where goods are trafficked through."

"Why did ya fold all their garments? Their dead."

Lorelei shrugged. "You don't know that. There are no bodies. They could have escaped the creatures and be on their way back. It's the least we could do for using their flare hopper and tools."

"Whatever. Let's signal the others and be on our way to Iris."

A harsh voice rang out in the enclosure. "Just as I suspected." The trio turned toward the entrance to see Sophia and her two henchmen standing there.

Sophia unsheathed two octaos from a harness on her back. She twisted the handles activating the electromagnetic field in the center which made the eight-sided razor blade vibrate. Daleth eyed the ancient circular weapon from the days of the wars. The electromagnetic field defended against laser blasts while the octagon-shaped offensive blade could easily flay skin. It was a potent weapon that indicated these intruders meant great menace.

Lorelei immediately ran over and grabbed Armonia pulling them both closer to Daleth. "Sophia!" she cried. "What're you doing here?"

Sophia signaled to one of her lackeys and he tossed Lorelei's dreaming log at them. It landed heavily on the ground. "Found this at your place. Took me longer than I liked but I used it and some dreaming to locate your hiding spot."

"Why?"

"You were a Yowgn spy and you brought the Way down on all of us you filthy traitor."

Lorelei gazed at the book for a moment and then turned her eyes toward Sophia. "I am a traitor but I have no ill will toward you. If you dreamed properly you would know that."

"Please I know all about you now," scoffed Sophia. "You only look out for what serves you best. I could admire that if you hadn't crossed me."

"I didn't do anything to you."

"Don't lie. I know how things work. You disappeared right before the Obstruction decree."

"It was a coincidence. You're not going to fight me over a coincidence, are you?"

Sophia raised the weapons in her hands. "Two things you should have already realized about me. One, I don't believe in coincidence, and two, I'd rather spill blood than let a score go unsettled."

"Don't you know who is behind me!"

"Doesn't matter." As Sophia spoke those words her two goons took out laser guns and pointed them at the trio. In the blink of an eye, Daleth's crystals were in the air. Two deflected the laser blasts. Another two went in between the two henchmen's ribs, severing their aortas. The fifth stopped in front of Sophia's chest. It then dropped to the ground with the other four.

Lorelei turned to Daleth. "What happened?"

It was Sophia who answered. " He's depleted. Used the fear residue from this camp to kill my underlings but it will take more than that to kill me. I wasn't a Follower but I took a healthy interest in their ways."

"I don't need special powers to rip your head off." Daleth unsheathed his trikilldo and started forward to face Sophia. Lorelei reached for his arm to stop him but he yanked it away.

Sophia swung with her right arm and Daleth leaned back and swerved to his left. He stabbed with his trikilldo but Sophia spun away.

"Shame you crossed me, Daleth, someone with your talents would have been very useful in my business."

"Your business is over with or are you that dense?"

Sophia shrugged. "Nothing ever changes all that much. I'll find a way to go on which is more than can be said for the three of you."

"If you are so confident about the situation why come after us."

"Cause I'm still annoyed."

They circled each other for a few moments before Sophia went on the attack once more. She swung both blades in front of her. Almost like she was drawing figure eights in the air with the base of the handles. Daleth tried to maneuver away and look for an opening but she caught him on the shoulder with the weapon in her right hand. Lorelei immediately moved to them but Daleth turned on her. "Stay out of it!"

"Oh, she'll get her turn soon enough, once I'm finished with you."

Daleth clutched his wound and tried to compose himself. Sil had packed his previous leg wound with herbs which helped ease the pain but he now had two gaping wounds. It was more than he had suffered in quite a while.

He grabbed a broken spear that was next to him, leftover from the vacated tribe. "Wish these primitive Uprights kept more lasers but this will do just fine."

With a weapon now in each hand, he made another lunge. Sophia and Daleth whirled around the tent like tornadoes. One of Sophia's weapons got stuck in a wooden chest. Daleth brought his hands together and raised his combined weapons high to bring down on Sophia but she surprised him by lashing out with her bare hand. Her serrated nails tore into Daleth's chest and he stumbled as she ducked under him. Sophia went to bring her weapon down on Daleth's backside but he rolled away at the last moment. Sophia stared at him, and a cruel smile crept across her face. "So sad that you are nothing without your powers."

At that moment, Daleth realized it wasn't just the fact that he didn't have any powers or was injured. It was also because, for the first time, he cared about the outcome. Sophia yanked her weapon out of the chest and appeared ready to make another advance.

"Stop and leave now or I'll kill ya." All turned to see Armonia holding out her hand which contained Daleth's crystals that she had collected. Her face glistened with perspiration.

"Armonia don't!" Daleth shouted.

Sophia smirked and gave a haughty chuckle. "Clearly, not the brains of this outfit. I'll get to you soon enough, dearie."

Sophia turned her attention back to Daleth who had gotten to his feet. Sophia and Daleth began to duel fiercely once more.

"I warned you." Armonia squeezed her eyes shut and concentrated hard.

"It won't work, Armonia, she's not a—" Lorelei's words were cut off by the spectacle of light beams emanating from Sophia. They seemed to be cutting her entire body into various segments.

Sophia and Daleth halted their fight. Sophia looked down at herself. "What is this?" She then let out a shrill cry as her body appeared to turn to light and scatter. Sophia was gone.

Daleth and Lorelei stared in disbelief. Armonia opened her eyes and smiled. "Oh goodie. I always get afraid I won't be able to."

"But how?" Lorelei asked. "She wasn't a Twin Flame."

"I thought she was your old boss who you betrayed?"

"From my time in the darkness trade, not my time as a Twin Flame."

"Whoopsie. I got confused with all these groups."

"Whatever. She's out of our way, it's all that matters."

"But she —?"

"It's over!" Daleth moved to a circular kite that looked like it was made of a paper-thin sheet of shiny metal. "Help me with this beam catcher."

"What's that?" Armonia held out the crystals for Daleth.

He took them from her. She noticed it was more gentle than usual. "Washan scouts use it to reflect the light of Iris and signal other tribes."

"We're not Washan scouts."

"We're going to use it to signal Gimeld that we are ready so he can defer attention away from us," Lorelei explained. She turned to Daleth. "Shouldn't we attend to your wounds first?"

"I'm fine. We can't waste any time and risk others showing up."

"Others who?" Armonia asked.

"Uprights," Daleth coldly answered.

《 》

THE BRIGHT GLINT OF light from the beam catcher danced across Gimeld as he stood atop his ship. It was time. He still wasn't entirely sure why he was doing this but it was the same feeling he had when he met Arjan. That gave him some hope at the very least. He opened the hatch and descended into the ship.

《 》

HE ENTERED THE BRIDGE. Arjan was fiddling with the holographic system interface. "We got the signal. Where's Sil?"

"Getting our new crew situated. Just give me a moment, whatever is on this stupid server M.A.T.O. gave us took forever to connect and load."

Gimeld sat down in the pilot's chair. He noticed something carved into the silver alloy that made up the console. He ran his fingers along the engraving which read: Wayward Star II. He turned to Arjan who was watching him.

"You changed my life once and I never looked back. Why not do it again?"

Sil entered the bridge. "They're all set."

"As am I sir." It was M.A.T.O.'s voice and it seemed to come from everywhere. They looked around and at each other.

"That wasn't just me who heard M.A.T.O.'s voice was it?" Sil asked.

M.A.T.O.'s voice rang out again. "You are all hearing me. The server you uploaded to this ship contained my consciousness. When we survived that polar shift on Dooga I began to contemplate my mortality, as well as my effectiveness to you all. Some time ago, I calculated that the system was heading for abrupt changes based on the trend of current events. Since I was always a liability due to my programming being tagged by my manufacturer I decided to create a backup of all my necessary programs and memory files. In that way, if the industry which created me ceased looking the other way on piracy I would still be able to serve. I would also still be able to serve if my primary casing and CPU were ever damaged beyond reasonable repair."

"So wait to do you remember us?"

"I consistently backed up the server. My last memory was us agreeing to help Daleth, Lorelei and Armonia steal a trans-dimensional drive, which I assume was successful since I can detect it on this craft. Of course, I assume my original version did not make it since the server was used."

Arjan slowly shook his head back and forth a broad smile grew across his face. "You stupid robot, I can't believe you did all this."

"It's good to have you back on the crew, M.A.T.O.," Gimeld said.

"This ship is equipped with biosensors and I detect many more life forms aboard."

"They're Washans who want out of this system too. We're about to take off and give the drive we stole a try. We're also a decoy for Daleth and the others who are using the second drive for something else so wish us the best."

"I can do more than that captain. I reconfigured my O.S. within the server to be able to operate any component on any ship. I will help guide you against the enemy craft and fire the weapons. I can also activate the drive upon your request."

"Just as long as you let me steer." Gimeld placed his palms on the console. The craft hummed and began to use its EMF weaponry to bore through the dirt in a U-shape. Within moments they were leaving two big holes behind them on Washa. As soon as they got into the upper atmosphere Gimeld began to loop around the Orbit's borders. As was expected guardian craft began pursuing them.

"Pursuant craft are trying to get through on the communicator to have us identify ourselves, captain."

"Ignore it and blast any you can to pieces."

"Affirmative. The ship should be cable of maneuverability up to and including three hundred sixty degrees."

"Excellent." With that Gimeld spun the craft one hundred and eighty degrees in mid-flight. MATO activated the antenna at the tip of the cone and destroyed most of the pursuant ships.

Arjan's eyes went wide as he watched the view screen. "Whoa, that's what I'm talking about."

"I calibrated the frequency to get the maximum amount of range while still maintaining an effective impact."

"Looks like it got their attention. Here comes a whole other wave."

"The Washans are probably all affright," Sil said.

"They'll have to deal. I'm trying to keep us alive," Gimeld snapped.

"I took the liberty to broadcast soothing frequencies in the compartment where I detect the other life forms."

Arjan placed his hand on Gimeld's arm. "It's time, sweets. Let's see something new."

"Arrupat indicates to me this is indeed what we need to do. It's the best course for us." Kristal popped out of the band on Sil's arm and let out a squeak. "Kristal agrees."

Arjan smiled at Gimeld who gave a quick nod and drew in a deep breath. "M.A.T.O. activate the drive—now."

There was a shimmery wave of light and then the cone-shaped craft was gone as if they had never been there.

《 》

IRIS ORBIT

Lorelei stared intently at a view screen on the bridge of the flare hopper as Washa grew smaller. "Looks like Gimeld and his crew did their part, nobody is following us."

"Maybe we should call this off," said Daleth.

"What? I just told you the plan is working."

"Exactly. Maybe The Spark wants us to do this. Maybe this is all a setup to get rid of us."

"It's not," Armonia blurted out.

"How do you know?" Daleth sneered.

Armonia shrugged. "I feel like we're being watched. My stomach's twisting up in knots and my skin's getting all prickly."

"See we should abort this mission."

"No. I don't know anything, except we have to do this."

They flew in silence for a bit. Lorelei toggled through the view monitors to ensure no ships were nearing them. Daleth concentrated on piloting. Armonia sat in the far corner strapped into a seat. She watched her two shipmates in silence. She tried in vain to figure out how they all came to this surreal moment. Nothing came to her but a knowing that they were somehow on the correct path.

Finally, Lorelei broke the quiet that seemed to saturate them. "We're approaching Iris." Lorelei held her palm out to Daleth. He gave a heavy sigh, dug into his pouch, and dropped the crystals into Lorelei's waiting hand. She in turn went over to Armonia who fidgeted uneasily.

Armonia shifted her eyes to the view screen with the fast-approaching Iris. "There's a lot of them, isn't there? She turned her attention back to the crystals in Lorelei's outstretched hand. "I don't like doing this."

"We're about to kill the entire system!", Daleth barked.

"Ya don't know that!"

Lorelei's eyes met Armonia's. "You have to set them free so they can start over. So we can all start over." She slid the crystals into Armonia's palm and took her hands inside her own. She gave a little squeeze. "You're not killing them. You know this because your dreaming revealed it." Armonia nodded slowly. Lorelei smiled and then went back to her seat next to Daleth. She buckled herself in and turned her focus to the view screen.

"How close do you think they have to get for her to do—whatever she does?"

Lorelei didn't take her eyes off the view screen. "I don't know, just watch out for EM disruption cannons and fusion grenades."

"They have them on Iris?" Lorelei nodded not taking her eyes off the images on the monitor. "Now you tell me?"

"I know it rotates, but stay away from the citadel and the long flat shaft to the right of it. Those are the most heavily guarded areas."

"I'll see what I can do," Daleth scoffed.

"Are you fully depleted or did you just not want to use up the last of your reserves back there with Sophia?" Daleth didn't answer. "Feed off me. I know you don't want to but otherwise, you both die and this was all a waste." Daleth remained silent. "Do it, Daleth. We have incoming ships."

Since any craft that wished to approach Iris had to give advance notice as well as register with the citadel where The Spark resided, these ships were immediately hostile. Daleth gritted his teeth and fed off Lorelei's fear. His senses became sharper. He pressed his palms into the console's sensors and the flare hopper began moving erratically. Flare hoppers didn't have weapons so their only chance was to avoid enemy fire and get close enough for Armonia to destroy the Twin Flame pilots. Fortunately, no guardians would be present to contend with. Guardians were considered unnecessary in the sanctity of Iris.

Daleth weaved in and out of the wave of craft coming toward them. He managed to avoid their fire using every piloting trick he knew. Some of them weren't even shooting. They were just trying to collide with the flare hopper. Armonia squeezed her eyes shut and clenched her fists around the crystals. She knew she could be dead in an instant but she had to empty her mind and concentrate on getting rid of the Twin Flames.

"It's working the ships are dropping off. Floating away like they are asteroids." Lorelei's words encouraged Armonia but not Daleth. An EM disruption blast and a fusion grenade were launched adjacent to one another. The EM disruption blast was deadlier, for it would disable the craft and make them helpless. He veered away from the EM disruption field. However, by launching them adjacent Daleth couldn't get as far away from the explosion the grenade emitted as he would have liked.

"If the heat shields get damaged we won't be able to get close enough to Iris," Lorelei reminded him.

"I know! We're still good." It was the same problem Daleth had with Sophia. He cared about the outcome. "We'll have to go lower."

"If we go lower I won't be able to make out what section of Iris we're nearing, there are some heavily fortified areas we need to avoid."

"This isn't one of them?"

"Besides it won't do any good their range is too great. Trust me, you'll lose yourself if you go so low as to get out of their range. Bear left, to the right is a large cluster of laser canons and concussive missiles."

Daleth complied jaw clenched. Even with his senses enhanced he couldn't match the sheer quantity of hostilities. Suddenly an idea popped into his head but he pushed it out. Daleth quickly jerked the ship up just in time to get it out of the blast radius of a fusion grenade.

"Space dust! I was afraid of this. Even with your and Armonia's powers, there are just too many weapons on Iris. If only you could throw up your shield around the craft. You could then fly close all around Iris so Armonia could wipe out the Twin Flames." Daleth blinked several times and twitched involuntarily. It was the same idea he had but he knew the cost. His reaction was not lost on Lorelei. "Is there some way you can do that?"

"I—" Daleth swerved again to avoid a ship's laser blast.

"Daleth, we're not gonna make it another way. If you can do it then do it already!"

"It may be possible but it would be a tremendous drain especially if I only siphoned from one. It might kill them."

"Not a problem for me so do it!"

Daleth quickly glanced at Lorelei's pleading face. "I don't know if you even have enough fear and pain for me to create that strong of a shield."

"I have plenty and you know it." Daleth averted his eyes and concentrated on piloting. A nearby blast shook the ship. Lorelei put her hand on Daleth's bicep. "Please, make me count for something in this life."

Daleth glanced over to Lorelei. He took a deep breath and concentrated. He fed off Lorelei. Devoured all the regret, worries, and hurt she carried. The stuff they used to talk about lying in the dark together. He took it all inside. Lorelei swooned and reached out for something to steady herself. She gripped the console and tried to catch her breath. It felt like all the blood left her head and her legs were turning to liquid. She went limp and lost consciousness.

Armonia went to leave her seat and help Lorelei but stopped cold when Daleth bellowed, "Leave her be and focus on the task at hand! I'm going in!"

Daleth concentrated and drew up every last bit of energy he had stored. He envisioned it flowing down his arms and through his hands. It was the same visualization techniques he had been taught to shield himself. It was second nature to envision an impenetrable barrier around his own body but now he had to see the ship in his mind's eye surrounded by an invincible wall of energy.

When a ship blasted them with its laser cannon to no effect Daleth grew confident and dove the ship toward the artificial ring around Iris. The weapons fired at them but to no avail. Daleth still avoided the EM disruption blasts to be safe but it was much easier knowing that it was all he had to worry about. His natural pilot skills took them in close, so they were only a few meters above the Iris halls and buildings. Sure enough, Armonia, who squeezed Daleth's crystals with all her might, did her thing. A silent death was left in their wake with ghostly flickers of light fading out of the structures behind them. All around the ring of Iris it looked like the last flames of a roaring campfire dying. After Daleth had made a complete circle there was no more laser fire, no more explosions, no more whizzing ships, just a silent emptiness.

Daleth quickly turned the ship full speed toward the fiery glowing orb at the center of the system. He then got up and unbuckled Lorelei from the seat. He cradled her body and brought it gently to the floor of the ship. He looked down at her face which was starkly drained of color. He checked for pulse and breath. He found both. "Armonia you can stop. It's over."

Armonia's eyes burst open. She saw Daleth holding Lorelei and crawled over to them. "Is she?"

"Still alive, just very weak."

Lorelei's eyes slowly fluttered open and she gave a small smile. "Did we do it?"

"It seems so. Just rest so you regain your strength," said Daleth.

"What for? It's done. Now Armonia can release me too."

"What?" Armonia wiped the sweat from her forehead with the back of her hand.

"End me, Armonia. It's time."

"You want me to kill you?"

Lorelei closed her eyes and moved her head up and down slightly.

"Don't be dramatic," said Daleth.

"I can't die, so what is left for me after you two burn."

Daleth averted his eyes but Armonia answered. "Daleth and I may survive."

"Based on what you two told me, I choose to believe we will find one another again. Either way, there's nothing more for me in this life. My life has been so long and I knew nothing but ugliness till I found you two. You freed them, now free me." Lorelei lifted her hand weakly and put it on the stethoscope she gave Daleth for Grevolios still tucked in his belt. He looked down at it and then back at her.

"This is foolish," Daleth blurted out.

"I have done so many foolish things, I know this isn't one of them. Please, I need to let go of it all. I've spent too much time in loneliness. "

Daleth's eyes locked with Lorelei's. They stared intently at each other. Armonia spoke again, " You're not alone you have us."

Lorelei drew up a wider smile. "That's true but there's a difference between being alone and being lonely."

In a hushed voice, Daleth said, "Just do it, Armonia."

"Warning. Heat shields are nearing their maximum capacity," the onboard computer squawked.

"Shut up!" Daleth then turned to Armonia and in a somber voice said, "Go ahead."

Lorelei reached her hand out and put it over Armonia's heart. "You won't destroy me. Remember body, mind, Yowgn." They nodded softly at one another. Armonia squeezed the crystals and fought back tears as vapors of golden glowing light wafted from Lorelei's body. Lorelei's eyes closed softly. There were only two left in the tiny craft.

Armonia sobbed until the computerized voice announced, "Heat shields at critical level automatic override commencing."

Although her vision was smeared by her tears, Armonia heard Daleth get up to move back to the console so he could override the automatic safety feature and keep the ship hurtling toward the center of Iris. Armonia wiped her eyes so she could give one last pristine look at Lorelei who had never appeared so serene.

With a tremble in her steps, she walked up next to Daleth. She went to hand him back his crystals but he did not move to take them. It was then Armonia noticed the pools of water in his eyes. She had never seen those eyes so expressive, even when they dreamed together. Ever since she had met Daleth and Lorelei she could never quite figure out what kind of relationship those two had. She now no longer wondered.

The alarms which began to blare sounded like a knife cutting through the hushed bridge of the ship. The same automated voice announced, "Heat shields have been breached. Repeat, heat shields have been breached. Damage to the ship imminent."

There was suddenly an overwhelming heat in the tiny compartment of the craft. The air became fuzzy and the walls began to warp and give. The view screen which had shown nothing but blinding brightness shorted out. It now showed only a pure reflection of Armonia and Daleth.

Armonia looked at the two of them in that dark reflection and strangely felt calmer than she had ever remembered. She placed her hand over Daleth's. He didn't move it away. She wrapped her fingers around his. She was surprised to feel him squeeze back as he activated the trans-dimensional drive. Immediately they were engulfed by warmth and peace which felt like it would never leave them.

《 》

COMQWO ORBIT

Leon sat in the abandoned ice tavern and slurped up the last drop of nectar from his glass. The various concoctions of fruit juices from Baabcrest were just as good as he remembered them being. He reached behind the counter and pumped his glass full of another round. He then turned back to the view screens which still showed coverage of the giant vortex swallowing

DREAMING

up the whole system. Since Iris was gone he wondered if the other Orbits which still hadn't been sucked into the abyss had grown colder. He was always intrigued by how much heat in a given Orbit was generated internally and how much came from Iris. Alas, Comqwo was too cold and too distant to provide much good data.

He did get very interesting data about the fungus that grew on Comqwo and the ecosystem as a whole. He learned the fungus not only fed off the decaying organic matter that existed on Comqwo but also had a feature that attracted organic matter toward it. It pulled minute organic particulars from the reaches of space into the ecosystem to feed. Leon had observed it himself firsthand. This proved that life was abundant outside the system, which he had always suspected. He felt vindicated for his held beliefs.

The fungus not only pulled in organic matter but as part of its metabolism emitted a small amount of vapor. This vapor was what gave Comqwo its thin atmosphere and the little bit of warmth that kept it from absolute zero. This was all a byproduct of the metabolism of the fungus but it proved indispensable for making Comqwo what it was. Leon always found the byproducts of organisms to be the paintbrush to the masterpiece of life.

Just as intriguing, if not more so, was the discovery that the fungus went through not only metabolic changes depending on the quantity of food available but also molecular changes as well over some time. It constantly seemed to reinvent itself.

The process was excruciatingly slow. Leon had been fortunate. The excess of decaying organic matter left by the introduction of the Breathless had somewhat sped up the process. It was just enough for Leon to stumble upon it. Normally it would have been very nearly undetectable. Nonetheless, based on his calculations under regular conditions the fungus would be an entirely new organism in just a matter of a few gremrevs. Leon had wanted to further investigate and perhaps play with the adaptability but alas it all seemed to be coming to an end.

Leon couldn't understand why more of the inhabitants of the system weren't taking advantage of the circumstances and indulging. The media reports said many were trying to get on ships to flee the vortex that was growing and swallowing everything in its wake. Leon couldn't help but smirk at the foolishness.

The view screens announced that Circapto had just been sucked in and was now nowhere to be found. Leon raised his glass in a salute to his origin Orbit. He took a long swig and savored the melody of tangy flavors on his palette. He noted the slight variations in colors as the various fruits had blended. He glanced back up at the view screens. The voice which blared out of them explained the remaining Twin Flames were going to mount a unified assault on the vortex. They planned to project an unprecedented wave of light toward it, in an attempt to stave off the darkness which was growing more and more rapidly. Leon shook his head and took another sip. *Doesn't anyone in this system besides myself understand, that life is inevitable,* he pondered.

Acknowledgments from the Author

I want to first show my gratitude to Free Minds Publications for giving both me and this story a chance. A huge thank you to Kevin Basile, Allison Basile, George Zeo, Gerrad Bohl, Tony Perry, and Josh Burkey for their unwavering support. It meant the world to me. I want to also show my immense appreciation to Logan Shirley, Alla Ilyasova, and Jean Minuchin for their feedback which not only helped me shape this story but also gave me the confidence to keep moving forward with it. A special shout out to Rachel Evans for creating that safe space for me to share this work of mine. My unending gratitude to Coryelle Kramer, Molly, and Buddy for opening up my world so I could have the pallet to create this book. And lastly a special thank you to the real-life Lorelei for giving me shelter till I found my true harmony.

About The Author

Matthew A. Basile is a storyteller, nature lover, and pop culture aficionado who owes his inspiration to the Grandmothers of the Sea. You can find him on Twitter @MatthewABasile.

SNEAK PEEK
Goode Oliver Dooley and the Quest to Save Hobcomney
Gerrard Bohl
Chapter I
Darkness Rises

 Far away from Hobcomney Palace above Odullum's dark and lifeless kingdom, a thunderous storm surged with wrath and fury as never before. Booms and cracks tore through the skies as if the sky itself was being ripped apart. Odullum's ominous castle, hidden among the Forgotten Cotton Woods, was invisible in the darkness until flashes of lightning suddenly illuminated it, whereupon it would fade back into the darkness. Though it appeared as if this storm was going to bring a downpour of rain at any moment, not a drop of water fell to the scaly, cracked earth that surrounded his parched kingdom.

 Odullum paced with rage through the cold and hollow foyers of his decaying castle, ruminating over the failures of his accomplices, Lord Manchineel and Aiden Brodenhugh, both of whom met their ends in service to Odullum's will. Their mission, as was the mission of all those who served Odullum: to stop Goode Oliver Dooley from ascending to the throne and forever destroy Hobcomney Palace. Odullum seethed with hatred at being continually thwarted in his plans.

 "This has gone on long enough," whispered Odullum through his feral teeth and clenched jaw. He circled his large pearl, the Pearl of Rancor, which sat perched upon the mouth of the Pity Well in the center of his main court. He occasionally glanced down at the giant pearl as he paced and brainstormed. Wisps of fog curled and twirled around the pearl, as if responding to his rage, seemingly encouraging it, and waiting eagerly to be unleashed.

 "Without Lord Manchineel in the Royal Council, we can no longer know what their plans are," lamented the wretched voice of a woman who was hidden in the shadows. "Was it really necessary to kill him? Maybe we could have used him for another purpose," she asked.

 Odullum looked in the direction of her voice, his white eyes squinting with disdain at her question.

 "He was pathetic...weak in every possible way," he growled at the woman.

"Weak?!" exclaimed the woman. "He dragged his broken, battered body back here to beg your forgiveness!" She emerged from the shadows and walked towards Odullum. Her green and greyish sagging skin was marked with sweeping burn scars on one side of her face.

"Yes, Madame Wyemei," he replied, "and for his loyalty, I repaid him with a swift death, which was more mercy than he deserved for failing me as he did." He touched the Pearl of Rancor with his boney hand. It shimmered with delight under his icy palm.

"You call having your flesh consumed by the fog of the Pity Well merciful?" she asked with a snort.

"Oh yes," he answered her, looking up from the pearl, his eyes wide. "Believe me, it would have been far worse for him if he had failed me any more than he had."

Madame Wyemei said nothing in response to this remark, knowing well that he meant what he said. She knew he was capable of far worse. She turned away from him, fearing him, yet still feeling loyal to him.

"So, the boy is flourishing...," said Odullum, continuing his pacing around the court. "The royal bees have been released for yet another year, and I've lost influence over the Royal Council therein..." he thought aloud. "How could this be?" he whispered, looking back at the pearl.

"We still have Clarke," added Madame Wyemei, turning around over her shoulder.

"Ah, yes," said Odullum, "the Corpse Flower boy. He has pledged his allegiance to me, but I question his commitment. Time will reveal if he follows through."

"Follow through?" asked Madame Wyemei.

"Yes," hissed Odullum, walking towards a dead tree branch which leaned against his stony and skull-clad throne. "He has been given instructions...," he said, pausing and examining the small pods which adorned the branch. They had the appearance of miniature skulls. "Let us hope he does not disappoint as well." He plucked one of the pods from the branch and put it up to his grey lips, biting it in half. Small black hairs shot out from the pod and squirmed about, whipping around the corners of his mouth and he consumed it.

Madame Wyemei looked away in disgust. "So, we leave Clarke alone to see if he delivers?" she asked, doubting Odullum's plan.

Odullum shot a glare at Madame Wyemei for questioning him. "Don't be stupid," he hissed, "I will see the end of Goode Oliver Dooley, and I will not let that pleasure be at the hands of some sniveling peasant boy," he paused and consumed the other half of the pod. "Clarke will serve a purpose, but there must be something else…some other way to stop Dooley from claiming the throne." He looked at the pods on the branch again. He plucked another with his thin fingers and held it up in the air, turning it over with a smile forming on his face.

"Mold," he whispered in delight.

"Mold?" repeated Madame Wyemei, not sure that she had heard him correctly.

Odullum ignored her for a moment as he mulled over the details of his new plan which began to form. He finally nodded at her. "Yes…mold," he replied, smiling at Madame Wyemei. "And you will deliver it."

Available now in ebook and paperback. For more information visit www.freemindspublications.com

FREE MINDS PUBLICATION is a boutique publishing company created by writers for writers. At Free Minds Publications, we strive to help writers from all walks of life achieve their literary dreams. Find more interesting books to read or learn more about our company on our website.

www.freemindspublications.com